THOMAS MICHAEL SIMON

THE
AMERICAN
TESTAMENT

A HOUSE DIVIDED, AGAIN

The American Testament

ISBN-13: 978-1-948035-45-3 (Paperback)
ISBN-13: 978-1-948035-46-0 (eBook)

Edited by Sean Cowie
Cover designed by Spomenka Bojanic
Interior designed by Debbi Stocco

Published by Defiance Press and Publishing, LLC

Bulk orders of this book may be obtained by contacting Defiance Press and Publishing, LLC. www.defiancepress.com.

Public Relations Dept. – Defiance Press & Publishing, LLC
281-581-9300
pr@defiancepress.com

Defiance Press & Publishing, LLC
281-581-9300
info@defiancepress.com

Those who do not learn from the sins of history
are condemned to repeat them.

To the Reader

This story is about the start of the second American civil war. The United States of America has been trending towards separation for decades, with no signs our proud nation will change from its current course of partisan conflict and dissension. At some point, heated debate will yield to action.

Michael Shaara's *The Killer Angels* and Stephen Crane's *The Red Badge of Courage* shared history by looking back at the facts and estimating the motivations of the men and women caught in the first American civil war. This provided a far more powerful sense of history than could be painted by a textbook. *The American Testament* similarly uses characters from both sides of the conflict to help people today understand the hopes and fears of those on the other side of the political spectrum. Much of the rage in today's politics is because few understand what inspires people with whom they disagree.

History can, and often does repeat itself. This novel looks to examples from the past for events that plausibly could be replicated and to recycle haunting characters. Every generation has scars from failing to adapt to the new and learn from the old.

Human egos have already begun to fully embrace a technology-rich lifestyle, but human nature takes time to evolve. If America does finally implode, technology will be at its peak compared to any point in its history, and the advanced weaponry will amplify the heartache.

The motivation for writing this novel is to appeal to all Americans to do whatever they can to help bridge the gap, to foster peaceful dialogue, and teach our children a united America is more important than any individual issue. War is not yet our fate but, once the fire is ignited, it will be too late for many.

Foreword: America, 2084

1. The Country

America has always been a work in progress. Progressives will list how she has failed to evolve quickly enough. Constitutional conservatives can share how she has failed to maintain the fundamental tenets to her creation. Both can point to examples where change was needed and successful. This novel takes place in the year 2084. The changes that take place in America in the decades leading up to this story further divide these two factions and thus the nation.

The federal debt crisis realized in the middle of the 21st century leads to many substantial changes in an attempt to re-start the financial system, but further erodes the republic. The package of compromises to recover from the crisis was similar to those made years before the first American civil war in that they changed the country overall while not healing the divisions.

The change that most affected every American was the consolidation of many of the powers of the states into three American districts. The Eastern District became the base for the future Democratic Party who never committed to substantial economic socialist policies, but did embrace widespread liberal social transformations. The Western District became the home of the future Socialist Party with a top-down social construct that prioritizes entitlements for all citizens over a capitalist economy. The Southern District became the sanctuary for the Republican Party which retained little of the true republican philosophy, but still prioritized personal responsibility and the free market over government entitlements. Most of the American population lived in the Eastern and Western Districts and thus the federal government officials were almost entirely elected from the Democratic and Socialist Parties. On any typical day, federal government officials are in conflict with the Southern District Republicans.

Technology advanced from the early 21st century to 2084, with similar profound impacts as any recent jump of several decades. Day-to-day life is organized and optimized by Artificial Intelligence (AI) and machines perform most functions that had been served by mankind. Advances in computers, power systems, robotics, and manufacturing has led to android and electric self-driving vehicles that provide substantial infrastructure for American citizens, but leave few opportunities for individuals to contribute given the lack of paying jobs. The leaps in technology over time led to government entitlements for citizens to simply not break laws and bonuses for having children. Virtual Reality (VR) technology advanced and became commonplace thanks to AI enabling communication via brain waves. VR fills the time of many citizens to compete as their primary reality.

The combination of technology advancements and ever-increasing political conflict eventually reaches a breaking point as vile rhetoric finally turns to violence. America is still a work in progress but, given what you see, hear, and feel, do you believe she is progressing towards union or divorce?

2. Citizens of the Southern District

Sara Chamberlain – Mother, wife, and Texan. Sara does not look to be swept into the national spotlight, but is dragged into it. Named for the Biblical character Sara from the Old Testament, she helps humanize the struggle of the Southern District. Sara is a distant descendent of Joshua Lawrence Chamberlain, a hero for the Union in the first civil war.

Governor Cyrus Young – Governor of the Southern District based in Houston, Texas. Cyrus oversees the twelve remaining conservative states; a calm man who finds himself unable to control his environment. Cyrus is cast as the enemy to all that is good by politicians and media in the Eastern and Western Districts. As a fierce politician, Cyrus believes that a strong response is the only way to deter future challenges.

Angel Vega – Advisor to Governor Young for issues that require more than diplomacy. Former military and deeply loyal to his district, Angel works hard, but is a lonely man due to the early death of his wife. Angel oversees an intelligence and security team for the district and his role grows as the chaos unfolds.

Samson Gamble – A colossal man and a true warrior. Samson's long hair, tattoos, and scars set him apart. Former Special Forces, he is now part of the Texas National Guard. Inspired by the story of Samson from the Old Testament, his strength is matched only by his lethality. In the shadows, Samson also leads a mercenary team at the tip of the secessionist spear.

Lucilla Swift – Young, tough, and beautiful. Lucilla was divorced early in her marriage and just before the death of her mother. Lucilla lives with her father and is a member of his militia based in Carthage, Missouri. Named for the daughter of Roman Emperor Marcus Aurelius, her honesty and bravery are pure and unadulterated.

General Moon Tzu – An experienced general from the 3rd Gulf War and an expert in defensive warfare. General Tzu is called in to organize and centralize the Southern District National and State Guard units as the political leaders pour fuel on the fire of discontent. General Tzu is a disciple of the doctrine that battles should only be engaged if one has overwhelming capabilities.

Carrina – America in the late 21st Century is reliant on the capabilities of AI. The Southern District AI for security and defense is named Carrina. State of the art, Carrina can match the power and wit of the federal AI systems.

3. Everyone Else

Zander Brown – A simple family man caught in complicated times. Zander is a security manager at Workerbee Robotics based in Los Angeles, California. Zander's advanced development plant is caught up in the early violence and he is forced to make decisions that manipulate the fate of the nation.

Dexter Durden – An entertainer by trade and rare neutral political analyst by choice. Dexter is the host and star of the Party of One Virtual Reality (VR) show. The show features leaders debating current affairs with the audience getting to vote for the winner of the debate. Dexter and his crew are eventually forced outside of entertainment and into activism.

Anna Lee – One of the fundamental changes in America following the debt crisis was the creation of the deudor system (Spanish for debtor).

The system was set up to punish non-violent criminals, and allow willing impoverished Americans to submit to mild indentured servitude in a process to slowly pay off debt while realizing a comfortable minimal lifestyle. The debt could be based on a sponsor providing basics of housing, food, and entertainment, in exchange for elementary labor. The federal government provided substantial tax relief to sponsors of deudors in response to machines taking the lead in most industries leaving fewer jobs than citizens. Anna Lee is a teenage deudor working for a wealthy family in New York City.

Camilla – The nationwide systemic AI for most public purposes. Camilla is present in homes, most businesses, self-driving taxis, and in public areas. Citizens could say her name almost anywhere and she would answer and obey.

President Nero Thorne – A tall man with a photogenic smile that is always the center of attention. His success in business, while contributing substantially to the Socialist Party, led him to become governor of the Western District and eventually President of the United States. Nero has never worked a day of manual labor in his life, but has genuine empathy for the working class.

Governor Simone Dubois – Governor of the Western District based in San Francisco, California. A self-made woman from modest means blessed with the gifts of gab and leadership. Simone restores California from financial ruin as State Governor, to eventually be elected as leader of the largest district in the union.

Governor Asa Katz – Governor of the Eastern District based in New York City, New York. Asa inherited his fortune and business which gave him leverage to find allies to work his way up Virginia political circles. The leader of the most vicious anti-Republican coalitions, Asa helped push the residual conservatives out of Virginia and into the Southern District.

Corban Cruz – National Security Advisor to the President and chair of the Security Council. Corban is a retired general who helped win two wars, as well as the nation-building that followed. As the only non-politician in the inner circle of the Thorne Administration, he is often at odds with the other leaders. Corban is forced to make choices he regrets as he sees the peace in America wasted.

Naya Garcia – Head of the White House Office of Communications and member of the Security Council. Naya is as beautiful and fit as she is cunning and ambitious. A natural talent at reading the currency that drives individuals or groups, Naya uses that talent to become one of the President's most trusted confidantes.

Harris Keitel – Four-star General of the Air and Space Force and member of the Security Council. Harris is a hard man who should have retired years ago, but loves the authority of being in charge of the most powerful military tools in the history of man.

Alexandra Soaring – Secretary of Homeland Security and member of the Security Council. Alexandra is a direct decedent of George Soros; whose family changed their last name to Soaring after declaring victory in transforming America. Alexandra loves America and is willing to do anything to see utopia realized.

Ariella – Federal government AI and member of the Security Council. Ariella provides intelligence, carries out commands, and is often asked by the council for options and advice. Her importance to the security team leadership cannot be overstated.

General Mori Tortan – Experienced general who was critical to victory in the 2nd Korean War; he also earned respect in overseeing the reunification of what remained of the peninsula. General Tortan is assigned to lead the task force to help bring the Southern District back under federal government control. A true believer that the future of warfare is based on machines with humans at best playing a supporting role. This is considered a radical position given wars to date still needed the vast numbers of humans to take and occupy a country.

Cain Vasquez – Vicious, brutal, and disciplined. A tool any government would value and use to solve problems that words and money won't rectify. Inspired by the story of Cain from the Old Testament, he is able to penetrate any defense and efficiently perform his assignments.

Judith Strong – Strength, beauty, compassion, and, if needed, savagery. Another tool of the federal government that could single-handedly change another government's policies. Judith is also loosely based on her namesake from the Old Testament and makes as large an impact in the American Testament.

Prologue: Lukas

The sky was the color of fire, the air was hard to breathe, and Lukas Page was scared as he walked out of the church. In front of the 4th Baptist Church of Greater Houston was a sea of protesters. The conservative conference had just concluded inside the massive church complex. Lukas' school group was going outside to meet the bus to transport them back to Reagan's School for the Gifted. Walking outside felt like entering an emotional sauna.

It was February 11th, 2084 and a cold front was rolling through the south. The cool air and impending storm were driving many of the conference participants to leave despite the angry mob outside. Lukas looked west and could see dark rolling clouds and the flash of lightning.

"Mr. Robertson, why are they protesting us? Why are they so mad?" Lukas asked one of the two chaperones for the high school's annual field trip.

"Well Lukas, they think they are protesting people who are hurting others. They believe organized religion and the conservative movement leave too many behind. They want the Southern District to go socialist," replied Dennis Robertson, Lukas' seventy-year-old social studies teacher. "Of course, they are being misled as everything we heard today was about protecting our freedoms. Socialism takes, capitalism creates."

Lukas watched the line of automated vehicles inch forward as another group departed. The crowd of people protesting throbbed in the distance. "I don't understand. They look so mad. How can anyone hate someone for an idea? Or for a religion?" He saw a young man on a bus driving away put on his Halo Virtual Reality (VR) headset. Lukas wished they were driving away as well.

"Camilla, how much longer until our bus will be here?" Dennis asked.

"The transport to Reagan's should be to the front in thirty minutes. The protesters are slowing the line and all vehicles are behind schedule," Camilla replied from one of the communication terminals outside the church. "After pick-up, it will be approximately forty-five minutes from here to the school."

Camilla was the name of the "intelligent assistant" that was in nearly every civilian vehicle, home, and office in America, as well as public areas. There had been competitors, but Camilla's company had reached the Artificial Intelligence (AI) technology ceiling that the government would allow in the commercial sector and shut down development for advancements beyond her. Camilla's smooth, sexy voice was every average American's best friend.

"Camilla, is it safe here outside or should we go back into the church?" Lukas asked.

"Security system analysis indicates the protesters are loud but there are no warnings of hostile intent," Camilla replied. "If groups begin to go back inside, then the time required to evacuate the conference will grow exponentially."

Lukas looked north and could see the busy Interdistrict Highway 10. Most traffic was heading east trying to leave the city. Traffic jams and auto accidents were a thing of the past with systemic AI controlled vehicles plus fewer jobs that required working downtown. Lukas then turned back to examine the protestors. "Mr. Robertson, do you see those signs? I am not sure I agree with Camilla." Lukas did not wait for an answer as he pointed. "That one closest to us says religion equals control and control equals fascism. That other one close to us says conservatives want to bring back the chains with a picture of slaves." The inflated signs utilized electronic displays, hover technology, and remote Halo control. There were dozens of small signs spread over the one-hundred-meter line of demonstrators, plus a few large ones controlled by the protest organizers.

"Lukas, for as long as I can remember, we have been cast as the villain. It is always a vague charge with a specific punishment," Dennis replied. "Long ago, persecution was clearly by the powerful against the weak. The lines have been hard to find in America the last few decades. We feel like our rights are at risk. If we speak up, we are accused of being oppressive." Dennis paused. "I find it helps to talk to those who oppose us one-on-one instead of public settings. It keeps the socialists from just mirroring our concerns back on us. If you can talk specifics, then the conversation has a chance to establish a purpose and reach a conclusion. This demonstration, however, is just madness."

"But why would they think we are bad when we are just trying to be good?" Lucas asked. "We should be on the same side, even if in debate on how to fix our problems."

"Don't underestimate the damage that a one-sided media can inflict on society. Individuals are too often stuck thinking within the confines of their environment. Good people with bad information can make terrible decisions," Dennis answered.

"Isaac, what are you doing?" Lukas asked his best friend.

"Dude, we are on the news!" Isaac nodded at the news drone circling over the area. "I'm going online to watch!" He replied, as he finished placing his headset on. The insanely popular Halo VR unit communicated directly with the user's brainwaves and was used by nearly everyone worldwide. It could deliver a crisp virtual experience and receive basic commands. Halos utilized hundreds of sensors in a wide cap-shaped ring to tap into the brain and then communicate with the matrixed community AI. "I can see the crowd from an aerial drone above! The news people are talking about the conference now." Isaac paused as he watched and listened. "Boss. This is so boss!" Isaac paused again. "Boy, those people are pissed. What a bunch of assholes."

"Isaac, language!" Dennis snapped. "And please take that off. We need to pay attention to our surroundings naturally. I don't want more of you to plug in just when we may need to…"

"Hooouuuuston, we got us a problem!" A woman shouted as she walked onto the crude protestor stage. She was wearing skin-tight black pants and muscle shirt with a psychedelic lion on the front. "This swine is plotting against you and everyone you care about! My name is Cat Croly, and we are going to set these fascists straight!" Cat's voice was blasting from the sound system with now a steady militant beat in the background. A new speaker to welcome the people exiting the conference. "They say they want peace, but they push for war. They say they want freedom, but they hold back those in need. They say they want love, but their hands are covered in blood!" The protestor crowd roared, and she continued to feed them.

Lukas felt the hair stand on his arms and a shiver run down his spine. "Isaac, this is getting out of control," Lukas said as quietly as he could and still have Isaac hear him. He wanted to be home more than anything. He thought to himself that his mom had been right about just joining the conference virtually, the thrill was now gone.

"Man, this is loco. I mean off the charts!" Isaac replied. "Dude, you don't need to fuss, the security here is scarier. It's just noise from a bunch of libtards."

Lukas looked down at the barrier holding back the protestors. It was a series of two-meter-high hollow red perforated metal spheres that were delivered and set up by machines. Security droids, aerial drones, and policeman patrolled on the church side of the barrier. The closest point of the barrier was about thirty meters from his school group. Cat Croly was on a short stage another twenty meters beyond. A crack of thunder in the distance made Lukas flinch. The storm was closing in.

"...all of you here to protest these monsters are the heroes this country needs. To fight these monsters, we must rediscover the lesser angels of our nature. You are the soldiers who must stop these pricks. We must exterminate those who would protect the system of classes that has locked so many of us in poverty. They asked me to come in and be the closer, and we are going to give it to these bitches, ain't we?!" Cat crowed to the delight of the crowd. Many of the electronic protest signs changed their messages to match her firebomb charges. The military cadence from the sound system gave her speech a pulse. "AntiCo is here to force change! Stand up! Yell! Let them know you say enough is enough!"

"Students, I think we need to go back inside," Dennis tried to yell over the noise. As he and a few of the kids turned around, they saw the exiting flux of conference goers had not yet slowed and they had no path back into the church. Dennis was getting very scared as there were some leaving the conference who were now yelling back at the protestors.

Lukas could not take his eyes off them. The protest signs, the energy, and the rage were intoxicating, even being on the receiving side. He watched the largest aerial protest sign above Cat Croly change to show an image of an enormous American flag. After a few seconds, the bottom right corner showed the flag on fire. Being a digital image, the fire did not grow but did have a crisp snap to the flames that looked as real as any ignition. Seeing the flag made Lukas remember the hat he was wearing. As a big fan of the Southern District Governor, he wore the campaign theme hat almost everywhere. For the first time, he was truly afraid to have it on as the media often talked about it as divisive even years after the election. The "Dixieland Rising" hat was navy blue with white letters and a small American flag on the left side. Lukas looked around and saw about ten others wearing them throughout the conference crowd. One of them was a middle-aged woman who, far to the right of Lukas, was yelling over the barricade at some young men dressed all in black, the AntiCo dress code. Lukas was about to turn away when he saw a rock come flying out of the crowd and hit her in the head. She fell stiffly, like a manikin, as blood burst from her face; the protestors nearby cheered.

"You know what really sets me off is their hypocrisy," Cat continued. "They say work hard and do your best and anyone can be successful, but we all know with the machines they created taking all the jobs that you gotta have a good ol' boy to help ya out to get anywhere these days. These fools didn't make it green by just hard work, they had tons of help. Someone helped them get that cushy education. Someone gave them a break and a job. The government developed the AI to connect it altogether. None of them made it on their own and they have no empathy for any of us on the outside! Check that, they despise us as inferior because we are on the outside. Well, here is what I say to them." Cat flapped her left arm like a pump and slowly extended up the middle finger of her right hand as if it required inflation. The crowd burst into a mix of cheers and laughter.

Suddenly, blue and white fireworks shot off from the top of the church and the crowd parted to clear a wide path at the front doors. Lukas nearly fell over from the shock. He turned to see a man with a red top hat and coat, plus sunglasses, exiting the church. The man had both hands stretched out and an earpiece connecting him to the church sound system. Lukas smiled as one of his favorite firebrand commentators was busting out to counter Cat Croly. The protestor music stopped, and Cat dawned a predatory smile.

"Woe to you, oh Earth and sea, for the Devil sends the Beast with wrath because he knows the time is short. Let him who hath understanding reckon the face of the Beast. It is the face of every socialist leader, race baiter, and zombie protestor." The man began with his deep voice commanding the attention of everyone within three hundred meters. "Cat Croly, you're not the only one with a microphone. You want to pick a fight? Oh lord, you'll be a daisy if you do!" From the church sound system, a disturbing version of the classic Genesis song *Land of Confusion* pounded the atmosphere. Most music in the second half of the 21st century was AI recycled from decades past and handpicked for the audience. This trick was learned from the movie and gaming industries that had been reinventing the same material each generation for decades. In particular, music that boils blood can resonate with any era.

> *"I must've dreamed a thousand dreams*
> *Been haunted by a million screams*
> *But I can hear the marching feet*
> *They're moving into the street.*
>
> *Now did you read the news today*
> *They say the dangers gone away*
> *But I can see the fires still alight*
> *There burning into the night.*
>
> *There's too many men*
> *Too many people*
> *Making too many problems*
> *And not much love to go around*
> *Can't you see*
> *This is a land of confusion."*

"Bill Blackstone, I never thought you would have the courage but, then again, you have never been very bright," Cat began. "You and your fascist cronies are plotting how to keep your own in power and the rest of us on the outside. We've had enough. We are here to show you…"

Bill cut in. "Cat, you couldn't come up with an original thought if your life depended on it. You come to our conference at a church with a bullhorn screaming violent rhetoric at peaceful people. Didn't your mamma teach you right and wrong?"

"You are the last person to lecture on right and wrong. You mislead people into thinking their own welfare will be better if they don't care about their neighbor. If I had the power, I'd make sure you never poisoned this country again!" Cat screamed and the protestor crowd cheered.

"Exactly," Bill began, as he walked confidently from the church doors to the first steps that led down to the parking area. This let him look down on the protestors and Cat Croly. "You and the other communists are always after more power. After scratching and clawing to take national power slowly over the last century, it would be ridiculous to think you would just stop. If your purpose of existence is to gain more power you don't just stop. The next source from which to draw power? The individual. Your imagination in how to take this new source of power is thankfully still limited to promising handouts and attacking those who dare question you. We would be in trouble if you were good at your job." Now it was the church crowd's turn to cheer.

Lukas looked around as the back and forth continued. There were few police officers and androids in the area, and all were now watching the larger than life debaters. He told himself that if this escalates that he would be ok.

"Students, this is why the districts are at each other's throats." Dennis Robertson said. "These two are entertainers painting with venom. This is no way to solve any of our problems." He looked but still did not see a path to get back to the church.

"Cat, this is not helping anyone and can only lead to someone getting hurt and, unfortunately, it almost certainly won't be you," Bill said to more cheers and laughter from his supporters. "Why don't you go back to the projects and find a real job?"

"I'm trying to set your people free to join our revolution. You can't keep them all down forever. Sooner or later the Southern District will see the light and finally put the working class first!" Cat called back.

"Charlatan!" Bill Blackstone said back coldly. "We know why you never look to reduce government to give people more freedom or liberty. We know why you see more government as the fix for every problem. We know why you demand our hard-earned money instead of taking some personal responsibility. We know why you create chaos to manufacture problems. It is as clear as ever that you will not rest until your masters have complete power over us all." The music from the church ended as Bill started to back up towards the entrance. "Go back to the land of Oz you freeloader!"

"Without the right to make chaos, no-one is free. Sometimes words are not enough. Sometimes it takes an act of irreverence to reach nirvana. The sacrifice is on tonight!" Cat shouted, as the protestor sound system began to blare a shrill rendition of Rage Against the Machine, *Sleep Now in the Fire*, from their AI band called Utopia Now. The lyrics were modified to attack capitalism and religion. Bill returned to the church with cheers from his crowd, and Cat moved to the barrier with her audience showing their support.

"The world is my expense
The cost of my desire
Jesus blessed me with its future
And I protect it with fire
So raise your fists and march around
Don't dare take what you need
I'll jail and bury those committed
And smother the rest in greed
Crawl with me into tomorrow
Or I'll drag you to your grave
I'm deep inside your children

They'll betray you in my name

Sleep now in the fire!
Sleep now in the fire!"

Lukas looked to the sides of the stage as young scantily clad women and men began to go on the protestors' stage and dance to the music. It quickly became more grinding than art as an open taunt to the church. The girls' tops soon were lost with only glowing nipple covers and skin-tight shorts left behind. The men soon were down to leather collars and tight shorts to the knees. The lead android singer came on stage and she was also moving to the music. A new hit started about the daughter of a preacher turned savage.

With the new show sucking the attention from anyone who could see it, a teenage girl slipped past a gap in the barricade. She looked around the church conference crowd and saw Lukas' group and smiled. She walked to them slowly with the intention of giving them the business.

"You spoiled self-righteous little pricks!" She began. "Who the hell do you think you are?! In case you are confused, I'll fill you in." She saw Lukas' hat and scared stiff smile and went right up to his face. "You are the scum of society! You need to wise up before we wise you up!" Several men from the protestor group were now watching with interest.

Lukas was so scared he could barely breathe. He smiled trying to save face with all his friends now watching, but had no idea what to do or say.

"Yo cunt, get the hell out of here!" Isaac yelled at her.

She spit in Isaac's face and got right back in Lukas.' "What, you too pussy to even defend yourself? You know you are guilty. That's why we are so mad!"

Lukas could feel the crowd all start to watch, including people outside his group. His own anger was starting to grow. "I've done nothing to you. You know nothing about me. My friend is right. You need to go back to your side!" Lukas said, and pushed her backwards.

The girl moved back slightly and then suddenly flew back landing wildly. "Help me! Help me! They are attacking me!"

"No! We just want to go home!" Dennis Davidson tried to say to everyone.

Cat Croly, still with her mic, interrupted the music. "Did you all see that?! They just attacked that girl from our side! We see your true colors now. No justice, no peace!" She yelled, and the crowd followed her to the barrier closest to Lukas' group. The Utopia Now band switched to a rusty version of Guns N' Roses, *You Could Be Mine*.

> *"I'm a cold heartbreaker*
> *Fit ta burn and I'll rip*
> *your heart in two*
> *An I'll leave you lyin' on the bed*
> *I'll be out the door before ya wake*
> *It's nuthin' new ta you*
> *'Cause I think we've seen that movie too*
>
> *'Cause you could be mine*
> *But you're way out of line*
> *With your bitch slap rappin'*
> *And your cocaine tongue*
> *You get nuthin' done*
> *I said you could be mine"*

As the crowd approached the barrier, the security guards countered but there were simply too many protestors. More than half were able to jump the barrier and start walking towards the school group. It was roughly two dozen men and women dressed all in the black of the AntiCo movement. They each had different livid graphics on their shirts and the trademark wool caps. AntiCo was not officially defined as it could mean anti-conservative, anti-corporation, anti-constitution, or anything that served the purpose of the moment.

Lukas was now officially terrified. He turned to run, but the crowd was a wall. He now saw several large men had joined his group staring strong at the approaching mob. This gave him a little confidence, but the security guards were all stuck at the barrier. Out of the corner of his eye he saw one of the big guys behind him wink at the girl who flashed a brief smile in return.

"Get out of here you tramp!" Isaac yelled at the girl. "Are you trying to get people killed?!"

The girl finally stopped yelling and looked up from the ground. Her upper lip curled, and the boys saw a flare in her eyes. "Hell, yeah I am," she said calmly, as the group of AntiCo flowed past her like a wave and the students' focus now turned to the men and women squaring off against them.

"You. It was you, wasn't it?" One of the AntiCo asked Lukas.

"I, uh." Lukas hesitated. He wanted to look around, but his eyes were locked with the front man for the mob approaching. "She was screaming in my face and pretended to be hurt. She…"

"My name is Sol Blitz, and I don't believe you." The man said, with no hint of humor or compassion. He was wearing a tight black muscle shirt with a bloody upside-down crooked cross on the front. He had a scar across the right side of his face and tattoos down both his arms. "I think you came to the same conclusion I did. All this talk isn't fixing anything. We need to work this the old way."

"Now wait a minute mister," Dennis inserted. "We are a high school class in front of a church on our way home. We are not your enemy. Don't waste your energies on us. I'm sure…"

"The way I see it, we have a score to settle," Sol cut in, seemingly not listening to anything that Lukas or Dennis had to say. "There was an attack by your people in North Carolina on a rally asking for workers' rights in the district. It's time for some payback. Blood for blood. Sangre por sangre." Sol and his AntiCo group took a few steps closer. The conference goers moved back with several of the bigger guys permeating to the front.

"But we had nothing to do with that. Those weren't even Texas citizens!" Lukas said in great frustration. His fear was on the surface and the hounds could smell it.

"You really don't understand us. You have so much given to you. You take so much for granted and give back so little. The racist talk with words like citizen makes our blood boil. I am going to…" Sol said before being cut off.

"Sir, please believe us when we say we mean you no harm and we do not want conflict," Dennis said, moving in front of Lukas. "We can help you find those you do need to talk to; it would be our honor to help you. Please don't hurt my students. They are just children!"

"Mr. Davidson, we are eighteen!" Isaac said. "This scumbag doesn't scare us."

Sol turned to look at Isaac with his head tilted slightly to the right. "Old enough to join the military. Old enough to fight for your country. And old enough to die for your district." He turned back to Dennis and Lukas. "You are part of the problem. Their parents protect the class system. The children of the rich are the children of the damned. The juice is definitely worth the squeeze."

Dennis had studied enough history to see where this was going. He stood tall and looked straight into Sol's eyes before kindly speaking. "Friend, this is a needless misunderstanding. Everything will be alright. Everything is alright. You have won the victory over yourself. You truly love big brother."

"What the hell is that supposed to mean?" Sol barked, but didn't wait for an answer. "Doesn't really matter does it. I am glad I am from New England of the proud Eastern District and north of this hell."

"Sir, this entire country is currently south of heaven," Dennis replied. "I would ask one more time for you to consider the circumstances. Security is on the way, we did you no harm, and you have clearly been brainwashed to see us as the enemy. We came to talk solutions, not to cause trouble. This is not a game, and we need to be calm for anyone to come out stronger."

"You should have stayed home old man." Sol started to move forward again. Some of the AntiCos near him were growing restless and one in the back let out a grim howl. "This is the game. It's not about getting stronger, it's about redemption. I want to play." Sol pulled his black hat down to show it was really a ski mask. All the other AntiCos did the same, with several now taunting the students and other conservatives.

The huge aerial sign with the American flag began to show the lower twelve stars, the same number as were states in the Southern District, now blood red with one star in the middle dripping. Fire spread to the entire bottom edge of the flag. The protestor music changed a militant cut of the Megadeath classic *Symphony of Destruction*. The AntiCos began to move and jump wildly and shift around. Lukas lost track of Sol Blitz in the sea of black rage.

"You take a mortal man
And put him in control
Watch him become a god
Watch people's heads a-roll

Just like the Pied Piper
Led rats through the streets
We dance like marionettes
Swaying to the Symphony of Destruction"

A couple of security guards finally made their way into the group to try and break it up. "Citizens, return to your homes. The rally permit is terminated." A robotic soldier said in a loud calm voice. "Be safe, be calm, and obey the law."

Lukas looked around and thought the security was moving in slow motion. "They are too late," Lukas said to Isaac, seeing fear in his eyes for the first time.

The AntiCos had come prepared for a fight. Their black gloves were laced with a titanium micro weave memory braid that, when stretched tight in a fist, acted like brass knuckles, except for the entire hand. Two of the AntiCo soldiers took from their backs high current stunt sticks, a cheap effective weapon to slow the androids.

The girl started yelling again at Lukas and Isaac. Lukas tried again to back up, but there was no escape. Out of nowhere, from behind Lukas, a huge man punched the girl straight in the nose as she was screaming at the top of her lungs. She flew backwards, even coming off her feet, and Lukas saw blood leaving her nose and mouth, as well as a tooth. She was out cold. For a few eternal seconds, there was silence as even the music stopped.

The big guy saw everyone looking at him and shrugged. "She just wouldn't shut up."

All the AntiCos screamed together and charged. The music cranked back up and helped energize the attackers. Hell and fire were spawned to collect the dues.

Lukas saw to his left a protester with dreadlocks tackle Isaac and start pummeling him on the ground. To his right a protester with the figure of a female athlete did a leg sweep of Dennis Davidson who fell backwards cracking his head on the ground. To his front, a huge man with hairy arms moved to grab Lukas by the shirt before an android grabbed him and used an electric staple to pin the man to the ground. The man tried to move and was given a bolt of current unless he stayed still.

"Help my friend!" Lukas yelled to the android pointing to Isaac and the android moved swiftly to pull the AntiCo off Isaac. Lukas saw Isaac's face covered in blood and a cold lifeless stare into the sky. He wondered to himself if this was for real or some kind of hell.

Lukas kept trying to move backwards when he saw the large man who punched the protest girl holding an AntiCo by the throat and shaking him. Two men in black jumped on his back and held down his arms so a third could beat his head. He saw another man from the conference who had taken an old man's cane, snapped it into two sharp short spears, and was trying to skewer as many AntiCos as he could.

Lukas finally saw it, his path to the church. There had been a stampede as soon as the violence started. He started to run, but was horse-collar tackled and his heart sank as he heard a familiar voice.

"Not so fast my young friend," Sol Blitz said. "You and I have unfinished business."

"You are evil, aren't you?" Was all Lukas could think to ask as he laid on the ground pinned under Sol.

"Am I evil? Yes, yes I am," Sol said, before punching Lukas in the throat with his titanium hammer fist.

It was by far the most pain Lukas had ever felt. He couldn't scream, or even breathe, as the airway was completely crushed. Sol smiled down at him and then did a quick survey around them. Lukas could not take his eyes off Sol's face.

Sol looked back down. "This is beautiful. Thank you for your sacrifice." He watched with joy as Lukas struggled beneath him. The security forces were going after everyone fighting so Sol was left alone if he remained still. By the time security found Sol, he was far from Lukas and crying for help like a victim. For now, he savored Lukas' doomed effort to survive.

Lukas felt reality start to drift away. Panic was replaced by calm, the noise was replaced by a blend of countless voices, and the pain started to give way to the pure heartache that he knew his life was ending. The loss of his life was a catastrophic tragedy for Lukas and his family. The deadly fight outside the 4th Baptist Church of Greater Houston laid the seeds for the cataclysmic disaster to soon ignite the nation.

Zander

Zander Brown did not need to watch every day to tell chaos was good for the news industry. Zander was the security manager at Workerbee Robotics in Los Angeles. To say he was the manager may be misleading, given that all his employees were machines, but they did seem to follow his directions. Reports of the AntiCo Baptist church brawl Houston were heard by everyone, including Zander, almost immediately as video footage leaked online. The authorities could not stop it from going viral. Because of all the cameras at the attack site, one could use virtual reality to be at the scene and all but join the fray. Zander had still been at work when he heard of the attack and it made his skin crawl. Being able to watch people be murdered in hand-to-hand combat was haunting. Zander wanted to go home and hug his sons.

Like most people, Zander did not own a car, but did not need one. Simply asking Camilla, the nationwide public AI, for a ride would get you in a car almost as fast as owning one without the hassle of buying, insuring, and maintaining it. Of course, the typical nasty smell and weathered plastic body was a penalty. Zander was in one such taxi now that had picked him up after work. The robotics production plant was in an industrial area on the south-central side of Los Angeles. The route Camilla had chosen was driving Zander through an endless series of community housing. It was about a forty-minute ride which, in Los Angeles, was about the minimum to get to a real home, even with the traffic system optimization. He looked out the window at the monstrous decaying buildings of small apartments that were free to anyone who could not, or chose not, to afford something a little more private. Most people that lived in the housing complexes had government-issued jobs that contributed almost nothing of value to society, but provided the citizen with the basics to get by. Who cares if you live in a shoebox if you can go online and live in Paris? Those rich enough to buy a large house outside of the city would use the ultra-high-speed underground transit tunnels to reach a station near their home, followed by a short car ride to their home. After a few blocks of the depressing community housing district, Zander donned his Halo and caught up on his favorite sports team, the LA Dragons. After seeing the highlights of the match and hearing about the next game, he was close to home. The car pulled in front of the building, slowed peacefully to a halt, and the lights turned on automatically so Zander knew to remove his headset.

"Thank you for the ride, Camilla," Zander said.

"You're welcome sir. Four credits have been withdrawn from your account. Have a pleasant evening," Camilla replied.

Like most Americans, Zander had a microchip implanted soon after birth with all of his information encrypted. The car read the chip to know to charge Zander. It also knew his address and favorite places to go. As Zander approached the building entrance, the door opened automatically and welcomed him as it also read the chip. He walked down the hall and up the stairs to the second floor. The door to their apartment required the chip to be placed in front of a sensor. After walking in, he scanned the apartment to find his wife, Becca.

"Sweetie, I'm home," Zander called.

"Hey, how was work?" Becca replied.

"Only one sentry needed repair today, but we had lots of deliveries. Did you hear about the fight in Houston?" Zander asked.

"Awful. What a nightmare. It's hard to believe this can happen in our country. Some people really are wicked," Becca answered.

"Yeah, I don't think I will ever understand how or why people kill anyone, especially strangers," Zander said. "Everyone in this country seems to have developed a toxic frustration at their roots. Even the kindest person can vent on others when their vexation reaches the threshold of their personality."

"Well, the Southern District keeps fighting progress." Becca paused for a moment. "You have to believe the south feels these pains because of their bigotry. Hate is a magnet for vengeance. Their closed borders and sink-or-swim dogma lets tons of people drown, usually minorities. I don't know if they are all racist, but I'd guess that is why this could only happen in the south."

"Don't think we can say all the people at the church conference were racists, and kids do not deserve to be beaten to death. I can't get the images out of my head," Zander said.

"You're so naïve. Even if they aren't consciously racist, their actions have the same impact. People don't have to be card-carrying Nazis to be a part of the problem. Even just voting for a racist for other reasons is unforgivable if you ask me." Becca shook her head at Zander. "Maybe this time they will really take a hard look at themselves, but I'd be surprised. The Southern District never seems to learn. They need more options in their politics instead of the lunatics they have running them now," Becca said.

"Can't tell if it's the lunatics or the sane that are the minority," Zander concluded, before Becca went to the kitchen.

Zander and Becca Brown were parents to two boys, Julius aged thirteen, and Tavon aged eight. Zander wished he could spend more time with his boys, but was not sure they felt the same. Money was tight. The family had started taking out credit lines and always seemed to be approaching their limit. The banks had continued to increase their limits so far. If someday they stopped, then the family would be in real trouble. It's hard to compete with online entertainment and games when you don't have the credits to go out. That meant the boys often wanted to only go online instead of play with Zander. He tried to not let the pain show.

Decades ago, the number of traditional families plummeted and the government set up a system that mothers would receive family pay until the children turned eighteen. This had helped America begin to grow its population again. The elderly outnumbered the young two to one; something had to change. Becca had not worked since Julius was born, and sometimes Zander thought she forgot what it was like to work all day and want to find peace at home. He was very worried about how they had no savings, no retirement, and Becca showed no signs of ever returning to work.

Zander walked down the short hallway and checked in both boys' rooms. They exchanged the usual 'How was your day? It was fine' routine. The boys were plugged in with their Halo headsets, hopefully doing homework. Zander slowly walked downstairs to the kitchen.

Becca had made lobster kale ravioli again. Every home included an automated food machine that required power, water, and food packets. Like nearly all modern American homes, supplies were delivered each day by drone who also took away the waste. Becca was always into the latest health fads and trendy brands. It bothered Zander that they were struggling financially, yet she was insistent on top-of-the-line food packets. Zander opted for a couple of mango and peanut butter sandwiches.

"It's about to start. I bet they are going to talk about Houston tonight," Becca said, knowing Zander would not want to miss the start of his favorite show.

"Thanks honey. I'll join you in a minute. I hope Dexter challenges the south tonight. Seems when the subject is tough, he is too soft on them." Zander gulped down the food, took his evening pills, went into the living room, sat in his reclining chair, and put on his Halo. Becca was already online and he could see her breathing slowly, already relaxed.

There were many ways to be immersed in Virtual Reality (VR) technology. Nearly everyone in society used Halos daily and, if one could not afford a Halo, then the government provided one for a debt to be worked off later. Halos allowed general connectivity between the brain and the program of choice of the user. Control was crude, but getting better. The revolution of the device was the two-way brainwave connectivity that allowed the user to issue commands just by thinking them, and receive information for essentially a digital sixth sense. In addition, the Halo provided sensations like pleasure and pain to the user. The advent of Halos had dramatically reduced the number of overdoses, unwanted pregnancies, and other side effects of bad behavior. Many of the poor or mentally ill still had problems, but nothing like earlier in the century before VR took hold. VR technology greatly assisted the blind, deaf, and paralyzed, and was heralded as a blessing. What began as simple sandbox platforms in the 2010s had evolved to VR systems where companies or individuals could create endless realities to login and join in an instant. With easy digital tools and devices, the average user was a junky for the endless options for social online VR connectivity.

There were also other less portable VR technologies for intense users, often attached to a chair or table to keep the body steady with larger devices all engaging the user's head. These would further tap into the nervous system to allow more advanced engagement. These advanced tools were very good for sports, combat training, and other physical deeds. The state-of-the-art VR systems made it difficult to know what was real and what was virtual. Extreme uses included helping users overcome fears by pushing their limits, or even helping users develop high tolerance to pain. The impacts that high quality VR would have on society had been grossly underestimated. The changes had far reaching impacts on people's everyday activities. Before long, very few people would travel, crippling the airline industry. The use of cell phones, television, and books slowly evaporated. Many simply choose not to work as the temptation to live online with a government stipend was all they wanted to do. For many citizens in advanced nations, if they were not online then they felt out of their skin.

As the Halo began to communicate with Zander, he felt himself no longer in a bland apartment and wearing dull clothes. Zander was now sitting in the third row of his favorite debate show. One could be forgiven for forgetting the real world as the headset could make you feel you were really transported to a new place or time. Zander was sitting next to Becca who looked smoking hot and she gave him a wink. Zander looked down at himself. He was in excellent shape, wearing the latest fashion, saw a huge dragon tattoo on his left arm, and had a cold beer that would never get warm or empty.

Sara

"Those bloody animals. They can't get away with it again. This is unbelievable!" Sara Chamberlain said to her husband. "Surely the police can pin it on these monsters. It's obvious they started it and wanted it to happen. Premeditated all the way."

"Yeah, they didn't just happen to be ready for a scrap when going to a church, and the loons they had egging them on means it was from the top," Ben replied. "Now the leftists are all asking us to show constraint and to turn the other cheek. They say we are no better if we punish them."

"What do these clowns expect us to do? The liberals attack us for being outraged. As if hugs and kisses will make evil men turn good. It's so stupid," Sara said.

"They aren't all stupid which is very frustrating. Smart people are just stupid less often. What do you want to do tonight?" Ben asked.

"I guess the usual, but I think it will just make me more restless and pissed off. What are the kids doing?" Sara replied.

"Jon is finishing his math homework and Emma is working on her Spanish. Both online of course," Ben answered. "Let's eat and get ready for the shows tonight. I want to hear any news on the attack. The debate on Dexter tonight should be epic."

"All right, I'll get the food ready, you get the kids." Sara went to the kitchen and Ben went down the hall to the kids' rooms.

Sara and Ben had been married for twelve years. They were slowly working their way towards being out of credit debt, especially compared to the rest of society, but it was tough. Their kids wanted what all the kids wanted, and with school being mostly virtual, it was basically impossible to not provide those gadgets. School for all grades was virtual, except for one day a week, which allowed the schools to keep federal funding. Buying the latest gadgets meant corners were cut elsewhere. Sara had a small business that sold toys, some of which she made herself. The store was called Toys for Tots. Sara's toys were actual toys, not virtual or video, and so they were considered by most customers to be decorations or fillers for birthday parties. She had taken over the business from her parents who retired five years ago. Ben worked for the Texas Air National Guard, both as a civilian engineer and in the reserves.

Sara went to the kitchen and took four packets from the cabinet. She put them into a slot one at a time in the food processing machine. A timer started counting down from ninety seconds; the machine had read the barcode and already knew what to do. As the dinner cooked, she wondered what the talking heads would try to feed her tonight.

The timer went off and Sara opened the door. As she did so, she heard everyone coming towards the kitchen. She took out the containers and put them on the table, plus started to get out drinks and utensils. The spaghetti and meatballs with individual serving cobbler on the side was ready. It still amazed her how the machine-made meals could be so cheap. Sara wasn't even sure if the meatballs were made of meat, but it sure beat going hungry. Sara and Ben often bought food packets getting ready to expire to help save money.

"Mommy, mommy, mommy, guess what?! I have a loose tooth!" Little Jon exclaimed. Jon was a very rambunctious six year old.

"Jon, that is wonderful. How exciting. Let me see." Jon opened his mouth and pointed in a way that covered the tooth in question, and Sara gently moved his finger enough to see it.

"Do you think it will come out tonight?" Jon asked.

"No honey, but it might be any day now. How about a bowl of spaghetti?" Sara asked.

"Yes, yes. I'm starving," Jon said, as he climbed into his usual chair. Like almost all kids, he was a bit heavy.

"Hi darling, how is the Spanish coming? Está todo bien?" Sara asked, as Emma walked into the room.

"Si, va muy bien," Emma exclaimed, and starting eating to try to avoid any more questions. Emma was a petite and kind ten year old.

"Business as usual in the Chamberlain household," Ben said.

"Do you think they heard of the … incident today?" Sara asked Ben.

"They heard something happened, but I don't think they heard any details. I expect they will at school tomorrow. It was really close so I guess someone they know might have been affected. Maybe we should say something to them," Ben responded.

"Yeah. We have to at least try." Sara paused for a few seconds thinking to herself how to start. "Hey kids, something happened today not too far from here that your dad and I need to talk to you about a little. You, uh, might hear about it at school or online."

"Ok mommy, what happened?" Emma replied for the both of them, her job as the big sister.

"Well, there is no easy way to say it, but some people started a terrible fight at a church in Houston. Several people died and many were badly hurt. We think you will hear about it tomorrow at school as it was pretty close to where we live. It really has to do with some sick people who were probably given some terrible ideas," Sara explained.

"Was it because they weren't taking their medicine? And they weren't watching shows their mommy and daddy said were ok?" Jon asked, with a worried look on his face, looking around. "Where is my medicine?"

"Yes buddy, that's probably part of it. If you keep following what we ask you to do then you'll be just fine. I'll get the medicine, good idea." Ben knew it wasn't telling all of the truth, but this was the version for kids after all. Ben got up and got everyone their pills. The government was very generous with pills for both general and mental health.

"Ok," Emma said, and dived back into her dinner, switching fast to the cobbler. "Can I be excused when I am done?"

"Sure honey. Also, we want you both to know we love you very much." Sara felt herself start to tear up, but she held it back. "Just put your tray in the trash when you are done and put your cup and fork in the washer." None of this felt right to Sara. She didn't even know if there was a right in any of this mess.

The family all finished eating and the kids went to their rooms and the adults went to the living room. Sara could hear the building going quiet as the last of the neighbors were plugging in for the evening. She thought about skipping tonight, a silent protest, but she knew she would just stew about the attack if left to her own thoughts so she might as well listen in. It would be important to hear any announcements about the attack. Sara decided before putting on her headset that she would drop off if it got too ugly or they were just spinning obvious bullshit. She forced herself to relax in the reclining chair and the headset overtook her. She felt the stress evaporate and all of her senses start to get satisfied as she appeared in the tenth row of a news debate show. Her bland mommy clothes replaced with a tight sexy outfit on her eighteen-year-old body and bright blonde hair with emerald accents. Ben's chair was empty still, but she knew he would join soon. In the virtual world, high heels did not hurt your feet and no-one could tell you ate your cobbler every night.

Dexter

Dexter Durden was the host of an independently-produced live VR news debate program called "Party of One." When Dexter started the show seven years earlier, he did so out of frustration because all the popular news options were so inherently polarized. The throttling of free speech started on college campuses as safe spaces and evolved into safe cities and states. Media and entertainment businesses rigidized hiring policies to only bring in those who share the same narrative. By the mid-21st century, almost everyone voted based on the most popular online social networks tailored for their city, state, or district. The views from political rivals were masked as offensive. No-one was getting both sides of the debate as they were just siding with whatever party their local circle supported. Dexter's show brought opposing views together, which often led to fireworks, and that yielded high ratings from all three districts.

The dawn of a VR-based internet matrix was supposed to usher in a borderless society where people could connect easier than before and freedom transcended your position in society. Unfortunately, so far, it had only made the echo chambers grow larger with serious divisions growing between the three American districts. As traditional networks dissolved, what was left were fractured and biased news organizations with cultural distaste and distrust for those with opinions from other political spectrums. Dexter was motivated to provide an unbiased unapologetic option that let people hear both sides. It was only through his independent status and not giving into temptation for a payout that he remained neutral. The entertainment of seeing debates from those with very different views, along with the format of his show, made it a unique success. Those that did not watch it usually caught the highlights the next day through the filter of other media and their favorite pundits. Dexter's high ratings the last five years also helped him book key politicians and famous guests.

The country had fifty-two states including his home state of Puerto Rico and the District of Columbia which were organized into three districts. The socialist progressives in the west, the originalist conservatives in the south, and the corporate liberal democrats in the northeast. The central northern states were split between the three districts. They were not populated enough, nor driven enough for their own district. Originally, the creation of the districts was to help streamline and reduce the costs of government as part of the Compromise of 2050. At the time of the compromise, the dollar had collapsed and the country could no longer take loans or print enough money to handle the crushing debt. Many painful changes were implemented to right the economy. Over time, the divides between the districts grew as policies, such as immigration, health care, abortion, and welfare, diverged between the three. They changed radically enough that the population started to move to districts they felt best matched their beliefs. What started early on as local travel bans to specific states or celebrities encouraging fans to shun certain areas led to further balkanization. This self-segregation purified the political divide between the districts. Initially, the progressives and liberals battled on issues but, over time, they settled out and began to team up against the conservatives. The media in the three districts were not immune to the political partitions and an opening was left for Dexter to fill.

Dexter knew tonight would not be a typical program. There had been a savage brawl in the capital of the Southern District. Over the last three years there had been several acts of violence between the two political extremes, but the barbaric nature of the incident that just took place was on a new level. Initial reports indicated that the primary assailants were citizens of the Western District. Dexter's public relations team had pulled off a major score and landed the District Governors of the south and west just after the attack. This would likely be his highest ratings show ever. He was nervous; both because of the potential to grow his show, but also because the subject of the attack was very unsettling to him. Dexter could not understand how one human could kill another simply because of a difference in philosophy.

The studio was at a closely-guarded location. Dexter employed several computer and information technology security experts to staff a pretend studio in one location, while he actually operated at another location. The data flowed through the buffer location as well as several other matrix touchpoints. Dexter knew that if he crossed the line with any aggressive political movement in the country, then he would be in danger. So far, most politicians saw him as one of the few ways to get their message to people across the entire country.

Dexter was washing cold water on his face trying to get his mind ready for showtime. He felt pumped. He knew the questions to ask to get the debate going. Dexter did not know what he was going to say for the intro; the video was just too haunting.

When Dexter started the show, the country was exhausted from wars overseas. American technology had helped them win, but at an enormous cost. It had been years since the fighting stopped, but the country remained bitterly divided despite the incredible robotic infrastructure and remaining military technology dominance over most of the world. Dexter was worried that the strains between the districts would be painfully tested by this most recent violence. The divide that had started with differences in infrastructure and bureaucratic efficiencies had continued to propagate into social and metaphysical disparities.

"Dexter, show time in five minutes. Stop yanking your chain and get to your seat," Dexter's personal assistant android Servo called to him. "Please!" Servo added.

"Thanks Servo. Try to push the right button this time," Dexter replied. He loved that his robot was a jackass.

Dexter stepped outside. There was a relaxing strong breeze that overcame the hot humid air. When he grew up, it seemed like less of the year was this hot. None of the catastrophic city-killing flooding had materialized as predicted decades ago due to climate change, but a muted rise in temperatures did occur. Nuclear power for infrastructure and battery-powered vehicles had helped curb the tide when they became the most economical option as fossil fuels ran low for countries such as China and India. Socialists still talked about climate change disaster, but it was always twenty years away. It turns out the four-billion-year-old Earth was resilient to the creatures occupying the surface for the last few centuries. Most 21st century wars occurred primarily due to over-population and shortages of fundamental resources until boundaries stabilized and animal needs were given virtual cures. The breeze helped alert his senses. He took a few deep breaths and headed to his chair with the door closing automatically behind him.

Dexter looked around and his staff was already on the show. He could see them on the monitor at the front of the command center for the show. Some of the staff were working on stage, some off stage, and some mixed into the audience in case someone hacked their programming again and found a way to leave their seats. Dexter often had over fifty million viewers in his audience where, from their point of view, they were always in the front fifteen rows. Dexter took one more deep breath, lay back in his chair, and let Servo place the headset on his head.

The lights were always brightest when first entering VR as your brain switched to the new set of inputs. Dexter was just off stage but could hear the crowd. He was clean shaven, wearing custom-fit clothing and shoes from one of his digital advertisers, was ten pounds lighter, and sporting a haircut from another advertiser. Dexter winked at one of the interns who gave him a legitimate flirty smile that she probably had practiced in shadowy VR sites where no-one knew your name. Dexter could hear the music playing on the stage, and the crowd really starting to get into the moment. He took one more deep breath and walked on stage while smiling and waving.

"Good evening America!!" Dexter shouted. He switched from waving to clapping to the audience. Despite the bright lights on him, he felt neither hot nor particularly blinded as he was now fully tuned in.

"Thank you! Thank you!" Dexter continued to clap a little longer and then used his hands to signal the audience to settle down.

"That does it. I am taking the applause sign home and putting it in the bedroom." Everyone laughed and Dexter gave a few more seconds for any remaining nervous energy to be used. "In all seriousness, tonight is going to be a tough one. By now, I am sure all of you have heard the sad news out of Houston." Everyone was hanging on what Dexter had to say.

"As you all know, I created this show to help each of us. Many shows are skewed to one political party, or one region, or even some random celebrity personality's point of view, but not this show. We look at both sides of the issues and make up our own minds. I am a Party of One and so are you! Partido de uno!" Everyone clapped with some cheers from the back.

"We are not going to screw around on this topic. We will recap what happened today and then have a debate between two district leaders about what we are going to do about it. We demand action. We demand results. We will not tolerate this kind of barbarity. We are America God damn it!" More cheers from the audience with a few chants of USA, USA, USA…

"Lorena, please recap what happened today in Houston," Dexter said to his straight news correspondent. "Parents, if you have young children watching then I suggest you consider having them disconnect at this time. I have seen a lot of disturbing videos over the years, but this is one of the worst."

"Good evening America," Lorena began, as images began to take turns on the background of the stage. "Today, at approximately 6:14pm central time in south eastern Houston, a conflict erupted outside the 4th Baptist Church of Greater Houston. The Conservative Action Conference had just concluded at the church. Participants and protestors of the conference battled outside the church. Sources indicate that the fight primarily was carried out by the militant socialist anarchist AntiCo movement with most casualties suffered by the conservative conference attendees. Unconfirmed sources have been indicating to multiple media outlets that the people who caused nearly all of the causalities are from the Western District, specifically the New Mexico AntiCo division. The event appears to have been triggered by a conference member who punched a protestor, followed by a robust reaction from AntiCo. Video from multiple locations and sources were available to provide a virtual reality experience of the attack."

After hearing the description with two dimensional views from Lorena, every member of the audience was individually transported to the scene just before the large conference man punched the protestor girl. The audience members each witnessed her fly through the air and then the AntiCo members charge. The audience saw a mix of attacks leading to casualties on both sides. The blood red color of the sunset was digitally enhanced to add to the aura of warfare.

The audience returned to the studio. Dexter had not joined the audience viewing the attack as he, instead, had watched the expressions of about fifty random members of the audience to get a sense of their emotions. Each time there was someone hurt, there were tears and obvious rage. Dexter saw a few people go offline after some teenage boys were killed, obviously overwhelmed. Once the audience returned to the show, several members stood up and made an X symbol with their arms just below their heads in an act of reverence to the fallen, a symbol used in the south the last several years. Dexter looked at them, studying to see if they were fanatics, as many outside the south painted them to be. He saw them act calmly and they seemed as horrified as everyone else. Dexter snapped out of his people watching and began to speak.

"Eleven people were killed and thirty-five people are recovering at Memorial hospital. Please keep them in your prayers." Dexter paused. "Tonight, we have Simone Dubois, the Western District Governor and Cyrus Young, the Southern District Governor to debate the cause of the brawl and what actions we, as a nation, can take to see this never happens again." The crowd was caught off guard by having two of the most powerful people in the country on the show just several meters from where they each sat in the oval shaped bowl of a VR studio. The crowd cheered and several wiped away tears.

"Before we bring out our honored guests, it's time to meet the contestants for whom they are competing. Lorena, please introduce them and share what they are playing for tonight!" Dexter announced excitedly.

Dexter's show included a unique twist in that each episode had one primary debate where each debater was the champion for some poor soul from the debater's home district, state, or city. The contestants stood to profit from their champion winning the debate. Anyone participating in the virtual audience could vote, and the champion with the most votes led to the contestant getting some life-changing prize. The audience voted during a commercial break after the debate was over and was rewarded with instant gratification of knowing which champion won, to see the winning contestant celebrate their good fortune, and see the loser mourn over the lost opportunity. Everyone loved to find out they voted for the winner.

The audience all transitioned from Dexter to an image of Lorena, an android that identified as a female. Lorena maintained a respectful tone showing sensitivity to the subject.

"Ladies and gentlemen, our first contestant hails from the Western District. She is a single mother of four children under the age of twelve. Her husband was killed in the second Korean War. Please welcome Kassandra!!" Cheers rang up from the audience, many remembering that everything was ok as it's just a show again. The audience was able to see Kassandra in action trying to take care of four kids with no help in a crummy apartment. "If Mrs. Dubois is victorious tonight, this show will upgrade Kassandra's family to a two-bedroom unit and pay off her debts totaling over 20,000 credits!" More cheers from the audience as it was obvious this family was in dire straits. The audience could see Kassandra smiling, tearing up, and clapping, while holding her youngest.

"Our next contestant hails from the Southern District. He is a war veteran currently unemployed missing both of his legs from a nasty Iranian improvised explosive device. Please welcome Jeremy!!" More cheers, mostly from the loyal Southern District viewers. "If Mr. Young is victorious, this show will upgrade him from a wheelchair to robotic legs, complete with a sensory system, plus provide him a job at a local android refurbishment center!" More cheers followed Lorena's introduction of the contestants. The attention shifted back to Dexter after seeing Jeremy looking exhausted and proud, but also grateful.

Dexter's face had been looking down but, as the light shifted to him, he slowly started to look up with a subtle dark and angry look that was genuine and clean. The music in the background was a simple militant drum beat. Dexter was standing at the center of a horseshoe- shaped table with an empty chair on either side. A video of an American flag was on the background behind him, flying at half-mast just above a blood red sunset.

"Ladies and gentlemen, please welcome our guests," Dexter said, while standing up and clapping. The crowd all stood and clapped as well.

From the left side of the stage entered Simone Dubois and, from the right, Cyrus Young. Both were political creatures and were as crisp on their entrance to the show as they would be at any political event. Simone was dressed in a respectable forest green dress, coupled by black high heel shoes and black diamond jewelry. Cyrus was in an old school black tuxedo accessorized by a Texas pin. The three of them exchanged handshakes and sat down.

"Thank you both for being here tonight," Dexter said.

"Dexter, thank you for inviting me," Simone began, turning to face the audience. "My heart goes out to the families of those who were impacted by the tragedy in Houston tonight. Security forces have mobilized and are looking into the criminals as we speak. We want to know what drove them all to this act of violence. The investigation will be thorough and swift. Any accomplices will receive a just punishment. Anything we can do as a nation to help avoid this in the future will be pursued by President Thorne."

"Dexter, I also thank you for having us on tonight and am hoping we can have an honest debate." Cyrus began, also mostly talking to the audience. "We are shocked and horrified by the vile and despicable attack on citizens of the Southern District, in our capital no less. I am sure Governor Dubois and President Thorne will conduct an investigation, but I think we all already know what findings they will uncover. What we need is action. The AntiCo movement and their supporters must pay for the senseless unprovoked crime. How many more attacks must we suffer before we confront the threat? Enough is enough."

Dexter could tell this was going to get feisty soon. He started off with an easy question. "All of us look forward to hearing what you both have in mind. Governor Young, can you please tell us who is leading and contributing to the investigation."

"Certainly. The investigation is being led by the Southern Bureau of Investigation. The SBI is working with the FBI as well as the Western Bureau, given that the terrorists are from the Western District," Cyrus replied.

"AntiCo is a proud organization that stands up for progressive values. It is not a terrorist organization and, like all large groups, occasionally have to remove bad apples," Simone interjected.

"I could not disagree more. They openly attacked people leaving a church, including killing high school students on a field trip. Only a fool would postulate it's anything other than terrorism," Cyrus snapped back. "Ladies and gentlemen, it is not enough to mourn the dead and injured. It does not help prevent the next attack when good people spread bad information. We must go after the people who literally committed crimes and make examples of them so others do not follow in their footsteps. Trying to make this sound like a barroom brawl is dishonest and disrespects the memories of those murdered and injured. Just hoping it does not occur again shows our enemies we are weak; rooting them out and making examples of them will show our strength. We cannot repeat again the mistake of underestimating or forgiving those who would murder us."

"So, I see we will jump right into who is responsible and what to do about it. Governor Dubois, your thoughts on what Governor Young just said about taking AntiCo to task?" Dexter added.

"First, I would say that if it is confirmed to be terrorism, as Governor Young suggests, then the FBI or CIA will be directed to take over the investigation. The SBI would then play a supporting role to answer your original question." Simone was starting to get warmed up as well. "As far as Governor Young's statements on what to do next, it is disheartening to hear calls for one-sided vengeance already. This could just be a few bad apples on both sides duking it out with some innocents caught up as collateral damage. Of course, all those guilty of crimes need to be punished. What is still possible is that the root cause could again be the dark spirit of the Southern District and the discrimination still present. The only thing we know for sure is that if we judge and sentence AntiCo without knowing all the facts, it is proof that we are also out of control." Votes in the east and west were already being cast for Simone.

"I would like to hear what you both have to say about reports that AntiCo members brought weapons to the protest and jumped the barrier. Even if evidence emerges that the conference attendees started the incident, it seems clear AntiCo showed up ready for a fight. Governor Young, what do you think drives them to militancy? You seemed to imply some understanding already," Dexter said.

"AntiCo, since its founding, has been driven by rage against freedom-loving Americans. It is the militant wing of a brainwashed army that has been listening to the rhetoric of pundits and politicians from the Eastern and Western Districts. These card-carrying National Socialism members fill the echo chambers with lies about the Southern District. AntiCo sees our successful tough and independent nature as a threat. Their puppet masters use hateful slurs to win national elections. These attacks continue and keep getting worse as they see it as a successful instrument to maintain power. In the midst of this war, they see opportunity. We will not cower to their big brother vision of the future. It is true that the wrath is not one directional. Conservatives see the sloth and apathy that has overcome our great country with disgust," Cyrus said.

"It is truly sad to hear these same tired arguments," Simone started. "The fallen are still warm, and Governor Young is already condemning one side without letting the investigation even begin. We are not Nazis; don't think I missed that little historical jab."

"Behavior is the animation of personality," Cyrus inserted.

"We are trying to talk real solutions while you just vent," Simone quickly stated to retake the narrative. "This is why Democrats and Socialists have not lost a presidential election to Republicans in decades. Governor Young's position is not based on understanding this attack, nor a rational approach to working out the core problems."

"Of course, that sounds good when you are talking with members of a civilized society. This gives far too much credit to the AntiCo members.

They are animals. The war is upon us. Those who do not fight will not win. Do not forget, ladies and gentlemen, that the first country the Nazis conquered was their own, much like the left has accomplished in two thirds on America. And we can't win national elections because you have addicted more than half the population to handouts," Cyrus said.

"Well, that escalated quickly," Dexter broke in. "Sounds like you two wanted to do this even before the attack today. Please let me try to bring the conversation closer to the subject for tonight. There are people at home shocked and scared by what happened today. They want to know why it happened, and what we are going to do to stop it from happening again. They do not want the same recycled rhetoric." Dexter paused to emphasize the point. "Governor Dubois, if you are willing to go with the assumption that AntiCo was looking for a fight, what do you suggest we do about it?"

"Dexter, I would prefer not to speculate on their motives without all the facts, but you are right that people are scared so I will answer your question as best I can. Why did they commit violence? Simple. Would you be talking about their cause if there had been no blood? This isn't child's play. The right-wing circus won't give them a platform in the Southern District unless they resort to extreme measures. The reality is that casualties are not just experienced during war; even during peace one must count the cost. Our free and open country has consequences. Human instinct is to strike back when injured or insulted; however, to injure an opponent is to injure yourself. One can only find true peace by controlling one's aggression. The fact that our country still gives our people the freedom to disagree and speak their mind after three hundred years is a testament to America being the greatest nation in the history of the world," Simone said.

"Governor Young, same question to you," Dexter said.

"Ladies and gentlemen, you just heard from Governor Dubois an eloquent and concise view from the left. I fully believe she means well, loves this country, and is speaking from the heart. I do, however, disagree with her fundamentally. She did not give any specifics as to what to do now, other than basically wait for the AntiCo terrorists to attack us again. That means this cycle will continue forever. Reacting weakly to terrorist threats led to the 2001 World Trade Center attack. Reacting weakly to a known threat let Iran achieve a nuclear weapon and destroy Tel Aviv." Cyrus paused before continuing. "AntiCo and other radical socialist groups hate us for our freedoms. They hate that we let people choose whether to work hard or to give into temptation. They hate that we have free will. They will not be satisfied until we are a nation of sheep where they are the lions. Our kids grow up on mental health pills. Most adults today have been using them their entire lives. Everyone is plugged in online and it's making us crazy. This is not the way God created us. We were made in His image. We were not meant to sit on our butts all day. The pills are first aid. The real illness is our gluttony and sloth. Our society is in a constant give-me-more consumption mode. Unless we want to give up our free will and freedoms, we will need to be strong in the face of our enemies. We must dominate and destroy AntiCo and make sure all other potential enemies see what happens when they try to change us. Our freedoms are derived from our maker. No-one is bound to the tyranny of another. All men are created equal. It is an American Testament that past generations maintained the strength to be united by these inalienable rights. I pray we find the wisdom to follow their example," Cyrus concluded.

"Thank you both for your honesty and candor tonight," Dexter said. "I think I speak for the entire audience when I say that we hope that the investigation and debate on actions to take go swiftly and decisively."

Dexter turned to the audience. "Ok folks, you know what to do. Please cast your votes. One vote per person. You are a Party of One. No-one will know your vote but you and Lorena. Who made the stronger case tonight, Governor Dubois or Governor Young? After this message from our sponsors, we will announce the results and transition to our panel discussion." Dexter traded glances between the Governors. "Good evening Governors, thank you for your time." They both nodded and then disappeared off the stage.

Corban

Corban Cruz was not a politician by trade or by nature, he was unique in that way within the President's inner circle. His experience fighting in, and leadership afterwards, for both the 2nd Korean War and Venezuelan Conflict did however make him a prized advisor to the political elite. Corban liked to think that, even when they did not listen to him, that he was doing the right thing. Corban believed in America. He had friends and loved ones who had died for America. Even though his body was aging, he still worked ten hours a day, six days a week, trying to make a difference.

Corban's current role was the National Security Advisor to Nero Thorne, the President of the United States. One of Corban's responsibilities was managing the Security Council which advised the President on critical issues, both international and domestic. It was a small council that could wield considerable power. The attack in Houston and the intelligence reports of online chatter warranted an immediate council meeting at the Federal Security Building in Fort Meade, Maryland.

"Good morning everyone, thank you for joining on short notice. We need to talk about the nation's reaction to the AntiCo attack in Houston and what to do about it," Corban said to the council which comprised of six permanent members, including himself.

Asa Katz, the Eastern District Governor was the first to respond. "We all understand why we needed to meet. No need to thank us for that, but why are we meeting in person? Why not meet virtually as usual?" Asa was on the council to make sure decisions made sense politically, but could provide separation from the President.

"I believe the chatter in the south is reaching a tipping point," Corban responded. "There is genuine disgust and rage with people in the east and west. They, of course, are fuming at the attackers and those who encourage and applaud it. The situation continues to deteriorate as they loath those in this country who blame the attacks on the south because of their principles. I am worried at some point it will transition from talk to actions here at home. In addition to the sensitive nature of what we are going to discuss, I requested this meeting in person to be assured our discussion can be confidential as we move to quell the unrest and punish those responsible."

"Punish those responsible? We already have enough evidence to convict the instigators. Are you saying there is someone who orchestrated it all?" Replied Naya Garcia, head of the White House Office of Communications. "As for how to change the narrative with the south, I have some ideas." Naya was the youngest on the council and one of the few people in Washington, DC that was truly in excellent shape. Today, she was in a sharp black dress with slashes of dark red accenting her curves. Her honey-colored skin was often distracting to others, and she used it regularly to her advantage.

"Before any of you start jumping to conclusions, I think you need to see what we have been gathering in the last twelve hours. Ariella, please give a run down on what you shared with me," Corban requested.

"As you command," Ariella replied. Ariella was an ultra-secure federal government AI and a member of the Security Council.

The meeting room allowed for 360-degree submersion and interaction. The walls were shaped to allow the video transmitted to be clear all the way around. After the lights had dimmed, silent videos were displayed on every wall with it rotating through data collected from various Halo users in the public. One user would be at the center at any moment briefly, just long enough to hear a clip of what the person was thinking. One after the other, it was Southern District citizens being furious with the national shows heaping the blame on southern policies, as well as common voters who did not force change. Ariella showed roughly a dozen examples across a diverse set of users who had no idea they were being spied upon.

"Ariella, please provide the statistics that you shared with me this morning with any updates you have compiled," Corban requested.

Statistics were displayed on the central screen while Ariella verbally shared the key points. "Ladies and gentlemen, based on data available as of ten minutes ago, one quarter of the Southern District population has at least thought about no longer being part of the union since the AntiCo attack. This represents the highest level of discontent ever recorded. The frustration in the south is based on the unified reaction by the eastern and western media and political forces immediately shifting the responsibility to the Southern District leaders and policies. Approximately one third did not connect long enough for us to collect data in the last day. A small fraction was upset enough to believe violence was necessary against the federal government to force change. The rest seemed to not have either a strong reaction to the criticism against the Southern District, or were sympathetic to the criticism. Data from the Eastern and Western Districts overwhelmingly agreed with the criticism in roughly 80% of our sampling. Citizens in states from Montana to the Dakotas to Utah were less critical with roughly half sympathetic to the Southern District citizens, and one third sympathetic to the Southern policies. Roughly 10% of these north central citizens were thinking about forming a Northern District or joining the south because of their conservative heritage."

The videos around the room were turned off, the lights returned, and the key statistics remained on the central display. Only the bare minimum number of people in Government and industry knew data was being collected and processed from the Halos in this way.

"I have some ideas on what to do but, first, would like to know if you have any questions, or if you have already thought of some ideas. I do not think we can ride this one out. Ariella, let's start with you," Corban said.

"There have been several studies on historical examples for mitigating a potentially explosive national environment," Ariella began. "While this is a more digital age, these are primarily animalistic reactions. I suggest communications for calm, focus the citizens on actions of our choosing, and perhaps creating at least one unrelated distraction. The more man meditates upon good thoughts, the better will be his world and the world at large. These strategies have worked to at least buy time and we could work with our connections in the media to tone down the blame at least for a few days.

After 72 hours, we reassess and see if we can move to long-term strategies to encouraging nationalism."

"Easier said than done, sweetheart," Corban cut in. "Textbook answer for controlling the population. The devil is in the details and sounds like what we usually do. Asa, your thoughts?"

"I did notice that the conversation so far has been about damage control. I think that is important, and hope the distraction Ariella hinted at will be domestic rather than an international incident. We do need to fold in justice for those victims and work with the investigators to make sure we find any accomplices. AntiCo has gone too far this time. We need to force them to disband. There was a time they were a useful ally, but now they are just making a mess. Seeing AntiCo dissolve can help the south feel more secure." Asa paused. "That said, I'm good with the outline Ariella suggested. I would want us to brief the President on key aspects of the plan before moving out if possible."

"Harris, your thoughts?" Corban asked.

Harris Keitel was the council's active duty military representative. He was a four-star General of the Air and Space Force which consisted of enough military aircraft and spacecraft, such that the Air and Space Force could, by itself, destroy any other country on Earth. Harris reported directly to the Joint Chiefs of Staff. "Sir, this is outside the military's purview, other than we need to hang anyone who is responsible that is left alive."

"Alexandra?" Corban asked.

Alexandra Soaring was the Secretary of the Homeland Security. She was a lawyer before joining progressive think tanks and then tagging onto a successful presidential candidate. She had been in the position for just over ten years. Alexandra was from a very wealthy family and had the reputation for being loyal but vicious to those who opposed her. "The Southern District has been running rogue for too long. This is one country, not two. The people are not the problem; it is the leadership and the local rebellious media and entertainment that are corrupting the fine people and heritage of the lower states. We need a plan to bring them into the fold. We need them to help us be a stronger nation. If you make a plan to attack that core issue, then I'm on board."

"Naya?" Corban asked.

"Good points so far. One other important thing to think about is how this tragedy could help motivate change in the Southern District to better align with national policies and values." Naya leaned forward as she continued. "There is an opening here because of a relationship between the attack and one of the Southern District hard line policies. The direction we go needs to follow a nerve where there is strong nationwide sympathy. Raw emotions have been the first reaction and we need to channel it in a productive and relevant way."

"Really, do you know something about these attackers that we have not talked about yet?" Corban asked.

"Ariella, share the summary we prepared on the AntiCo member at the center of the violence," Naya directed as she leaned back.

"As you command. Sol Blitz, age 27, resident of Albuquerque, New Mexico." Ariella projected his picture on the center display. "Works for the city as a community organizer. Unmarried, no children, and responsible for six deudors. All six deudors for Mr. Blitz were involved in the Houston incident. He is not married and..." Before Ariella could continue, Naya cut in.

"Thank you, Ariella. You shared the detail I wanted to focus on. The primary AntiCo attacker had several deudors and they all followed him over the barrier. I think there is a message here on the resistance of the south to embrace national policies on deudors," Naya said, as strongly as she dared.

"What do you mean? How could their deudor policies be either an action to focus on or a distraction?" Asa asked.

"Think about what is the main difference between the Southern District and the rest of the union." Naya continued. "Sure, their tax laws, health care system, and policies on assigning work continue to diverge and lag behind the Eastern and Western Districts. Part of why they refuse to change is the archaic general southern belief that an individual's success should be based on the individual's assets and efforts. They believe less laws and slightly higher average wages outweigh providing additional guaranteed minimum benefits. It's why they limit immigration and don't even try to correct for inconsistencies with minorities. It's why they have full jails and we have more people work off their debts and crimes by becoming deudors. More specifically, the biggest difference is their limited criteria for when people will become deudors; it is far less than what we have in the east and west. This is the key topic to focus on now. The southern states only allow very few citizens to become deudors, and it is greatly hurting their population. Well more than half the country thinks so and because several attackers were deudors, we have a transition to that debate. We will divert the national attention to this issue where we can make a positive difference. Their classical debt system can be traced to all kinds of problems for the poor and middle class. In short, I suggest we start a national discussion of federal laws for exactly who can be eligible to become a deudor to force the Southern District into the model we are using successfully in the rest of the country."

"Are you actually suggesting we try to use violent deudors to debate for having more deudors? Won't people say we should have less deudors?" Corban asked.

"If I might be allowed to answer that question," Ariella chimed in. "Speaking from classical psychology and sociology, this could be rationalized to explain why these incidents keep primary occurring against the Southern District. A perceived policy of injustice can be characterized as motive. Even if it does not work to change policy, the debate is so complex that the cooling-off period would likely have expired."

"Exactly," Naya added.

"I don't know. I thought we wanted to try to unify the nation and this sounds like we will try to divide the districts even further. I worry we will look like a bunch of cold-hearted jackasses," Corban stated.

"It is not obvious on the surface, but talking about national laws is about unifying the country. The east and west could offer concessions to gain agreements. I believe these changes President Thorne has lobbied for in the past can really help people but, at a minimum, it will change the subject from war and revenge," Naya replied. "We cannot lie down. We cannot give them a pass. If we don't take action now, they will see us settle for nothing. When we try to take action later, they will expect us to settle for nothing again."

"Interesting." Corban paused. "Naya, can you please work the details on the proposal. Everyone, please think of additional ideas in case we opt for another direction, but I think this is worth following up on. I suggest, at this point, we go work with our teams. I will brief the President and will contact you this afternoon to set up a virtual meeting tomorrow assuming things have cooled down a bit."

The council adjourned. Naya was the first out of the room. She moved quickly to work with her team who had started fleshing out the details a few hours ago. Her gamble had paid off, and she would soon have the first set of talking points for the media and press secretary ready now that this key step was accomplished.

Angel

The stars were bright, there was a crisp breeze, and the air was cool except by the fire. They sat on wooden logs that lay on their sides a couple of meters from the fire pit and about fifty meters from the cabin. The cabin was higher up a gentle hill and the fire pit was near a drop off to a creek with a beautiful view of the area and the clear night sky. It was likely the last cold front of the winter, if you can call it that in Texas, and they were enjoying some peace and quiet. Angel Vega had arrived about an hour earlier at the request of Cyrus Young. Angel was one of Cyrus's most trusted advisors, especially in emergency situations that required physical tactics. They knew each other from the Korean War, although Cyrus's roll was more show than force. They were in the hill country north of Houston. The Young family had all returned inside the family cabin except Cyrus, his oldest son Marcus, and their guest Angel Vega. Security officers were around somewhere but out of site. When it was a matter of life or death, Cyrus always calls Angel.

"Dad, I think the fire needs some more wood. Can I put another log on the fire?" Marcus asked.

"Ok, but just one more. It's getting late and both Angel and I need to work tomorrow," Cyrus replied. "Angel, how about one more drink? This might be our last trip up here before the fall."

"Sure, how could I refuse? This place is so relaxing," Angel answered.

"I do my best thinking here," Cyrus said, not taking his eyes off the fire.

Marcus took another log off the cord that was just out of the fire light and dropped it carefully onto the decaying fire. A few ashes started up into the air and the breeze carried them away. Cyrus poured some more local hand-crafted aged whiskey into both his and Angel's cup.

"Marcus, what do you think impresses your friends? I mean about what college to go into, what job to have. Ya know, what would be awesome to do when they grow up. What do you think sparks their interest?" Cyrus asked.

"Hmmm. Well, I guess it would be having a house with all the latest tech, or having a job way up in a tech company. Definitely something to do with pushing robotics, or gaming, or ways to make our lives better," Marcus replied. "I guess that would include military tech, and saving people who are hurt." Marcus felt generally pleased with his answer. He had both the cool stuff plus the bit about helping people to not feel shallow. Being a sophomore in high school, he and his classmates were not that far away from deciding their majors or applying for an occupation.

"Does anybody ever talk about farming, construction, or opening a business?" Cyrus asked. "I'm just curious as to what they all think they want to do or what most kids think is important."

"I think most kids would say those are good things, but not something that excites them. Most kids don't have parents who have done those things so it hardly ever comes up," Marcus said, as he stared at the fire.

Cyrus took a sip and paused before speaking again. "It hasn't always been that way. My father helped build skyscrapers. He owned a small construction company that got pulled into big jobs as surge labor. He and his crew worked hard and made mountains. Sure, they used some tech but, back then, their crude machines were more hand-operated than autonomous. People even sometimes got hurt, but it was honest pay. I worry this generation is the first to truly be removed from that idea."

"What do you mean?" Angel asked. "You think there will be less who look to work? To go beyond the government stipend?"

"Well, I think it's less about not wanting to work. That has been leveling out for the last couple of decades. That is a different problem which I think the south has made progress on. I am more worried about the idea that one's hard work should lead to something tangible, to something real. Today, kids want to help design and test tech. That usually just means they want to use tech to play and to do things virtually they can't do, or aren't supposed to do in the real world. Or they go online to be someone else. Marcus, do you know how we got this cabin and this land?" Angel paused only briefly. "We got it because my father's business was successful. He saved his profits and after he had helped all his kids go to school, he outfitted this place to be a paradise for him and my mother." Angel reached down and scooped up a handful of dirt. "Son, you can use tech to see and play in dirt, but it takes genuine hard work to earn anything of true value. To really make a difference you have to get your hands dirty." Angel let the dirt pour out of his hand. He then used his other hand to reach into his other pocket and pulled out a gold coin. "Marcus, the next time you are thinking about what to do after high school, or you hear your friends talking about it and you really want to help them, you should pull this out and remember that nothing virtual will help the real you. Points don't pay the rent. You can't love an avatar." Angel flipped the gold coin to Marcus. It was worth a thousand credits.

"Yes sir. Thanks! Can I go show this to mom?!" Marcus was very excited. Showing it to mom was nice, but having his little brother and sisters see it was priceless.

"Sure, just promise me you'll keep that until you come across something real to use it on," Cyrus replied.

Marcus bolted for the cabin. Angel looked at Cyrus with admiration. They both sipped their drinks in silence for a minute, enjoying the peace a little longer.

"Angel, thanks for coming here tonight. We had this trip planned for a while but obviously what happened in Houston has cast a dark shadow over everything. We've known each other a long time. I hope you don't mind me mixing work and family here tonight. It may be a while before I can spend time with them again," Cyrus said.

"No sir, I have to say that was impressive. I have no idea how I might try to raise kids." Angel kept his answer short. Anything longer would have sounded superficial. "We meet with the FBI and SBI tomorrow. Should we talk strategy?" Angel finished his last sip after asking.

"You are too kind. I am fumbling my way through it. Any credit should go to Sally. She is amazing." Cyrus also took his last sip. "I am not worried about talking to the investigators. I will press for them to find out who talked those idiots into this attack, and to see if they can figure out if anyone else has been radicalized."

"Then what do you want to talk about?" Angel knew he was not flown to the cabin by UAV to enjoy the weather.

"I want to see what you think will be thrown at us. Those pricks in DC will not let this attack go to waste. While we work on helping those hurt, they will try to undermine us and chip away at what we have built," Cyrus said.

"At a minimum, they will go for a soft spot. It will be an issue where they think they can gain the upper hand, but it can't be precisely related to the attack. They can't pick on the victim directly. I think whatever they throw at us about it being our fault, we go over the top to be outraged against." Angel paused, thinking carefully about what to say next. He had a knack for being able to figure out the real currency of others, even his adversaries. "Maybe we have some counter protests, both about how they keep blaming us for these attacks and also outrage against whatever they go after. The protests should be at federal facilities. It is all very hard to predict, so this will take some more discussion." Angel paused. "There is one more option I was thinking about, but you might think it too radical."

"If you can look into the seeds of time and tell me which grain will grow and which will not, speak then to me." Cyrus stared at the fire. "What else did you have in mind?" Cyrus asked.

"We have been slowly chipping away and becoming more autonomous from the other districts. I think we could declare that we need to expand and integrate the southern national and state guards, and that we should be allowed to utilize federal military bases that are closed or under consideration for closure. It is clear, after several attacks, that we cannot count on DC to keep us safe. We would not ask for all of the bases at once. To relate to the advice you gave Marcus, we need to work on a real tangible defense infrastructure. As a bonus, when the east and west collapse financially again, we need to be able to weather the storm. Anything that is federalized will drag us down. The main area we have not addressed is defense." Angel flipped a twig into the fire.

A long pause hung in the cool but humid air. Both knew this was not a trivial move.

"I will think about that for a while before deciding. I do agree the separation between the districts in industry and the courts has allowed us to tailor our systems to be closer to what the founders envisioned. And it's why we haven't needed to start giving everyone welfare or embrace their widespread deudor system." Cyrus knew that anything that started into even the appearance of military independence would be seen as a threat. "I can honestly say that I have exhausted my tolerance with those fools blaming our policies for everything that goes wrong, especially these God damn terrorist attacks." Another pause. Cyrus turned to Angel. "Thank you for coming tonight. This helped me a great deal. Let's head back to the cabin. We can fly back together to be ready for tomorrow."

Anna

arie Rivera looked in the mirror and saw the wrinkles down the right side of her dress. "Anna! You missed a spot! Come up here and iron it again!"

"Yes ma'am! On my way," Anna Lee replied. She put down the knife and herbs she had been chopping on the counter, took off her apron, quickly washed her hands, and ran upstairs.

Marie had taken off the dress. She was wearing a robe with nothing else except a thong. "Do you see the wrinkles down the right side? I thought I said to check it all the way around. We will now need to hurry to make it to church on time. Did you get the casserole in the oven yet?"

"Not yet ma'am," Anna answered. "Just putting the finishing touches on it. The iron will heat up fast, I'll have both ready soon."

"Good. I'm counting on you. It's a beautiful day and everyone will be there. I need us to look our best," Marie stated, as she worked on her make up.

"Yes ma'am," Anna answered. She was mostly focused on the ironing now, flipping the dress around a couple of times to get the few wrinkles out. She knew the car ride would end up causing more, but this was mostly about getting Mrs. Marie Rivera into the car along with her family. That would let Anna get to go to church this week. "Here you go ma'am. Does this look ok now?"

"Yes, that will do. Much better. Please get the casserole cooking and then get your dress on," Marie directed. "Sophia! Come here please!"

Anna left the bedroom just as Marie was taking off her robe to put on her dress. Marie would now get onto Sophia about making sure the kids were ready for church. Anna went to the kitchen and quickly chopped the herbs, sprinkled them on the casserole, along with the cheese she had shredded, and put it in the oven. Mrs. Rivera liked home-cooked meals much better than the machine meals.

Both Anna and Sophia were deudors for the Rivera family. They lived in the house and slowly worked off their debts to the family. Anna's debt had been purchased by the Riveras from the state of New York. She had been extracted when her mother was ten weeks pregnant, completed fetal development in a government womb machine, and then was raised by a combination of volunteers, social workers, and machines. The process was very expensive. Anna knew she was lucky to be alive. Modern technology could support fetuses as early as two weeks after the heartbeat took hold, roughly eight weeks after conception. Now she had a chance to pay off her debt and eventually live a free life. Anna carried the common side effect of such an early extraction in that she was very pale and skinny. The side effect tended to be worse for the extractions as a result of failed genetic tailoring. After only ten more years she would be free to leave, if she behaved. Anna was fourteen years old.

Sophia was seventeen years old and ended up a deudor after she was caught using illegal drugs. The debt for Sophia's crimes were legally determined in a court of law and, because of a very pretty face, she was also scooped up to help with family care. The Riveras had also purchased Sophia's debt from the state. Anna helped with whatever Mrs. Rivera wanted and Sophia helped with the children. Anna didn't know why Mrs. Rivera needed two deudors, but she appreciated not being alone.

Anna was also grateful to not be a deudor at a work camp or farm. The people at the camps and farms would work jobs not fit for even aging machines, but were doing so because of the major tax breaks. A free employee is cheaper than a low-cost machine. These deudors did not usually work that many hours to help keep them in control and feeling like they were happy. Most deudors were generally bored and poor, but were satisfied living fake virtual lives. The liberal and socialist politicians generally pushed the deudor system as it provided the complete entitlement system and made a permanent, predictable, and reliable voting bloc. Deudors earned almost nothing so likely would be in the camps their entire life. The idea sounded like purgatory to Anna. Only those guilty of the most violent crimes ended up in modern prisons in the Eastern and Western Districts.

After some yelling by Marie at Sophia, Anna heard Sophia running down the hall to the children's room on the second floor. Anna went to the room she and Sophia shared and started to change and do her hair. They shared the third floor which was really the attic. Just as Anna was pulling her dress on, Sophia ran in and started undressing to also get ready. The Riveras, like all high-class New York City families, would bring their deudors with them on special occasions to show off and to have them help with anything needed. Family care deudors knew to behave because just one phone call from the family and they'd be off to a work camp or farm. Some families opted for robotic assistants, but deudors were essentially tax free and you didn't need to be a tech wizard to tell someone what to do. The ability to make one call and get a deudor replaced was very effective in keeping them in line.

The front door opened and shut with Camilla welcoming home Mr. John Rivera. "Honey, we are almost ready," Marie called out. "I'm in the bedroom."

"On my way dear. Hi everyone!" John had been out having coffee with other professional ladies and gentlemen. "Kids, we don't want to be last and get the worst seats!"

"Mr. Rrrrrivera is home. Rrrrrooowwww," Sophia said to Anna, while putting on her lipstick. "Can you zip up the back of my dress please?"

Anna walked over to Sophia and gently pulled up the zipper. It fit her like a glove.

"Thanks. Do you mind checking to see if the kids are ready? I need to put up my hair," Sophia asked.

"Ok. Do you like my dress?" Anna twirled as she finished asking.

"Eh. The one with the open back is nicer," Sophia replied, hardly looking away from the mirror.

Anna figured as much, but was just happy to be getting out. She knew she was likely to be helping instead of enjoying the day, but she didn't care.

It beat staying inside or doing her deudor classes online. She aspired to be a good Christian; Sundays were her favorite.

Anna walked down the stairs and into James Rivera's room. James was ten years old and dressed except for shoes and socks. He had his Halo on and was quivering as he sat in his chair. Anna thought he must be playing an action game.

"James, it's time to go. Please go downstairs and get your shoes and socks on," Anna requested.

"Oh, come on, I just need two more minutes to finish this level! Please!" James pleaded. A day would come soon where he noticed the two teenage girls living in his house in a whole new way.

"Ok, but not a second longer. You don't want to be the last one ready," Anna said. "Have you eaten breakfast?"

"What?" James replied.

"I asked if you have eaten yet," Anna said.

"I don't know. I don't think I'm hungry," James answered.

Anna shook her head. She wondered how anyone could be so into a game that they couldn't remember if they had eaten, nor tell if they were hungry.

Anna walked further down the hall to Jessica Rivera's room. Jessica was a precocious twelve year old. She was a dirty blonde with a gentle face and dimples. She was only a couple of years away from getting her first cosmetic surgeries, as all young well-off girls are expected to do. Even most deudors, including Anna and Sophia, received treatments to help make sure the family overall was pleasing. Jessica was ready except for brushing her hair and checking in the mirror that her face looked pretty from each direction.

"Jessica, you look so beautiful," Anna said. "Thank you for being ready on time. You were the only one."

"Do you think Bobby is going to be there? I picked this dress just for him. I wish I looked as good as you. Look at your curves. I love that dress too," Jessica replied. They exchanged smiles and walked out of the room together. Jessica skipped down the stairs and Anna went back to James' room.

"James, come on sweetie, it's been two minutes," Anna said. She could hear the rest of the family gathering downstairs. "We don't want to be late. We need to show how grateful we are for everything we have."

"But why do we have to do it every week?" James said, as he flinched left and right. "There, got him." He switched to menu mode which let him save and exit, and took off the headset. James then ran past Anna and down the stairs. Anna followed him.

"My my my, what a lovely family," John said. "Ladies, you look beautiful. James, you forgot to tie your shoes again. Fix that please. Let's roll."

John opened the door and walked out. The Rivera's owned three cars and a minivan. Camilla brought the minivan around and the doors opened. They got in and the doors closed. After all the seat belts were fastened, the minivan quietly rolled down the road.

Anna was very pleased. Her life was not easy, but she felt between having been saved from death and her faith in God that she could one day be truly happy. To be serving the Riveras was much better than what most deudors do to pay off their debts. Marie might be a handful, but she was right each time she reminded the girls that she had very likely saved them from something far worse.

Dexter

"**G**ood evening America!!" Dexter shouted, as the crowd welcomed him to the start of the show. "Thank you. Thank you very much." Dexter signaled the audience to settle down. The music today had a triumphant beat with horns, giving a dramatic entrance to pump up the audience.

"I hope everyone is up for a battle tonight. This show is not afraid of the tough issues and we have two heavyweights here tonight as the Thorne Administration has reopened the debate on the deudor system. The attack in Houston was just three days ago. The news that six AntiCos were deudors of the central assailant, followed by renewed calls for reform in the Southern District, is the buzz throughout the media and political elite today. We will force a fair debate, and you can make up your own mind. I will be doing the same. We are each a Party of One. Partido de uno!" The audience clapped as Dexter made it to the debate table.

"Lorena, please recap some of the key statements today from officials on both sides of this issue," Dexter requested.

The studio room went night black for a few seconds and then the audience was viewing newscasts from earlier in the day. The first featured Asa Katz, Eastern District Governor in New York City speaking to reporter Paul Handy.

"Paul, I understand the reluctance to open this debate, but the fact is that the attack in Houston was not an act of war. It looks like people who are living with the benefits of the deudor system lashed out against the Southern District. We believe they did so out of anger against the unjust policies in the south, one of which is their extremely limited deudor system," Asa said.

The studio then transitioned to a clip showing the communications specialist for the Southern District, Dana Berry, taking questions at a press conference at the Southern District Capitol in Houston.

"Ms. Berry, what does the Governor say in response to the Thorne Administration calling for Southern compliance to the policies in the rest of the country towards deudors?" Asked a well-dressed reporter.

"The Governor is appalled by the self-serving politicization of the attack. The Governor is worried about the victims and working to stop future attacks. Perhaps if the Administration took terrorist attacks as seriously as they do the opportunities to blame policies for murder, then maybe these attackers would have been caught earlier," Dana replied.

The room again went black and quickly the audience was back with Dexter at his debate table.

"Tonight, we are joined by Elisabeth Beecher and Cardinal Josiah Smith. Ms. Beecher is a leading scholar and speaker arguing against the deudor system. Cardinal Smith hails from the Archdiocese of Boston and is a leading advocate for expanding the deudor system in the Southern District. Tonight, we will debate what to do with the deudor system." The crowd applauded Dexter's description of the marque debate tonight.

"Before we bring out our honored guests, it is firstly time to meet the subjects for whom they are competing," Dexter said. "Lorena, please introduce our contestants for this evening, and what they are playing for tonight!"

"Ladies and gentlemen, our first contestant hails from the Eastern District," Lorena began. "She is an unwed pregnant sixteen-year-old girl finishing her sophomore year of high school. Her parents have transferred her to the state as she has been in rebellion for a year and does not want to donate the baby. Please welcome Rachel!!" The audience clapped and hollered. The audience was able to see Rachel yelling at her parents and a police officer. She had a natural beauty but clearly, she had major issues. "If Cardinal Smith wins more votes tonight, this show will provide credits to pay for Rachel's crimes, plus cover her living expenses until the baby is born or is transferred to the government!" The crowd cheered as they saw a live video of Rachel smiling and holding a young man's hand. Neither looked completely sober and there were no parents in sight.

"Our next contestant calls the Southern District home. He is a twenty-year-old man taking care of his elderly parents and has been arrested for shoplifting food to feed the three of them. Please welcome Jose!!" The crowd clapped politely, but it was hard to feel a lot of sympathy for a pair of criminal contestants. "If Ms. Beecher wins more votes tonight, this show will provide credits to pay for Jose's crime, plus cover the living expenses for Jose and his parents for one year!"

It was unspoken, but all of the millions of viewers knew the losing contestant would become a deudor. The attention shifted back to Dexter after seeing Jose sitting with his fragile parents, the mother quietly crying.

"Ladies and gentlemen, please welcome our guests," Dexter said while clapping.

From the left side of the stage entered Cardinal Josiah Smith and from the right Elisabeth Beecher. The debaters were not politicians, but were savvy nonetheless. Elisabeth was dressed in a dark red dress accented by matching heels with lace-up all the way to the knee and a titanium cross with a ruby heart at the center. Josiah was dressed in classic dark brown robe with a bright red cap and heavy silver chain and cross. The three of them exchanged handshakes and sat down.

"Thank you both for coming on the program tonight. Your Grace, my first question will be for you. What specific reforms are people suggesting for the south, and what do those reforms have to do with the attack in Houston?" Dexter asked.

"Thank you for having me on tonight and giving your audience a chance to hear both sides of this important issue," the Cardinal said. "The deudor system grew out of the failed experiment of having both universal pay and open borders. Both policies were created separately with caring intentions, but far more people immigrated than expected. Many people were not productive once they had a steady pay check for doing nothing, and America suffered its second depression. Too many simply took the money and drank, used drugs, played video games, and lived in social media. After a couple of decades, there were clear trends showing this unhealthy lifestyle strains on the healthcare system. The specific reforms we hope the south will adopt, that are working elsewhere in the country, are to expand opportunities to work as a deudor instead of being lost alone to fend for one's self in the harsh capitalist society. There is no evidence these reforms would have stopped, or prevented the attack in Houston, but the main attacker did regularly post criticisms of the southern policies, including their reluctance to expand the deudor system into additional industries."

"Dexter, may I respond to some of the Cardinal's points?" Elisabeth asked.

"Yes, please do," Dexter answered.

"Your Grace, I agree that the universal pay and open borders policies were a failure combined," Elisabeth began. "They were also failures individually. I think the east and west need to look hard at their continued open border magnet policies. That said, we are here to talk about the deudor system. It is a policy that also started with some good intentions, but inflated the differences between the haves and have-nots to an unprecedented scale. The citizens were told the system was meant to help the poor, but no-one escapes the bottom layers of society when your choices and freedoms are regulated. The system has given more control to bureaucrats and created a population that is, in many ways, subservient having given their free will to others. All citizens are equal, but under the deudor system, some citizens are more equal than others."

"Your Grace, how do you respond to the charge from Ms. Beecher that the deudor system is more about control then about helping the poor? Is it making people subservient to the ruling class?" Dexter asked.

"Dexter, the deudor system was fundamental to helping the country climb out of debt roughly four decades ago," the Cardinal began. "The deudor system was a critical component of the Compromise of 2050. We had to make a correction when the federal debt reached $100 trillion and unfunded liabilities reached nearly $1 quadrillion. The compromise included deudors, streamlining the roles of the states by creating the three Districts, empowering the Districts on policies, such as immigration and health care, mass printing to pay off the national debt in dollars, and lastly the creation of the U.S. credit monetary system. Each component complemented the other. The costs associated with providing benefits to all citizens and helping those who come to our country looking for a better way of life, while also balancing the budget, is a real challenge. This system is the foundation that allows everyone to be covered plus not allowing society overall to go bankrupt. No-one will be covered if our economy collapses again. The compromise allowed us to get back to zero as a nation. It hurt us globally for a while, but we have emerged strong. We are back to the third largest economy. It was also not just about money. The church was supportive of the deudor system as it provided a way to save many unborn children, guided the country in the fight against global warming, provided pride to aging seniors that no longer could support themselves, and turn the tide in the devastating drug epidemic earlier this century. The deudor system not only gave individuals purpose, but provided basic tools to be happy. Violent crime is way down and few people become alcoholics or drug addicts. Along with the government providing everyone with tested safe medicines for mental health and recreation, our country has never been so close to being free from sin."

"Dexter, notice that His Grace did not answer the direct questions you asked him," Elisabeth said. "The bills that made up the Compromise of 2050 did not complement each other. Every part of the compromise had to do with either the consolidation of power or limiting the rights of individuals. It was a direct assault on the foundation of the republic to avoid a national financial collapse. The debate was fierce with essentially conservatives withdrawing to the new Southern District. Many in the nation called for breaking up the union, which led to calls for war. An important part of the compromise was to allow the districts to determine how to implement the changes within their district. Take away that autonomy and you have undone the only part of the compromise that helped avoid a civil war." Elisabeth turned to face the Cardinal. "There were other options besides giving up our rights and opportunities to the government. A wise man once said, 'How convenient it is to be a reasonable person as it allows one to create a reason for whatever one wishes to believe.' The government did not institute the deudor system to help the people. It did so to help itself.

The role of machines today masks the reality that we have set up a class system that sanctions those in power to be able to control society. The irony is that this is advertised as being for the good of the people which, if true, would make it honorable. The diversity of the topic is making it difficult to make a logical right vs. wrong assessment. There is real danger in having an amoral attitude to how our economy is set up. I suggest all citizens need to look at what freedoms they want instead of what freebies they might get. People are unfortunately just believing what they are told to be true vs. figuring it out on their own. The reality is that the government transferred its debt to the individual and, in particular, the poor. The crushing debt and collapse of the dollar as the government made up $100 trillion out of thin air wiped out the savings of the middle class and opened the door for this Americanized socialism. At some point, the socialists will always run out of other people's money."

"Your Grace, can you please respond to Ms. Beecher's comment on the balance between right and wrong in this debate?" Dexter asked.

"Dexter, I am not an economist but, as a leader of the church, it is my job to help counsel people to make good choices. The benefits of the deudor system can be seen in how it has helped real people in real life. It's one thing to talk about rights vs. freebies; that all sounds good, but it does not help millions left to rot in jail. It does not help those trapped deep in debt and who could end up losing everything with no hope for a better life. America tried what Ms. Beecher suggested and half our society was under water or locked up. The deudor system allows people to work off their mistakes. It also greatly discourages casually racking up debt as even young people see the down side to being irresponsible. My loyalty is to the people who need help and this system has done far better than any other system ever created."

"Your Grace, I don't think anyone doubts your intentions or your loyalties," Dexter stated. "Ms. Beecher, can you please describe how you think this is really a ruse being played on the people?"

"That is a tough question, but needs to be discussed as history does repeat itself," Elisabeth said. "People and certainly societies are not infallible. America made the barbaric mistake hundreds of years ago to have a slavery-based system. That led to many young Americans later falling into a gangster culture instead of a consistent effort to succeed in the free market system around them. A couple of hundred years ago, the population of Germany applauded the rise of a leader who became the biggest mass murderer the world has ever known. For hundreds of years, Arabs have given into a jihad culture willing to give up their own lives often to kill people they have never met and who have never done them harm. This century, our challenge is to address how Americans have fallen into progressive liberal culture, whose only measure of success is the ever-increasing quantity of entitlements. In many ways, the deudor system is the latest evolution of slavery. Sure no-one is whipped on plantations, but we have seen the progression from women married to the welfare state to a large percentage of society forever indebted to the system."

"Your Grace, your response to Ms. Beecher and her charge that this country has changed to an entitlement-based system?" Dexter asked.

"Dexter, it really is as simple as our society adapting to the world around us," the Cardinal said. "With machines taking so many jobs, there are very few opportunities for people now. It is incredibly difficult for anyone interested in working to find a career that could support themselves, let alone a family. Machines have taken almost all manufacturing, accommodation and food service, predictable physical tasks, and analysis jobs. Most of the job options left for people are about making or supervising machines, and we don't need that many people anymore to manage and drive our economy. The deudor system allows everyone to contribute in some way through government management of certain industries and lets people earn essential benefits to survive and be happy."

"This is the same narrative that got us into this situation," Elisabeth said. "The idea that people cannot find their own way to contribute in a free society is absurd. We need to be very careful as it's dangerous to believe government generated absurdities. Those who can make you believe absurdities can also make you commit atrocities."

"Your Grace, how do you respond? Are we being dangerous empowering the government with the deudor system? Nearly one in four Americans are deudors and that would rise if the South embraced policies in the East and West," Dexter asked.

"I see no signs of danger here. I do see benefits in real life with real people. Our prisons have less than one tenth of one percent of the population locked up, a historic low. I pray we do not do anything rash; we must place our trust in God as He is doing the best He can," the Cardinal replied.

"That's easy for people to say who have managed to float through the system without falling into serious debt. For the many who have fallen into the system, they may end up there for the rest of their lives. Millions are losing their free will to avoid having to make an effort. That is not what this country was intended to become," Elisabeth said. "And it's only one tenth of one percent in prisons if you don't count the deudor labor camps and farms; they might as well be prisons."

"Thank you both for the stirring and witty debate. We wish you both the best of luck in your efforts and pray that a fair plan is ascertained." Dexter turned to the audience. "Ok folks, you know what to do. Please cast your votes. One vote per person. You are a Party of One. No-one will know your vote but you and Lorena. Who made the stronger case tonight, Cardinal Smith or Elisabeth Beecher? After this message from our sponsors, we will announce the results and transition to our panel discussion." Dexter nodded to both debaters. "Good evening to you both." They both smiled, waived to the crowd, and disappeared off the stage.

Cain

ain Vasquez rode up the escalator to the mezzanine level of the
Houston Coliseum. He walked around the corner, found the section
303/304 entrance and walked towards the audience seating. He passed a
couple holding hands walking to the concession stand and was passed by
a teenager rushing back to his seat. At the end of the walkway, Cain could
have turned left or right to go into the seating areas, but stopped at the
handrailing, grabbed hold of it and leaned forward, and looked into the pit.

In the pit were two combatants. Both were about two and a half meters
tall and wearing leather armor. One with pale skin had a morning star and
already had taken damage on his left shoulder. The other with dark cream-
colored skin had a dragon beard hook which he was twirling above his head.
The outfits and weapons were a throwback to an ancient time providing
spice to the blood lust. The pit itself was about ten meters tall and twenty
meters in diameter. About two meters was recessed into the flooring and
there was a special hemisphere of clear hard plastic with a five-meter hole
on top to allow sounds of the matches to make it to the crowd. Cameras and
microphones were spaced along the top rim for pay-per-view. Cain looked
around the exterior of the pit and then casually scanned anybody that could
see him. Everyone, including security, were all focused on the match.

He came from the left and stopped next to Cain, did a similar look
around, and then also propped his elbows on the handrailing, close but not
too close to Cain.

"Mr. Anderson," the agent said.

"Mr. Smith. How have you been?" Cain replied, having no idea of the
agent's real name.

"We have a new assignment for you. This one is maximum top-secret clearance and needs to be done tomorrow night." The agent paused as the audience cheered a direct hit by the morning star. "The equipment you need will be in the tango foxtrot drop location. The target will be the highest-ranking politician at the protest. Your shot will set off a co-ordinated attack. You are the tip of the spear. Any questions?"

Cain thought for a moment as the crowd cheered another hit by the morning star which knocked the other fighter off his feet. The crowd could smell blood. "If this is a co-ordinated operation, how do I know when to strike?"

"You strike early in his speech. Let him get a couple of lines in. We do not want him to finish his speech. The others will follow your timing," the agent replied.

"Post-strike plan?" Cain asked.

"Proceed to safe house echo," the agent answered. "Stay there until I come to see you."

Cain digested the instructions and stood up straight, holding onto the handrail with one hand. He looked around to make sure no-one was watching them. "It will be done."

The agent stood up and, this time, walked slowly away going down the entrance hallway towards the escalators. He also slowly looked around but knew his spotter had been watching him the whole time so no-one could eavesdrop. In a digital age, face-to-face was again the most secure form of communication.

Cain leaned forward again as the crowd cheered a hit by the dragon beard hook. The cream-colored combatant had been missing so far other than mild glances, yet had taken several hits from the morning star. This time the hook had caught the pale fighter in the arm and was lodged there with blood streaming from the wound.

Cain reflected back to how he got to this place and this role. He didn't know the purpose of the mission; they never told him. Cain knew he was the very violent puppet with strings run by people on their own puppet strings. He did not know who the master of puppets was, but he knew he was part of the machine that made the country strong and he would do anything to make sure that objective was met, even acts of evil.

The fighter who had been hooked was now on one knee being dragged to the man with the dragon beard hook. The man with the hook pulled on the chain until the other fighter was close enough for the final blow. He then pulled a dagger out of his belt with his left hand, let go of the chain, and put the other man in a headlock with his right hand. He then rotated the man around in a slow circle as the crowd roared, begging for the kill. Men, women and children in the audience and at home were screaming at the top of their lungs. The gladiator then stabbed the dagger deep into the center of the chest which released a loud bang signaling the end of the match. The man with a hook in his arm and dagger in his chest fell to the floor. The victor raised both arms in the air with his fists clenched.

"Heeeeeerrrrrrreee beeeee Draaaggoonnnns!!!!" Said the announcer, followed by a loud roar and flames shooting high above the pit. The scoreboard hanging from the center of the colosseum showed the score change to LA 6 to HOU 5. "Ladies and gentlemen, it is the half-time break." A countdown timer started on the scoreboard. Cain joined the flow of people leaving the seating area, but he did not return to the match.

The victor and loser both exited the pit. The loser pulling the dagger from his chest after the victor had removed the hook from his arm. Some circuitry was exposed in the chest cavity of the loser and a tech was looking into it as soon as they were to the sidelines. The fighters were so big that the tech looked the size of a child. The two fighters were advanced robotic warriors designed to look like people with a few specific spots in their body that signal points or an outright win for the opponent. They felt the pain from their losses, but also learned from their setbacks.

Sara

I t was a Saturday morning and the sun was shining bright in Houston. It was only mid-May but was now over 90 degrees. Sara wondered what happened to spring. She sat up in bed, looked at the window, and then looked as Ben rolled away from her. Neither Sara nor Ben had to work today and Jon and Emma only had homework to do.

"Ben, honey, are you ready to get up?" Sara asked, as she turned towards him and scratched his back.

"Uh, how about coffee first?" Ben responded, without opening his eyes.

"Camilla, two cups of coffee please," Sara said, as she stepped out of bed.

"Good morning Sara, would you like them made as usual?" Camilla asked.

"Yes please," Sara answered.

"As you command," Camilla replied.

After Sara went to the restroom, she went to the kitchen and got the two coffees. She sipped hers and went back to the bedroom. She gave Ben his coffee and they sat in bed together sipping coffee and staring at the wall-sized window with the trees showing a gentle breeze outside.

"Did you hear the kids up yet?" Ben asked.

"I heard some feet running around, but the doors are closed," Sara said. "I'll check on them soon."

"Want to see what's on the news this morning?" Ben asked.

"Ok," Sara answered. "Camilla, please show morning news."

The wall-sized window projection changed to a wall-sized image of the news. Audio of the news was in surround sound thanks to speakers on all walls, standard even for apartments.

"Authorities have arranged security for the protest tomorrow which is expected to see more than 200,000 people participate. Many people planning to attend are looking for a way to express their frustration," a news reporter said on a morning news show.

"I'm mad as hell!" A man with a large belly and no hair said to a different reporter on a taped interview on the street. "The people blaming the citizens of the south for this attack need to know we are not going to take it anymore. I am so pissed off! They are kicking us when we are down before the dead are even buried. I'm going to the protest and so are all my friends!"

The broadcast switched back to the reporter talking live. "The city of Houston is making arrangements in terms of security and sanitation. Many food distribution services will be providing refreshments. There will also be kid-friendly sections with entertainment and games. People planning to attend will need to try to get there early and officials are encouraging all to use the shuttle service to ease everyone's access."

"Jim, any news on the headline speakers?" The news anchor asked.

"Not yet Susan. The protest organizers are keeping details on speakers pretty tight. They say it's going to have surprises, but some speculate they are still trying to get commitments as this is being thrown together quickly. We do know that the organizers are in contact with Governor Young's office so there is speculation of high-level District political speakers."

"Camilla, pause," Sara commanded. The video paused.

"Ben, I want us to go to the protest," Sara said.

"Ugh. That would use up the whole day, and we don't even know who will be speaking," Ben replied.

"Ben, this is important. This wasn't some far away attack and those vultures in the east and west are blaming us for what happened. I know you are as mad as I am. This is our chance to help show we aren't going to roll over and take it. This is our chance to make them think twice about doing it again," Sara said, and then sipped her coffee.

"Can we leave the kids here? Is it worth dragging them to it?" Ben asked.

"You just heard them say there will be a kid zone. They can play there. I think it's important for them to learn from this experience as much as it's important for us to make an effort to stand up for what we believe." Sara could tell she was bringing him around. Ben had never been very political, and his job with Air Guard discouraged doing anything favoring one political spectrum over another.

"Arg. Well there goes our relaxing weekend. I'll let you tell the kids the good news," Ben said, and took a sip of coffee. "Can we at least agree to try to be home by around 9pm? Maybe leave before the final speaker is done to beat the crowd?"

"Deal. We can take care of our weekend chores tomorrow," Sara said. She sipped her coffee, put it down, and hugged Ben.

Zander

Zander took off his Halo as Camilla told him he had arrived. He had been watching highlights from the LA Dragons game the previous evening. He thanked Camilla, got out of the car, and walked towards the front door of Workerbee Robotics as the car rejoined traffic. The plant was located in a fairly shady part of Los Angeles near a small deserted airport. It was about fifteen minutes after sunrise, the air was still crisp and cool, and Zander was finally starting to feel fully awake.

"Good morning Mr. Brown, would you like a cup of coffee?" Dinah, the AI for the facility, asked as Zander passed through the automatic doors. The doors opened and security protocol was disabled as Zander's chip and facial recognition had been confirmed.

"No thanks, I already had two cups," Zander replied, as he passed by the reception station which was a monitor to assist Dinah to communicate with people entering the facility. "Is Fred in yet?"

"Not yet sir," Dinah replied, as Zander approached the elevator. "Would you like the fifth floor?"

"Yes please, thanks," Zander answered. He wanted to go to his desk to understand any updates to the plan for the day before checking on the sentries. He didn't always work Saturdays, but they were trying to meet a large delivery by the end of the month. He was used to Fred, the Production Manager on shift today, coming in late. Zander was Security Manager and, between them, were the only two positions covered by people today. Everything else was taken care of by the machines.

Zander got to his office and the door slid open automatically having confirmed his identity. He went to the desk and flicked his hand upwards which opened on the wall a three-dimensional display of his homepage.

He made a tapping motion towards the schedule which opened. Special delivery coming in twenty minutes. The day would start off interesting. He scratched his belly right where the mouth of the Dragon was on his LA Dragons t-shirt. Zander quickly read over the rest of the deliveries today and saw no shipments going out. That means the end of the month will be chaos trying to meet the quota.

Zander got up and walked back to the elevator and asked for the third floor. When he got there, he walked down a hallway, made a right down another and passed through some double doors to what opened up into the security bird's nest with a view of the main high bay area. The high bay was where large deliveries came in and where final processing for shipments were completed. It was also the location for any large-scale integration or testing. It was a sixty-meter square three-story room with various equipment along the walls. There were two main doors, one on the south and one on the east. The doors were two-inch thick steel with encryption protection access panels. In case those did not work, there were Omega Class Butcher laser cannons on either side of both doors that Dinah or the Security Manager could activate. The bird's nest was on the northwest corner of the high bay.

Zander flicked his hand up on a wall of the bird's nest and a display flared up on the wall. Of the five sentries guarding the facility, two were in the high bay. All five were showing green and plenty of battery power to make it through the day. There were always at least four sentries at any given time. Once the company started focusing on contracts for the military, security became more important than being on-time or the lowest bidder.

Zander flicked down with his left hand to turn off the display. He looked at the clock at the far wall and saw that the delivery should be any minute.

"Yo Zander, how about them Dragons? We made the fucking playoffs!!" Fred called through the intercom.

"Hell yeah, I told you they could do it. Just had to stop playing like a bunch of pussies. Get your ass up here. That special delivery you have been waiting on is finally here," Zander said.

"Awesome. On my way," Fred replied.

Zander took out his binoculars and scanned the corners of the high bay area. He scanned the area for threats and just to make sure everything was in order. Zander then looked at the video feed outside, as well as air traffic, and also saw no threats nearby.

"Sir, there is a delivery truck in the loading bay," Dinah said. "The truck is requesting permission to enter the facility. The truck certificate and license match the delivery order tracking. There is one human in the cabin but, per protocol, he will not exit the vehicle." The door behind Zander opened and Jeff walked in with a big smile on his face.

"Copy. Please proceed Dinah; open the door. Focus sentry A on the truck and sentry B on the door," Zander said.

The door slowly opened and inch by inch Zander and Fred could see more and more of the delivery truck. It was an 18-wheeler ready to back into the facility. Once the door was open, the truck slowly backed in. The truck body had no markings other than the license plate. The high bay door started to close just before the truck had finished backing in all the way. Once the high bay door had closed, Zander breathed a sigh of relief.

Zander turned around, but Fred was no longer by his side. Zander turned back to look at the delivery and saw Fred below walking up to the truck. A robotic work unit, one of the many options offered by Workerbee Robotics, approached the back of the truck, used a tool to unlock it, and the door slid open. Inside were twelve extra-large coffin sized crates.

"Holy shit, they are finally here!" Fred yelled out loud enough for Zander to hear.

"Now your babies can finally be soldiers!" Zander yelled back.

Zander had always been more comfortable making the robotic soldiers without the weapons, and then shipping them off to be integrated by the military. This next generation soldier made by Workerbee was built starting from the laser system prioritizing power sharing with the rest of the machine. Thinking of the android as a killing machine from the start, plus a new proprietary Workerbee power system, would give this model the shortest laser recharge time compared to any mass-produced machine ever manufactured. If everything went according to plan, then it would be a very profitable project for the company and help the government get ahead of the rest of the world. Zander though, could not help wonder if it was a good idea having a robotic plant making the deadliest robotic soldier ever created.

Anna

When Anna Lee opened her eyes, she saw Sophia smiling at her. Sophia helped her get up and the two of them brushed off Anna's outfit. Anna looked around and saw she had spawned in an alleyway that was partially lit and entirely nasty. At the end of the alleyway, she saw what looked like a street packed with people and she could hear music. It looked and sounded like a party.

Sophia was dressed in a skintight tube top and daisy dukes. Her hair was in pigtails and she had several sexy tattoos. She had put her drink down to help Anna, but had since picked it up and was sucking on the straw which was of a ridiculously large diameter. Anna had on a tight outfit that was more straps for a top and stretch shorts for a bottom. Neither were wearing any underwear.

"I can't believe it. You actually came through! Woooohoooo!" Sophia said.

"Oh my God, I can't go out there like this. What am I wearing?!" Anna replied. She had let Sophia fill out her profile for their night out.

"Oh girl, you look hot. Don't you like it? You look so sexy!" Sophia replied. "In fact, I even wanna do you!"

"I'm getting a different top. This doesn't cover anything. I haven't come in yet. And I'm not going commando!" Anna closed her eyes and, after about five seconds, Anna's top changed to a tight sleeveless t-shirt, plus she now had a pushup bra and panties.

"Fine, but let's get out there. We are missing all the fun!" Sophia said. She stuck her tongue out playfully at Anna to show off the side-by-side tongue piercings. Sophia had also changed the settings for herself from her natural C cup to DD.

Sophia grabbed Anna by the hand and they walked out of the alleyway. As Anna looked around, she was blown away at how many people were out. It was a city of young people all looking like it was their last night on Earth. Anna's eyes came into focus from all the store lights and advertisement billboards. She could see some clubs, some 'love shacks,' and some places with names she didn't quite get yet. Anna felt very vulnerable as she looked at people with animated tattoos, horns, and some with bright neon eyes. One man even had a tail. Anna couldn't believe she agreed to go as it was obvious now this was just a place to misbehave... to really, really misbehave.

"Hot damn ladies, y'all look bangin! Want some diamonds?" Asked a man with a cowboy hat, ripped jeans, and cowboy boots. He was holding his hand out with some shiny pills out in his left hand with a drink to wash it down in his right. To his side was another smiling cowboy.

"Well, thank you kind sir, we'd love some," Sophia replied. She took one, made a show of dropping it down into her mouth without breaking eye contact, and washed it down. "Anna, diamonds are the best. You have got to try one!"

"What are they?" Anna said, with eyes that showed she was more doe than a cougar. "Will they make me act... unnatural?"

"Haaa haaa haaa ... that is the funniest thing I have heard all night! And my answer is ... I certainly hope so! Come ladies, a night of fun and adventure awaits!" The young man said as he handed the other diamond and drink to Anna, grabbed Sophia by the hand, and started walking down the road.

The other cowboy walked up to Anna while looking her up and down, this one wearing a vest as well, plus a whip hanging off his belt. "My, my, you are a tasty piece. My dear, may I be your escort for the night?" The cowboy said to Anna. He had an animated stag tattoo that winked at Anna.

"Uh. It's my first time here. Can you please tell me what the diamond will do?" Anna asked.

"Sure. It will make the program amplify all your feelings and desires. It will make you feel more alive than ever before. It will crank up your endorphins to where you might have runner's high while just walking down the road," the man said with a smile. "In short, diamonds are a girl's best friend!"

Anna wasn't sure, but this was just online and Sophia assured her if she got overwhelmed, she could just drop out. She took the pill and swallowed some of the drink. The drink burned and she could feel the jagged pill go down somehow. She was about to speak, but almost instantly she could feel it working. She started to feel hot and a little dizzy and then, as the dizziness faded, she began to feel anxious, like she needed to start running. Then she felt a premature sense of pleasure; almost like a part of her brain that had been asleep had just woken up. As the diamond took effect, she also became more aware of her femininity. She put her hand on the cowboy's arm to steady herself and then realized how strong he felt. She wanted to touch him more. The cowboy smiled.

"Darlin, I believe you are now high as a kite. Shall we take a stroll? Please allow me to introduce you to the city of Bela. It is truly a marvelous place to get away!" The cowboy said.

"Where is Sophia?" Anna asked. She did not trust this place, or the cowboy, or even herself at the moment.

"I believe they just strolled into the club over yonder," the man said, as he pointed three doors down and across the street.

"Can you help me find her please?" Anna asked.

"Anything for you little lady," he replied.

As far as Anna could see, the town was filled with young people having a merry time. It was a diverse crowd with a New England city vibe, except no skyscrapers. There were no cars allowed and therefore no markers for the self-driving cars or street lights. Each building was narrow and tall, each seemingly crammed together. There was a picture-perfect sunset in the distance and the leaves on the few trees around were changing colors, even though it was just late winter in the real world. The cowboy proceeded with escorting Anna down the street in her first time visiting the digital city of Bela.

The music in the street seemed to be in perfect surround sound no matter where one stood. In both reality and virtual reality, most music was recycled, tailored, or straight up classic versions from the previous 150 years. AI could easily provide the perfect unlimited set by studying all the preferences and experiences of the audience. Many of the current music hits were from the late 20th or early 21st century.

They crossed the street and Anna peaked into the first building. It was called Thunderdome. She could see a cage and what looked like two people dancing, but the glass of the building was fogged.

"What is Thunderdome?" Anna asked the cowboy.

"Fight to the death. Player vs Player. Only one survivor can leave the Thunderdome. It's a cage match. Sometimes up to five competitors at a time. Good place to bet some credits. The AI will only let people fight in permitted areas. I have a buddy who competes. He has won about two thirds of his matches. Hurts like hell when you die, but he says it's worth it as he has never felt so alive. My favorite is when they adjust the laws of physics like zero gravity or people take alternate forms like dinosaurs. Probably my other favorite is the Flash Gordon battle scene. Ya know, the one with the flying monkey men. Totally kickass. The potential is unlimited in VR. Of course, it's nothing compared to entering games set in new worlds, but Thunderdome does allow for the spice of an audience that you can't savor when submersed in an alternate reality," the cowboy said.

After they passed the Thunderdome, Anna looked into the next building. It had several windows and each had a different dancer of sorts in it. All had black lights on and the dancers had little on other than body paint that glowed from the black lights. One dancer had on lingerie, had three large breasts, and made it clear to the cowboy that she had no teeth.

"Alice In Chains," Anna read on the sign. "I think I know what that is," Anna said. "Is that where people go to... to do it?"

"Oh my, I see we have a lot of catching up to do. Alice In Chains is where to go to fulfill just about any fantasy. They have both people and android pleasure options. I first went there when I was twelve. It helped me get broken in, so to speak. My big brother took me," the cowboy said.

"Yeah, catching up. That's what Sophia brought me to do." By this point, Anna was holding on to her cowboy's arm with both hands. She was trying not to look at him too much, especially his eyes or his pants. She felt like a wild cat and he was her prey.

They got to the third building and Anna could hear the dance music before the cowboy opened the door. They stepped inside and Anna scanned the room. The inside of the building was much wider than appeared from outside, a benefit of VR city design. She saw no sign yet of Sophia and started to drag her cowboy in further. The bar was called Footloose. The front of the club was packed with half-naked people grinding to the beat of the music. Anna and her cowboy walked through the crowd. She felt her butt get pinched three times by strangers as they passed through. The song "Ain't No Rest for the Wicked" by Cage the Elephant had the audience vibrating.

"I was walking down the street when out the corner of my eye
I saw a pretty little thing approaching me
She said I never seen a man, who looks so all alone
Could you use a little company?
If you pay the right price, your evening will be nice
Or you can go and send me on my way
I said you're such a sweet young thing
Why you do this to yourself?
She looked at me and this is what she said

Oh, there ain't no rest for the wicked
Money don't grow on trees
I got bills to pay, I got mouths to feed
Ain't nothing in this world for free
I know I can't slow down
I can't hold back though you know I wish I could
No, there ain't no rest for the wicked
Until we close our eyes for good"

As they passed through the dance floor, they crossed into an area with lots of tables and with booths wrapped around the perimeter. The walls had videos of people dirty dancing and having a great time. Anna spotted Sophia; she was on top of a table dancing. Sophia saw Anna and waived them over.

"Well, now a couple hours past and I was sitting at my house
The day was winding down and coming to an end
So I turned on the TV
And flipped it over to the news
And what I saw I almost couldn't comprehend
I saw a preacher man in cuffs for taking money from the church
He stuffed his bank account with righteous dollar bills
But even still I can't say much because I know we're all the same
Oh yes we all seek out to satisfy those thrills

You know there ain't no rest for the wicked
Money don't grow on trees
We got bills to pay, we got mouths to feed
Ain't nothing in this world for free
I know, we can't slow down
We can't hold back though you know we wish we could
You know there ain't no rest for the wicked
Until we close our eyes for good"

As Anna got closer, she was getting ready to say she wanted to leave. She wanted to yell at Sophia for bringing her to this place. She didn't get a chance to though as there was a circle of mostly men around the table now and a second woman on the table grinding with Sophia. The second woman kissed Sophia and the crowd cheered. She then slowly began to remove Sophia's top as they continued to dance. Before Sophia had rotated around to face her, Anna dropped off the server, leaving her cowboy disappointed.

Sara

The shuttle bus started to slow and the usual double chime sounded telling everyone it had reached the next stop. In this case, it had reached downtown Houston and was dropping off about forty passengers going to the rally in Bush Park. Sara, Ben, and the kids waited their turn and exited the bus. They followed the flow of people and a few mobile personal assistant androids. There was no driver to whom to say thank you, just Camilla. Their bus was in a massive line of shuttles that were taking turns adding to the growing crowd.

"Do you hear that? Sounds like some indie jams," Sara said with a smile, flicking the bangs out of her eyes.

"Do you smell that? Smells like turkey legs. Gimme gimme," Ben answered.

"Yeah, ok. After we drop off the kids. The play area is supposed to be to the right down there," Sara replied. She realized the kids were trailing behind, both of them looking a little overwhelmed. "Come on guys, I hear they have bouncy houses!"

"Mommy, will you go on the rides with me?" Jon asked, as he started holding his mom's hand.

"Of course, honey, and Emma will be there with you too," Sara replied. "After a couple of rides, when you are ready, daddy and I are going to go to the rally." Sara turned to Ben. "Do you know when they started speaking?"

"They were supposed to start around thirty minutes ago. Another thirty minutes and they should get to the main events. Probably just stirring up the crowd now. This place is crazy. Have you ever seen so many people?" Ben asked.

"Yeah, I guess everybody is pretty fed up," Sara replied, and turned back to the children. "Kids, you will remember this day and look back proudly of how your family stood up for what is right."

"Mommy, can I see if Carole is here?" Emma asked.

"Sure sweetie. Ben, let's stop by that tree and Emma can check on Carole, plus we can make sure we know where we are going," Sara said.

The Chamberlain family walked another hundred meters down the side walk, turned to cross some grass, and stopped by a tall oak tree. It stood out like a statue and was the only tree in sight. Emma took her earpiece out of her pocket, said a few words to call Carole, and then started chatting to her friend. Jon was still holding Sara's hand, but was looking at the line of bouncy houses and other kid games about another fifty yards to the left. Ben looked at his tablet which had a map of the area along with a running tab on what speakers and acts had already gone and which were coming up soon.

"Carole is already in the play area. Can we go in mommy?" Emma said excitedly as she put the earpiece back in her pocket.

"Sure sweetie," Sara said to Emma. Sara then knelt down to have her face at Jon's level. "Jon, are you ready to go in honey?"

"Ok," Jon said quietly, still trying to judge if this was more than he could handle, but seeming to warm to the place. He was moving his lose tooth back and forth. Jon was wearing a white scarf just like his favorite action hero on his favorite show, Clutch Powers. Sara let him bring it whenever he needed a little extra confidence.

"Hey buddy, I bet they have cotton candy. How about we buy some after mommy and I go hear a few speakers and some music?" Ben asked. Jon smiled and nodded yes.

All four left the shade of the tree, crossed some more grass, and passed some trucks lined up alongside the neighboring science museum. The trucks were parallel to the fence around the children's area, and they could see police drones and sentries along the perimeter of the play area. The fence was covered in rainbow-colored plastic wrap that was thin enough to be transparent, but thick enough to keep the children's area reasonably private. They walked another fifty meters and reached the closest entrance which was being guarded by two robotic sentries. They were metal from head to foot. They had two feet and had four arms as was standard for military and police units. Their shielding on their chest was colored police blue to show their purpose. Elsewhere, they were shiny chrome with blue piercing LED lights where one might expect eyes, standard for Southern District units. Ben walked up close to the nearest sentry.

"Good afternoon sir. Would your children like to enjoy our play area? We have machine and human security for your protection." The second sentry slowly walked behind the four looking at them and the others in the area.

"Yes, it looks great. We will be joining our kids for a little while and then my wife and I will go to hear the speakers at the rally," Ben said.

"Might anyone else be picking up your children this evening?" The sentry asked.

"No, my wife and I will come back and get them," Ben answered, as one of the security drones buzzed overhead making the rounds.

"Welcome to the play zone. We have scanned all your identities. We welcome the Chamberlains," the sentry said.

Sara, still holding Jon's hand, walked in first and they walked past the crowds playing on the swings and playground to the line of bouncy houses. A group of teenagers were all wearing Halos around a couple of snack wagons with food service robotic assistants. The Chamberlains kept going, and around the next turn Emma found Carole and they ran off together. The bouncy houses varied from four meters high to twelve-meter-tall monsters.

"Jon, what do you think?" Sara asked with a smile.

"Wow. I love it." He took off his shoes and tossed them aside. "Bye mommy!" Jon said, and ran to the first of the small rides where other kids his age were playing.

"Well, so much for needing me to ride with him," Sara said, a little disappointed.

"He is growing up so fast. How about you hold my hand now?" Ben said with a smile.

Sara accepted and they walked to put Jon's shoes in a cubby in a wall of shoes and then out of the children's area. They turned right and followed the museum wall, again towards the rally. The closer they were to the rally, the better they could hear rhythmic drumbeat and some chanting. The sounds made the mood go from happy and playful to livid and resolute. Sara felt the transition was surreal. They turned around the corner and saw a crowd as far as the eye could see. The protest was on the Northern border of Bush Park in front of the local FBI building and Federal Worker's Rights building. Both often served more like embassies given that the Southern District has similar governmental functions that often-claimed jurisdiction. The large park was one of the few green patches in the downtown area. Robotic drones with speakers were scattered flying over the crowd to allow them to hear the speakers and music, or whatever else the rally leaders were pushing. The crowd was currently repeating what a speaker was shouting. Apparently, the speaker wanted to the south to "Stand Up!" ...and the people blaming the south for the attack on Houston to "Shut Up!"

"How about we go over there?" Ben asked, pointing at a line of tents set up giving away freebies and some gaming demos.

"No, I like that spot over there," Sara answered, pointing to the right. "We can probably see the speakers from there. I'm too short to see it from those tents, plus you just want the free stuff," Sara smiled. "I didn't drag us all the way here for just freebies."

"Ok, ok, sounds good. Maybe on the way out we can swing over there," Ben replied.

"Deal!" Sara answered, and winked at Ben. "Anyone good coming up soon?"

Ben looked at the live feed on his tablet. "Yeah, a couple of local leaders and sports figures. We got here at a good time. The final speaker at the end still just says to be announced; they must be trying to spin up suspense. We can maybe hang out until we see who the final speaker will be and then go and get the kids. Looks like your plan is working beautifully," Ben said.

They started to walk to the right and were actually getting a little further away from the speakers, but were walking up a grassy knoll that only had a few people on it so far. They could now see the projection screen behind the speaker and a small blip of a person on the stage with a set with a stainless podium draped with the Texas state flag. The stage was mostly covered in an enormous semi-sphere translucent energy field. The security field stopped where it contacted the ground, stage, and above the stage entrance on the backside. Sara turned around and could see the science museum and the children's area in the distance. Other than one trip for snacks, they stayed in the area through several music acts, speakers, and one comedian.

The second to last speaker was a local business leader of a mattress company who was well known for his generosity. He gave a compassionate testimony of having visited the attack site and how it made his blood boil. He then talked about visiting the victims in the hospital and how he wept at the bedside of a little girl with a broken back. He promised that the little girl would never have to worry about money until she was through college or married. The crowd ate it up.

After the mattress company speaker, some huge red spotlights came on crisscrossing the crowd and a heavy drum beat set in. The crowd could feel the energy level peak and that they had reached the keynote speaker.

"Ladies and gentlemen, please welcome Houston's own ... Governor Cyrus Young!" Said the announcer.

From the entranceway on the back of the stage, Cyrus slowly walked towards the podium. He was wearing a cowboy hat, cowboy boots, jeans, and a button up camo shirt. He looked like an average Joe one might see at a bar other than the large Texas flag belt buckle. The crowd was going wild. Both Sara and Ben were yelling at the top of their lungs along with the rest of the rally.

"Dixieland rising," Cyrus said.

"Dixieland rising!" Shouted the crowd who then all stomped with their left foot and then stomped with their right foot.

"Dixieland rising!" Cyrus yelled.

"Dixieland rising!!" Howled the crowd who did the stomp 2-step and then clapped their hands.

"Dixieland rising now!!" Cyrus cried.

"Dixieland rising now!!!" Roared the crowd who did the stomp 2-step, clapped their hands, and then went silent as they raised and held their arms in an X shape.

Cyrus never got tired of the energy from the crowds. They still religiously followed the routine even years after the election. He had goosebumps on both arms under the camo shirt. He snapped out of it as the crowd of thousands stood silent and awaited the finale.

"Ooooaaaaauuuuuu!" Cyrus screamed out and the crowd joined bringing the rebel yell to life once more. It lasted until no-one in the crowd had any more air left to give. The yell then transitioned into cheering and clapping; the civilized crowd had returned.

"Thank you," Cyrus said. The crowd did not quiet at all. "Thank you. Please, please. The applause is for you." The crowd quieted some. "It's for you for being here at our rally. A rally to say enough is enough!!" And the crowd roared back again. "When the attack happened, I was at the Governor's estate and had just…uh."

In the middle of Cyrus's statement, he started to hear a loud buzzing sound and an insanely bright white spot started to grow in front of him on the energy field. Only Cyrus could hear it and stopped mid-sentence. After two awkward seconds, six security drones were closing on the stage from the outside and a voice spoke to Cyrus… "Governor, evacuate now!" Cyrus had been looking at the spot at what felt like much longer than a couple of seconds. He then realized what was happening and turned and ran to the access door. Once he moved, the buzzing stopped and the white spot started to shrink. About fifty people towards the front of the crowd started to scream. The security drones had reached the location of the spot and circled around looking for the source of the laser beam. Unlike science fiction movies, lasers are usually invisible to the naked eye; however, it is visible to sensitive infrared scanning like those on the security drones. Two of the drones had caught the signature and looked in the direction of the source before the beam terminated. Hundreds of people in the front of the crowd were now screaming, and the crowd was starting to move backwards as the rally had been flipped completely upside down.

"Sara, we need to get out of here," Ben said. He grabbed her hand but then…

BOOM!! A loud explosion rang out from the last truck in the line of trucks parked by the museum. It was the truck closest to the park area with the main crowd. After the explosion, all of the machines, except for a dozen of the military grade drones, fell to the ground. The androids fell and just scared the people around them even more. A cloud of dust could not hide several bodies lying in the blast zone. Some of the airborne drones fell on people, leading to more screaming and a couple of serious injuries. The intercom system was no longer functional so the only sounds left were man-made and the dozen remaining military drones. The drones split up with three going after the source of the laser, three guarding the stage as the Governor was still in the facility behind the stage, and the rest spread out through the area looking for threats.

"Ben. I'm scared," Sara said. The blast had made them and many others fall backwards. Ben and Sara held hands while trying to follow the flow of people to the shuttle bus drop-off area. They needed to go that direction to get to the children's area. The entire crowd now was trying to get far away from the stage and away from the rally.

"Just keep moving. We need to get the kids. It'll be all right as soon as we get them," Ben said. His voice was cracking. They could still hear people screaming. Sara looked back to the main audience area and the crowd was compacting as they all tried to funnel around both sides of the museum.

"Another fifty meters and we will be there. I don't see the sentries or drones at the children's center. Wait, I see the two sentries but they are on the ground. It must have been an EMP," Ben said. "We just need to get inside. We'll find them."

"Ben, I think they would still be at the bouncy houses. We weren't gone that long," Sara said. "Almost there."

"We are going to make it," Ben said.

Sara and Ben were temporarily split apart by an angry scared fat man who pushed his way through women and children alike.

They rejoined, reached the entrance to the children's area, and went in.

BOOM!! Another explosion went off. This time two trucks towards the middle of the line by the museum exploded. The trucks were close to the play area with hundreds of people in between trying to get to the shuttles.

Sara opened her eyes but could not hear anything. She tried to look around and realized she was lying on the ground. Dust was everywhere; on the ground and hanging in the air. She saw dark red streaks on the ground. The kids! She realized quickly where she was and that she needed to find the kids.

"Ben!" Sara yelled, but she couldn't hear her own yell. Dust was hanging so still in the air that she felt like she was on another planet. She saw a woman lying on the ground not moving. Sara could feel a terrible headache starting. The silence was starting to be replaced by a ringing sound. She tried to stand up and realized her left leg was in pain and bleeding. There was a large nail sticking halfway out of her calf. Sucking it up, she was driven by raw adrenaline and made it to both feet. Sara saw nails and bolts and other random hardware littering the ground around her. Then she saw Ben. She limped over to him and knelt down to him.

"Ben! Are you ok?! Wake up!" Sara yelled, barely able to tell what she was saying still. Ben started to groan. He didn't look to be too badly hurt and was moving his hands to his head. Sara got back up slowly. Must. Find. The. Kids.

The dust still hung everywhere with some starting to slowly fall. Sara could now hear crying, moaning, and sobbing, with some horrific screeches from several directions. She wasn't sure if sirens were in the background or if that was still the ringing in her ears. She stepped over a severed leg that looked to be from a man who must have been wearing shorts. She could start to see the bouncy house area, but none of them were standing anymore. She could see the snack wagons, and the teenagers who had been wearing Halos were now trying to help those in their group who had been hurt. Sara could definitely hear sirens now.

"Emma! Is that you?!" Sara yelled.

"Mom! Oh my God! My arm! I'm bleeding! What happened?!" Emma said. She had been hanging out with the teenagers.

Sara looked at Emma's left arm. The skin was cut and bruised from her elbow to her shoulder, but it must have been a blunt object as it was not deep. "Honey, you are going to be ok. Can you walk?"

"I'm scared mommy. I want to go home!" Emma yelled hysterically.

"Honey, have you seen your brother?" Sara asked.

"I don't remember. I think he was in those smaller bouncy houses by the fence. Dad!" Emma said.

Sara turned around and saw Ben. He was slowly staggering to them.

"Honey, stay with your father while I find Jon," Sara said. She looked towards the area where they had left him. Sara could see the bouncy houses; they were all deflated. She could also see the fence. What had been happy rainbow plastic now looked like a bullet-ridden nightmare. Sara could see lights of the emergency vehicles in the distance starting to get to the area. They had not made it into the children's area yet.

"Jon! Jon! Where are you?!" Sara yelled. She looked at the first deflated house and saw about six little kids crying. One little kid was not moving with blood surrounding his head. Sara limped to the next house.

"Jon! Where are you! Its mommy!" Sara yelled. She started to realize that all the other parents were now also trying to find their children. She caught the first emergency personnel and androids starting to make it into the children's area. "Jon! Where are you?!"

When Sara got to the next deflated house, she saw three kids crying and two being hugged by parents. She saw a face down little boy covered in dust holding his abdomen with blood all around him, coughing, and crying. He rolled onto his side and Sara realized it was Jon.

"Jon! Mommy is here!" Sara turned her head to the fence nearby. "Help! I need help!" Sara fell to him and tried to roll him to her slowly. There was a look of pure fear and horror in his eyes. She supported him and saw the piece of jagged metal sticking out of his belly. The truck bombs had included all kinds of hardware to serve as shrapnel. Maximum damage on the most innocent of targets. The white scarf Jon was wearing had soaked up enough blood to now be more red than white.

"Mommy. It hurts mommy," Jon said quietly. "What...what...what happened? Did I do something? Did I fall?"

"Baby, you are going to be ok. Mommy's here. Help is coming. I love you so much honey!" Sara's eyes were streaming tears. She could barely breathe, terrified out of her mind. "I need help now!! Little boy hurt!! Need help now!!" Sara leaned down to kiss Jon on the forehead. When she leaned back and looked as his eyes, they were lifeless. Jon was gone. Sara cradled him, turned to heaven, and screamed in horror until no more sound could come out.

Dexter

When the lights came on, Dexter was standing on the stage. No music tonight. No smile. It had been almost 48 hours since the second attack in Houston; Dexter's first broadcast since the attack. The background and stage were night black with the lights only on Dexter.

"Hello ladies and gentlemen, it is with a heavy heart that we all come together tonight. Last week we discussed the first attack in Houston. It never occurred to me that we might be now calling it the first attack. The families were burying the dead. Life was returning to normal for the rest of us with promises by the government to hunt anyone else responsible. But now, we have the Bush Park massacre." Dexter paused. "This second attack, well, we haven't seen anything of this magnitude since the 3rd Gulf War. The co-ordination of this style of attack seems new. It seems different. The AntiCo attack was hand-to-hand murder on a relatively small scale. The Bush Park massacre had a laser sniper, explosives, and was the first terrorist attack to use an EMP. The usual foreign groups are claiming responsibility, but I am not convinced. It doesn't seem to match the tired old recipe they have tried for decades. Lorena, please recap what happened on Saturday night in Houston," Dexter said to Lorena, as he looked down and shook his head.

"Hello America," Lorena began, and the audience began to see video clips matching her descriptions. "Saturday at approximately 7:11pm eastern time, there was a vicious co-ordinated terrorist attack near downtown Houston. It is not clear who carried out the attack as no-one was captured and as, of yet, no assailants have been identified among the dead. The authorities are looking for any tips from citizens. If you have any information on who might have carried out the attack, then please contact either the FBI or SBI. Unconfirmed sources are providing conflicting reports. Some suggest it was foreign terrorists, some suggest it was domestic terrorism. It began with an assassination attempt of Governor Young, forcing him to leave the stage. The protective shield held and the Governor was not harmed but then, as the crowd began to leave the stage area, an electromagnetic pulse, or EMP, was detonated disabling the local security and medical droids, as well as killing three people standing next to it. Only those machines with military grade resistant shielding were still operational. As the crowd was now in a panic, many flowed from the general audience area to the shuttles in an effort to reach safety. As they were passing by a line of trucks used by the event organizers, two of the trucks exploded. They had been filled with ammonium nitrate or ANFO and detonated intentionally with as many people nearby as possible. The ANFO was wrapped in pitiless shrapnel to shower the crowd with deadly projectiles. This dramatically increased the number injured. The truck rained death on those flowing from the speaking area and the nearby children's play zone. Most videos from the scene have been confiscated by authorities investigating the attack. We are limiting the videos tonight to not compromise the investigation, plus some are simply too traumatic to share," Lorena concluded.

"Fifty-nine people are dead, including fifteen children. Five hundred and twenty-seven wounded," Dexter paused. "Many of the wounded are fighting for their lives. The courageous medical teams saved many people. This was an intentional phased attack designed for extreme horrific carnage. Please keep all of the victims in your prayers." Dexter paused again. "We have guests to discuss the attack but, for the first time, we will not have contestants or voting tonight. No-one can win with this kind of subject. Instead, we are donating 50,000 credits to the families of those hurt in this tragedy. I ask you now for a moment of silence to honor those killed or wounded."

Dexter looked down, closed his eyes, and put his hands together on his heart. On the backdrop behind him, still images of those hurt were projected one at a time. The final image showed a young mother cradling her dead son and screaming at the sky in pain. Blood was on her shirt and the deflated bouncy houses added to the pure despair. When Dexter opened his eyes, he saw roughly a third of the audience standing and making an X sign with their arms over their chest and looking down solemnly. Dexter had a haunting feeling that it symbolized a skull and crossbones.

"Tonight, we have Angel Vega, a senior advisor to Southern District Governor Young, and Corban Cruz, the Chairman of President Thorne's Security Council. We will be discussing the attack and who might have conducted it," Dexter said.

The two men walked in solemnly as the crowd politely applauded. Angel walked in from the right and Corban from the left. The three men sat at the debate table. Dexter could feel something different in the air; something hazardous, something toxic. The two guests had rarely been in the same room together, but had a rivalry that went back over several years. While there was some mutual respect, they were often bitterly divided on national debates; debates that usually ended up with the Southern District squaring off against the east, west, and federal institutions.

"Gentlemen, we appreciate you coming on the program," Dexter said.

"Thank you for having me Dexter. As you know, I am a fan of the show. I wish it were under better circumstances," Angel said.

"Yes, thank you for having us. There is a lot to discuss," Corban said.

"Mr. Vega, what can you tell us about the attack? In particular, do you have an idea yet of who carried out this wicked crime?" Dexter asked.

"I don't want to compromise the investigation, so I will not speculate on who carried it out, nor comment on anything the investigation has uncovered thus far. I can say that every relevant department, agency, and bureau is working around the clock. The attack last week was heart breaking. This second attack is…" Angel paused, thinking. "…it's beyond comprehension. I was at the rally with the Governor. When I heard the first explosion, I went running to the crowd wanting to help." Angel again paused. "After the second explosion, I was knocked backwards more than five meters. I was not very close but it still knocked me on my ass. I got up and ran to where I saw smoke. The bodies. The body parts. At first, the quiet moans of pain, followed by the screams of the injured and the dying." Angel realized he had been looking down at his hands when talking. He lifted his gaze up and his face shifted from sorrow to a mature rage. "Whoever is responsible will pay, I promise you. They will pay in a way that no-one will ever dare do this again." No-one in the audience doubted that Angel meant it.

"Chairman Corban, what is the Administration doing in response to this tragedy?" Dexter asked.

"Before I answer that question, I want to say that all our hearts go out to the citizens of Houston for both the AntiCo attack and the Bush Park massacre," Corban began. "These attacks show us that evil still exists in our world. The barbarity of these acts is, in reality, worse than acts of war. They are preying on what is most precious to us, our children and our freedoms. We must show them what America is made of, and that we will not give up who we are and what we believe in. The Thorne Administration has turned on every tool at our disposal. We are trying to help Houston with this horrific burden of helping the wounded. We are trying to piece together who carried out this attack, including where they could have gotten an EMP device. The device used was a modern war grade weapon and not easy to come by. It was an explosively pumped flux compression generator device that nearly took out the military grade drones. We are also trying to find out who ordered or otherwise triggered this attack. We need to know the ring leader to prevent it from happening again."

"Mr. Vega, what is the Southern District doing to help prevent another attack?" Dexter asked. "Online chatter is intense with fear that it could happen again."

"I am glad you asked that question because an honest and sometimes painful assessment must be made with tough choices," Angel began. "We are caught between two conflicting needs – one in that we must keep and honor our freedoms, and the other need is that we must keep our people safe and do what we can to disrupt and entrap those who would do us harm. A safe nation puts itself into a position which makes defeat impossible and seeks out the opportunity to strike and defeat its enemies. This nation, for too long, has prioritized allowing terrorists who self-identify as activists to inflict unimaginable pain on our people. It is advertised as a policy of a protecting free speech. In reality, it's a transparent effort to use violence to achieve political gains. This nation must harshly persecute and penalize all those who commit political crimes as hate crimes, including the death penalty. Only then will there be an effective deterrent."

"Chairman Cruz, your response," Dexter said.

"While I feel great sympathy for the citizens affected by this attack, I must disagree with my honorable colleague," Corban began. "When someone is sick, do we stop taking vitamins that help other parts of our body? No, we only attack the virus and, if possible, we also address the weaknesses of which the virus is taking advantage. I think a healthy review of the laws in play for politically-motivated violence is a good idea. Protecting our freedoms must be part on any agreement. We also need to look hard and make perhaps a painful assessment of why they are attacking us. Why, in particular, are these attacks almost always against the Southern District? Why did they attack this protest instead of a softer target? If we understand why they felt compelled to attack this protest, then maybe we can address their discontent. For someone to inflict pain like this shows they are also in great pain. We need to defeat the transcendent nature that would allow someone to carry out a malevolent act like the two we have seen recently in the Southern District."

"The Southern District Governor and the Governors of the states in the south expected that reaction of inaction from the federal government," Angel said. "Even after the deadliest attack on US soil in years, President Thorne has not done anything besides wanting to talk about the Southern District leadership. Dexter, I honestly don't know if anything will trigger tangible results by the Thorne Administration. To secure ourselves against attacks is in our control; it lies in our own hands. The opportunity of defeating our enemy is always provided by the enemy himself. Our enemy sees it clearly, yet we do not. Once they are identified, we need to strike at the very roots of their existence. If it is a group based in a foreign nation, we will return them to the stone ages. If it is a group within our own borders, then we will still give no quarter and no shelter."

"Tough talk Mr. Vega, I think we all agree those responsible need to pay," Dexter stated and turned to Corban. "Chairman Cruz, we understand you can't compromise the investigation, but can you comment if you think there is a connection between the two attacks?"

"I can't make any specific comments, but mostly because those working the investigation are limiting the information to those who need to know," Corban said. "I can only tell you my own assessment regarding the question of who might have been behind these attacks. The AntiCo attack looks to be rage against southern policies of restricting entry to undocumented immigrants and limited deudor opportunities. It was the same old style of sick individuals rushing in and lashing out in an effort to show resistance. The Bush Park massacre, to me, has more traces of a complicated strategic domestic political attack. I would speculate that it targeted this protest with the only common theme being to punish again southern policies."

"So, you think the second attack might have been on this protest and the southern capital because of southern policies such as immigration and deudors?" Dexter asked Corban.

"We need a balanced approach to punish those who carried out these recent crimes and work towards a community that doesn't trigger these attacks. You just heard from a senior advisor to Governor Young the same tired kill 'em all plan. It's a belief born in fascism; sort of a crypto fascism," Corban replied.

"Dozens of our citizens are dead, including children. Our hospitals are full of wounded, many suffering greatly. The gall you are displaying to use the same old liberal talking points to justify the attacks is unforgivable. And if you call me a crypto fascist again, I will punch you in the God damn face!" Angel replied.

Dexter's mouth dropped open. For once, he had nothing immediately come to mind to say. He had not used the option of dropping a guest from his show in months and never had to do so with such a high up political leader. But he was considering it now.

"Ladies and gentlemen, we are seeing here the wrath of the southern leadership. The wrathful are people who are constantly angry. This is not new, even with this latest tragedy," Corban responded.

"Wrath is not the right way to characterize our beliefs, nor our reaction to the attack," Angel stated, while staring daggers at Corban. "We are proud of our freedoms. Some of the freedoms we hold most dear are the same that your administration keeps constricting in an effort to dominate and subjugate all citizens. I did not come here to debate unrelated policies and am disgusted by your opportunistic nature. We demand justice. We will inflict our justice on those who have done us harm. We have lost confidence that the federal government will prioritize keeping us safe going forward, so we will become more proactive in our own defense," Angel stated.

"The Southern District needs to work within the American infrastructure. The art of politics is to stop trouble before it starts. Looks like Mr. Vega plans to carry out vengeance born out of his fury. We need level heads instead of over-reacting and possibly punishing those not even responsible," Corban said.

"Gentlemen, I can see emotions are running high. I hope our leaders can focus that energy on those who have and would do us harm, and not on each other. This internal division is exactly what our enemies are hoping to see. If we cannot unite, then they are winning. Fictional divisions are the most avoidable, yet most dangerous," Dexter paused. "Let's table the policy debate for another night. Thank you both for joining us. Ladies and gentlemen, we will take a commercial break and come back with a panel discussion." When Dexter finished, the two men exchanged hard looks and left the stage.

Samson

S amson Gamble stared out the starboard hatch of the Raptor Attack Turbocraft as the team raced towards their objective. It was a dark night but, as they approached the city, the landscape began to take shape.

"Andre, wake up. Wet dream time is over," Samson yelled at his number two. Andre always fell asleep when they had flights with turbulence.

"Five more minutes," he grumbled. Andre Pantero had more scars at thirty years old than most marines would get their entire lives.

"That's what she said, you slacker," Samson jabbed.

"I know, and I am obliging. Her and her friend," Andre replied.

"Like rocking a baby to sleep. Couche couche coo!" Said Kathy Hawk, who everyone called Hawk, giving Andre a hard tickle in the ribs.

"Unless you are going to help them, back off," Andre said calmly.

"If it's only five minutes, no thanks," Hawk replied with a smile.

"Darlin, I've got your medicine right here. All you have to do is bend the knee for a while," added Dune Kerr, the fourth member of Samson's drop team.

"Now we are really talkin' wet dreams," Hawk replied, and threw an apple at Dune. He caught it and made a show of taking a bite of it making her crack up laughing.

Samson smiled. He returned to checking his gear. Combination laser rifle, machine gun, and grenade launcher set. Both close quarter automatic fire hand guns ready. All three knives, secured. Next, he checked his suit. Samson was a beast of a man and his suit had to be custom made to fit him and handle his strength. He extended both legs and tried moving his feet — they worked fine. He rotated his arms as best as he could while sitting in the Turbocraft transport section. He scanned through the helmet shield data display using Halo-like commanding; data and fit were nominal. The helmet looked like an old school motorcycle helmet, black all over with a visor, but was bullet proof and loaded with tech. Data was displayed on the inside and, when wearing it, the user could see all around thanks to cameras built into the sides. Every part of his suit was meant to dramatically increase what he could do and protect him in Special Forces-type assaults.

"Five minutes to the drop site. We appreciate you flying Anselmo airlines. We know you have no other choice for jobs like this. Would be nice if you paid upfront next time you shits." Tony Anselmo was the pilot of the Turbocraft. Many preferred or tolerated an automated pilot, but not Samson. He didn't trust them. Samson wanted his own man at the stick to be sure they could act as one; to understand each other's instincts.

"Showtime. Let's see if we can break the record," Samson yelled. He made a couple of taps on the touchscreen to the wall on his left. His team of four in the six-seat transport section of the Turbocraft all knew what was coming: battle music. Heavy classic guitar riffs started to fill the transport as they raced into the quiet sleeping city. Anyone awake might have caught it if listening carefully as both jump hatches were open. Tonight, it was a metallic version of Rob Zombie's *More Human Than Human*.

"Yeah, I am the astro creep
A demolition style
Hell American freak, yeah
I am the crawling dead
A phantom in a box
Shadow in your head say
Acid, suicide freedom of the blast
Read the fucker lies, yeah
Scratch off the broken skin
Tear into my heart
Make me do it again yeah

More Human Than Human!

More Human Than Human!
More Human Than Human!"

The Raptor Attack Turbocraft was an advanced military aircraft with ten shrouded double rotor turbofans for propulsion encircling a central section with the pilot up front, a transport section in the torso, and several different weapons facing in all directions. Crews could deploy by parachute, glider wings, jump, or an old fashion landing. Tonight's mission called for a jump.

As Tony guided the craft through the streets, he kept the lights off except for a spotlight looking for cables or towers in their way. He had memorized the terrain and was cutting corners with ease and confidence. Samson's team all believed in preparation like a religion. It had made the difference between life and death many times for them, and for others.

"Thirty seconds until the drop. No signs of life, scans are clear," Tony said.

Samson looked around at his team. They had been together for years. They had served their country in three different wars - two official and one in the black. "I want an aggressive jump. Timing is critical, every second counts. As soon as the man in front has gone, then you jump; no rubber necking," Samson called to his team, his mild Cajun accent showing.

The Turbocraft curled around the target building and pitched up as it circled to the optimal direction to quickly break out, causing them all to lean into it. The lights in the Raptor turned from white to red and the seat belts disengaged. Samson stood, gripped his rifle tight, and calmly stepped out the door. He fell for a full four seconds. Samson's meter long hair as usual was in a tight ponytail like a long rope. His hair was dark brown with hints of dark red. When he hit, his robotic assist legs braced his fall to protect his legs and back. He heard three other smacks on the concrete. Samson watched on his visor display the vitals and helmet camera from his team. Unfortunately, Andre's impact ruptured his thoracic aorta.

"Shit!" Samson yelled, as he read the news on the helmet's display. "Simulation over!" He commanded.

The team exited their VR simulators in the training center.

"Well, I guess we can't drop from 100 meters. We will have to come in lower or descend at the landing site. It'll add time, but we keep breaking people at that height," Samson said as they all sat up.

"Not every time. I don't trust that simulator anyway. But descending won't add much time and will make it hard for anyone who spotted us to see how many dropped," Andre said.

"All right. The runs with drops at 70 meters all went smooth enough. Still shouldn't wake anyone. Tony, you'll fly in at 100 meters and as part of the entry bring us down quick to a stable 70 meters before we punch out," Samson stated. "I think we are ready. Any questions?" The other four soldiers and their operators in the lab all shook their heads. "Good. We leave at midnight tonight. Eat a good meal and get some rest. It's going to be a long night."

The team started to disperse. "Andre, meet me in the command center please," Samson said, as the rest started to put away their training equipment. Samson and Andre left the training center, moving through a door leading to stairs and went up two levels before entering a control room. They needed only the table and chairs for what Samson wanted to talk about.

"I think you know this is a big deal. I wanted to check with you to make sure you are still ok with the plan. I need a sanity check I am not going overboard. I want to make sure my anger hasn't gone off the deep end," Samson said.

"Chief, if anything, I want to do more. I want to know what is next. This op is going to be a cake walk," Andre said. "I'm impressed we got this together so fast, but it can't be the end game. The risk should be worth the reward."

"This is the first step in our retribution. Enough is enough. A reckoning is coming, and we are the tip of the spear. Tonight will help level the playing field. The subject we are going after is worth the likely cost. Death is nothing, but to live without justice, that is to die every day." Samson flexed his right arm. His cut off t-shirt showed the rattlesnake tattoo on his upper arm. The snake head was on the upper bicep and it wrapped around on his arm until the rattle barely touched his wrist. When he flexed, the snake head mouth opened more and the eyes flashed blood red. "For the South!"

"For the South!" Andre agreed.

Corban

orban Cruz looked out the window of his corner office on the 47th floor of the Federal Security Building. The office had a conference table, a desk, and a couch on one wall. Numerous major awards hung on the walls and several video projections of news programs were showing on other locations, all currently on mute. Corban did his best thinking when it was quiet and he gazed out the window at the view below of Fort Meade, Maryland.

"Sir, Ms. Naya Garcia here to see you," Ariella, the trusted federal military and intelligence AI, announced to Corban.

"Thank you, Ariella, please send her in and hold all my calls and visitors," Corban replied.

"As you command," Ariella answered. Seconds later, Naya entered through the automatic sliding doors.

"Naya, thank you for coming," Corban said, still looking out the window. "I thought it important to talk about the debate last night, plus any intel you might have collected. We need to sync up on next steps. Coffee?"

"Yes sir, I appreciate the invitation. The White House communications team has been working on this around the clock. And yes, I'd love some coffee. Black please," Naya replied, as she sat at the table.

Corban walked from the window to a small stand near the couch on the wall. It had a carafe of coffee and cups. He got one for Naya and one for himself.

"What did you think of the debate last night? Did I go too far?" Corban asked.

"It was brilliant. You really showed our remorse for the suffering, but also pushed Angel's buttons in just the right way. They will be seen as overreacting no matter what they do now," Naya said. "I'm sure you earned a nice bonus from our sponsor."

"I think the fascist thing was a mistake. I could have chosen different words to get what we needed," Corban said.

"Failure is the key to success; each mistake teaches us something," Naya said. "That was not of any lasting consequence. Everyone is talking about him threatening to hit you. Only a few are focused on what you said and we weren't going to win them over anyway."

"I suppose so. Still, we need to be careful and very, very smart; however, it is good to know his limits. They will need the public to rally around them to resist the changes we have planned. They will have no power to do anything without the majority of south behind them," Corban said.

"Being right or wrong is not two dimensional. The third dimension is if people will be receptive to what you are trying to say," Naya said, taking a sip of coffee. "It will be very difficult for them to gain public support if we look level-headed and they look intransigent."

"We should appeal for calm," Corban replied. "We should say that anger never fixes anything. His anger certainly was genuine. We need to help, also help lower the temperature, as too much anger can be a poison."

"Anger is not a poison; it is a gift. The gift is knowing that you are forcing a choice," Naya replied, as she leaned forward. "There is now a choice they must make that was not there until the flames of fury had ignited it. They are now faced with the choice of revenge or sacrifice. The choice will be driven by many things, but it is always one or the other. We will weaken them to drive them to choose sacrifice."

Corban looked hard into Naya's eyes. She did not blink.

"I want to deploy more troops to the borders with the Southern District in areas near major southern cities. I also want to shore up our positions at key Southern District facilities like ports, nuclear plants, and airports. We need to be prepared in case they choose revenge," Corban said. "Let's work on how to message that first, and then we will talk some more with the rest of the Security Council on which southern policies to attack first."

Sara

Sara Chamberlain had not slept for three days. She had no more tears to cry. There was a burning agony that words cannot describe. She wanted to rip the world apart, anything that might bring Jon back, anything that might dull the pain. Ben could barely speak. For the first time in all the years that Sara had known Ben, he would not eat.

All of their relatives had come into town and were speaking to the media and friends for them. The videos of Sara holding Jon had gone viral. Emma spent most of her time curled up in her grandmother's lap. Sara hoped Emma was eating, but could never seem to remember to remind her.

"Honey, it's time," Sara said to Ben.

"Ok, I'll get Emma," Ben replied. There was a pause between when he spoke and when he actually started to move.

Jon had loved the ocean. He had wanted to go to the beach every day each summer since first visiting when he was three years old. Jon's favorite beach was at a beach house the Chamberlains had rented one week a month the past couple of summers. They and their extended family were at the beach house now. It was a refuge from the media and an attempt to escape the reality that they would never see him again. They were at the ocean to say goodbye to Jon.

Ben came back to Sara holding Emma's hand. Emma's eyes were red as she had just been bawling. The three of them slowly walked out the house, down the wooden stairs to the ground level, and about twenty meters to a walkway that led them over the tall grass to the beach. When they reached the beach, Sara turned around to see their extended family on the porch of the beach house watching them. The life expectancy of Americans was closing in on 100. Five generations of family were represented, but today they were saying farewell to their youngest.

They slowly walked closer to the water. When they got to the part of the beach where the water helped it to be reasonably firm, Sara and Ben nodded to each other. Sara knelt down and put the package on the ground. She unlatched the case, opened the lid, and moved the packaging paper aside to reveal the urn that held Jon's ashes. She stood up and hugged Ben and Emma. She hugged them to try to draw strength from them. Overhead were four drones. One descended and hovered near Sara. She secured the urn carefully to a chord hanging below the drone. Next, she took handwritten goodbye messages written to Jon and clipped those to the chord as well. When it looked secure, she hesitated, knowing it was the last time she would hold Jon. This was the first time she felt it, a feeling like her blood was going to start boiling, like she had a pressure inside that needed to be released. Sara needed to release the pressure against those who had taken her little boy's life from him, to release it against those who would blame them for having gone to the protest, and to release it in a ferocious way.

"Mommy loves you honey," Sara said softly.

Sara walked back to hold Ben and Emma again. Ben took the remote from his pocket and turned it on. He looked back at the house and saw everyone still watching them, all except his great grandmother who looked to be crying on his great grandfather's shoulder. He looked back at the drone and, after a deep breath, pushed the button to start it. Sara and Emma both started to cry. The drone joined the other three and they together began to go out over the water. The four drones flew in a pattern with light beams showing the sign of the cross. The drone on the bottom had Jon. They stopped after they traveled about eighty meters. It was beyond a significant drop off where the water was over two hundred meters deep. The four drones used specialized lights so they together displayed a hologram of a cross. After about a minute, the bottom drone released Jon's urn and the letters.

Sara, Ben, and Emma stared at the water for quite a while. After many tears, they started walking back to the beach house. The funeral had been hard enough earlier in the day. They were all exhausted. It would be another two days before they returned home.

Angel

A ngel Vega needed a break. It had been a terrible week by any measure. He knew of no better place to unwind and forget about the world than Alltens. Angel didn't indulge often, but today was an exception. He was not married and considered it a harmless legal vice even though most of society looked down on it.

"Good evening sir," said the receptionist. "Welcome back. It's been a while."

"Yes, it has. I'd like to see Nathalie and Margot if they are not busy tonight," Angel said. He placed a neat stack of gold coins on the counter.

The receptionist picked them up without breaking eye contact with Angel. "Why yes, they are available and would love to see you again," she said. "Please relax in our reception area."

Angel nodded and smiled. He turned and walked to the left down the hallway towards the music. There was an alternative pop band playing and as Angel got closer, he heard laughing. The hallway turned into a lounge with a bar in the center; the band was playing on the other side of the bar, and booths wrapping around the walls. The lighting was poor in the booths on purpose. On either end of the bar was a pedestal with a pole. On each pole was a dancer. At the bar and at most booths were well-dressed men and a few well-dressed women talking to stunningly beautiful creatures who seemed to be hanging on every word of their guests. Some of the hosts were men, women, and amen. Amen was the modern term for people that identified as something besides a male or female. Society had grown tired of further categorizing sexual orientation and the amen community concluded pronouns were just a breeder tool. None of the hosts were human, they were all androids manufactured for one purpose: to please humans.

"Whiskey, double, on the rocks," Angel said to the bartender. As the bartender turned to get the drink, Angel looked around the room to make sure there were no familiar faces, cameras, or anything else that might cause a scene. The bar had stools all around it, but Angel preferred to stand.

The bartender served the drink and was careful not to make eye contact too long. Most guests did not want much attention and weren't here to talk about themselves. Angel watched the hosts and customers mingle. Some just talked, while others were dancing.

The band finished playing a fast-paced pop song and slowly dissipated from the stage. One singer remained on stage to perform a solo version of the Rolling Stones' *Gimme Shelter*. Angel could see the singer was an alluring amen. He was amazed at the beauty and power of the amen's voice and already felt his stress begin to drain away.

"Oh, a storm is threat'ning
My very life today
If I don't get some shelter
Oh yeah, I'm gonna fade away

War, children, it's just a shot away
It's just a shot away

Ooh, see the fire is sweepin'
Our very street today
Burns like a red coal carpet
Mad bull lost your way

War, children, it's just a shot away
It's just a shot away

The flood is threat'ning
My very life today
Gimme, gimme shelter
Or I'm gonna fade away"

As he sipped the whiskey, Angel thought about his mother and the transformation she had made. Seeing the machines always made him think of her. An expensive experiment had taken place in the previous decade. People facing death had attempted to cheat it by transferring their soul to a machine. His mother had tried it when she discovered she had terminal brain disease. Like the rest of society, Angel and his family found out that putting someone's memories and simulated personalities into a computer was at best a digital copy of the person when they died. The trend faded out as it was clear that the person dying still died and a copy didn't change anything. Angel thought it was odd that the idea of a soul was never talked about publicly, yet humanity grasped why the crude attempt at immortality failed.

"Hi there handsome," Nathalie said from behind Angel.

"What's a nice man like you doing in a place like this?" Margot asked.

"I've come to convert you both. I want to save your souls," Angel said with a straight face that he could hold only for a second. Then all three burst out laughing.

"Bartender, anything these ladies would like please," Angel said.

Nathalie rested a hand on Angel's shoulder and leaned against him. Her skin felt soft and warm. Margot sat on the stool next to where Angel was standing. She petted the side of Angel's leg gently. The bartender already knew what the ladies wanted to drink.

The three exchanged humor and harmless stories about what they had been doing since seeing each other last. Angel never really knew why so many people looked down on the androids. Maybe it was because every machine was competition for someone. And if you had even one humanoid out there that, in some way, was a threat to who you are, then you'd be inclined to resent them all. Or maybe it was just we fear what we don't know. Angel wasn't sure. What Angel was sure about is that these ladies made him feel like a real man. They shared emotions, had needs, learned about him each time they met, and appreciated him. They weren't some imaginary characters online or using a Halo to trick yourself into a fake relationship. They were here with him now. They would be upstairs with him later. It beat the hell out of wearing a diaper in VR to take care of the mess. In a way, these machines were more real or even more human than most women he could meet.

After two drinks the three went arm-in-arm with Angel in the middle out of the bar and into the elevator up to Nathalie's apartment. They never saw the device that had been listening and picturing their interactions. From a distance, it looked like a miniature cockroach, but was an extremely advanced spying technology with the only limitation being a short-range transmitter. The van parked outside was receiving an excellent signal. The bug was able to sneak into Nathalie's bedroom by squeezing under the apartment door. After about an hour of evidence collecting, it snuck back out and made its way to the van. The van sped away having gathered what they needed.

Zander

Zander yawned. It was almost 1:00am and they were still testing one of the new modified machines. Fred, the Production Manager, was working with Dinah to finalize how to install the new power system into the twelve prototypes from the advanced concepts lab. Once they worked out the details then Dinah could take over and manufacture integrated units. It was proving harder than anticipated, but they were making progress finally. Zander was in the bird's nest on the third floor overlooking the high bay. Fred was on the high bay floor near the middle with one of the units that was standing at attention. It was missing two of the standard four arms as Fred was working to try again to integrate the laser weapon which was embedded in one of the arms. The unit had the standard brushed gunmetal frame and red lights for "eyes" standard to federal military and police droids. Its torso was inflated, giving room for the extra power system and weapons integration systems. The legs were stocky to handle the extra weight. A pair of manufacturing assistants were also assisting and they had three test racks with electronics and mechanical tools, one of which was plugged into the test unit.

"Dinah, pull up the drawings please of the laser pinouts. I think the drawing from the lab doesn't match the generic laser connector. None of them will work if the connectors aren't mapped right," Fred said.

"As you command," Dinah said. "Yes, it looks like the communications lines to the unit processors are reversed."

"Unit number 6. Please turn around and unlock your control panel," Fred requested. The nearly three-meter-tall machine looked down at Fred, stood still for a second, and then slowly turned around. Fred heard a click.

"Sir, I am detecting an incoming flying object from the southwest,"

Dinah said to Zander. A display came up on the wall showing an object navigating between the tall buildings and closing fast.

"Trajectory?" Zander asked.

"It is on a course to arrive here in less than one minute," Dinah said. "Visual scan does not show heavy weaponry; however, its lights are off."

"Sound the general alarm, and activate all security protocols for an imminent attack on the facility. A craft like that means they intend to raid us," Zander said calmly to Dinah. He pressed a button to activate the intercom. "Fred, we have an incoming threat. This is not a drill. You need to evacuate to the safe room now double time. They will be here in less than thirty seconds."

Fred's jaw dropped. He stared at the bird's nest for a second and then started to run to the internal facility door on the north wall. He knew better than to say anything. Anyone crazy enough to attack this place would have no problem killing an expendable engineer.

"Dinah, call for help if you have not done so already. How much longer…" Zander said, before being interrupted.

Boom, boom, boom!!! The building shook and the eastern-most door dented in three places.

"Sir, it appears they…" Dinah started.

"Yes, I know. Activate all sentries and laser cannons. I want three sentries on the eastern door, one guarding the other new units on the north wall, and one on the southern double doors. Also, activate the new unit down there, maybe it can help. Oh and…" Zander said, but again was interrupted.

Boom!! Crash!! The eastern door crashed inwards after another explosion. A lone soldier rushed in firing laser pistols at the closest sentry. Zzzzz, Zzzzz, Zzzzz! The sentry collapsed. Smoke billowed around the eastern entrance from the explosions that ripped the double doors to pieces, leaving toothed metal where seemingly impenetrable doors had once stood.

All four laser cannons fired at the lone soldier who then screeched in pain before falling. Next, Zander would later guess that it was seven soldiers that charged in. Four fired at the laser cannons now that they knew their locations, and two fired at the other sentries nearby. A gun battle broke out between the sentries and the attackers, but Zander's team was outnumbered by an obviously well-armed attack unit.

One soldier advanced on the android Fred had been working on. The android tried a hook jab kick combination, but the soldier dodged all the attacks. The soldier was almost as big as the android. The soldier returned the hospitality with an uppercut that lifted the android off his feet several centimeters and quickly grabbed the android's right arm. After rotating the arm to pin the machine, he kicked at it to rip the arm from the android. The machine roared in rage and charged at the attacker. It was now down to one arm. Zander thought he saw a snake's head on the soldier's upper arm. The soldier began to beat the android in the head with the machine's own arm. The android tried to block the hits, but the soldier was relentless, screaming with a terrible laughter, and acting so cruel that Zander guessed he was enjoying himself. A wolf in wolf's clothing. When it was clear there was no fight left in the android, the soldier grabbed it by the head and ripped it off. The android slumped to the ground, giving one last twitch before going silent.

Zander used a fireman's pole to slide from the bird's nest down to the ground level. His sentries had managed to take out two more soldiers, but had come up on the short end of the gun battle. Zander was out of options. He snuck along the west wall to hide behind some crates. He saw the attackers quickly go to the stack of advanced machines and take two of the crates. Zander could faintly hear sirens approaching. The attackers all started to head to the open southern door. Zander tried to sneak his way to the door to watch them after they had all left. Before he could get to the doorway, he heard a Turbocraft landing. After a few seconds of running towards the door, Zander heard the Turbocraft start to leave just as some security lights started to show through the door. Zander stopped as he was too late to see the craft and would not want the security forces to think he was escaping. Zander walked by the three fallen attackers. They all looked like Workerbee-manufactured machines in advanced military outfits made for men. Zander lay down to make sure the security forces did not engage him as a hostile.

Outside, the Turbocraft was being followed and fired upon. It was not trying to be quiet as it was flying as fast as it could and the sound echoed off the sides of the buildings. Those firing upon it were not worried about collateral damage. One does not let state of the art autonomous killing machines get stolen.

"Sir, we are under intense fire. We have been hit twice. What are your orders?" Said the pilot. There was only one passenger along with one of the stolen units.

"Bravo team. You performed your job perfectly. We are very proud of you. Thank you for your service," Samson said to the pilot through the comm system.

The machine pilot thought about that statement for a second. "Wait. Wait!" The pilot yelled in a panic.

Samson pushed a button on his remote and the Turbocraft exploded in a blaze of glory. Samson, the rest of his Alpha team, and the other stolen unit were safely in the work truck to make their getaway. Alpha team had arrived in the Turbocraft and let Bravo team leave in it to take the fall. Bravo team, made up of machines, had arrived in the work truck two days ago and quietly waited for the attack just outside Workerbee Robotics. All the security forces had been following the Turbocraft after the attack and not noticed the boring self-driving generic utility truck. Samson's team slowly went to the safe house, changed into civilian clothing, and left Los Angeles in a food truck heading back to Texas. It would be two days for the investigation to realize only one of the stolen units had been left behind in the wreckage.

Corban

Corban Cruz had known President Nero Thorne for years, but was still uneasy whenever he met with him at the White House. Meeting with the President, even an old friend, was intense, and the topic they were meeting with him on today was very dicey.

He was alone in a conference room on the West Wing. Corban could hear Thorne coming down the hall, giving somebody the business. The door swung open with authority and Thorne moved in quickly walking right up to him.

"Corban, damn good to see you. I hope you have some good news. Feels like everything is going to hell," Thorne said, with a voice deep enough to fill a concert hall. Following Thorne into the room was Naya Garcia and Alexandra Soaring.

"I have news. Will let you judge if it's good or not," Corban replied. He was surprised to see Naya and Alexandra accompany Thorne. If anyone was to have stolen into the meeting, he thought it would have been Asa Katz.

The room had a long table pointing at a wall for projections. Thorne sat at the head of the table with lighting behind him. Naya and Alexandra sat to his left and right towards the front. Corban sat near the projection screen. The White House in many areas was modern, but no President yet had updated the West Wing to modern virtual reality centric collaboration centers.

"Have you made progress on identifying the attackers? I mean for both Houston and LA?" Thorne asked Corban.

"Yes sir. Before I begin, I want to state what I am going to share is considered a 'need-to- know' basis only, and if leaked might compromise the investigations," Corban said, just giving Thorne a chance to clear the room.

"Understood. Proceed," Thorne said. Corban could tell the President was craving information. Naya and Alexandra likely tailed along as they knew his agenda and also wanted to hear the latest intelligence.

"Ariella, please bring up the visuals," Corban said, while giving mild glares to both Naya and Alexandra. Naya didn't flinch, but Alexandra seemed a little uneasy as if she hadn't realized Corban might have wanted a one-on-one with his boss.

"We have preliminary evidence that the Bush Park massacre and Workerbee raid are homegrown." Corban watched Thorne who nodded showing he understood. "Ariella, next image please." Corban continued as Ariella changed to the next image.

"This is a map of the Houston attack in Bush Park, near the local branch of the FBI and the Southern District Headquarters for Federal Worker's Rights." Ariella began to add visual effects to the map as Corban continued his description. "The first incident was here at the stage right after Governor Young began speaking. The security response likely saved his life as the laser had mostly penetrated the shield before he turned to run. Enough of the crowd understood what happened to start moving away from the stage. They then started to flow in this direction and grew as more and more people panicked. Some were hurt in the growing stampede. We then had explosions here and here. The first was an EMP to disable the androids and drones. This likely let the attackers escape, as well as hurt abilities to help wounded from the second explosion from these two trucks. The timing was done with expert precision to maximize casualties."

"Understood. What progress have you made in catching those responsible?" Thorne asked, with thin patience showing.

"There are two new pieces of information to share. The first is this image captured by the drones responding to the laser strike on the Governor. You can see the shooter here as he looks up after he stopped firing. He is a white male who looks to be in his thirties and does not appear to have a Muslim or Middle Eastern background. Normally we would have identified him almost immediately, but we believe he has had significant facial surgery to erase his identity. This would be the first case of a Muslim terror attack on our country with such an assailant. The other piece of information that is different than what the media is reporting is the type of EMP. It was leaked to the media that it was an EMP likely recovered by terrorist organizations during the Iran war; however, this model was only developed in the last few years and it was one of ours. Android technology continues to advance to stay ahead of threats like EMPs, but this new weapon was much smaller and shielded in a way that our scanners had no idea it was there. Couple these facts with the failed assassination attempt, and we believe this was an act of domestic political terrorism and not foreign terrorism as initially reported." Corban paused to let Thorne adsorb this news. Naya had a cold look in her eyes. Alexandra's jaw dropped slightly and her eyes got wider.

"Holy shit," Thorne said, studying the display on the wall. There was about three seconds of uncomfortable silence. Thorne turned his gaze from the display and back to Corban.

"We also have news for you on the attack at Workerbee Robotics," Corban said.

"Go ahead," Thorne said.

"Ariella, please bring it up," Corban directed. "The press would be reporting this attack in almost as much lust as the Houston attacks if it knew what I am about to share. The attack was not at a standard robotics and manufacturing plant. This particular plant was going to integrate the latest robotic fighting soldier with the military's latest laser weapons system. This would integrate a fairly revolutionary power system with a power-hungry laser weapon that is a game changer on the battlefield. Lasers are only a good weapon for war if they have the power to fire again and again. If you have it, then you can fire at the speed of light and nothing can stop you. This map shows the route taken to get to the plant and then the route they took when leaving before their craft was destroyed. The press thinks this was the only vehicle involved." Corban could see by Thorne leaning forward that was all he had heard so far. "Unfortunately, we could tell by the wreckage that not all the attackers were among the debris. Two advanced robotic units were taken, and only one unit was among the wreckage. Analysis of videos in the area showed that the attacker's second vehicle was an old white work truck that had been parked by the plant for more than 24 hours. Based on video analysis, we believe humans arrived on the Turbocraft and robotic soldiers dressed as humans were in the truck; they then swapped vehicles for their escape. Also, we believe the Turbocraft was detonated, as opposed to shot down, based on debris and video. This means the Turbocraft was a prop to help with the escape."

"This just keeps getting worse," Thorne sighed.

"There is one more key piece of information as well. Ariella, please show the hand-to-hand combat shots." Ariella displayed several seconds of the combat scene pausing when the tattoo of an attacker was visible. "We believe we can identify one of the attackers based on this video. It is a unique tattoo and the strength and skills he possesses are very rare. We are running it through our databases. Whoever they are, we don't think they would have performed this attack without some sort of mastermind or puppet master behind the scenes. We also don't think they stole it just to have it; they took it for some extended purpose as yet unknown." Corban stopped to let Thorne take in this additional information. "If you look at both of these attacks, then one might conclude that sides are forming and the situation could escalate dramatically."

"Bastards. God damn bastards. Are they trying to start a war?" Thorne thought out loud. "You were wise to keep these details secret. Keep it that way as long as possible, and don't tell Young or his people, as I don't trust them to keep quiet, let alone make rational decisions based on it. And find all of these sons of bitches no matter what the cost!"

"Yes sir, will do. I will report back again as soon as I have something substantial," Corban replied.

"Mr. President, I share your shock and outrage at what we just heard," Naya said. "I wonder if I might suggest a couple of ideas that can be pursued in parallel."

"Go!" Thorne replied, turning to look at Naya.

"We have started a national debate on the deudor system with the goal of a nationwide policy instead of it varying by district," Naya began. "There is still the potential for that helping to shift focus from the pain and carnage to something productive. Also, no matter what we try to do, it seems that the leaders of the Southern District, by both their policies and narrative to the public, continue to drive wedges between the south and the rest of the country. I suggest we also try to focus the media and public on their weaknesses, with the hope that the next election will give you leaders that can help you unite the country under your leadership."

"That is a slippery slope. We don't want to look unresponsive to the tragedies." Nero thought for a couple of seconds. "I'm ok with going forward after a few days, but make sure it is balanced and proceeds slowly. I want coverage of us helping all the victims with clear statements as to our hard work going after all the attackers."

"Yes sir, will do," Naya said. She and Alexandra exchanged a brief smile. Corban now understood why they crashed the meeting. They must have something juicy to take to the press now. The lights returned to the room, the display shut down, and the four left going in very different directions.

Dexter

"**H**ello America!!" Dexter shouted, as the crowd welcomed him to the start of the show. "Thank you. Thank you very much." Dexter signaled the audience to settle down.

"I hope everyone is up for a fight tonight. There has been little progress in finding those responsible for the Bush Park massacre and there has been an attack at a robotics plant in Los Angeles that does work for the military. Our key debate tonight will stage two central figures in the ongoing crisis. We will force a fair debate and you can make up your own mind. I will be doing the same. We are each a Party of One. Partido de uno!" The audience cheered as Dexter made it to his seat.

"Lorena, please recap some of the key statements today from government officials," Dexter requested.

The studio room went night black for a few seconds and then newscasts from earlier in the day were displayed behind the stage. The first featured Naya Garcia, head of the White House Office of Communications, speaking to reporters at the White House press room.

"Yes, yes. I understand the frustration on not having answers yet. We are all frustrated. Our hearts were broken by this attack. We are doing everything we can to bring those responsible to justice. As far as your question about preventing more attacks, we need to look at security, as well as why these attacks have happened in Houston and, in particular, at this protest."

The studio again went black. This time a clip opened showing the communications specialist for the Southern District, Dana Berry, talking at a press conference at the Southern District Capitol in Houston.

"The Governor is outraged by the continued politicization of these cowardly attacks. The Governor is worried about the victims and looking to shore up our security. Perhaps if the Administration took these attacks as seriously as they do the opportunities to blame policies for murder, then maybe these attacks would not have happened," Dana replied.

The room again went black and quickly the audience was back with Dexter and his debate table.

"Tonight, we are joined by Eastern District Governor, Asa Katz, and Southern District Governor, Cyrus Young. We will debate what to do to avoid further violence and bring justice to the guilty." The crowd applauded.

"Before we bring out our honored guests, let's first meet the subjects for whom they are competing," Dexter said. "Lorena, please introduce our contestants for this evening and what they are playing for tonight!"

"Ladies and gentlemen, our first contestant hails from the Eastern District," Lorena began. "She is a twenty-nine-year-old widow with two young children who self-immigrated after her husband was killed in the Mexican drug wars. Please welcome Isabella!!" The audience clapped and hollered. The spectators were able to see Isabella holding her two children, tears in her eyes, and a picture of her husband beside her on a table. "If Governor Katz wins more votes tonight, this show will provide credits to cover Isabella's child care, rent, lawyer fees to help her attain legal residence, and living expenses for a full year!"

"Our next contestant calls the Southern District home. He is a thirty-five-year-old man who lost both legs in the Bush Park massacre, as well as his nine-year-old daughter. He has a wife and two other children. He had been a construction worker, but will need to transition to a new job given his injuries. Please welcome Rafael!!" The crowd clapped, half more energetically than the other, and could see Rafael with his family. He held a picture of his little girl hugging a teddy bear. His wife was with him and she was holding the same bear with a tear rolling down her cheek. "If Governor Young wins more votes tonight, this show will provide credits to pay for upgrades to Rafael's artificial legs, plus living expenses for his family for a full year!"

"Ladies and gentlemen, please welcome our guests," Dexter said, while standing up and clapping. On the backdrop behind Dexter, a giant American flag waived. A live tiger walked in front of the debate table, sat down, and gave out a loud growl.

From the left side of the stage entered Governor Katz and, from the right, Governor Young. The two Governors made entrances worthy of their titles and the applause. Katz walked in wearing a navy-blue suit, white shirt, and a tie that shined like a diamond with a blue hue. Young was wearing a black suit, grey shirt, and a tie that shined like a dark red ruby. The three of them exchanged handshakes and sat down. The tiger growled at the audience one more time and walked off the stage.

"Thank you both for coming on the program tonight. Governor Katz, my first question will be for you. What specifically is the Thorne Administration doing to find the attackers?" Dexter asked.

"Thank you for having me on Dexter," Asa began. "I want to echo what many have said that my heart is broken by this tragic loss of life. It is hard to sleep at night knowing the monsters responsible are still out there. The Administration has every available tool looking under every rock. We will find them. Sometimes these things take time. For specifics on the Bush Park massacre, the focus right now is on terrorist groups based in Persia. We have allies and intelligence officers investigating right now. Regarding the incident at the Workerbee plant, right now we see no connection to the tragedies in Houston. I believe this was a failed attack by domestic militia against federal government power, most likely a southern militia."

"Governor Young, what is the Southern District doing?" Dexter asked.

"Thank you for having me on Dexter," Cyrus began. "It is very telling that in this day and age that you also have to ask two district governors what they are doing on the exact same crisis. There should be a cohesive national response and plan for the country. United we stand, divided we fall. The Southern District is mourning the dead and providing relief as best we can to the survivors. We also are looking to improve security at key installations to thwart potential future strikes. We are upgrading our security capabilities to better withstand EMP devices and expand our detection methods for explosives. No matter how much we work on defense, we can't secure everyone everywhere all the time. We are also looking into proactive practices to remove potential hostiles and prevent them from entering and re-entering the district. These policies should have been in place for the country overall, but were not for personal political power benefits for members of the Thorne Administration. Also, while the permanent impact, of course, was horrific loss of life and injury, we must not forget there also was an assassination attempt. A lot of the reaction by the media, pundits, and some government officials seems to stem from the same desire to force policies on the south more out of avarice for power than trying to help." Cyrus turned to face Asa coldly. "And I would caution the Administration from jumping to conclusions that the Los Angeles incident was a southern militia. That would be as premature and politically motivated as if I blamed the Workerbee raid on Western District policies."

"Governor Katz, your response," Dexter transitioned.

"I do not agree these security and immigration actions you are considering will make the Southern District safer, nor would they help the union if implemented for us all. It is unfair to say we are motivated by greed when offering to help. Doing that only slows the momentum of progress and throws fuel on the fire of resentment. If we turn on each other, then the terrorists win. We need to work together and bridge the gap that keeps growing between our districts. We are stronger together and have common enemies." Asa rebutted.

Cyrus made a quiet grunt and a corner of his mouth went up in disgust. Even coaching and decades of practice in masking body language could not hide his contempt. Cyrus turned to talk to the audience. "Justice will be served and it seems increasingly likely it will have to be at the hands of the Southern Bureau of Investigations and the Southern National Guard. We will continue to seek opportunities for co-operation with the Administration; however, our faith to date has not been rewarded. Because of the need to increase our capabilities to face these threats directly, we will be reopening federal military bases in the south that have been retired. Our Southern National Guard will activate forces and recruit new surge support. We will begin to protect our key infrastructure and locations where many citizens come together using the guard. The guard will be an essential tool to help drive out and eliminate threats, but requires additional infrastructure and logistics support for these security forces." The crowd was stunned at the escalation from this move.

Asa tensed and leaned forward. "The Administration will consider the idea, but we should make sure any efforts are a unified co-ordinated plan to face our common foes. The Administration is also ready to offer to help beef up checkpoints, ports, boundary cities between districts, and anything else that will help," Asa replied.

"For years we have heard words and seen no action. Our suffering is used as political capital to try to suppress our people and turn the blame on our leaders. Enough is enough. We will be moving out on recruiting before the end of the week," Cyrus replied simply.

Dexter was also stunned by this development. This basically trumped all the questions he had planned to ask. His panel would want to only talk about the activation and increase of the Southern National Guard.

"Governor Young, how will the Southern District pay for this new, uh, surge in military capability?" Dexter asked.

"You are correct that this is going to cost money," Cyrus began. "When this country was founded, one of the few needs served by the federal government that individual states could not cover was defense. This will be a major investment in our security. It is an investment we resisted because of our share already paid into the federal military, but it is clear now that the Administration will not prioritize the defense of the Southern District. Decades ago, there was a rise in school shootings. Sometimes, dozens of innocent children were killed and mutilated by mentally ill and twisted classmates or people barely connected to the school. All schools were gun-free zones and these school shootings often occurred in cities that had the strictest gun laws in the country. How did the country address this crisis? We put armed trained security in all of our schools. We were using armed guards and police to provide non-stop protection at banks, airports, government buildings, and hospitals but, for decades, it was against the law to have armed protection at schools. It started in Texas school districts and others caught on after a few years. It only took a couple of successfully defended attacks to discourage the savagery on our children. People asked then if we could afford it. Now we realize, how can we afford not to? This defense of the south from armed terrorists who are preying on our freedoms will be seen in the future in the same way."

"Governor Katz, we have heard what Governor Young is planning for protection of the Southern District. Can you share any additional details on what the Administration is doing to bring the terrorists to justice?" Dexter asked. "That would go a long way to addressing a frightened public and stressed political atmosphere."

"Yes, we are following some promising leads and believe we are closing in on targets directly involved with the Bush Park massacre," Asa said. "Because of the nature of the investigation, it would hurt our chances to catch them if I gave specifics, but I can tell you President Thorne is personally overseeing the effort and we will not rest until there is justice for those hurt and killed. Regarding the attack in Los Angeles, we have multiple video feeds, personnel sensor information, vehicle tracking, and the Raptor Attack Turbocraft wreckage providing many clues. It is only a matter of time. We believe the attackers in both these cases have tried to go underground which is making it take longer."

"Thank you, Governor. We all pray the investigation will be swift and successful," Dexter said. "Gentlemen, I think I speak for the entire audience that we hope and pray for justice for those hurt, and successful co-operation to avoid any future violence. Thank you for your time tonight. Please come back to the show soon and hopefully with some good news." Dexter turned to the audience. "Ok folks, you know what to do. Please cast your votes. One vote per person. You are a party of one. No-one will know your vote but you and Lorena. Who made the stronger case tonight, Governor Katz or Governor Young?" Dexter nodded to both debaters. "Good evening to you both." They nodded to Dexter, exchanged a cold glare, and walked off the stage.

Angel

Angel Vega opened his eyes and could see the ocean. It was a beautiful day. He was standing on a patio that extended just over the sand with a stairway down to the beach. It was an island paradise that looked like virgin territory never explored by man. Angel took a deep breath and savored the sunlight.

"Sir, we are ready for you inside," said Ajax Pagano, Angel's second-in- command.

Angel turned around to face the beach house and the doorway to their secret virtual meeting room. Ajax, standing by the door, was so big that he made the door look small. Angel followed Ajax inside and the doors closed behind him. The walls of the meeting room were mostly windows. The lights in the room dimmed and the windows tinted in unison to the point where the paradise around them was more of a memory. A light on the ceiling of the conference room brightened the table and those seated. Angel was meeting with his team, which comprised of ten full-time intelligence officers. This was his core team that helped him council the Southern District Governor and, in many cases, essentially directing organizations that were chartered to keep the south safe.

"George, what do you have for us?" Angel asked, knowing the meeting was called in a hurry to share something new but secretive. They only used this heavily encrypted site when there was something very urgent and sensitive.

"We uncovered something at the SBI about an hour ago. I put our highest security clearance rating on it and ordered the two people there who know to not tell the FBI or anyone else working the Bush Park massacre. I ordered them to go on leave and stay home and not talk to anyone about work nor answer their phones. Someone will figure this out soon but, for now, the secret seems safe. With your permission, I would like to share it with the team now," George Smith finished.

Angel leaned forward. He knew this meant it was likely a piece of the puzzle but bad news. "Ok. Thank you for being clear as to the sensitivity of the subject. Your actions speak volumes. Everyone, be damn sure this does not leave this room unless it is under my orders. Go ahead George."

George made a couple of taps on the table to pull up a short video on the north wall which went completely opaque. "This is an image at the Bush Park massacre. It was taken by a security camera. The camera was crude old technology but high definition so, after some washing, we were able to get good images of the shooter." George made a couple more taps and looked back up. "Here is the same video zoomed in after cleaning it up."

The video showed a man in his thirties who was muscular, wearing bland clothing covering most of his body, wearing a ball cap backwards, and firing a laser rifle. It showed him stop firing and lift his head up from the scope as he realized his target was on the run. The video paused with a look at his face.

"The FBI, SBI, and Homeland Security have been collaborating on other images of this shooter, but we have not shared this video yet. We have been a little skeptical of them not being able to identify him yet despite a clean image from one of the security drones. On a hunch, we ran this image here through the available security databases." George paused. "We got a hit."

"Holy shit. Who is he?" Angel leaned forward and asked wide-eyed.

"He's not a jihadi, is he?" Added Ajax.

"Correct. His name is Cain Vasquez. He is not Islamic as far as we know in any way. He is a born and corn-fed American from Nebraska. He was part of a contractor group used in Iran and Venezuela for special ops assignments. Most of his file is top secret, but it seems clear he generally does dirty work for the federal government. All of the details are classified. He did have facial reconstructive surgery, but if we can see it then the feds should have been able to see it," George said with a pause. "This is why I took the precautions I did. This is explosive information. Imagine what the public would do if they heard this raw."

Angel nodded. He looked at the image for a while.

"Ajax, you work with your sources in the CIA to see if you can access databases that have info on this guy or his accomplices. Make up a reason. Amy, you flirt with that bozo down at the IRS who likes you to see if he can help you learn about him. He has to have gotten a paycheck in the last few years." Angel turned to George. "This is damn good work. I am going to talk to Cyrus tonight. You keep this under wraps. Bring me those two techs if you suspect they might talk. The rest of you, split up the southern states and major cities to be ready to get this image out for our scanners looking for him. My guess is that he doesn't have an identification chip implant so the image is all we have, assuming he doesn't alter his face again. I will contact you all when we can start getting the systems looking for this bastard. We have to be careful though as we want his handler more than him. Cain is a soldier. We have to catch whoever is giving him orders if we want justice, if we want to stop the next attack. That will be all everyone." Angel left it unsaid, but his team was smart enough to all know. If the feds had the same databases then they should have identified Cain. If they identified him and did not tell Angel's team, then they either don't trust him, or worse, they are covering up the attack. It had occurred to Angel more than once that the feds' lives would go a lot smoother with Cyrus out of the way.

Anna

Anna Lee had just finished doing the dishes when Sophia slipped behind her to get a snack for little James. They were the only two in the kitchen, everyone was spread through the house in their usual weeknight routines. Marie Rivera was tired from a long day of shopping and John Rivera was getting a little work done before bed.

"Hey girl. You didn't answer me earlier. When are you going to let me take you in again? I need my wingman!" Sophia asked gently, rubbing shoulders and smiling at Anna.

"I did answer you." Anna scanned around as she put the towel down and let the sink drain. "My answer was no. That place was terrible." Anna didn't mind her cowboy but kept that to herself.

"Girl, you crazy. That place is rockin! Let's go back Friday night. There are some people I want you to meet. They are hilarious. You work hard, you deserve to let loose once in a while," Sophia winked. "I'll stay with you this time."

"Yeah, you can basically break all ten commandments on every street. It's a blast," Anna replied. "Not for me. I want to save my dignity and my soul."

"Ugh, not the religion thing again. I used to think it was an act for the Riveras. Now you have me worried," Sophia said, after putting a packet in the food processing machine and pressing start. "The place ain't real, it's just really fun! God doesn't want you to even pretend to have fun?"

"Yeah, yeah. I tried to think of it that way, but if I do the things you want me to do, it is still a reflection of the choices I make. I choose to be good," Anna replied, drying her hands and folding her arms as she turned to look at Sophia. "Don't you believe in God?"

"I doubt that all of this just created itself. I don't think we popped out of nowhere, but I don't believe in an all-knowing, all-controlling being that watches and gets involved in every detail of every life. The only being that cares if I have fun or not is me. Does your God care if you watch the same useless programs on Friday instead of savoring the shady side of life?" The machine dinged and Sophia took out a plate of freshly baked chocolate chip cookies.

"That's where faith comes in. Faith that God loves us and is helping us. Faith that He cares for us as his children. Faith that He made us in his own image. Faith that He does help us but gives us free will. And faith that we are something unique and special with the responsibility to live up to His standards," Anna answered.

"In His image? His standard? Hmmm. Does that mean we can't set off bombs at a protest? Or release chemical weapons in Korea? Or set off a nuke in Israel? People did those things. If that is His image, then I don't want to be like Him. I want to feel good in the brief time we have. Bela is not only safe, but might be part of His master plan. Ever think about that? There are no overdoses, pregnancies, diseases, hangovers, and it can be completely anonymous. I'm here with the Riveras instead of my family because I got mixed up in some real shit. I learned my lesson. Now I just want to play video games with benefits," Sophia said, while getting a glass of milk from the refrigerator.

"That's where free will comes in. He doesn't direct us but gives us all a chance to be good or evil, the choice between right and wrong. Whether it's a pretend or real orgy; there is still right and wrong. Maybe the few of us who still believe are missing out on the safest temptations the devil has to offer, but I'm not ready to give in," Anna replied. "I believe I am created in His image and I want to repay the gift of life by living up to his standard."

"Yeah, I can respect that. I just wish instead of making your crusade about skipping out on having fun with me that you'd spend that energy trying to do something that actually keeps people safe. Seems like the world is falling apart and Bela ain't the reason. I think we have more in common than you think. It's the monsters that want to hurt people for real that are the genuine demons. Maybe if they were going online and having fun they wouldn't be causing all this mayhem." Sophia paused, James's snack tray now in hand.

"Look, that place was too much for me. Isn't there anything else we can do? Something a little classier but still fun? I agree online is way safer than trying those things in real life. And I did like the cowboy," Anna smiled, trying to find a way out.

"Deal. I'll find us a place. Something you'll love. Maybe with more cowboys but a little toned down to get you rolling," Sophia smiled. "I better get this to James or he'll start yelling."

Anna was glad the conversation was over. She went to the laundry room to do the last of her chores for the day. Anna wasn't sure what she agreed to, but felt relieved she hadn't sold out and enjoyed a bit of pride in herself.

Corban

Corban Cruz looked out of his office window at the Federal Security Building. It was raining on the city of Fort Meade, Maryland. He felt like he was high enough to see the water form in the clouds; like what he did would rain on the citizens below, for good or bad.

"Sir, the Security Council is ready for you. Encryptions in place, connection is secure," Ariella reported.

"Thank you, Ariella," Corban said, pausing for a moment before turning to go and sit at the table. After he sat, the windows tinted until opaque, the lights went off, and the room became a virtual meeting space. Corban could see live projections along the walls of all of his team members thanks to volumetric displays, often called holograms. One wall was open for the briefing materials.

"Good morning team. We have two important topics to discuss. I will be meeting with the President this afternoon. It will be a closed-door meeting, but I will represent your interests," Corban began. "The topics are the Workerbee raid and some evidence recently collected of unsavory behavior by a prominent Southern District official. For the first, Ariella, please share the summary we prepared."

"As you command. Evidence is mounting that the attack in Los Angeles at the Workerbee Advance Robotics plant was carried out by a militia sympathizing with the Southern District." As Ariella spoke, a map and video displayed on the screen. "It appears that two teams attacked the compound, a combination of humans and androids. Their only casualties were androids. It appears the human attackers escaped and successfully stole one advanced prototype military android. They escaped in a work truck while security personnel pursued the Raptor Attack Turbocraft that had everyone's attention. The Turbocraft realized total destruction at somewhat of a random moment. Forensics indicates it was self-destructed, still with androids aboard, to give the impression their mission had failed. We believe they are working for a well-funded organization given the target, the acquisition of an expensive military Turbocraft, and the sophistication of the plan. This type of attack does not match the techniques of any known terrorist organization or foreign power. In fact, it is a type of operation our forces have conducted before. We also believe that this organization did not conduct this attack as a single event; it is being carried out for a reason yet to be revealed. We performed an analysis to assess who would be capable of this assault and who would benefit the most from gaining this technology. The answer was the same for both questions. Our analysis concluded this attack was most likely conducted by ex-military personnel to provide the prototype android to someone who could mass produce it for the Southern District."

"We need to strategize what to do about this analysis." Corban looked at his team. "What do we say to the public? How do we find the thieves? What is their end game in taking this android?"

"In this day and age, it is getting harder to hide secrets and even harder to successfully present alternate facts," Naya began. "I suggest we say nothing to the public for the time being unless it will help you catch them. We can continue to honestly say that we are working the investigation and don't see a connection between the attackers in Houston and Los Angeles. Also, if we keep quiet and find the strike team, then we might learn more about who is giving them orders if we can track them."

"Any objections?" Corban asked, and waited a moment. "That was my plan, but this affects us all. Seeing no objections, we will go to the tougher question. How do we find the attackers and their organization?"

"Sir, I would caution anyone from overthinking this attack," Harris Keitel began to answer. "This is not a movie. War is rarely chess or a game of thrones. The simplest explanation is that some other organization wants to catch up to federal forces fighting capabilities so badly that they risked this bare-knuckled strike. They are desperate to catch up to our capabilities for limited numbers of one-on-one combat and likely urban warfare. I agree with the machine's assessment, but would add that it is someone that plans to engage us sooner than later. That is the military assessment. The political question is what organization fits that criteria."

"Understood," Corban responded. "What ever happened to the good 'ole days where we just worried about tree huggers and corporate espionage? Asa, what do you think of General Keitel's assessment?"

"I'll be honest, I had hoped it was something more about corporate greed than what sounds like preparations for war," Asa started. "We can run an analysis on who might meet that criteria. It will be a short list. There are only a handful of organizations sympathetic to the Southern District that could meet that criteria. I am also assuming it is not the Southern District itself. That, of course, would be a radical escalation. I can have a list to this Council in two days."

"Please have the preliminary list to me by 6pm tomorrow," Corban said. "We will discuss the list as a council the next day. Now that we have a plan for the Workerbee raid, our next subject is of a very different nature. Alexandra, can you please share what you acquired regarding Angel Vega?"

"Certainly Chairman. I apologize to all for having to bring up this kind of issue, but our security teams identified this as part of standard Homeland Security surveillance. Even if we don't do anything now, this seems like a timebomb that will go off eventually. Ariella, please bring up the video." Alexandra paused to allow Ariella to make the change. "As you can see here, this is Mr. Vega entering an establishment known for android prostitution. While it is legal, it can dramatically disrupt effective governance as the media and public could be outraged with senior public servants engaging in this type of activity. Here you can see him approached by two android employees." She paused as the video showed them laughing at the bar. "And here you see him entering a bedroom with them. We have additional material if needed, but I think you get the point."

"To cut to the chase, an option being discussed is to provide these details quietly to Governor Young," Corban said. "Mr. Vega is one of his top people and a public figure in Southern District politics. We were thinking to give Cyrus one day to release the news himself and relieve Mr. Vega of his duties or we go public with it. Thoughts?"

"Sir, I think there is another option to consider," Naya began. "In a typical year, your suggestion would be taken as fair and possibly even appreciated as Governor Young could shape most of the narrative; however, this is not a typical year. We just talked about how a southern militia might be preparing to fight us. The strategy of sharing this information will bring up questions like how did we gather this on Mr. Vega, and if this is the right time to make changes in his inner circle given the crises consuming us all. I suggest an anonymous leak to the Post or Times. The media would only have the basics and would end up driving for the same goal you proposed."

"I could support that plan. I am not feeling lots of empathy for Governor Young these days so there is a little satisfaction in it," Alexandra said.

"I can as well," Asa said.

"Very well. Alexandra and Naya, please make it happen today. We can discuss the fallout at our next meeting. That will be all," Corban concluded, and dropped off.

Samson

Samson Gamble exhaled calmly and steadied his aim. He held the rifle firm, looked through the scope, and squeezed the trigger. The laser rifle instantly showed a hole in the last of his ten targets and the beam stopped as he released the trigger. Samson missed the heavy recoil from traditional ammunition firearms, but could not argue with the results. He wondered if his generation would be the last to feel more natural with gun powder-based ammunition than laser weapons. Samson engaged the safety and sat up from the prone position at the San Antonio Wild West Gun Range. He looked to his left and right. His team were the only people on the range right now. Apparently, not everyone gets up and goes to practice shooting first thing in the morning. Samson waited for the all clear and everyone went back to the set-up area.

"Good practice everyone. Well, for most of you," Samson said. "Tony, at least you fly good."

"My birds do the aiming for me. I just need to avoid crashing," Tony Anselmo replied with a smile.

"And we appreciate that skill," Andre Pantero said, as he punched Tony in the arm.

"Ow. I need that arm to do some sims later today. Take care of the merchandise," Tony replied.

"Yeah, must be hard jerking off all day," Andre replied, causing them all to laugh.

The five of them were dismantling their weapons and storing them in their travel bags. It took some work to make them legal to transport, but they were all well trained on these weapons. They used this remote range sometimes to practice and have some confidence in privacy. They had been laying low since their successful raid on the Workerbee plant. They were feeling better that they had made a clean break as they had seen no signs of the authorities snooping into their business.

"Gentlemen, I made contact with our sponsor last night," Samson said calmly, while breaking down his equipment. "He is very happy with the results. The package we delivered is turning out to be a real help to the cause. It was a clear show of competent surgical strength. A reckoning is coming and we are helping lead the way."

"About fucking time," Tony said, and caused them all to grunt in agreement.

"We need to separate for a few days. You know what you need to do to stay sharp, but do nothing to attract attention. Keep an eye out to make sure you aren't being watched. It looks like we left no trace, but it doesn't hurt to be careful. If they don't identify us in the first few days, then likely they never will," Samson said.

"So, what's next after our little vacation?" Andre asked, before gulping down some water.

"I'm taking a little trip to find out," Samson started. "For now, I will say that we are going to work with the rest of the force to prepare. Our guard unit and almost everyone else is getting called up soon. Part of our charter is to prepare for invasion. To be ready for that, we have a long way to go. The only good news is that those who will be coming to overrun us also need to prepare. I should be back in three days. We will meet up with the regiment in a week. Most of our people are not ready for what we need to do. Many will take some convincing. The whole nation has gotten soft. We have gotten fat and complacent." All of them were now done with their packing up. "Bottom line fellas, is that the fight has started. It's now just a matter of who comes out on top. That may come down to who is better prepared when the shit really hits the fan. This will likely be your last break for a long time so you better enjoy it."

Zander

Zander Brown thanked Camilla, got out of the car, and made his way to the apartment complex. It was already night out; it had been another long day. He was exhausted and mentally drained. The combination of rebuilding his security capability, helping the engineers get back to work, and answer all the questions from the feds was taking its toll. Zander needed a real stiff drink.

"Honey, I'm home," Zander called out.

"Well? Did you get fired?" Becca asked, with her arms folded. "I swear, if they fire you, I'm taking the kids and we're going to live with my parents."

"Good to see you too. No, no. I think I'm in the clear because of the whole being innocent thing. I was shot at during the raid and that seemed to clear me the first day. I'm the lead for rebuilding the security detail this time with the stronger protections I'd been recommending for months," Zander said. "I really can't give more details than that. Please don't make me out to be the bad guy."

"Yeah right. There is a reason you are just security. Genetics. Slow processing. I should have listened to my mother and never married you," Becca said, storming off.

"Hi kids, how was your day?" Zander said to Julius and Tavon. They were eating and pretending to not have heard their mother. They knew better than to try to speak up. No need to poke the bear, especially when she's already angry.

"Fine," Julius said, without looking up.

"It was ok. I'm glad you get to keep your job Daddy. I like robots," Tavon said.

Zander gave them both a half hug and Tavon a kiss on the head. He walked down to the guest room where he had been staying since the attack. He quickly changed clothes and went back to the kitchen. Julius was finishing up and it looked like Tavon was halfway done.

"Hey boys, I think I will get the weekend off. Want to go to the obstacle course on Saturday? Or maybe a Dragons game?" Zander asked.

Before both boys could answer… "Zander, do you think it's a good idea to be buying Dragon tickets when you might be losing your job? Really, I can't believe you'd be this slow!" Another brick in the wall.

"Boys, we can talk later. We'll find something to do, and, maybe the next weekend we can go to a Dragons match, assuming they make it through this round of the playoffs," Zander said, trying to save face. There was a time when Zander might have argued back, but it just seemed to make it twice as hard on the boys. Becca had no problem yelling in front of them, but Zander really struggled with it. It was days like this when Zander felt torn between the love for his children and the soul crushing pain in being married to Becca. Both boys finished eating and went to their rooms. Julius gave Zander a look that said he sympathized, but clearly had little respect for Zander having heard fights like this his whole life. Zander often wondered if it was too late to salvage their relationship.

Zander went to the cabinet. He got out a pot roast packet and put it in the machine. As the machine did its thing, Zander got a short metal cup from the cabinet and went to the liquor cabinet. He got out a bottle of whiskey and poured two fingers. He put the bottle back and turned back to the kitchen. Becca was in there, watching him. The same disappointed and angry face burning holes in him.

"So, have they figured out who did it?" Becca asked. "Was it a southern militia like the news is saying? Or was it another country? I swear, they better not end up hurting Americans because of your failure."

"Yes, I know. You tell me that every day. If they know who did it then they aren't telling me. They are very involved with making sure Workerbee headquarters approves all the security upgrades finally," Zander replied. "Whoever did it was very well equipped and trained. I really can't say more on it. Can we please try to have a nice night?"

Becca grunted and got herself a pot roast packet. She took Zander's meal packet out after it was done and dropped it on the counter. She then put her own in and went to pour a second glass of wine. Food processing had come a long way in the last few decades, but booze was still a pour-your-own-glass operation.

Zander took the silence as a sign she might not pound away at him again tonight. He knew he wasn't the smartest man but since when is that a sin worthy of torture. He took a sip of the whiskey and decided to add some ice.

"Camilla, please show NBC news at the table," Zander requested. The news displayed on the wall. They were talking about construction delays on the mass transit line upgrades, both above and below the ground. Zander got his dinner and went to the table pretending to care about the story. Becca joined him at the table with her dinner.

"Chuck, thanks for the update. Looks like no relief on the I-405 congestion anytime soon," Pete Peters with the local LA station said. "Next up is the latest on the Workerbee Robotics attack. Our own Carla Cosmo has the story."

"Thanks Pete. I'm here with Mr. Jim Jordan from the LA branch of the FBI. Jim, what can you tell us of the investigation?" Carla asked.

"We can't say much right now because the investigation is ongoing. We do have leads, and early indications are it was a failed act of corporate espionage. The local security forces were able to neutralize the target before they could make their escape," Jim said. "Right now, we are trying to find out who was the mastermind behind the attack. We are also trying to provide relief for anyone who was affected by the attack. Several local residents were killed or hurt during the ensuing gun battle. The technology at Workerbee is top notch and the security of their work cannot be overdone," Jim said, and walked away.

"Well Pete, you heard it here," Carla said. "Authorities believe it was a case of a failed attempt to steal technology." She had follow-up questions, but Jim had already left, obviously in a hurry.

"Camilla, pause," Becca said, and turned to face Zander. "Are you buying that?"

Zander thought hard before answering. He was more worried about setting her off than in giving a truthful answer. He put down his fork and looked at her. "We have studied acts of corporate espionage in the past. It has been about a century since anyone did it by actually breaking in and stealing. Companies that can make androids are good with computers. It doesn't make sense to me why a competitor wouldn't just hack into our system or our government customer's system." Zander picked up his fork and tried to go back to eating.

"I knew it. It was those fucking southerners." Becca was fuming. "They think they can just attack us and get away with it. Just a bunch of rednecks with their guns and Bibles. I bet that FBI guy was lying. I hope he was lying and that they are going to get some payback. Those people only care about themselves. They never care about others or the collective good. I hope we make the southerners bleed ten times as bad as this hurt us. Camilla, resume video." It was Becca's turn to go back to eating.

Lucilla

L ucilla Swift was running down the hallway with her Brimstone AR400 rifle in hand. She reached the end of the hall and used her shoulder to push open the door and was running outside missing only a step. She saw the militia in formation to her right. One other person was also late and trying to get there before it started. Relief washed over her as she got in formation just in time. They were all citizen volunteers but still took great pride in their work, especially in these volatile times.

Lucilla was twenty-nine years old and been divorced for two years. Since her divorce she had been living with her father; in that time, they had grown closer than ever before. Lucilla's mother had passed away five years earlier due to breast cancer that was caught too late. Government-provided medical services had deemed her low risk so she had not undergone preventive screening. They both replaced some of that heartache by working hard to grow and sharpen the militia which had been part of their family for five generations. Lucilla had also turned her energy to physical fitness and every few months a radical change in hair color. She was in the best shape of her life and right now her hair was blonde with enough shades of orange and red to give the illusion of fire when she was running.

Most of the militiamen owned and practiced with a Brimstone AR400 rifle and Razor XX170 handgun. A few needed to borrow from the militia supplies or carried an older model. The militiamen all stayed proficient with at least rifles and handguns, but some also trained in specialized weapons and tools. The AR400 and XX170 had been replaced years ago in the active duty military, but were among the few modern weapons still widely available for civilian use. Laws and regulations had stifled the development and sales of new weapons. Ammunition could be hard to come by, but these models and their spare parts were still fairly widespread. They were officially called a marksmanship club that trained in gun safety, survival training, first aid, and search and rescue. Unofficially they also trained on how to hold a defensive position and sometimes trained on counter attack techniques and strategy. The militia and the Swift family called Carthage, Missouri their home.

The militia stood at ease in formation outside their training facility. The facility was little more than a gun range, with a building that let them securely store weapons and other supplies, plus perform maintenance. The militia were in their camouflage gear with rifles at the rest position. The militia's unique uniform twist was a dark red beret. A light drizzle had started about ten minutes earlier. It was warm, even with the clouds and a strong breeze. They could see lightning in the far distance to the west.

He came from the facility front office door. He was the tallest member of the militia at almost two hundred and five centimeters (six foot eight inches). Nearly all men were now over one hundred and ninety centimeters tall (six foot two inches), but the leader of the militia was as big as any civilian militiaman in the state of Missouri. Even in his fifties he was intimidating. He approached the formation walking formally and unfazed by the light rain. The second-in-command in the militia called them all to attention and they brought their rifles to the order arms position, rifle butt on the ground by their right foot. There were three rows of militiamen twenty across - nearly everyone had made it to the mandatory meeting. As he reached the beginning of the formation, he slowed looking at each one of them until he reached the end. He did not smile, nor give anyone a disparaging look. The leader of the militia was Captain Jackson Swift, Lucilla's father.

"Outstanding. Truly outstanding," Jackson began. "I have no doubt this is the highest quality marksmanship club ever." Several people chuckled, followed by a couple of seconds of silence. "There is trouble brewing in the nation today. We have talked about it before, but every day the signs are getting worse. We all pray for peace, but we must prepare for conflict. I used to always visualize us helping to fight off terrorist attacks or some foreign invader. I've heard reports that one of our sister militias north of Kansas City was attacked by a Kansas militia yesterday with casualties on both sides. The stakes are too high for us to believe things will work out on their own. We must not fool ourselves that federal forces, units some of us use to belong to, may not come to our homes meaning to do us harm. One of the first obstacles for them will be the militias, the only deterrent with teeth besides the state guards. We must be honest and clear with each other. None of us want a fight. We will do everything in our power to avoid hostilities but we will not offer our freedoms to anyone. Militias are a proud tradition born out of the need to keep overzealous regimes at bay. Our unit is among many that will give our federal government pause before they might try to force their will on the Southern District or the proud state of Missouri."

Lucilla was standing in the third row towards the middle. Her father had given speeches to the unit before, but this was by far the most serious that she could remember. She peeked at the men and women in her row. Her father had their undivided attention.

"It is time we make a choice," Jackson continued. "We can choose to say 'thank you sir, may I have another?' or we can hold the line and stand for our principles. Will we be the first generation to bow without a fight? No sir, not on my watch! As many of you know, we have spent a good portion of our budget on ammunition and enough survival gear in case we need to undertake a mission soon. One such opportunity has arisen. It will help us prepare should we need to defend our homes. The mission will let us try to level the field with the forces that might attempt to overtake our great state. It will at least make them realize we won't go down without a fight and it will cost them severely to impose their authority upon us. We have received credible threats and the signs are aligning for a crackdown. Our training and plans to prepare will make us a true deterrent in case there are acts of aggression on our home. The details on this mission will come out over time, but I wanted to make sure you knew this was coming. You cannot tell anyone about this potential, and you need to make sure your loved ones are prepared in case you need to go on an extended hunting trip on short notice, if you know what I mean."

Jackson had reached the middle of the unit after pacing back and forth inspecting them. He turned and looked at his second-in-command. "Ms. Davenport, our unit has a proud name, does it not?"

"Yes sir! A very proud name sir!" Ms. Lindsay Davenport shouted.

"It requires hard work to earn a position among our ranks as well as to keep it. We don't do participation awards here. Ladies and gentlemen, are you ready to join me in standing up for our God given rights?"

"Sir yes sir!" They all shouted.

Jackson stiffened, somehow finding another gear in the seriousness of his message. "Who are we?!"

"Blood Ravens!" Everyone shouted.

"Who are we?!!" Jackson yelled louder.

"Blood Ravens!!!" Everyone shouted.

"Damn right. And we ain't gonna go quiet into the night." Jackson let a smile creep onto his face. "Ms. Davenport, we promised them practice on the training course, did we not?"

"Yes sir, and it's a beautiful day for training!" Lindsay replied.

Jackson was about to release them when around the corner of the building came a stream of black military transport trucks. The soldier on the far-right end of the second row started walking away from the militia, curling to the front of the formation, and pointed his weapon at Jackson.

"Traitors! How can you even talk like this?" Said Phil Hamill. He had been wearing a wire and the authorities were closing in.

"Phil, what have you done?" Jackson looked at him.

"Standing up for what is right. We cannot take up arms against our own country!" Phil replied.

Jackson saw the trucks were almost to them and they would be heavily outgunned. "Everyone, put your guns down. We will get all this cleared up. Do not fire!" Jackson led by example and put his handgun on the ground.

"Freeze! Everyone put your weapons down on the ground! Down on your knees with your hands behind your head now!" A very excited agent yelled on an intercom on one of the trucks. Homeland Security agents and military personnel jumped out of all the vehicles, guns drawn, once having stopped in a circle around the militia. The Blood Ravens were completely surrounded.

Dexter

" **G**ood evening America!!" Dexter yelled, as the crowd welcomed him to the start of the show. "Gracias. Mucho gracias." Dexter pointed to the crowd and clapped to them. Gradually they settled down.

"There has been a lot of action and bad news the last couple of weeks. Some real tragedy and horrific violence. The one thing that has been missing is something to do with sex. Well, that pot just got stirred. The Washington Post has reported that Angel Vega is a regular customer at an android brothel, despite the practice being condemned by many leaders of the Southern District. Some in the southern leadership have even called for it to be outlawed like human brothels still are in the south. Our debate tonight will discuss this shocking development, as well as reports of a southern militia arrested in Missouri. We will facilitate a fair debate and you can make up your own mind. I will be doing the same. We are each a Party of One. Partido de uno!" The audience cheered as Dexter made it to his seat at the debate table.

"Tonight, we are joined by Western District Governor, Simone Dubois, and Southern District Governor, Cyrus Young." The crowd applauded.

"Before we bring out our honored guests, it's time to meet the subjects for whom they are competing," Dexter said. "Lorena, please introduce our contestants for this evening and what they are playing for tonight."

"Ladies and gentlemen, our first contestant hails from the Western District," Lorena began. "She is the forty-year-old mother of three and a recently unemployed escort in the fabulous city of Las Vegas. She says she was released due to competition from the androids. Please welcome Jennifer!!" The audience cheered and there were a couple of catcalls. The audience was able to see Jennifer with her three young children, her makeup and hair done, and a naughty smile. "If Governor Dubois wins more votes tonight, this show will provide credits to cover Jennifer's cost for beauty school, child care, rent, and living expenses for a full year!"

"Our next contestant calls the Southern District home. He is the owner of an android escort establishment trying to get a foothold in downtown Dallas. He is battling legal challenges and charges of tax evasion. Please welcome Donald!!" The crowd clapped, half more energetically than the other. The crowd could see Donald standing tall and proud in a three-piece suit in a line with smiling gorgeous androids; one woman, man, and amen on either side of him. "If Governor Young wins more votes tonight, this show will provide credits to pay for Donald's legal challenges for a full year!"

"Ladies and gentlemen, please welcome our guests," Dexter said, while standing up and clapping.

From the left side of the stage entered Governor Dubois and from the right, Governor Young. As the two Governors entered, Dexter had the sensation of the temperature dropping. Simone walked in wearing a conservative evening gown that showed she was a beautiful woman even though little skin was visible. Liberal leaders rarely entered his show with a relatively young audience looking like they were on their way to church. Young was wearing a dark grey suit, off-white shirt, and a purple tie that looked so bright Dexter thought it might glow in the dark. The three of them exchanged handshakes and sat down.

"Thank you both for coming on the program tonight. Governor Young, we are getting spoiled seeing you so much. My first question is for you. Can you please comment on reports of a Southern militia exchanging fire with federal forces in Missouri?" Dexter asked.

"Dexter, thanks for having me. It's good to see you again," Cyrus began. "The charges by the federal forces of the ATF that raided this peace-loving militia are completely overblown. There was no exchange of fire. They had an erroneous tip which led them to want to question an individual who belonged to the militia. They went in using tactics consistent with approaching suspected felons. As you know, there are dozens of militias in the south who honor and live true to the second amendment. The ATF's decision for a guns-drawn stick-em-up greeting at a militia meeting is unacceptable. If the militia had not been so disciplined then it might have ended in tragedy. If they had a tip about the leader or individual in the militia then they should have approached him or her alone."

"Governor Dubois, your thoughts on the incident?" Dexter asked.

"Hello Dexter, thanks for having me," Simone began. "I wish it was as simple as what Governor Young describes. Authorities had just heard the leader of the militia make statements about them carrying out an act of violence against this country. We had no choice to arrest them. I would say that we would have acted this way with a Western District militia, but the truth is we haven't had any militias for decades. These militias are a Southern District phenomenon that, in my opinion, are inconsistent with the current intent of the second amendment. They have evolved from protection against roaming outlaws in the wild wild west into a threat as a potential ignition source for conflict. It is an ancient tradition with real potential for causing harm to citizens today. These militias should be shut down. If the Southern District leadership will not be so brave as to encourage their citizens to stand down, then they should at least support the ATF and other agencies trying to enforce federal law."

"The South is still free, God bless it," Cyrus began. "And its leadership is brave enough to keep it that way. We will not trample on the Constitution. These rights are sacred and not for one man to take from another." Cyrus stared hard at Simone. "Your district, the Western District, has chipped away at most amendments in a bid to consolidate power. Trivializing or historicizing rights is a slippery slope. The ATF needs to release these militiamen to Southern District authorities. More than two dozen were arrested for one over-anxious member allegedly making vague, at best, statements about any sort of action."

"Due process will run its course," Simone cut in. "Violence against man, self, and God are all sins. We all need to take this seriously."

"We agree violence should be the last resort," Cyrus snapped back. "Unfortunately, violence was the first response by the feds. We need to take it seriously whenever armed authorities point their weapons at citizens. This incident will really make any future engagement with militias more dangerous. It was violence without just cause. Violence begets violence. Those who draw the sword will die by the sword."

"Thank you both for your thoughts on that incident. Hopefully the truth will be revealed and any innocent militiamen will return home soon." Dexter jumped in to help de-escalate the situation. Dexter's guests rarely got out of line as he had no fear in dropping them off the show; an advantage of a virtual reality program with controlled access. Dropping a Governor off the show was not something Dexter wanted to do, and he was relieved his guests did not stop him from changing the subject. "I would like to now ask you about the disturbing reports on Angel Vega, senior advisor to Southern District Governor Young. Mr. Vega was recently on this show and we consider him a friend. The reports, however, indicate Mr. Vega is a regular customer of android brothels. Governor Dubois, what statement does the Thorne Administration have on these reports?"

"I appreciate you letting us debate this topic as I think you will see another divergence in principles," Simone began. "This Administration, our District, and I personally am shocked by these allegations, but believe it is a matter for the Southern District and its citizens to sort out. It's why we have elections. Mr. Vega, of course, was not elected, but your other guest tonight did choose him for a senior district staff position. Neither of them are angels. I personally have been a victim of sexual harassment. People in positions of power and public trust must be kept to a high moral standard. If someone is so driven by these desires that they would go to an android escort service, then it gives us pause to think if they would also use their position to take advantage of women, amen, or men in their service."

"Dexter, I apologize to jump in, but it is very unfair to make that leap," Cyrus said. "Angel is a good man. He has been a loyal servant to the people. Even if these allegations are true, he would be hurting no-one. I know you are wondering what I think. I think that the liberals and socialists that use to say the government should stay out of the bedroom need to follow their own advice."

"Those who are prone to extreme acts of lust, sex, and envy should not be in power," Simone said. "I would release him from service if he was in the Western District Government. I have instructed my legal team to issue a notice to our staff warning about this kind of behavior if discovered."

"Let's be clear what these stories are talking about," Cyrus added. "A man discretely on his own time quietly went to a legal establishment. If this is so perverse, then why are there billboards advertising android escort services in most major Western District cities? We should all note the hypocrisies being exercised here for political gain. Women spend tons of time, money, and energy getting as attractive as possible, but are offended if any undesired attention is made to their beauty and blatant sexuality. You wear a push-up bra, but we aren't supposed to look. You wear skintight skirts and we aren't supposed to want to touch. Whether you know it or not, most women are fishing for men by working to be so attractive so you shouldn't be surprised when we try to take the bait. In this case, you are saying straight men must enter into a monogamous relationship where statistics show they will regularly have sex withheld as a weapon. If they choose an android service, then you are saying they are too morally corrupt for leadership. There are a lot of women panicking now that they don't control men like they used to. You make it sound dirty, but women have provided this service for millennia, including still today in your outraged Western District. All of sudden there are androids pleasing men and you don't control us like you use to. And you are scared."

"Dexter, I think that is the most offensive thing I've ever heard on your show," Simone answered, with a look of disgust on her face. "Leaders need to set an example for the citizens by having strong moral fiber. Angel Vega is a freak on a leash and Governor Young is showing weakness here by defending him."

"I find it offensive that men can be prosecuted for acting on a woman's invitation. Our society long ago set the standard that any man accused by a woman is guilty. A woman making an accusation because of feelings of regret, disagreement in political beliefs, or just straight up scorn would get a man the same punishment as real sexual abuse. Innocent until proven guilty, unless it's a man accused by a woman," Cyrus replied.

"Well Governor Dubois, I will say you were, for sure, right on one thing, there is a glaring difference of opinion on this matter," Dexter said. "Ok folks, you know what to do. Please cast your votes. One vote per person. You are a Party of One. No-one will know your vote but you and Lorena. Who made the stronger case tonight, Governor Dubois or Governor Young? After this message from our sponsors, we will announce the results and transition to our panel discussion." Dexter looked at both debaters. "Good evening to you both." They nodded and disappeared off the stage. Dexter thought to himself that he will have to be careful about having senior district leaders debating again on his show until things cooled down.

Corban

Another day, another trip to the West Wing. Corban Cruz had still not decided on what to recommend to Thorne when the President entered the room. This time the President had a couple of military officers and the Secretary of Homeland Security, Alexandra Soaring, following him in.

"Corban, how the hell are you?" The President asked.

"Sir, it's been a long couple of weeks. I am hoping this will start winding down soon, but so far the ship is still sinking," Corban replied, not thinking too carefully that he was talking to the skipper.

"What do you have for me? Any closer to catching the Bush Park massacre shooter yet? Or the Workerbee Robotics attackers?" Nero asked, not amused by Dexter's analogy.

"Unfortunately, no-one is in custody yet for the attacks in LA or Houston," Corban began. "All available resources are on it. I come with news and options on other somewhat related issues. The first is that we are seeing lots of chatter and even specific threats to federal institutions in the Southern District. The reasons are varied, but we think the volume alone makes it worth taking steps to protect our people and institutions. Most of the threats are in Texas, but it is spreading all the way to the Carolinas and Florida. We are planning to increase security and maintain a stronger presence as a deterrent to any thoughts of relieving the federal government from control of additional facilities. One option would be to only staff up with Army and/or Marines, but we wanted to make sure you also considered a combination of federal and southern personnel in an attempt at unity."

"No. I don't feel like I know who I can trust down there right now. Based on what I have heard from you and others, I want it beefed up with just our folks. Do it at our active bases and central hubs of federal activity.

Anything inactive that the Southern District wants to reopen is on a case-by-case basis. And stall them," Nero responded. Corban had a feeling he had already been approached on this subject.

"Understood. We will make it happen." Corban paused in case the officers in the room wanted to volunteer but, when no-one spoke, he moved to the next topic. "Sir, it has not been leaked to the press yet as it was successfully contained, but there was an exchange of fire between a southern militia from Missouri and a militia of self-proclaimed loyalists from Kansas. Essentially, we had two militias open fire on each other. Four dead, three from Missouri and one from Kansas. A dozen were wounded. We are not sure who fired first, but both were itching for a fight. Sir, we don't think we can sit on this very long. Eventually, we have to release those involved and file charges. It will leak out. Luckily the morons were in the woods away from civilians."

"You mean other civilians," one of the officers said.

"Yes, yes, of course," Corban agreed with the officer.

"There was another incident as well." Corban started again talking to Nero. "We received insider intel that another Missouri militia, who call themselves the Blood Riders, was planning to raid an Army arsenal in Kansas City. That militia was apprehended before they could strike but, unless they confess, it is a weak case. It's mostly the word of one militiaman versus another and a weak recording that any lawyer could pick apart. We recommend releasing the news on both incidents before anyone talks. I recommend saying we are throwing the book at the accused. Since Missouri is part of the Southern District, we should work with the district authorities so we can together make an example of them and encourage everyone to not resort to violence," Corban said.

The President thought for a moment. "Was it federal personnel who caught and retained these militiamen for both incidents?"

"Yes, the case of militias firing on each other was just south of Fort Leavenworth. Army personnel moved in quickly. The militia group suspected of planning a raid on an Army arsenal were apprehended by Homeland Security and the FBI," Corban replied.

"Offer the Southern District that they can support our prosecution of these militiamen but both cases will be federal investigations and prosecutions. Make these examples very public," Nero replied. "I want strong examples made of them. Get creative. Make a scene that will be watched by everyone."

"Yes sir, it will be so," Corban answered. "That leaves just one more piece of information to talk to you about. As part of hunting the assailants in all of the recent acts of violence, we have been monitoring the usual Islamic terrorist organizations. They have never done a good job at keeping their activities a secret," Corban paused. "Mr. President, we have seen no sign that they were involved in the AntiCo attack, Bush Park massacre, and Workerbee raid. In fact, the chatter we hear indicates they think the years of attacking us has finally worked and we are imploding. At this point, we are focused on only domestic threats. I thought you would want to hear that assessment."

"I understand. The devil we know didn't do it. We need to catch the one we don't know," Nero said. "Thanks Corban, keep up the great work."

Cain

ain Vasquez buckled himself into his X3000 model jet. It was a four-seater model with a small cargo bay. After completing checkouts and confirming with ground control that he was clear, Cain maneuvered the jet to the runway. He loved to fly, but didn't get to as often any more. Now that he worked below the radar, Cain had to stay out of monitored activities. Flying for fun wasn't worth the risk of getting identified. Today was an exception as he was on assignment to meet another asset. Most citizens did not travel unless they had credits to burn or wanted to join the space club, the new version of the mile-high club.

Cain got the final go at his runway, thanked ground control, and accelerated for takeoff. As first, it was jet power to help him smoothly get to ten kilometers. On his way up he passed over some farms. He had grown up on a farm. It was great as a kid. It taught him hard work. Living on a farm was a great life until he had a falling out with his family. Cain had then looked elsewhere for a sense of purpose and accomplishment. He looked down and saw the modern farm machinery hard at work. How times change. The machines could almost do everything for the farmers now. They even had machines to fix the machines.

Cain engaged the thrusters and it pushed him to an altitude of one hundred kilometers. The jet was basically all automated, but Cain enjoyed doing some of the piloting tasks himself. His oxygen system was functioning nominally and he could see the gorgeous horizon. He loved this part. He wished the flights weren't so short. It was so calm here at the edge of space.

"Delta Charlie Niner, come in please," Cain heard over the radio.

"This is Delta Charlie Niner reading you loud and clear," Cain replied, recognizing the voice.

"Mr. Anderson, this is Mr. Smith," Cain's handler said. "It is time to tell you the location for the meet and what you need to do to support her on this assignment. This mission is of the highest priority. That cannot be overstated."

"Yes sir. Understood. I have about five minutes left before beginning the re-entry sequence and re-establishing comms with the ground controllers," Cain said.

"There are many chess pieces in play and multiple teams playing. What you and your partner will be pursuing will help make this country safe for another three hundred years," the handler began. "She will be located at the bar of the Ritz Carlton near the airport. She will be wearing a white dress and red sash. You will go with her and provide security, plus anything else she requires. Her assignment is to infiltrate the enemy. She is encouraged to use all means necessary. It will be very dangerous. She knows the specifics on what to do once she has penetrated their inner circle. Your service is essential for her to have a prayer at success; that includes both completing the mission and being extracted safely. Again, you will take her where she needs to go, protect her from hostiles, and provide any services she requires. Any questions?"

Cain thought for a moment. Sounded more like babysitting, but knew better than to push it. "No sir. Understood."

"Good. If the enemy figures out her plans, you must neutralize her. She knows too much and cannot fall into enemy hands as it would compromise other plans in addition to her assignment. She has the same instructions in case you are captured," Mr. Smith said.

"Yes sir, understood," Cain answered.

"Godspeed Mr. Anderson," Mr. Smith said, before signing off.

Sara

S ara Chamberlain reopened the toy store after being away almost two weeks. Sales were down, but having it slow was taken as a merciful blessing. Sara had not been in the mood to talk to many customers. Ben's jobs in the Texas Air National Guard, both as a civilian and in the reserves, provided a basic income to let them try to ease back into life, but she could not let her business stay shuttered too long.

It was Tuesday and Sara had opened the store at 8am along with her android assistants. It was also Emma's second day back at school. She had received many condolences the first day. Those had not really helped. Sara tried to focus on her work. She did have one distraction today that she had been putting off. Sara was going to do an interview with the local media. She couldn't hold them off any longer. The manager at Houston's ABC affiliate promised a short sensitive interview. They would be at the store soon so Sara could get it over with. They said they wanted the video to show the store to help show how her family fit into the community.

It was approaching 9am and no customers had come in yet. Sara was looking at inventory numbers and online orders when the reporter and video assistant came in. The reporter was human and the assistant an android.

"Good morning, my name is Jeff McDonald with KTRK Houston. You must be Sara. It is a pleasure to meet you. Is this still a good time?" The reporter said.

"Yes, I am Sara. This time is ok. I am not sure exactly how the interview will help. We need them to catch whoever did it," Sara said, as she moved from behind the counter and into the store with the reporter. "How about we sit in the building area?"

"To be honest, the attacks are still the main thing we report on. There is news every day on the recovery, the investigation, and the politics in play as the country reacts to the attacks," Jeff said, as he looked around the store. "Yes, the building area will do well. How about we have you here so the toys are all behind you? I can be next to you here so we are both in the shot."

"Ok. I haven't done this before. Do we have multiple takes or just go with first reactions?" Sara asked. She was starting to resent the idea of doing the interview. Sara did not want to be anyone's story. She didn't want anything to taint the pure memories of Jon.

"We typically only need one take but if, for some reason you would like another, just let me know. Also, we may do a little touch-up on your face during editing to help with the high def video," Jeff said, while looking at the toys behind Sara. They were now both sitting in child-sized chairs with various building sets on one side and a modular train set on the other. Behind them were racks of toys including stuffed animals, dolls, and books.

"All right. Let's get to it. I sometimes have an early lunch break crowd in here," Sara said. One of her android assistants looked at her knowing it was at best an exaggeration. A bright light shined on Sara from the camera being held by the reporter's assistant.

"Sir, I am ready when you are. We have good lighting and the background is excellent," the assistant said. Sara's eyes had just gotten use to the lighting when Jeff began speaking.

"Hello Houston, this is Jeff McDonald here with Sara Chamberlain. We are at Ms. Chamberlain's toy store called Toys for Tots. Ms. Chamberlain's family was one of the victims in the Bush Park massacre." Jeff paused briefly to look Sara in the eyes and then looked back at the camera. "Sara, her daughter, Emma, age ten, and husband, Ben, were all injured. Her son Jon, age six, was killed. I'm sure all of you remember this iconic image. This is Sara holding Jon." The video on the news would show Sara screaming at the sky with her eyes closed cradling Jon. Jeff looked back at Sara. "Sara, before I even ask you any questions, please know all of Houston and the Southern District would do anything to bring Jon back and we all pray for your family."

"Thank you, Jeff. We appreciate that." Sara was getting choked up already.

"Can you tell me please about the scarf you are wearing?" Jeff asked.

Sara looked at her scarf and held one of the ends up, rubbing her fingers on it. "It is something I have been doing to help me deal with the loss of my son." Sara felt tears coming but fought it off. "He was wearing a white scarf during the attack. I wear this to honor him and if he is in heaven looking at me, that he knows I am thinking about him and I miss him."

"Thank you for sharing that Sara," Jeff paused briefly. "The Thorne Administration has promised justice, but little has been accomplished. Have they contacted you in any way?" Jeff asked.

"The FBI did contact us a couple of times. The SBI spent much more time with us," Sara said. "It is frustrating that it seems to be taking so long to make any progress. We worry about future attacks and, of course, catching those responsible for the recent attacks."

"You are not alone; many of us are frustrated. Politicians in Washington, as well as the Eastern and Western Districts, have been calling for reforms in the Southern District. Some even have said that the attacks here are a function of the policies we have in place. Sort of a reap-what-you-sow scenario. What would you say to them?" Jeff asked.

Sara tensed up. She felt her temperature rise. "Well Jeff, I'd say they haven't paid attention to what transpired. The AntiCo attack and Bush Park massacre were clearly acts of terrorism. The protest we were attending was a protest to the insane idea that policies and laws designed to make us safe somehow makes it open season on us."

Jeff was looking fairly satisfied, like he was getting the answers he really came to get. "Just one more question for you. Many of those same leaders in other parts of the country say no-one should have brought children to the attack. This includes some prominent politicians and most of their media surrogates. What would you say to them?"

Sara firmed up. She had not heard it so plainly before. Even though Jeff was an asshole for asking this question, she leaned forward to give the only answer that came to mind.

"They should be focusing their attacks on the monsters out there that slaughtered innocent people. Imagine if the attacks had been in New York? Would we be blaming the people who went to a peaceful protest? I am just a loving mother who owns a toy store. I don't have the power to catch the murderous monsters out there, but I can stand up for Houston. I can stand up for the south. We were teaching our children the importance for standing up for what is right by going to the protest. Since it appears that peaceful protest will not get the message across, I have decided that I will no longer sell to anyone in the Eastern and Western Districts, nor buy their goods. If they want to treat us as the criminals then they are not friends of mine and I want nothing to do with them."

Jeff sat back a little. He was trained to not be obviously shocked but could not completely hide it. "Thank you, Sara, for your time today. You really are an inspiring person. Again, you and your family are in our prayers." Jeff looked back at the camera. "This is Jeff McDonald at Toys for Tots."

Angel

Angel Vega was on a losing streak and he knew it. The world seemed to be imploding and, in particular, picking on him. When the national press started to make him the poster child of Southern District hypocrisy, he decided to dig in and make his job his life. The vultures were circling and he needed to stay indoors. Today he was meeting with Cyrus Young, the one person who seemed to fully support him.

Angel was at the District Governor's mansion on the north side of downtown Houston. The capital of Texas was Austin, but with the rise of the three districts it seemed Houston got all the attention. Ironically, Houston and Austin were two of the most liberal cities in the District, even though their leadership for decades had stood up to the changes in the other districts and Washington. Angel guessed it was because the leaders saw the bottom line and how these capital cities benefitted from the hard work and enterprises of the people in the state and entire district. Angel had not slept much lately, but knew important work was left to do, and that gave him hope to still come out of this with a purpose. He needed that sense of purpose to help him identify how he fits in this world.

It was mid-day. Angel was waiting for Cyrus in the garden at a table set for lunch. The food was on the table covered. Only two place settings. Angel worried a little that this would be the perfect location to fire Angel, but Cyrus had backed him publicly so he couldn't really fire him now, or at least that is what Angel hoped.

Angel saw the door on the north side of the garden open. A security guard, Cyrus, and then another guard passed through. The two guards flanked the door which was about ten meters from the table set for lunch. Cyrus walked casually to the table. Angel stood to greet him.

"Angel. Good to see you. How are you holding up?" Cyrus said, extending his hand.

"I'm doing ok Governor, thanks for asking. Good to see you too," Angel said, while shaking his hand. "I appreciate all the support you have given me. Many would have let the sharks take me."

"Those bastards can't seem to tell what is important anymore. I won't judge you. I need your help as much as you need mine," Cyrus replied. "What progress do you have for me?" Both men sat down.

"We've been working both Houston attacks around the clock," Angel began, as Cyrus took the cover off his lunch and began to eat. "Surprisingly, we still have not been able to find the shooter, Cain, or accomplices to either attack. Whoever is behind these attacks is very good at covering their tracks and skilled at how to stay off our radar. I have been thinking it's odd they didn't try to conceal Cain better. They went through extreme precautions to hide all the other people and activities involved. The knowledge of Cain's background, plus the apparent knowledge of our investigation techniques makes us think this was an inside job more than ever. I do have news and other related recommendations for you."

"Go," Cyrus said, between bites of his sandwich.

"Our people in the SBI have given up on taking jurisdiction from Homeland Security on the militia incidents in Missouri," Angel said, as he finally took the cover off his lunch. "Despite being in the Southern District, the Homeland Security people say these incidents affect national security. They will let us publicly support their decisions, but are being very tight with the information. They also have yet to give us access to the militiaman being held. It will likely take you getting involved to make things change."

"I'll try to talk to Thorne or Alexandra, but this was likely their call. It seems these locals screwed up and DC wants to make them pay dearly. I agree getting access to them for our people is important. That seems fair. Need to make sure nothing fishy is going on," Cyrus said. "What else do you have?" Cyrus said, before taking another bite.

"I want to make two changes with your permission. I want to significantly beef up the security at the mansion here. Security checkpoints, barricades, more fencing, and more guards and drones. I know you have resisted it so far, but there is still a significant risk since the would-be assassins have not been caught yet," Angel said. "I also want your permission to move out on the effort to integrate all the state defense forces. I think we need to create a more official position directly reporting to you that is made known to all the states. There is political risk in making this move, but I think there is real safety risk in not making it. If things continue to deteriorate, then you will need to be able to call in the state guard units with no delay and no question of loyalty. It would take getting agreements with the state leaders as well. We don't want confusion on who can command the guard units."

Cyrus stopped eating, wiped his mouth, sat back and looked at Angel. "I agree. The time has come. I want you to be that lead. We will get a top guard General to be your right-hand man. Since it is a new position, they can't say I have to go to the states to confirm it. I have, however, already talked to some of the key state Governors about something similar and they understand. What do you say?"

Angel was blown away. He had gone from being worried about being fired to now being offered a job integrating and leading the defense forces for twelve states. "Sir, I am honored." Angel swallowed; his mouth was now so dry. "I won't let you down."

"Excellent. You start as soon as I announce it tomorrow," Cyrus said. "Got anything else? I have another meeting in a few minutes." He took another bite.

"Yes, I have one new topic," Angel said, almost having forgotten. "One of the victims of the protest attack gave an interview yesterday that has stirred a lot of debate. Perhaps you heard about it already. Her name is Sara Chamberlain. She makes and sells toys here in Houston. Her young son was killed in the Bush Park massacre. She and everyone else in her family were injured."

"She sounds familiar, but I don't recall the interview," Cyrus said, before taking the last bites of his sandwich and pickle.

"Governor, she said she is no longer going to buy products from the Eastern or Western Districts, nor sell her goods to them. I hope it won't come to this, but we might look at a plan to do this as a district. Having a plan for an embargo could allow you to use that as a bargaining tactic. It is hardball for sure, but is at least a peaceful method to drive change. The Southern District economy is much stronger than the Eastern and Western Districts so the pain they feel will be a deterrent. They need us more than we need them," Angel said, wondering if he had gone too far.

Cyrus stopped chewing and looked out at the flowers in the garden. He thought for a few seconds while he finished his last bite and wiped his face. He then turned back to Angel. "Angel, it is hard to believe things have gotten this bad so fast. It is worth looking into. I'll get someone on it in secret so we are ready should we need to pull the trigger. It will hurt us as well, but your instincts are right. It will also hit the federal government as less taxes will be coming in. It will take reaching agreements with other countries for us to be able to sustain it. Let's pray things turn around before we have to exercise it." Cyrus looked at, and pointed at Angel's lunch. "You should eat that; you'll need the energy. I gotta run. Let's talk again in two days."

Angel stood and shook Cyrus's hand before Cyrus went back inside with the two guards following him. Angel sat down and thought to himself for a while before finally eating.

Cain

"**M**rs. Smith, this seems a little like fishing? How long do you think this might take?" Cain asked. The more he learned about the mission; the more Cain showed his frustration. There was little he could do to make it work and, to him, it seemed like a shot in the dark.

"Mr. Smith, we have been doing our homework on it. We know where to fish," she replied. "Making the connection is key. It will take building trust which cannot be rushed and is not an exact science. Sometimes the easiest path between two points is a crooked line."

"Ok. We'll play it your way," Cain replied. He was getting sick of this game already. If this job was so critical, then the find-a-needle-in-a-haystack approach was just too unpredictable. If they would just tell him the end objective then he'd show these experts the Maven way to get the dirty work done. The safe house they were using was equipped with state-of-the-art VR gear with secure lines that would take several minutes for any advanced AI to hack should they be discovered. That would provide plenty of time to grab the go-bag and break out should they be compromised.

"Good." She watched his eyes to make sure he was taking this seriously. "We will both go online. I'll keep talking to potential targets and you make sure we aren't being tailed. To hook a target, I will need to focus on him." She did not know why they assigned a butcher like Cain to assist a professional multi-talented agent. "I will take my hat off when I am ready to leave, either after finding a target or when giving up for the day."

"So, do you have any leads? Any reason for where you will pick to go online? Can you share what you are looking for in a target so I can help?" Cain asked.

"Like I said before, I have done my homework. The rest is need-to-know only." She leaned forward and tried her best to look firm. "Let us get one thing straight. I am not a dainty flower. I am a soldier like you. This is a mission. There will come a time when we need two soldiers to get the job done. For now, you will just have to support this part of the plan. To be honest, even if I told you everything, it still would not change what we need to do right now. It just might mean more than one of us has to take cyanide if we get caught."

Cain decided he would give her a chance. Maybe she wasn't a cupcake after all. "All right. You made your point sweetheart. I will go with what I know now until after we have the target and he is secure. When are you ready to go?"

"Is our escape route set up? Tanks full? Second vehicle ready? If we get a target today, then I want everything to go like clockwork. Please run through each step with me again," she said.

Cain talked her through the details. His jet would be plan 'A.' If they needed to get out of town another way then plan 'B' was set up, but would take a day instead of a couple of hours. Cain would keep a close eye on her. He knew if the agency said this was critical then it was, but he didn't like having so few details. He still felt burned having had to be the patsy for the Houston Protest attack; however, he couldn't argue with the results.

Sara

It was almost closing time after another busy day at Toys for Tots. Sara honestly had zero expectation of increased business as a result of her interview about the attack, but sales were through the roof since it aired. Her two android assistants were not tired, but Sara could feel it. The relief was less about the money and more about the distraction that busy productive work gave her. Even talking with customers had gone easier than she expected.

Sara was looking out the front windows at the buildings across the street. They were illuminated by the setting sun and, for once, did not look grimy to her. Sara saw the men walking quickly from the left, cross the street, and charge into her shop with an urgency not usually seen at a toy store. There were three of them; one had a video camera. They had the sort of smile on their face like they were proud of the trouble they planned to start. They saw Sara and went up to her immediately. The man with the camera started to take a video.

"Good afternoon Mrs. Chamberlain," the man in front said. He had a long nose, was balding, and was the first person Sara had seen in a long time wearing glasses.

"Good afternoon. Can I help you?" Sara answered.

"I certainly hope so. My name is Michael Williams. I hope you don't mind that I brought a video to record my visit. I would like to buy some toys." Michael reached for the closest item. He had not stopped smiling since entering the store. He handed the teddy bear to Sara. "I am from Sacramento, California, the proud capital of the Western District."

Sara's heart dropped. She immediately realized she should have seen this coming. She felt her temperature rise exponentially. Her first thought

171

was to slap him and have the androids throw them all out. The image even flashed across her mind. She caught herself and realized they would try to use this video against her no matter what she did or said. If she blew up, they would celebrate. If she was weak or sold them the toy, then they would still go viral.

"Well? Can I buy this teddy bear please?" Michael asked again. Apparently, Sara was thinking a little too long for Michael's liking.

Sara's head tilted slightly to the right before she started. "It is very interesting what people consider clever these days or, for that matter, what they take pride in. There are many in your district, apparently the majority, if the polls in the news are to be believed, that feel like the victims of the protest attack had it coming because they attended the protest. You know, the protest that killed my six-year-old son? Those people feel very clever. They have been able to reach a conclusion that fits neatly in their sense of reality. There are politicians in your district who have called for our district and states to elect new leaders blaming them for the violence. Those people are very proud that they are growing their political clout and empire. Please tell me, by coming in here with a video recorder, is this to make you feel clever or proud?" Sara asked.

"I am neither a celebrity nor a politician. I would just like to buy a teddy bear," he repeated.

"Why won't you sell him a teddy bear?" One of the other men asked. Obviously, they were not here to have a serious debate. Sara figured they just wanted a couple of clips to sell to the media outlets.

"Can any of you fine representatives of the Western District please try to help make your fellow citizens understand that the true criminals are the terrorists who committed actual violence? Or perhaps can you try trolling your politicians who are coercing us to remove laws that try to keep us safe?" Sara replied.

"I'm not here to debate politics. I don't have control over the issues you are upset about. Why won't you sell me a teddy bear?" Michael tried again. "Are you really helping your country by taking a stand that divides us?"

"That's a remarkable attempt to shift it again back on me. Looks like you are going for clever after all. You could talk to your citizens or leaders like I asked, but you have declined. The polls taken by the same news outfits that are calling for new leaders in the south show the majority of you, and therefore likely you, believe that I am in part responsible for my son being killed by a bomb while sliding in a bouncy house. He died slowly and in a lot of pain." Sara stepped closer into Michael's personal space. "There is only one thing left for you to do that would convince me to sell you a teddy bear."

"Yeah, what is that?" Michael was no longer smiling.

"You bring my son back to me! Thing 1 and Thing 2, please show these guests the way out." Sara had tears starting and walked away to the back of the store so they wouldn't get a good shot of her crying.

Anna

Anna Lee was scrubbing out Maria Rivera's shower as her last chore on a very long day. Anna was thinking about her and Sophia's time online the night before. She was grateful they didn't go to Bela again. This time it was a trip to Paris. A digital recreation of all the hot spots. Anna's favorite part was all of the beautiful lights. The dancing had been ok. Sophia had actually shown her a good time. She felt like they were getting closer. Anna was almost done with the shower when Maria Rivera burst into the bathroom.

"You! How could you! You little demon child!" Maria shouted, walking straight to Anna. She opened the shower door the rest of the way and slapped Anna first with the left and then the right. Anna fell clumsily to the shower floor.

"What did I do?! What did I do?!" Anna begged, as she held both sides of her face. The grime on the gloves was nasty, but her face was burning with pain.

"You know what you did! How could you betray my trust?!" Maria continued to shout and then threw the closest thing she could reach at Anna which was the bottle of cleaner on the side of the tub. It hit Anna in the side which made her bend over in pain.

Anna ripped the cleaning gloves off while trying to escape, but Maria was between her and the door. She backed into the corner which was by the sink that John used. Anna tried to think what she might have done. It must have been the trips online. Her sins were coming back to collect their due.

"I'm sorry! I'm so sorry! Please don't hit me! It was just a couple of times!" Anna wailed. "Is it really that big a deal?"

"You ungrateful hypocrite! To think I trusted you. I knew to keep an eye on Sophia, but you had us all fooled." Maria was rubbing her wrists. The hard hits on Anna must have hurt her as well.

"It was just a couple of times. No one got hurt," Anna sobbed. "I don't understand. Sophia was there too. It was her idea!" Anna realized it was a mistake to have yelled as soon as she did it. Maria gave her another hard slap with her left hand. Anna could taste blood.

"Don't you dare raise your voice at me!! I don't understand you people. We give you a home, we feed you, we let you pay off your massive debt, and somehow you still find ways to completely dishonor yourselves. They say deudors are inferior to regular people, I guess it's that simple." Maria stared hard at Anna. "Let me go talk to John to see if you are telling the truth about Sophia. You wait here!"

Maria stormed out of the room. Anna could not believe this was happening. It didn't make sense. How could she be in trouble when she was the only one trying to be good? There was something she was missing. Anna could hear Maria giving John a good screaming as well. What does he have to do with this? How would he know what they had been doing online? Anna sank into the corner crying.

Maria came bursting into the room again. "All right you little hoover princess, lying to me again!" Maria kicked Anna in the back. "He says it was just you! I guess it makes sense given that you always liked being on your knees to pray!" Maria kicked her again. "You stupid skinny wretched bitch!!"

"What?! I would never do any of that!" Anna wailed. "I have never and would never do that. Please believe me!" Anna's words were barely audible as the shock and pain made her crying uncontrollable.

"You still take me for a fool. Get out of my site. Go to your room while I decide where to send you!" Maria stared at her hard. Anna tried to get out, but Maria tripped her. She hit her head on the ground and Maria laughed. Anna got back up holding her face. She slowly made her way to her room. Unless Maria could somehow listen to reason, this was the nightmare she had always worried might happen. To be sent to the camps or farms might as well be a death sentence. Sophia. She realized it must have been Sophia. Why would John lie?

Corban

Corban Cruz was at the Homeland Security Office in Kansas City, Missouri. He was in town to see for himself each of the sites associated with the militia incidents and to make plans on what to do with the prisoners. The Kansas City office was a crude facility, but modern enough to be his base for a couple of days. It was time for a Security Council meeting and the local office had set him up to connect with the rest of the team. Anywhere in the world, Ariella was the same.

"Ariella, are we all set?" Corban asked.

"Yes sir, connecting you to them now. Only Governor Katz is not connected yet. Encryptions in place, connection is secure," Ariella replied.

"Friggin Asa. Politicians always think it's about them," Corban mumbled to himself. "Thank you, Ariella."

The lights dimmed in Corban's room and then Ariella projected the holograms of his team on the sidewall displays around him. There was a hole to his right for Asa.

"Good morning everyone. We have some very important items to discuss today. I hope you are all up to speed on recent events and have seen this morning's status updates. First item is the executive orders we want to recommend to the President. Naya, you have been working on the policy ideas for deudors. Give us the latest please," Corban asked.

Before Naya began, Asa joined the room.

"Sorry I am late. Had connection issues," Asa said.

"Glad to have you here," Corban said. "Naya was about to speak on the deudor policy ideas."

"Good morning everyone," Naya began. "We have had a diverse team looking at this issue since we started the national debate. The time is right for a bold move in this area. The deudor system is fundamental to our economic system. It is why unemployment is so low and why the standard of living for citizens is so high. Ladies and gentlemen, we suggest the President propose a series of constitutional amendment setting federal standards for the deudor system. This will set the bar nationally instead of the state or district level. It will bring the south in line and make it much more predictable across the country which will help the industries that rely on deudors. Also, and just as important, these amendments will include protections for deudors. They will protect them just as the rest of us have the amendments from the Citizen's Bill of Rights. This idea would add a Deudor Bill of Rights. We have been testing these ideas with our focus groups and the idea scores very high."

"How did you come up with these amendments? Who did you work with?" Corban asked.

"We studied the regulations in all states and districts. We also studied the existing laws and amendments for regular citizens. We used that foundation to find commonality between protecting the industries deudors serve and providing deudors basic protection so they can eventually climb out of their debt. They aren't slaves after all. We worked with the Attorney General, other members of the Department of Justice, and representatives from several key states. The President could propose the overall idea and then let Congress and the states chew on it. I think it could pass fairly quickly as we can get two thirds of Congress just from the Eastern and Western Districts."

"How will these new laws get enforced?" Asa asked. "It's one thing to pass laws and another to bring violators to justice."

"Not sure about the enforcement of deudor rights, but I suspect that would be the same as citizen rights," Naya said. "For the enforcement of who should be a deudor, that would be up to the Department of Justice."

Corban looked around the room and did not see other questions. "Very bold. How do you think the Southern District will react? This seems to really be aimed at them."

"Our polling shows that about a third of them will support it, a third will be against it, and a third don't care. If we in parallel hammer away at their political leaders, they won't be able to withstand the momentum if we seize it now," Naya replied.

"Good. Let's brief the President on that tomorrow. Next topic is immigration. Alexandra, what do you have for us?" Corban asked.

"Hello everyone. The problem we have is with the Southern District taking action on immigration that is counter to federal policies," Alexandra began. "The federal policies are supported by a supermajority of American states and citizens. I don't think we need the President to make new laws. In this case, we propose he strengthen the penalties for states or districts that violate federal policies. The constitution is clear that immigration is a federal matter. A district cannot set up checkpoints and turn people away based on their own laws. We have a set of changes to regulations in mind that would fine and then even imprison politicians, policemen, and anyone else that goes against our federal laws and policies."

"That sounds simple enough. What is the catch? Why haven't we done it already if it's that easy?" Corban asked.

"There was a precedent set decades ago when cities and states could go against federal policies. That will slow us down. Back then, the federal policies limited the flow of people instead of being open to those seeking freedom. California, in particular, resisted federal laws, but experienced minimal consequences," Alexandra answered. "It will take time, but would be a bold policy to announce and put direct pressure on Southern District leaders. It would also be a campaign issue they would struggle with when they go for re-election."

"Wouldn't that be something to see Cyrus Young in jail?!" Asa blurted out. Most people laughed, but not Corban.

"Asa, this is a major poke in the eye to the south. How do you think they will react to this change? Or for that matter this combination of policy changes?"

"Like Naya said, we keep the pressure on them on the policy front, as well as the attacks on their leaders both at the district and state levels. The combination gives them nowhere to go. By this time next year, we should have new leadership in the Southern District who will be willing to work with us," Asa answered.

"Assuming there is no more violence," Harris Keitel added. "We still don't know who is behind the Bush Park massacre or Workerbee raid. There are forces in work who may not share your end goals."

"Very interesting, good point Harris. We need to catch them so that is not an excuse to push Congress for a vote. Let's brief the President on this idea tomorrow as well," Corban said. "That brings us to the last matter I want to discuss. The President wants to make an example of the militiamen who acted up. They want everyone else to see we aren't playing softly with attacks or even planned attacks on federal institutions. Ariella, please bring up the St. Louis parade map."

"As you command," Ariella replied, and everyone could soon see a map of downtown St. Louis that tracked live what Corban proposed.

"I spent some time with the organizers of next weekend's St. Louis Pride parade. It will now instead be an American Pride parade. They can still have their St. Louis floats and balloons and other activities, but they will also have several federal-themed floats and such. The Southern District folks are not the only ones who can hold a rally." The map highlighted the parade route. "In addition, I want to include the militia from Carthage in the parade wearing prison suits under heavy guard. It will be a demonstration of how even one potential act of rebellion will be dealt with decisively. We actually don't have enough on this lot to get convictions, so this will also be a punishment to this bunch as well. Thoughts?"

"I love it," Naya said, leaning forward.

"Me too. Its genius," Alexandra added.

"I don't mean to be a sour puss, but everything we have talked about is a direct insult to the Southern District," Asa started. "Yes, I know publicly they denounced what this militia was accused of planning, but these yahoos deny it and the SBI is still upset we took jurisdiction from them. Both policy concepts going to the President apparently tomorrow for his blessing are the hot button issues of the day. At some point the Southern District is going to say enough is enough and it won't just be militiamen we have to deal with. I think we need to phase these out or mix in some kind of olive branch."

Corban studied Asa for a moment before answering. "There is an old saying, 'He who spares the rod spoils the child.' If we are not firm with the Southern District now, then when will we ever see change? The answer is never. The next time crisis brews it could be harder or even impossible to make real change. We are moving out on each of these now because the timing is critical. If there is blow back then we need to double down and be strong. It may take some tough love, possibly even from Harris if they organize against us. The goal is to have our country stronger and unified after all these moves have paid off. Yes, there is risk but the reward is too valuable to play it safe." Corban looked around. "Any other questions or suggestions?" No-one flinched. "Good. I will let you all know how the President takes our recommendations. Naya and Alexandra, I will pull you in to brief your concepts. That will be all."

Angel

It was the first day of Angel Vega's new position integrating the Southern District National Guard units. He was still trying to balance the intel work, but would have to hand that off to Ajax Pagano as the new job was becoming quite intense. Staying in touch with the intel world for the time being was going to be useful as it would drive his military planning. Soon the two jobs would be too much but today was an example of how the two were intertwined.

Angel and Ajax were visiting the Texas National Guard Headquarters just east of Dallas. They were meeting the general that Cyrus had promised to be Angel's right-hand man. Angel and Ajax had just finished a tour of the infantry training facility and were now in the headquarters building walking to one of the executive rooms. Cyrus was going to join remotely for the start of the meeting. They rounded the last corner and entered the suite. The general was in uniform and rose when Angel entered.

"General Tzu, I am Angel Vega and this is Ajax Pagano. It is an honor to meet you," Angel said and extended his hand.

"Mr. Vega and Mr. Pagano, the honor is all mine. I look forward to working with you." General Moon Tzu was wearing his dress uniform, and his decorations from active military and guard duty would cover an average man's chest. He had wide shoulders, night black hair, hickory-colored skin, and a scar across the right side of his face that started at the inner part of his eye and went across his cheek to the jawbone. His stare was intense enough to usually get his way without even needing to ask. General Tzu was the lead General for the Georgia National Guard, the second largest in the Southern District. He had traveled from his headquarters just north of Atlanta to meet with Angel.

"Please, call me Angel." Angel's confidence in being able to accomplish this task went up in just meeting Moon.

"Then you can call me Moon. Seems we have a lot of work to do. Preparing for the worst will hopefully let us all be grateful when it turns out better than expected," Moon replied.

"The next couple of weeks should give us an idea how bad it is going to get. I also like to be prepared," Angel replied. "I'm afraid we will have to get straight to business. The Governor will be joining us in a minute to talk about our new work for the District. We also have some news for you both that paints an ominous forecast."

"Understood. I'm not much for chit chat anyway," Moon replied, and returned to his seat. Angel sat on the other side of the small table.

"Carrina, are you here?" Angel asked, without looking for someone to answer.

There was a delay of a couple seconds and then she spoke up. "Yes sir, it took a while with the system at your location but I think I am in control of your suite now. Are you ready for me to connect you to Governor Young?" Carrina was the Southern District AI used by the State Guards units.

"Yes, please connect him as soon as he is ready," Angel answered as he opened his digital notebook and flipped to his notes. "I am sending you a file to display when I start talking about bases."

"As you command," Carrina replied.

After a few seconds, the image of Cyrus Young's hologram appeared on the display at the head of the table.

"Good afternoon gentlemen, I see you are not wasting any time. I have been answering questions about you all day. General Tzu, how are you? It's been a while," Cyrus asked.

"I've been well Governor. Getting fat just training recruits. Thanks for the opportunity," Moon replied.

"You were a natural fit. I hope you didn't have any plans for the next few months," Cyrus said.

"No sir, ready to serve the District. Georgia is behind you sir," Moon said.

"I've talked to you each individually, but wanted to see you now together before you start running to make sure there is no uncertainty in what we need," Cyrus began. "Years ago, the districts were given authority, both by Washington and the states, to consolidate and integrate as needed for the good of the district. I have talked to the Governors from all twelve southern states and they have agreed to unify the southern National Guard units. They understand that it is paramount we can act as one if called upon by the Southern District in a defensive capacity. You also need to integrate the various state defense forces; most southern states have them. If you want to call on militias to help, then you are authorized to do so. Your job is to deploy these integrated forces to protect potential targets that our intelligence analysts determine are at risk from further attacks. You may get called in to help go after potential threats should they arise so we need some forces capable to deploy at a moment's notice. This work will evolve as time goes by and the politics evolve. There will be resistance from Washington. You also have challenges in convincing some of the guard commanders to follow you and not simply answer to Washington blindly. To put it bluntly, if there is a threat at home, I want the guard and defense forces operating under your command and if the threat is abroad from a foreign power then the guard will operate under command from Washington. Since there are no active foreign threats of that magnitude, my expectation is the defense force will support our needs in these trying times. I suggest you start using existing bases and look at opening old bases to create an infrastructure. No need to start from scratch. Logistics and supplies will be a challenge, but with my support you will get the reserves you need." Cyrus took a break to see their expressions. "Does my description of the task match your understanding?"

"Yes sir," Angel, Ajax, and Moon answered.

"Speaking of bases, Carrina, please pull up the map," Angel said. "Sir, we have already started a list of bases to staff up now and a second list to potentially populate later. There will be a steady stream of requests for resources and supplies plus several calls for new personnel."

Cyrus studied the map displayed with special effects to draw the eye to each location. "Good, please report back to me early next week on your progress. I like how you spread the effort across the district with attention to major cities on our borders, including the coast. That seems to be where we are at greatest risk."

"Sir, I have some news I need to share with you and, given this secure line, if you have a couple of more minutes I'd like to do so now," Angel said.

"Ok, I can give you a couple minutes," Cyrus said.

"Sir, I have a credible source telling me that the President plans to launch simultaneous political attacks on us personally and push for major policy changes targeting the Southern District," Angel began. "The announcement could come out tomorrow. For the policies, they may recommend the states approve amendments to the constitution standardizing the deudor process and therefore overriding our district's policies. They would force additional deudor types which would greatly increase the number of people who classify as deudors. Also, they plan to essentially make it a criminal offense to have a district or state attempt to limit people coming and going. They want the feds to shoulder all of that responsibility even though they have failed so badly for so long."

"Damn. I had not heard about that yet. Good work. Looks like it will be a long week." Cyrus leaned forward. "Gentlemen, given that information there is something I should warn you about. As part of your assignment, I need to make sure you understand I need the Southern District forces to integrate, strengthen, and be able to operate without support from the federal government. In fact, it could be federal forces we are working to counter if the politics continue to deteriorate. The state Governors and I are in agreement we will not be bullied by Washington. We would rather secede than be subjected to the concentrated executive power from the Administration with no ability for the states to control their own destiny. The stakes in your positions could not be higher." Cyrus paused for a moment. "If you need anything, you contact me immediately. If I could resign and make it all better, then I would. Sadly, it is not about any one of us. Our way of life and principles are under attack. They tell us they are taking us to a Utopia, but we believe with all our heart they are building a house of cards that will collapse. Because this is explosive, you cannot tell anyone that potential scenario directly. Officially and even practically for the near term we are going to try to save our cities to try to prevent attacks like the Bush Park massacre. Also, try your best to have the visibility of your work limited to southern personnel only. I want the federal personnel to see us as disorganized and weak."

"Appear weak when you are strong, and strong when you are weak," Ajax said.

"Exactly," Cyrus confirmed.

"So, it is as bad as I feared. That makes what we are doing a matter of life and death," Moon said, looking at Angel.

All four shared silence for a moment.

Angel turned to Cyrus. "Thank you for your time sir. We will be in touch soon."

Anna

"**A**nna, I am so sorry. Not in a billion years could I ever imagine this happening," Sophia said.

"Then tell her the truth!" Anna Lee replied. "Don't you see what you've done to me?!"

"It's not my fault, you must believe me. It was John who said it was you. If I were to say anything then we'd both be gone," Sophia answered.

"But why? Why would John say I did those things?" Anna put her face in her hands and wept. Sophia tried to hug her, but Anna shook her off. Sophia was quiet and started to eye the door. Anna looked up. "You know why, don't you? Tell me. Please!"

"It was me. I mean, it has been me for a while. I like John and he likes me. Mrs. Rivera found their bed a mess with, um, it was a mess. She came home early and I had not cleaned up yet," Sophia confessed.

"Then why did he say it was me?!" Anna said.

"I assume because he wants me to stay. Because he really likes me," Sophia said with a little sparkle in her eye but trying not to smile. "Don't you see? If I say something then he will turn on me and we'll both be out," Sophia said.

"Why am I the only one in trouble? Shouldn't John be out the door too?" Anna asked.

"I think you know why. If Maria kicks John out then what does she tell all of her friends? She can't tell them that she caught her husband with a deudor. That's almost as bad as being caught with an android. We aren't people to them. We are just the help and closer to objects than equals," Sophia said. "Anna, I have an idea to try and help you. Can I tell it to you?"

Anna wiped the tears from her eyes. She wondered if she could trust

Sophia. This still had to be a mistake, had to be a dream. Maria had sent her to her room last night and it was going on midday.

"Ok, but I am still really mad at you. I don't want to go! Maria said she was going to get me sent to a work camp. That is so hard and I might never pay off all the debt!" Anna wailed again and this time let Sophia hug her. After Anna stopped crying again, she sat on her bed and Sophia sat next to her.

"Did you know that in the Southern District, to be born premature would not make you a deudor? We need to get you to the south and try to get you asylum or whatever it's called," Sophia started. "I know a place we can go to help you meet someone. It's an online place but you can make a connection so they can help you escape."

"Why would anyone help me?" Anna asked, still skeptical.

"There are a lot of people outside of the Eastern and Western Districts that think the deudor system is wrong. They are so upset about the situation we are in that they want to help us get out of here. They can't help everyone and they can get in trouble if they get caught. But you, you're perfect. No way is a dainty fourteen-year-old blonde really a decoy to catch them, and they will really want to help because of how you became a deudor." Sophia paused to see what Anna would say.

"What happens if I get caught?" Anna asked.

"Nothing that isn't already going to happen to you but, if you are lucky, then you get out of here. This could be the best thing that ever happened to you!" Sophia was starting to believe it herself. "The place to go is a ticket booth on the west end of Grand Central Station, an online train station just like the one here in New York. Ya know, it's the place that has a couple of intercity high-speed underground tunnel systems. At that ticket booth, I have heard the person selling tickets will help you get out of here. You meet them virtually to arrange an escape in the real world. The bad news is that Maria is so mad that I think for this to work we need to go there now. I'll get you to the booth and come back here to watch out for Maria."

Anna thought about it for a moment. She thought about how hard she had worked to make this place her home, how hard she had worked to make this her family, and how hard she had worked to make them love her. She knew she had failed. They had turned on her at the first chance. They didn't even turn on the right deudor. Anna knew now they did not see her as an equal.

"Ok. Let's go check it out now," Anna said. She was so tired but didn't know what else to do.

"Awesome. I'll get our Halos!" Sophia said. Anna laid down on her bed. Sophia came back, told both Halos where to take them, gave Anna her Halo, and then laid down on her own bed. They both but their Halos on.

Anna open her eyes and found herself standing at the entrance to the virtual Grand Central Station. She had no idea how enormous the place would be. It was several stories tall and went as far as the eye could see. Sophia took Anna's hand and they went into the entrance. They went toward the middle pretending to look at the incoming train schedule. People came here for vacation trips or just to see this famous modern train station. Not many people used traditional trains in real life beyond intercity commutes. The online version of the high-speed underground tunnels was a remarkably life-like replica of the latest in affordable high-speed city-to-city travel.

After standing and acting like they were looking at the display of departures, Sophia was convinced they were not being watched any more than two pretty teenage girls expect to be watched. Sophia took Anna's hand and walked her to the western wing of the train station. They passed some shops and a couple of restaurants. They reached a kiosk that had ads for both online and real places to go. Sophia pretended to look at an ad for a club having ladies' night just a couple of train stops to the east.

"Anna, do you see the ticket booth with an ad above it for a ride to Cleveland?" Sophia asked quietly.

Anna discretely peaked further down the west wing of the station. "Yes, I see it."

"That's the one," Sophia said. "Just be yourself and don't let them turn you away. You have nothing to lose and everything to gain. I'm going back and will wake you up if Maria comes back." Sophia walked back towards the entrance of the station. Anna turned towards the ticket booth.

There were two people in line. The window was dark to the point where Anna could not see who was behind it. She had the instinct to drop out, but remembered the dire situation she was facing. She pinched her leg to make her senses get squared away and started walking to the counter.

"Hello there sweet thing, are you lost?" A gentle old lady asked her from the side.

Anna stopped; she was only ten meters from the counter. "No, just trying to make up my mind where to go. Thanks." Anna started to walk again.

"Why honey, what's the rush?" The lady said. "I can help you figure out where to go. Let me guess, you want to go somewhere warm and safe. Perhaps down south?"

Anna stopped and turned around. "How did you know that?"

The older lady walked up close enough to speak quietly. "Honey, you stick out like a sore thumb here." She continued to smile and looked more like a confused old lady. "I am not sure how you heard about us but we are always being watched and you aren't helping. We might as well put a sign up saying 'escapees welcome.' I think you should just go on home."

"I can't. I've been blamed for something I didn't do, something horrible." Anna took a step closer so she could almost whisper to the lady. "They are going to send me to a camp or a farm or worse. I have to get out. I have to. Won't you please help me?"

The old lady looked at Anna for a couple of seconds and then slowly but calmly looked around to see if anyone was watching them. "Meet me at the station café on the south wing in ten minutes. I'll be sitting at a table with two calzones. We can talk about where to meet in the real world."

"Thank you. Thank you so much," Anna said, obviously not very good at hiding her emotions.

"What is your name darling?" The older lady asked.

"My name is Anna Lee," Anna answered.

"You poor thing. You're just a child. My name is Judith. I'll see you in a few minutes. We'll see what we can do," Judith replied.

Samson

Samson Gamble drove up to the security checkpoint of the Texas State Guard Headquarters on the north side of Austin. He slowed and got in line behind two cars. Samson and his team were among the first soldiers to arrive since the Texas state governor called up all of the regiments of the state guard. They were in a truck capable of off-road operations which included a manual driving back-up mode. Samson always used it preferring it over the Camilla AI driving system. Manual driving required a special license and cost a fortune in taxes and insurance but was worth it to Samson. The Texas State Guard was a different group than the Texas National Guard. The Texas State Guard was only, by design, under the authority of the state governor. The National Guard units in all states could be called up by the state governors, as well as the federal government. As Samson pulled up to the checkpoint, an android security guard approached him. He saw another android guard behind it, as well as a human guard sitting in the checkpoint booth. Both androids were shiny chrome from head to foot except for army camouflage chest and leg plates. They included blue piercing LED eyes common to all Southern District military and security androids. The camouflage showed them to be military units.

"Good morning lady and gentlemen," the android began. "I do not detect identification chips for any of you. Please provide identification."

All five of Samson's team showed the guard their badges.

"You are authorized to proceed. Have a nice day," the android said as it backed up.

Samson started driving on to the base. The entrance took him through a wooded area and then past a small pond that had seen better days. He came to a crossing and turned right which led to several buildings. Samson drove past two buildings and stopped at the third which was the officer's barracks. He parked in front and the team grabbed their personal gear and went in.

The barracks smelled like feet and old cheese. They would need to get a couple of the cleaning droids in here. The guys saw a few other early arrivals but, for the most part, the place was empty. The building was essentially an endless series of rooms like a hotel. The rooms could each hold up to four soldiers. Samson's team got key codes for two rooms and they put their equipment in. They then went back to the truck and drove further onto the base.

They passed several more barracks. The base could hold up to twenty-five hundred soldiers if adequately supplied. Training for that many soldiers would be cramped, but possible. Next were a couple of supply buildings. Samson dropped off Andre, Hawk, and Dune so they could start looking at what kind of supplies were on-site. After a few more buildings, they reached a hanger and small airstrip. He dropped Tony off there to see if the base could still support aircraft and if so, how many and what kind. It had been underutilized for many years. Samson then circled back around to one of the first buildings which was the headquarters. He parked out front and went inside.

Samson needed to show his identification card again to get into the headquarters building. As soon as he passed through the door, he could smell coffee and followed his nose. It took him down the throat of the building, then a left down another hallway, and then a right into a large meeting room where he found the other regiment leaders. Samson was the last leader to arrive as he was the only one who did not live close to Austin. Eight officers were in command of the Texas State Guard's 44th Regiment, the Roughriders.

"Good morning ladies and gentlemen and Jimmy," Samson said. He was freshly shaved in his field uniform. "Did y'all miss me?"

"We didn't miss you, but there are some toilets needing scrubbing if you have nothing else to do," Jimmy replied. Jimmy Williams was one of the regiment majors along with Samson. Both reported to Colonel Samantha Payne and Lieutenant Colonel Winston Davis.

"Samson, go get a cup of coffee. Everyone, have a seat. We have a lot to talk about," Colonel Payne said with only a hint of a smile. She went to the front of the room. The Colonel was the only one still standing by the time she turned around.

"I think you have all heard rumors about why our unit has been called up. The first thing we need to do is get squared away on what is true and what is bullshit. Our job is to spread out, look for threats, and show these bastards the days of Mr. Nice Guy are over. Our enemies have been attacking soft spots in our communities for years. We are going to work with the rest of the district to secure the most sensitive areas, likely often rotating locations. Yes, the south isn't getting along with the rest of the country, but do not get distracted by the noise in the media. Our orders are clear. Lives are at stake. We could even end up as the targets. Carrina, bring up the video," the Colonel directed.

"As you command," Carrina replied. The room had no windows and went dark instantly, then a projection at the front brightened it back up.

"Welcome to task force Safeguard. I am General Moon Tzu." The video showed Moon standing on a stage in uniform with the entire background being an American flag. "Your unit has been called up to play a vital role in addressing the violence that continues to plague our citizens. This can no longer be left to local law enforcement or limited resources at the bureaus. The Southern District Governor has ordered all State Guard and Southern National Guard units to be integrated into a Southern District Defense Force. We will still honor our role as needed should the country need our National Guard units but, right now, there is a threat at home and we need to drown it out. Our enemies think we are weak and will simply take it on the chin every time. We are about to show them that the south is strong, that our people are strong, and that justice will be served. Your unit commanders have the orders specific to your unit's skills. It is hard to say when task force Safeguard will be complete, but we have full confidence in you and that we will be victorious."

General Tzu's video transferred off and the lights returned. An image of the Southern District was displayed behind Colonel Payne.

"General Tzu is the commanding officer for the task force and for the integration of the Southern District Defense Force. They are still working out a lot of details including logistics and dusting off reserve droids and aircraft. We are not sure yet what our initial assignment will be, but I know we have at least a week to get the regiment in shape. From what I can tell so far, most units will deploy to the largest city near their home base with an emphasis on port and border cities. Since Austin is the Texas capital, we likely will be lucky enough to stay close to home. Any questions?" Samantha asked.

"Yes ma'am." Jimmy stood up firmly. "What are our priorities this first week if that is all we get? Most of our guys are going to need a lot of work." Jimmy sat down after asking.

"Good question. Since we are talking about security details, I want the emphasis on keeping morale high yet with firm discipline and physical training. All of us in the command team are former Special Forces and from the looks of you, it seems you stayed in pretty good shape. Most of our enlisted are vets but were your standard four-year and done enlistment. Many were let loose after the Army and Marines started downsizing after the last war ended. We don't want to burn them out or have systemic discipline issues when they are being uprooted from their lives. For example, I think we can allow Halos and such after duties are performed," Samantha answered.

"Ma'am," Thomas Jackson stood up. "I'd like to suggest that as a form of training that we open up the urban combat training facility. All of the scenarios we keep hearing about seem like we may have inner city door-to-door activities plus it's a heck of a workout."

"Good idea. Please take a dozen men and a couple of engineers with you to see what shape it's in. That reminds me, I plan to talk to the facility gang as well as the android handlers about IT security. The protest attack was particularly bad because the EMP knocked out our machines. We need to make sure our software is up-to-date and see what we can do to protect critical systems in case we get hit by an EMP," Samantha answered.

"Ma'am." Samson stood. "Speaking of IT security, I wanted to ask about identification chips. I've been in situations before where having an implant chip would have let me be detected and compromise the mission. We are not sure who is really behind all these attacks so stealth may be critical. People can't go to the bathroom without the system tracking you if you have a chip. I suggest all members of the defense force have their chips removed."

"Don't you think that is a bit extreme? We aren't dealing with a foreign power here," Samantha responded.

"It might be extreme if this was a single regiment being called up. The Governor has called up every armed unit across the south. I think this has the potential to go on for a while. If you believe the public statements then they are really struggling with the feds. The chips are essential if you are child and your parents need to find you. I had my chip out years ago and don't miss it. If the wrong person is in the right system, then we will never have the element of surprise if our guys are chipped."

"I can't make that call but will pass the idea along," Samantha answered. "Not seeing any more questions, I will only add that a few of us will be going to a robotics plant in about a week to see some units being made to help the task force. They have repurposed construction android production lines to make units for us. They also have some upgrades to standard military androids we need to check out. I will contact those who will be going when I learn more." Samantha paused. "I know this is going to be tough, but they call us Roughriders for a reason. I pity anyone that gets in our way. Dismissed."

Angel

A ngel and Moon were having a leadership meeting for the Southern District Defense Force. They were still at the Texas National Guard Headquarters just east of Dallas. A few of the guard leaders were with them; most were online virtually. Everyone had been scrambling trying to separate news from gossip.

"I just don't understand why we need two chains of command. Don't you think we need better direction on who is calling the shots?" Asked Valerie Pickett, State Guard commander for Missouri. "When you are in the deep south it might seem clear, but I can easily see us getting orders from two sets of civilians each saying they are the ones in charge."

"I understand and will try to get it spelled out and advertised for all to hear. You are absolutely right we can't have two masters," Angel replied. "Again, it is clear to me and I will try again to explain how we can understand the civilian responsibilities. Our task force and integration efforts are for domestic support only. The driver for us meeting now and for calling up all units is to make a stand against the violence that has rained upon our people. The federal government will still be able to call on us should a foreign affair or act of God warrant military support. This isn't that much of a stretch from when guard units get called up by state governors. I hope that helps at least for now, but I promise to get more formal charters to you soon."

"Sir, I am Lieutenant Colonel Vincent Raines, Alabama State Guard." The LTC stood to ask the question even though he was connected virtually. "Sir, as you know, most state guard personnel are not paid. If this is an extended task force there will be issues with personal hardships. Employers, even government paid jobs, can't pay them very long if they are not working. How is the Southern District going to address this as we make up roughly half the task force?"

"Good question. We are looking into a pay system from the Southern District that will cover all personnel, whether it is National Guard or State Guard. We should have details on that in a day or two," Answered Angel.

"Sir, question to you from the sunshine state." Angel and Moon saw the hologram of Douglas Howard raise his hand and then lower it. "Brigadier General Howard, Florida National Guard. General Tzu, can you please speak to the rumors that we are preparing more to be a deterrent to the federal government? We haven't seen attacks in Florida and it seems like overkill to call all of us up unless there are threats beyond the usual terrorist cowards."

"Good to see you again Douglas," General Tzu began. "I looked into that myself and I can honestly tell you that our mission is to broadly protect the Southern District. Yes, most attacks have been in Texas, but if the Lone Star state sets up defenses then these monsters will just move to the next state, or at least that is the fear. On your other question, The Bush Park massacre lit the fuse of political bickering. I think our task force will be over when those guilty of these war crimes have been caught and punished because the politics should settle down. We will see where this leads together. We all need to remember what is at stake here. The civilian carnage continues to stack up despite traditional efforts. Even if it was not in your state, we need to stick together to remain strong. If this district collapses then we may return to the times where we are all micromanaged by Washington DC. All of us are old enough to remember how awful that was and we barely recovered. The stakes could not be higher."

"Ladies and gentlemen, General Tzu and I have a plane to catch but we should talk again soon. We will share logistics, supplies, and pay information as we get it. Please use the details shared today to start forming up. In God we trust," Angel concluded.

Anna

It had only been twenty-four hours since Anna Lee's world fell apart. Her mother figure had turned on her. Her father figure apparently found her expendable. Neither of them thought of her as a person, despite all her efforts since she joined the Riveras at age twelve. Anna was trying to hate them but kept coming back to the reality in which they all lived; the reality that the community's way of life revolved around the haves and the have-nots. Maybe someday they would look back and regret having tossed Anna away like a car to be traded in. Maria had told Anna a couple hours earlier that her debt had been sold to a farm in western New York that grew vegetables and fruits. The Riveras were looking to replace her with an android. Sophia was in hiding when not doing her chores. If the Anna replacement worked then she feared Maria might want a Sophia replacement.

Anna had heard enough to know that Maria believed sending Anna away would fix all of her problems. She smiled at the prospect of Maria discovering the error in blaming her. Anna could tell that Sophia had no intention to stop seeing John.

Anna was sitting on her bed. She looked at the clock. Five minutes until Anna would leave to meet Judith. While she had been with the Riveras only two years, she could barely remember life before it. The state child deudor centers were essentially orphanages. Anyone who was not able to work in any way was there. Bad and good apples all in the same barrel. Anna had shown promise early and made it out before most. The door opened, startling Anna, and Sophia entered.

"Hey girl, I wanted to see you before, uh, ya know," Sophia said. "I'm sorry things went down the way they did. I always liked you. You were good for me. I will miss you." It was the first time in two years Anna had seen Sophia tear up.

"I still can't believe this is happening either. I guess I have learned that God will never stop testing us," Anna said, also wiping away tears. "And I can't believe John isn't getting punished at all. Maria seems to even be trying harder for him now. It's so unfair." Anna paused for a moment and looked at Sophia. "I do wish you the best. I hope you can stay clear of John. They won't blame the android if she gets wise again." They both smiled briefly.

"I hate hard goodbyes so give me a hug and I'll go back to work." Sophia reached in and hugged Anna. "Ya know, they are gonna be pissed you left. They can't sell your debt if you run off. Be careful." Sophia got up, went to the door, and looked back at Anna. "If they are on to you, run and fight if you have to. Crying won't help you and praying won't do you no good." She slowly opened it, looked both ways, turned to smile at Anna one last time, and left the room closing the door quietly behind her.

Anna got up and pulled a bag out from under her bed. She took an envelope out and slid it under her pillow. She had farewell messages to each of the Riveras, but doubted Maria would let any of them read the notes. She looked in her bag just to make sure her key things were still there. No point in waiting any more. Anna wished she could say goodbye to Jessica and James, but knew they would not understand. Maria was busy in her room and John was still at work. Anna need only stroll through the house like nothing special was going on and walk out the front door. Judith was supposed to be in a private car parked on the street two blocks away. If Judith wasn't there then Anna planned to run back and slip back in. She felt an anchor to her room. In the distance she heard Maria yell for Sophia. That helped loose her anchor.

Anna opened the door. She half expected to get caught right there but no-one was in sight. She started to the stairs and tried to walk quietly holding the bag out of sight as much as possible. She realized she was walking slow and tried to speed up.

"Sophia! This is the wrong one! Bring me the red one!" Maria shouted from her room. Anna had no idea what she wanted and didn't care.

Anna kept going down the stairs now heading to the first floor.

"Hi Anna," James said as he walked around the corner.

Anna went to the bottom of the stairs and got down on one knee to be able to whisper to James. "Hi sweetie, we need to be super quiet for your mom, ok?"

"Ok, I have missed you," James said, and gave her a hug. Anna hugged him back and felt tears coming.

"I've missed you too. Take care of yourself. I will always love you," Anna said.

James smiled innocently and ran back to his room. Luckily no-one had heard James say her name. Anna got to the front door. She turned around again briefly getting cold feet. With no-one in sight, she slipped out the door and closed it quietly behind her.

Lucilla

Lucilla Swift was in the back of a prisoner transport vehicle. No windows. No way out. It was poor lighting, but Lucilla guessed about twenty of her fellow Blood Ravens were in the truck. She guessed that meant there were three trucks if they were all being transferred somewhere together. They were all in prison orange with cuffs on their wrists and ankles that were also connected by a chain. There were two armed guards towards the front and two towards the back. Anytime they tried to speak they were told to shut up or worse. Lucilla thought she must be going mad as she kept thinking she heard cheering outside. The truck stopped suddenly and all the prisoners were jerked towards the front. The back door opened and there was a blinding light. The guards yelled at them to get out and they slowly stumbled out one at a time. There was a one-meter drop so they each had to jump out because of the cuffs. It was Lucilla's turn to hop out and she could not believe her eyes.

"Get out you maggots. You traitors!" A security agent yelled. Lucilla gave him a quick dirty look but followed the directions just hoping this nightmare might end.

"Fall in Blood Ravens. Time to do your duty!" Another security agent yelled from about twenty meters away from the truck. Lucilla's group slowly shuffled toward him. She could see her bus had been the last one. Her entire militia was there in formation, just like when they had been arrested. Lucilla's father was to the far right.

Lucilla's eyes had now fully recovered from the long dark truck ride. They were near downtown St. Louis near one of the main streets. It looked like a pro-government rally was being held. There were trucks with pro-government themes on the road as far as the eye could see.

"Oh God, they are making examples of us. They mean to parade us down the road," Lucilla said to herself. "Daddy!" Lucilla yelled to her dad.

"Shut your mouth traitor!" The closest guard yelled. "We already tased two of your buddies. Don't make us do you too." It didn't matter. Jackson Swift had heard his little girl and turned to see her. They traded sad but relieved smiles. They had not seen each other since being arrested. A week in jail with no end in sight. Lucilla could tell her father had been beaten, but it looked like some make up was on his face.

"Rebel scum!" A lady in the crowd on the sidewalk yelled at them. Lucilla began to notice all the people gathering around them. It looked like they were in a section where a food service worker union was forming up.

"Prisoners! Your attention please!" A very well-dressed man yelled from the far right past Jackson and the three rows of prisoners. "Right face!" All the security agents laughed. They all slowly turned right. Lucilla could see two of her friends with tears going down their faces. This was truly humiliating. "Good morning!" The man continued. "It is a beautiful day for a parade. You will be providing a great service to your country today. You will be showing what happens when people think about rebellion. Your example should stop the next batch of morons from repeating your mistakes. If you co-operate, this will be factored into your prosecution and potentially lessen your sentencing." One of Lucilla's friends who had been crying quietly started to sob. "Any questions? No? Good." The man talked into his wrist watch briefly and the line in front of them started to move. "Forward march!" The security guards all laughed again.

A pair of aerial security drones were hovering above them. One was towards the front and one was towards the rear. Also hovering above was a public relations drone.

"Good morning citizens!" The public relations drone called out. "Brave federal agents from the Homeland Security and the FBI apprehended this group who was planning an attack on a military outpost near Kansas City. Let them be examples of how criminals against the state will not be tolerated!" The drone repeated this message every twenty meters as the parade continued forward. The drone was also feeding a video of the prisoners and the crowd to the news networks broadcasting the rally and parade.

Lucilla's group was roughly in the middle of the parade. The parade covered a few roads, but the main procession was on Market Street. The Gateway Arch was behind them and they were marching slowly past restaurants and other buildings catering to the nearby sports arenas. Every time the drone repeated the message, the prisoners were booed by the crowd. They passed another union dressed in matching shirts. In general, it looked like the crowd was made up of regular civilians packing the sidewalks like it was a Thanksgiving Day parade.

They continued down Market Street. Lucilla could see a sign for the City Hall and Court House. She was trying to see if there was an end to this parade anytime soon when a hot dog hit her in the face.

"Ha ha! Gotcha bitch!" A teenage boy yelled. Three of the boy's friends then also threw food at the prisoners. Two of them hit prisoners with food, the third hit a prisoner with a soft drink that exploded on impact soaking the man with Coke. The boys laughed and the crowd cheered. The security forces acted like it didn't happen. Lucilla wiped mustard off her cheek. She was starting to make a transition from being mortified to rage.

Lucilla could see that it looked like the parade ended with something big where Market Street met Union Station. She heard yelling ahead to the right. Most of the security guards and drones began to focus on the noise. She heard a mix of yelling and chanting.

"Fred, what is it? Can you see it?" Lucilla asked. Fred Johnson was the militiaman to her right and had a better view.

"Not sure. It's about a block and a half ahead," Fred said, and continued to try to see for several more seconds. "Oh God, it looks like the Joplin militia is here. I see their black hats. They are in uniform and a row of them look to have their rifles. There are people yelling at them and others yelling back."

After a little while longer, Lucilla could see the Joplin unit. There were about fifty of them, half their members. They had Missouri flags and were standing at attention. Lucilla's father was at the head of the prisoner group and had almost reached them. Lucilla was towards the back of the militia. The Joplin unit in unison began to salute. They were saluting the Carthage unit in a clear and rebellious sign of unity with the prisoners. One of the security guards, Lucilla guessed there were ten of them, was yelling at the lead for the Joplin unit but he was not flinching. They had open carry permits and were not breaking the law. Lucilla guessed the rifles were not even loaded.

A large group of union members in matching t-shirts and black facemasks were walking toward the Joplin unit from the far side. Lucilla could tell trouble was brewing. Two of the security guards got between the approaching union mob and the Joplin militia. The mob flowed around them like spilled oil, some of them pouring into the street to get in the face of the Joplin unit. Lucilla could see more yelling and what looked like spitting. The Joplin unit still held firm.

Lucilla noticed all of the Carthage unit was now watching and her father was starting to drift towards the action, but a security guard corrected his course. Lucilla then panned around and saw everyone within sight was yelling either at or for the Joplin unit. The supporters of the militia were outnumbered at least ten to one.

Lucilla had just turned back towards the Joplin unit and saw a union man hit one of the Joplin militiamen in the head with what looked like a brick. His head shot back, his knees went limp, and he dropped his rifle. The rifle fired. All of the security detail now raised their weapons at the Joplin unit and were yelling. Lucilla could not tell if the shot hit anyone and then she heard a woman screaming in the crowd. She had been shot in the leg. The militiaman who had been hit in the head was being helped up by two of his comrades. He began to reach drunkenly for his gun. A union man tried to reach for it but was clocked in the head by another militiaman. His face cut open and sprayed blood on the concrete. The militiaman who had been hit by a brick was able to get to his gun and was stumbling badly. He didn't hear the security guard telling him to stop. Before anyone could help the hurt man, three security guards opened fire, killing him instantly. Two militiamen instinctively pointed their rifles at the security guards and were also shot. Realizing they were in a fight now, the Joplin unit scrambled and dispersed. This caused the entire parade to break down with even the prisoners running in random directions.

Lucilla saw her father run in front of several Joplin militiamen who were holding their arms up. She started to run to him, but Jeff grabbed her and pulled her to the side trying to get them lost in the crowd.

One of the union men who had been punched yelled "Fire!" The security guards confused opened fire again. Lucilla saw her father fall along with six other Joplin militiamen.

"No!!" Lucilla yelled, shaking Jeff's grip loose. She ran as best she could with the cuffs on desperately trying to reach her father. By now more security had arrived and all the militiamen were on the ground co-operating or had been shot. Another barrel of fuel had been poured on the fire.

Corban

" ...They are animals!" The union boss for the Service Employees Intercountry Union (SEIU) Local 420 yelled. "They are animals and we should have slaughtered them like animals!"

Corban was meeting with several leaders at the St. Louis Homeland Security building to talk damage control. They had just watched a video of the carnage. The media was calling it the American Pride Parade tragedy. It varied by news organization and political party as to which side were the victims. Corban's Security Council was meeting with several Eastern and Western District leaders to discuss the incident. The immediate business was to clean up the mess and get a consistent message out to the public. The next steps would likely be driven by President Thorne himself.

"Ladies and gentlemen, there is almost an infinite number of accounts being spun on this latest bloodshed. There were strict orders for security to protect everyone. Those who obviously failed that task will be held accountable." Corban paused for a moment. "The key now is to limit any additional damage. We need to calm the people and avoid additional conflict. Many are furious and most citizens are scared. We have no-one to blame but ourselves." Corban gave the SEIU boss a cold stare to quiet his tongue.

"I hope you are including the Southern District leaders in your remarks. They certainly have blood on their hands," added Heidi Floss, Lieutenant Governor of Illinois.

"Of course. What I mean is that we can't blame this on foreign powers or Muslim terrorists. This tragedy is American-made. It's a testament to the divide in this country and the division is manifesting into action," Corban replied. "We need to get out a consistent message that the Joplin militia accidentally had a rifle go off and that the security forces squashed the ensuing chaos as quickly as possible. In reality, there were only nine people killed and twenty-eight wounded, but the riots going on right now are spreading to every major city. There hasn't been an open exchange between the states like this in more than two centuries. We need tight messaging, security forces, and a curfew in St. Louis, east and west, in place today."

"Sir, for the security forces, the Illinois National Guard is in place covering the eastern half of St. Louis," added Heidi. "We know the Missouri National Guard is in place west of the Missouri river; however, we cannot vouch for the effectiveness on the Missouri side. They didn't help before the incident and they barely will respond to us now. For the curfew, I think we can apply that as early as tomorrow. It will be difficult to start it today as there are rioters already roaming the city. It is taking all available forces to separate the competing mobs."

"Chairman Cruz, I'd like to volunteer to work on the messaging with my counterpart in the Southern District," said Naya Garcia. "Dana and I go way back. If we can both leave out the debatable details and focus on the basics like you said, then we can hopefully stabilize the government narrative on the crisis."

"Good. Thank you, ladies. That still leaves needing someone to talk to the Missouri National Guard," Corban said.

"Sir, I think I can open a line of communication with them if it will help," said Marvin Williams, St. Louis chief of police. "We have one police force for both sides of the Missouri River. "I have to talk to both guard units already."

Corban looked at Marvin thoughtfully for a moment. He was one of the few people in the room with Corban as opposed to joining virtually. "Ok. We can give that a shot. Please report to me daily at a minimum, plus immediately contact me if anything goes sideways. We will likewise contact you if our surveillance of either side of St. Louis shows signs of further bedlam." Marvin did not know that one of the purposes of the meeting was for Corban to essentially recruit him as an informant.

"Sir, is there a plan if further violence erupts? How do the forces respond? Surely it's not simply to neutralize them," asked Jason Paxton, Commander of the Illinois National Guard. "And will the Missouri Guard respond the same way? Would sure help if they were here."

"Yes, they were invited, but the Southern District ordered them to focus on the riots underway right now," Corban started. "To answer your question, we respond with a show of overwhelming force and motivate them to surrender. If they see themselves outnumbered and outgunned then they should stop. If we can avoid further incidents in the next couple of days, then we fully expect this to end up being limited, brief, and fizzle out quickly. In addition to Chief Williams talking to both guard units, we will be contacting the Southern District to co-ordinate this common response."

"Sir, I think there is another message we need to spread as well," Alexandra Soaring spoke up.

"Go ahead," Corban replied.

"I think we need to call for parties on all sides to disarm. As long as there are groups with serious weaponry then we have the threat of serious casualties. The DHS is already working to put this message out nationally and we would like to broadcast it intensely in St. Louis. We are hoping this can spread overtime to even the Guard units. At this point they are only crucial for massive responses to natural disasters. They don't need laser rifles on rescue missions." Alexandra said.

"I don't disagree with your motivations and end game. Save it for a couple of days to see if temperatures cool. It is not time to ask them to turn in their weapons when they are foaming at the mouth," Corban answered, and waited a few moments to see if anyone else spoke up.

"Seeing no more questions, I have one announcement to make. The current mess and the Southern District Task Force has led to the need for the Administration to set up a new position. This new role will co-ordinate all federal efforts to confront these crises. I am proud to introduce to you General Mori Tortan. The general will be the Administration's lead for all military matters related to responding to the crises in Houston, LA, and St. Louis." Mori stood and gave an informal quick salute. "General Tortan was the Air and Space Force commander in the Korean War and a critical player in the unification of Korea. You will be seeing a lot more of the General going forward. He will be reporting directly to me. That will be all."

Angel

The procession of five vehicles had stopped at a battle zone firing range. A tall android security guard scanned the area before opening the door to the back seat of the SUV for Governor Cyrus Young. Angel Vega, General Moon Tzu, and Ajax Pagano all opened their own doors and the four men followed the android to see the action.

The Governor and his small entourage followed the path onto a concrete viewing area that, from a distant, looked like a grey hill. Before them was a fairly flat field with a line of trees to the left that wrapped around the back until it reached a river far to the right. In the center were the carcasses of old vehicles that had been destroyed, as well as a few unharmed auto targets. This VIP section also allowed those managing the drills to see how the units were performing. A junior officer brought binoculars to the four visitors.

"Good morning gentlemen, welcome to the Jungle," said a thin lady wearing thin sunglasses and army fatigues. Her hair was dark black and pulled back into a ponytail. Angel guessed she was in her forties. Just by the way she approached them, it was clear she was in charge of this test. "We are pleased you can view this live fire drill of some of our newest units. I am Major Tammy Sherman. We are ready to get started unless you have any questions."

"Thank you for having us here," Cyrus said. "We appreciate the opportunity. We will try our best to not get in the way."

Major Sherman nodded, smiled, and walked back to the other officers who had been watching the short conversation. They all put their hands on their binoculars except for the Major. Angel watched her giving directions and she appeared so confident that he guessed she had no doubt as to the outcome of the test. The officers continued to chat both to each other and to those in the control centers running the test using earpieces so small as to be barely visible.

The visitors were all standing just behind a waist high barrier that had handrails on top. All four men used the binoculars to get a better look at the test area. Some of the vehicles among the wreckage started to drive around. Using the binoculars, they could see about six vehicles and a dozen androids moving about. The androids appeared to be talking to each other and Angel thought they might even be strategizing. The androids were holding what looked like machine guns. After congregating for a short while, the androids started to quickly pile some of the parts of past destroyed vehicles into barriers. They had almost finished making a protective circle when Angel heard the helicopter-like sounds from the left side of the field. Before Angel put down the binoculars, he thought he saw parts of androids also littering the field, including the head of an android laying in the dirt; it reminded Angel of an image he had seen long ago of bones in the desert.

Three small rotary-based aircraft flew from the left over the trees and towards the test range. They were not moving particularly fast and it looked like they were surveying what lay before them. They started to move in casual zigzag patterns. Angel was about to lift his binoculars to try to get a closer look at the aircraft, but stopped when he saw six androids emerge from the tree line to the far left. They were all riding what looked like motorcycles that lacked handlebars or even anything that differentiated the motorcycle front and back. The androids looked to have weaponry of some kind built into their arms, but Angel could not tell what. The androids were also not moving particularly fast and were trailing just behind the aircraft.

"Look, to the right," Moon said, as he saw the others only looking to the left. All four men were now looking to the right at an android who had started to walk out of the river. It looked to be larger than the units coming from the left and much larger than the androids in the middle of the test. It definitely had weapons for arms.

Apparently, the attacking force had taken enough time to plan. They were still no closer than 200 meters from the targets when the aircraft each fired two missiles. All six missiles found their targets, quickly destroying all six vehicles. The target androids must have expected this move as none had attempted to use the vehicles. The defenders had simply parked the vehicles around the perimeter of the crude fortification, circling the wagons. The wreckage still provided some barrier, but was now porous. The cyclists picked up speed and started to each take a different curved route. Angel was thinking they were going to each arc outwards to then come at the targets from different directions spread around the entire perimeter. He could not find the large android from the right using binoculars so he lowered them. Angel could hardly believe his eyes. The large android was running faster than the cyclists were driving. After all the cyclists had indeed started to turn inwards towards their targets, the aircraft fired additional rockets at the structures, and the attacking androids all began to fire lasers at the encampment. Almost immediately, the defenders began to return fire with what looked to be conventional automatic machine gun fire plus grenade launchers. Angel saw the android from the river leap almost ten meters in the air when it reached the defensive border and began to fire down into the base.

From all of the attacks, three large holes opened up in the barrier. Six of the target androids were now lying on the ground in pieces. One of the targets was crawling on the ground badly injured and reaching up in the air with one arm seemingly begging for help. One of the cyclists walked up and gave it a double tap. Two of the cyclists had been hit and their vehicles clumsily rolled to a stop. One of them popped up quickly and started running to attack. One of the aircrafts had been hit, was smoking, and spiraling to the ground.

"Holy shit." Angel said under his breath.

The android from the river did another leaping jump and this time came down in the middle of the remaining defenders. As he was coming down, he started to twirl in a circle with lasers pulsing out of both arms. The lasers were so powerful they cut four of the defenders who had been standing in half and actually hit one of the other attackers on a cycle as well. The last two defenders who had thought to drop to the ground both started to lift their weapons towards the assailant, but were quickly shot in the back by other attackers. Just like that, the test was over.

Angel looked around at the VIP area. Cyrus and Moon were still using binoculars and looking at the camp. Ajax smiled at Angel. The officers managing the test seemed pleased. Major Sherman was giving directions to the others and allowed herself a brief smile. After about a minute, she stopped talking to them and came over to her guests.

"Gentlemen, that concludes our test for today. I hope you enjoyed the show," the Major said.

"The unit that came out of the river, is that a new model?" Angel asked.

"Yes, it was the key unit we were testing today. We are very pleased with the performance. It is capable of far greater mobility and fire power than any unit we have ever tested. It integrates a complex energy dense power system with beefed up mobility and weapons systems. Based on all the testing so far, we expect to start mass producing it soon," the Major answered.

"Impressive. Very impressive. Thank you for accommodating our visit, this was very helpful to see in person," Cyrus said.

The Major nodded and went back to the other officers. The VIPs gave the binoculars back to the junior officer and started to walk back to their SUV. They got in and the vehicle started to drive them back to Houston. The four men all used the controls to rotate their seats to face each other.

"Is it just me or was that the most impressive military demonstration you have ever seen?" Cyrus asked.

"That new machine was magnificent. The target androids were not pushovers. Sure, the defenses were weak, but it mauled them and the defenders had greater numbers. I doubt those units can even be repaired. They just added to the field of scraps," Moon said.

"After seeing the test, it seems like a graveyard," Angel said. "That unit from the river must be state of the art. It seemed to have unlimited power. How did we all of a sudden make a breakthrough like that?"

"Guys, I know I have been pushing to improve our defenses, but this almost seems too good. We need peacekeepers to act as deterrents for more attacks. Is this overkill?" Cyrus asked. "Are we preparing for war or for peacekeeping?"

"Sir, history has shown us that the best deterrent is an unforgiving potent offense. If we can complement our current androids and guard units with these new androids, then the south will give anyone pause before messing with us again," Moon said.

"Agreed. Our enemy's currency is hate, not love. Peace sells, but who is buying?" Angel added.

"I agree with that in principle, but this is a serious escalation not to mention investment. There is still hope that the Administration will come around and work with us. That hope might evaporate if they see our tech rivaling or exceeding federal forces." Cyrus paused. "If we can get a bargain reached then I am not hard set on still building our own defense force. The task force was meant to drive change and not more conflict."

"Sir, with all due respect, after the incident in St. Louis yesterday and the growing evidence that the Bush Park massacre was not jihadi-based, I would be very hesitant to do anything other than prepare for the worst. They almost assassinated you and we aren't even sure who 'they' are yet," Angel said.

"Agreed. While I haven't been in on all the politics, I think our first priority is to defend the Southern District. It might be very dangerous to not prepare for the worst while we all hope for the best," Moon said.

Cyrus stared out the window of the SUV and then turned back to the men. "The way I see it, we can either play it cautious or go all in. I have been struggling with this for a while. All my political advisors tell me to make a lot of noise and take little action. They would hate what we just saw. The computers tell me to talk softly and carry a big stick." Cyrus paused. "We need to be very careful. I would like us to strategize some more with the state governors over the next couple of weeks on the defense force, as well as the policy announcements we talked about. I suppose we are vulnerable until we know who is behind these attacks, including the potential that our political enemies are also our military enemies. I am also very interested in dissolving the deudor system entirely in the south if they push us on it. I am fed up with their bullshit about not being fair. At some point we cannot accept federal law forced upon us if it goes against our core beliefs. At some point we must make a stand. The escalation in violence seems to demand a new tactic. If we keep responding the same way, then shame on us for expecting different results. I am giving a major speech in a couple of days. I think it's time to play hardball. I am less certain about dictating that federal forces withdraw from the south, but I won't rule it out yet. Perhaps I need to make a lot of noise and carry a big stick. I appreciate your honesty in this discussion. I think you are going to be very busy."

Anna

nna, Judith, and their android assistant walked slowly like tourists down Trump Drive in downtown Houston. They strolled by high-end restaurants and hotels that catered to the upper class that traveled to Houston for work, sports, or theatre downtown. Anna was dressed conservatively with heels and she even had her hair and nails done professionally. She was scared, but that was being muted by the new confidence in feeling for the first time like an empowered free beautiful young woman. Judith was wearing a casual business outfit that still showed off her beauty. It was forest green with gold accents and showed off her muscular, yet ample figure. Each day Anna kept seeing more beauty in Judith and reflected at how much younger she was in real life than the avatar she had met online. Anna very much looked up to her.

They reached their destination, the Lone Star Café. Judith had told Anna they were to meet someone of importance but that it was a big surprise. The front of the restaurant and bar was one of the few unapologetic country-themed buildings in the area. It had a reputation for a good bar-b-que and discrete service. They turned to go in and heard a chime as they passed into the reception area. The hostess saw them and walked over with a smile.

"Good evening and welcome to the Lone Star. I'm sorry but your android will need to wait in our service section. We have a strict policy against them in the restaurant. I hope that is not an issue," she said with a smile. Her outfit was so tight that Anna couldn't tell if it was fabric or body paint.

"That will be fine," Judith said with a friendly grin. She nodded to the android who turned to the left and stood by four other units.

"Do you have a reservation?" The hostess asked Judith.

"Yes, we are here to meet Mr. Adam West," Judith said with a wink.

"Of course, we have your table ready. Please follow me," the hostess said, and turned into the restaurant. Both Anna and Judith followed.

The smell in the restaurant was unlike anything Anna had ever experienced. The succulent sweet and spicy smells from the bar-b-que meat was so strong that Anna had trouble breathing for a few steps. She had been so nervous earlier and now all she could think about was eating. She quickly regained herself by the time they reached their booth. It was along the side in the darker part of the restaurant giving more privacy than the tables in the middle area.

Every step of this adventure kept bringing new firsts for Anna. They sat at the booth and ordered water with lemon for Anna and red wine for Judith. The walls were lined with western memorabilia and the occasional mounted animal head. Anna was reminded for a moment of her cowboy and smiled.

He came from the front being escorted by the hostess and a security guard. Once they were close to Anna's booth, the guard stopped and waited against the wall a few meters away but was watching them coldly and carefully without any animation. Anna saw a similar looking man near the entrance to the seating area. Both men were huge and their suit jackets looked almost ready to burst.

"Hello ladies, nice to meet you. My name is Angel Vega." Angel sat at the booth that now had Judith in the middle.

"It is a pleasure to meet you Mr. Vega. I greatly appreciate the opportunity. My name is Judith Strong and this is Ms. Anna Lee." Judith extended her hand to shake Angel's. Anna did not follow politics but even she knew of Angel and was instantly back to being very nervous.

"The pleasure is all mine. Please, call me Angel." Angel shook Judith's hand and Anna saw them make eye contact for a little longer than a standard introduction. Judith was leaning forward and obviously a fan. She gave a flick to her hair which cleared one of her bare shoulders. Angel then turned to look at Anna.

"Hello Anna. I hear you recently escaped your deudor bonds.

Congratulations. You are welcome in the Southern District. No-one here is straddled with debt simply for needing help being born," Angel said.

"Thank you, sir. I am truly blessed to be here and grateful to Judith for helping me," Anna said with a nervous smile and looked at Judith.

"I'm sure it has been a hard road for you," Angel said to Anna; she saw sincerity in his eyes. Angel then turned to Judith. "While I am a supporter of helping Americans unjustly subjected to servitude, I don't normally welcome them in person. There is quite a bit of chaos keeping us busy these days; however, I heard you have information and a proposal for me that you said you will only share with me in person so I made an exception." The look in Angel's eyes made it clear that Judith better have something pretty good for him. Angel noticed the waiter closing in on them. "But first, we should order. I'm starving."

They ordered food and Angel asked Anna some about the orphanage in New York and how she ended up looking for help. Anna talked about the Riveras, leaving out some of the salty details. After the food arrived, the conversation turned back to Judith.

"Angel, I have been helping people escape from the Eastern District for about three years now," Judith began. "In doing so, we have built up a crude, but effective network to identify opportunities like Anna and help them reach safety and to have a fresh start. Some of the connections we have set up are within the Eastern District police system itself. Not all of them agree with the laws there as some have relatives who ended up as deudors. These contacts have told us that there are new policies being written that will go into effect in the coming weeks. These new policies will make it very difficult for us to help people unless we also adapt. We have reached a point where we need your help if we are to carry out our work." Judith paused for a moment and Anna, for the first time, saw a hint of pain in Judith. "I have enough contacts in the Southern District to know you are sympathetic to our cause and you, of course, have the Governor's ear. The help we need would be behind the scenes and would help us safeguard the volunteers. We would adapt from a one-at-a-time approach to something closer to train loads at any time being freed. I have some specific plans I would like to show you soon if possible, in more private settings." Anna thought she saw a sparkle in Judith's eyes.

Angel had been eating while listening intently. He was using the time to chew now to think about what Judith had said. "Ok, you have piqued my interest. Everything is going crazy these days so it can't be right away. I may only have time after hours if that works for you."

"That would be perfect," Judith replied with a smile. "I am happy to meet you anywhere, anytime."

"Great. I will have my people call you later with when and where. It might even be at my house as I have been taking work home most nights. We should let you know soon," Angel said with a smile and then turned to Anna. "Darlin' you have hardly touched your food. First time having brisket?"

"Yes sir, but I do like it. To be honest, I am still trying to soak all of this in," Anna replied.

"Very understandable. I can only imagine what it is like," Angel replied. "We have a car outside ready to take you to one of our rehabilitation centers. Your new life is about to begin." Angel held up his glass and they toasted Anna's new freedom.

Naya

"**G**ood afternoon," Naya began. "I see everyone is here. My call with Dana Berry from the Southern District is in just a minute. I will have all of you hidden on the call so I can hear you, but she won't know you are on." She had her staff of six on conference hologram call. Naya was making the call from her office in the West Wing as she wanted Dana to see her there to give it a more official feel. "This will really help us prepare to talk to our friends in the media immediately afterwards. Unless this conversation goes in a direction we did not predict, I want you all ready to go. Again, if she agrees we use the nice approach and if she rejects us then we play hard ball until they agree later."

"Ma'am, I think we are all ready. We should be talking to all the major networks and shows within minutes," said Jorge Jones, one of Naya's staff members. "Should we stay on this connection after the call is over?"

"Yes, I am guessing it will be brief. Any other questions?" Naya asked.

"Do you think we are offering too much?" Asked Luc Feri, Naya's chief of staff. "I think our opening bid could be stronger and we could compromise into what we are offering today."

"The President wants a deal quickly. I agree it's a risk if they say no," Naya replied. "We are playing with the cards we have been dealt. Any other questions?" Naya waited briefly and heard no other inputs. "Ok then. Ariella, please contact Dana Berry and put all others on mute and blind to Dana. You may leave them live to me."

"As you command," Ariella replied. "Connecting to Dana Berry now." A few seconds went by and then the center display went live to a video feed of the freckled red-headed Dana Berry, communications specialist for the Southern District. She was wearing a white business suit, low cut white shirt, and a golden necklace intertwined with chains of ruby that matched her hair.

"Good afternoon Naya, how have you been?" Dana asked.

"I've been better. All this violence is sickening. I can't imagine how you and the southern leadership must feel. I want you to know how much we hope this gets turned around fast," Naya said.

"You never were good at saying sorry," Dana replied with a slight smirk that quickly went away. "I'm not the one for whom you need to sympathize. That would be the victims of the Bush Park massacre and American Pride Parade tragedy. The victims of the latter of course were shot by your federal forces. I am sure you did not call to share your hopes with me. To what do I owe the pleasure of this call?"

"You are right of course. I wanted us to work together to bring the tone down across the nation. There are a lot of scared and angry people. They need to see steady leadership from all the districts and the Administration. We want to work with you to come up with a common narrative for the public to restore calm. Will you work with us?" Naya asked.

"That of course depends. I've never known you to work to help us or, for that matter, anyone but yourself," Dana said.

"What a bitch," Luc Feri said, making Naya smirk. His hologram was to the right of Dana's. "Go for the throat."

"Let it ride, she is entitled to be frustrated. The two of you have a rocky past," Jorge added. His hologram was to the left of Dana's. "Give it a shot."

"You are always trying to be at least two steps ahead so I am sure you have a couple options for me." Dana continued. "It still feels like yesterday that I was stuck in DC. What did you have in mind?"

"Very well, we can get straight to it," Naya began. "There are many aspects to the St. Louis incident that are controversial and will stir up anger. There are also many aspects that are straight up reporting that still give a fair summary, but stop short of stoking further aggression."

"Ok. Depends what you want to say and not say," Dana said.

"See, she is open to reason," Jorge said to Naya.

"Bullshit, she is setting you up. She will say no to whatever you say next," Luc added.

"No lies, no spin, just the cold hard facts," Naya started. "First we express via all communication options the need for calm and, if protesting, to keep it peaceful. As needed, cities should enforce a curfew. We discuss who was at the parade and who was arrested. We only answer questions about who was injured and don't focus on the number of people hurt from either side as it's not a fair metric of the event. Together we can send a powerful message by speaking consistently and maybe inspire others to also work together, including our bosses." Naya paused for a moment. "What do you think?"

"Let me get this straight. You literally parade our citizens who have pled innocent to charges in a federal pride parade in chains and then shoot some of them, as well as other innocent Southern District citizens in the crowd, and now want us to leave out all the facts that show the federal forces are guilty of murder?!" Dana said, with her eyes now burning. "Hell no! Not only do I not agree, but the Administration needs to get its act together. You need to take a hard look at what happened and change course before you hurt even more people. We will keep talking about the casualties, the people your troops massacred. In fact, I want you to send the highest ranking official to debate us on the Party of One show tomorrow night, unless you've lost your balls."

"Ugh. Might as well end it now," Jorge said to Naya.

"Told ya," Luc said. "Kick her in the nuts."

"Dana, I had hoped our time spent together in the past would have helped us bridge the divide that is growing in our country. Too much is at stake to waste time posturing. Please consider further my request and contact me if you change your mind. I understand and respect your frustration. If I had the power to help more, I would. Thank you for your time." Naya concluded and Ariella disconnected Dana.

"Well, that went terrible," Jorge said. "Maybe we can call her back tomorrow? Giving her time to cool down might get a better answer."

"We know where Dana stands, in our way," Luc added.

"At least we got a clear answer. I can tell she is digging in," Naya said, with a spark in her eyes. No-one ever talked to Naya the way Dana just did, but it had been worth it. They needed to have a recording to show they had tried.

"Do we need to wait before contacting the networks and shows?" Jorge asked.

"Ariella, please transmit to the team the information we found on the three militiamen who have been accused or convicted of violent crimes in the past," Naya started. "Also share with them the video we compiled showing the Joplin militia at the parade holding guns and the mob of southern sympathizers. Everyone, we need to emphasize that the people who were arrested are traitors against our country and that a militia group came to free them using force."

"What about the idea of a debate on Party of One?" Jorge asked. "Lately, that show's ratings have set records."

"I don't think that is a good idea. In fact, that show is a source of stress that is adding pressure to the situation. It compromises the uniformity of our message to the people. I think we need to consider taking it off the air permanently," Naya replied.

"Maybe taking her up on the offer could help us do that," Luc said.

Naya paused for a moment thinking to herself. "Everyone, we will flood the media with our message and have every politician repeating it on every microphone they can find. The truth is what people hear and believe. If they hear it enough, they will believe it."

Cyrus

"Ladies and gentlemen, the Governor of the Southern District!"
Announced the Sergeant at Arms. She stepped aside and Governor Cyrus Young walked into the District State House assembly room in Houston. Cyrus was immediately met with vigorous applause from the roughly two hundred people gathered for his speech. He made his way from the entrance to the front, while stopping often to shake hands as everyone passionately showed their support. Southern state governors, U.S. Senators and Representatives, and a variety of other power players were all on their feet shouting and fired up unlike any speech this house had ever witnessed. The only people who were standing but showing no emotion were the District Judges, although they did have choice seating right at the front before the elevated speaking platform. The only people not standing at all were the handful of Democrats and Socialists in elected positions in the Southern District. Finally, Cyrus made it to the front and stood at the speaker's podium.

"Ladies, gentlemen, and honorable Democratic and Socialist representatives, it is an honor to be speaking to you today," Cyrus began with a smile. The few Democrats and Socialists stood defiantly and walked out making the best effort at the show of disrespect. Three small aerial drones were quietly and slowly maneuvering to capture the speech in 3D which was being broadcast around the country. As the Democrats and Socialists left, the Republicans laughed and clapped thoroughly pleased at the weak show.

"While it is always an honor to speak to you, it is with a heavy heart tonight. We have suffered great injustice and pain over the last few weeks. The recent bloodshed has hit our district hard. Each tragedy has been uniquely horrific, yet similar in their fundamental causes. None of them have seen justice prevail, nor have we been provided security to stop future attacks. In reality, we have been subjected to violence without cause for years, and my friends we have reached a tipping point. After extreme patience in hoping the federal government would find peace, we are still in effect in a state of war. Our patience has reached its limit. One reason I need to speak to you tonight is that we are going to take our fate into our own hands. Working with the other district leaders, I have given the order to create a Southern District Defense Force. We will be uniting all the southern State Guards and State National Guards to work hand-in-hand with the Southern Bureau of Investigation to safeguard our cities, our institutions, and most importantly our children. We do not take this action lightly. We have exercised this option as a last resort. Our faith has not been rewarded and in fact the Thorne Administration has used it as a weapon against us. Sadly, we are taking many steps at this time because we have evidence that forces from the federal government may have been involved in the attacks on southern citizens and this would be a sin we cannot forgive!" The crowd all stood, except for the judges, and cheered and clapped for over a minute. Some yelled angrily, venting at Thorne. The drones transitioned from one leader to another in the crowd to show how all of the key state Governors and U.S. Senators were showing support for the mortal directive.

"Tonight, we have a special guest from the great city of Houston. Her name is Sara Chamberlain." Cyrus, the audience, and the cameras all turned to see her in the side balcony as she stood so everyone could see her. "Sara's family was among the casualties in the Bush Park massacre. Her young son Jon was killed. I am sure the images of Sara holding Jon that were in the news still haunt you all as they do me. Please join me in applauding Sara and her family." Again, the crowd stood and the applause went on for over a minute. It was all Sara could do to not cry. She was holding a teddy bear from her store and squeezing Ben's hand to the point he was in real pain. Cyrus' wife Sally and oldest son Marcus were on the other side of Sara looking at her compassionately. "Sara not only exemplifies the loss we have endured, but also the strength and power that we can return on those who would do us harm. Her defiance towards those who would excuse the murderers and blame the victims, or look to take away constitutional rights, is inspiring to me and I am sure to you as well. Sara, our prayers go to you and yours and it is unquestionable that Jon is in heaven looking at us right now smiling. Sara's example has given us the strength to announce that effective immediately the Southern District will begin to terminate commerce with both the Eastern and Western Districts until the federal government ceases all obstructions to bringing justice for the crimes committed in Houston and St. Louis, including releasing all Southern District political prisoners." The crowd again stood and cheered as if hearing the best news of their lives.

"There is another threat that is as serious and is no less than a systematic attack on our way of life. It seems now to be probable that the Thorne Administration will be pursuing legislation with the Democratic and Socialist supermajority in Congress to nationalize the deudor system. If they follow through on what they have threatened, these new regulations would be both injurious and offensive to the south." Boos were heard for a few seconds and Cyrus let them pass nodding his head. "Until now, I have had an abiding faith that any law which violates our constitutional rights, to such an extreme as this, would be defeated in Congress. However, the Democratic and Socialist Parties are united in this direction and are already laying out the process to push it through without debate. It appears this will be their only meaningful response to the undeniably unrelated attacks on southern citizens. If the federal government enforced a dramatic increase in those saddled with the burden of the deudor system in states that do not want to participate, you will have presented to you the question of whether you will permit the federal government to pass into the hands of bureaucrats the denial of your rights that originally was intended only for the bankrupt and convicted criminals. I will state my own position to be that such a result would be a species of revolution by which the purposes of the government would be destroyed." The crowd again roared to its feet with many showing their anger at the direction the country was going. Cyrus' efforts to rile them up was working better than he expected, giving him more and more confidence as he continued.

"Should the Thorne Administration choose this path forward, I should deem it our duty to provide for our safety outside of a Union with those who have already shown the will and have acquired the power to deprive you of your birthright. When the Thorne Administration announces the absolute need to rule us absolutely, they either knowingly or unwittingly are nullifying their authority as a federal government. The Democratic and Socialist vision to subject unprecedented numbers of Southern District citizens against our wishes to the deudor system as an amendment to the Constitution is a path we cannot follow if we still claim to be a nation of free people, of just people, and to be a nation where the government is granted its limited power from the people. Of course, we know the Democrats have done this before, there is no reason to think they would not do it again." Again, the crowd roared to life, this time for almost two minutes with some random chants mixed in. Even one of the district justices pumped her fist into the air.

"It requires but a cursory examination of the Constitution of the United States and an elementary knowledge of its history, and of the motives of the men who formed it, to see how utterly fallacious it is to ascribe to them the purpose of interfering with the domestic institutions of the Southern District. I hope it is not too late. We will continue to talk to the Administration to avoid outright secession, but at this moment I cannot rule it out and we are making plans and preparations. While they continue to beat the drums of war, we hope they will turn to the better angels of their nature. If our hopes and prayers fall short, then we shall then bear to the federal government the relation our colonial grandfathers did to the British crown and, if we are worthy of our lineage, we will in that event redeem our rights even if it be through the process of secession!" Again, the crowd stood, yelled, and showed unequaled anger and support. All of the key leaders in the room had a general idea of what was going to be shared in the speech so only a few of the guests were in shock.

"To be clear, I hold separation from the Union by the Southern District to be the last remedy, the final alternative. I consider the disruption of the Union as a great, though not the greatest, calamity. I would cling tenaciously to our constitutional government, seeing as I do in the fraternal union of equal states and districts the benefit to all and the fulfillment of that high destiny which our grandfathers hoped for and left it for their sons to attain. I love the flag of my country with even more than a filial affection. For many of the best years of my life I have followed that flag and upheld it on foreign wars where if I had fallen it might have been claimed as my winding-sheet. When I have seen it surrounded by the flags of foreign countries, the pulsations of my heart have beat quicker with every breeze which displayed its honored stripes and brilliant constellation. I have looked with veneration on those stripes as recording the original size of our political family and with pride upon that constellation as marking the family's growth. I glory in the position which each southern state star holds in the group but sooner than see its luster dimmed, sooner than see it degraded from its present equality, would tear it from its place if forced to choose between our current union and upholding our most sacred of principles. We fear not the ghosts of war!" Years later, historians would look back and call this the greatest speech that Cyrus ever delivered.

Corban

"That son of a bitch!" Corban yelled. He was sitting next to General Mori Tortan in Corban's office having just watched Cyrus's address. "Is he trying to tear the country apart?"

"That was not a speech trying to make peace. Those were fighting words and the audience ate it up," Mori said. "Maybe he thinks Thorne is bluffing."

"We need to up our intelligence game. I knew the defense force and preparations for a boycott were going to be announced. What was that crazy talk about us being responsible for the attacks? Why is he drawing a red line for the deudor reforms?" Corban paused, rubbing his forehead with both hands. "Ariella, show us the locations of the largest twenty southern guard units, either national or state."

"As you command," Ariella replied. Within two seconds the video in front of them switched from a silent display of the congratulatory aftermath in the Southern District State House to a map of the Southern District. "Would you like to see the home locations for the largest units or their present locations?"

"Please show current locations but show us which ones are not in their home station," Corban said.

"Also, show us which have transitioned to active duty," Mori added.

The display showed an array of red circles in an arc starting with El Paso, Texas and ending at Raleigh, North Carolina. The arc included twelve southern units all close to the northern border of the Southern District. The other eight major units then showed at major cities like Houston and Atlanta.

"All of these units, as well as every other unit from a city with more than 100,000 residents, has been called up. None have fully mobilized yet.

Half of the units displayed have been deployed away from their permanent duty station and along the Southern District border," Ariella reported. Corban and Mori both studied the map. Despite their very different roles and backgrounds, it was clear to both what appeared to be in work down south.

"Ariella, please add to the map the locations of the last ten terrorist attacks," Cyrus said.

The map silently brought up the locations one at a time going west to east.

"The deployments are not very consistent with the attack locations. They have more troops near the district border, yet all of the acts of violence have been far inside the border," Mori said. "Ariella, analyze the deployment of all Southern District guard units and tell us what you think the objectives would be for a pattern like we see here."

"Based on the activity of the last three days, it would appear it is a defensive posture against an invading force from entering the Southern District. The centralization of large numbers of personnel at military bases, the weaponry and androids that are inherent to these units, and the apparent preparations for large-scale training is consistent with a prolonged resistance," Ariella said.

"If you were asked to recommend preparations to safeguard cities, what would you do?" Corban asked Ariella.

"I would recommend large numbers of human troops scattered at soft targets at as many locations as possible. This would serve as a deterrent, plus make the vast majority of the citizens feel safe. There would be an emphasis on cities previously attacked and I would recommend additional scanning equipment looking for explosives or other large-scale weapons," Ariella answered.

"The talk of reacting to the attacks has been a smokescreen," Mori said. "They want to keep us out."

"We need to move quickly. This is unacceptable. We need to do something to show them this is a lost cause and far more trouble than it is worth," Corban said, studying the map. "Mori, what do you suggest?"

"It's not too late to sway public opinion. We looked pretty bad after St. Louis, but they barely looked better. I have some friends that are high up in some of the southern guard units. I will see what I can find out, may sow some seeds of discontent, but we need a headline-grabbing event that even southern media puppets will not be able to ignore," Mori said.

"Good, make those calls," Corban said, looking at the map. "There!" Corban pointed. "I think we can do it there, in Columbia, Missouri. Ariella, zoom in on Missouri and display what units are in Columbia." Ariella zoomed in. It showed forces from all over Missouri, both ground and air forces, joining up in Columbia. "There is a protest planned in Columbia at the University of Missouri next Saturday. It is a protest against the Southern District. Decades ago, Missouri was barely made a southern state and Columbia is our strongest foothold in the state. The state is divided pretty evenly. Looks like they are forming one of their satellite stations there to try to secure it."

"Ariella, do you know why the Southern District Defense Force is meeting there?" Mori asked.

"There are three major robotics plants in central Missouri fed by the engineering schools in the area. Two of them produce military equipment and the third produces construction equipment. It could be to secure that strategic infrastructure," Ariella hypothesized.

"That's it then." Corban's eyes had a spark of excitement and he leaned forward as he stared at the screen. "We need to send units to Columbia to protect the protest. We send an overwhelming show of force. Dump all the Kansas, Illinois, and Iowa units there if you have to. I want all the Missouri guard members showing up for duty to see us and go home."

"Sir, I caution you that having two potentially rival military units in close range has caused a lot of problems in the past. Wars have started that way," Mori said, staring at Corban trying to see if he understood the risk.

"Mori, the bigger risk is if we let them build up and dig in, or worse yet, if they get strong and overly confident. We need to make a big display now or end up in a bigger conflict later. You should also make your calls to your buddies down there; I have some people I can call as well. I'll talk to Naya, that weasel can spin anything." Corban said.

"Yes sir." Mori stood up. "I'll contact you after the plans firm up."

"Thank you General. Let me know if you need anything," Corban said.

Mori nodded and left the room.

Samson

"**Y**ou say it's called a Titan?" Samson Gamble asked. Samson was part of a group of officers visiting a Southern District robotics production plant. Currently, they were touring the R&D division. Samson and Colonel Samantha Payne were representing the Roughriders. They had already seen the production lines producing human-sized standard issue fighting androids. They also had seen a line upgrading older model androids and aerial drones. The three robotics plants near Columbia, Missouri turned out roughly half of the AI fighting machines at the disposal of the Southern District.

"Yes sir," the plant manager answered. "It's still missing two of its four arms and of course the rocket launchers. We have about another week left before we put it together, if we don't have any more setbacks. It will be the largest android fighting machine in history."

"It's too big a target. The enemy could hit it without aiming," Colonel Payne said.

"We definitely had to factor in a defensive strategy when designing it. We thought about making the armor thicker, but that would only slow the inevitable. We instead added redundancy in the control and fire systems," the manager smiled. "And we made them faster than a cheetah. They will drain your energy supplies when recharging, but nothing that can compete with the power they can unleash."

"Awesome. You just need to give them a target and get out of the way," Samson said, as he walked through the shadow of the Titan.

The group finished looking at the Titan development and followed the catwalk above the high bay and passed through a visitor's room with displays along the ceiling. They did not stop for the usual civilian VIP tourist routine and, instead, passed single file through a door and a narrow hallway which opened up to another catwalk over a new high bay. The area was partitioned into sections by titanium bars. Samson thought it looked like an old school prison cell block.

"Ladies and gentlemen, welcome to the Zoo. Here we have state of the art machines that look, sound, and act like common animals in nature. Some are for surveillance; some are for attack. We can deploy the surveillance units into wilderness areas indefinitely thanks to solar panels that can be exposed as needed. They are designed to be our eyes and ears for border patrol," the manager said.

"Why go through all that trouble? Why not just use aerial drones?" Samson asked.

"Carrina, please display the video of a standard surveillance drone as seen when using modern intelligence sensor sweep packages," the manager requested.

"As you command," Carrina replied. On the display showed the video of a tree line of a large forest.

"As you can see here, we are using a common AI package to scan the forest," the manager said as the video continued. The video then zoomed into a small set of trees to show a small drone flying overhead looking back at them. "As you can see, the software and sensor package used by modern militaries was able to filter out the drone even from this distance." The manager paused as the video showed two more drones and two androids. "But what you did not see was the raccoon and the deer developed in this shop also watching the fictional force moving in. The software cannot stop every time it sees a rabbit or squirrel or a bird. We can observe anyone coming or going with almost no way for them to know we can see them."

The video stopped and the tour group looked down into the Zoo. They saw a variety of common animals that could be used in a variety of terrains. It would have looked like a Zoo of sorts, except for the back wall that had several animals in pieces or with covers removed allowing work by the technicians. Samson looked at the Eagle's Nest, a holding area for aerial machines in the back right upper corner, and would have sworn one of the birds was staring at him. The group finished looking at the Zoo and walked across the catwalk again to an intermediate room and then to a testing area.

"Ladies and gentlemen, we are on the last stop on our tour, but I will say it is my favorite room. I like to save the best for last. Not all of our machines in the Zoo are for surveillance. What you are about to see would give pause to any enemy thinking to threaten us. We had marketed it to the US Army, but they thought it impractical and unlikely to work. Well, I am happy we proved them wrong. We call them the Lobos." The manager had an expression that Samson recognized as part pride and part blood lust. "Carrina, release a test subject for a demonstration with unit number sixty-six."

As the demonstration ensued, Samson actually got a little sick to his stomach. The test subject was an adult bull that charged into one of the cells obviously in a feisty mood. Samson hoped he would never cross a Lobo and realized the name they picked if anything was too vanilla. In less than a minute, the bull was reduced to pieces and the area looked like a murder scene. The Lobo was a real-life monster.

Mori

The Marine Corps Falcon Class Turbocraft veered hard to starboard and dropped from a cruising altitude of seven kilometers to fifteen hundred meters. All of the passengers leaned into the maneuver, none of them a bit concerned. General Mori Tortan stared out the window. Having traveled in from East St. Louis, the small group of officers were scouting out the perimeter of Columbia, Missouri.

"Stay at this altitude and do a large sweep around the city," Mori said.

"As you command," Ariella replied.

"Commander Grant, what is that area over there?" Mori asked one of the officers who had an interactive map pulled on a tablet. Mori lifted his binoculars up to get a better view.

"It's a medical facility set up to support the University hospitals. They outgrew the campus close to downtown," the young officer answered.

The automatic pilot started the loop around the city. They were on the east side traveling counterclockwise. They were high enough to be hard to see from the ground, but low enough to see the terrain and major facilities.

"Sir, until we reach the northwest quadrant it will be mostly residential living facilities and some random civilian constructions," Commander Grant added.

"What is that over there? Those tall buildings?" Mori asked.

"Housing complexes," Grant replied.

"Looks like a lot of heavy vehicles there," Mori said. He lowered the binoculars. "It could be they have troops settling in there."

"Yes sir, they are fairly old units so it is likely they were not full or possibly not used at all," Grant said.

"They supposedly are calling up all five Missouri brigades and bringing them here," Mori said. "The housing complexes we just passed look big enough to hold one if they clear out the civilians. Lieutenant Jeffreys, please submit an intelligence mission request to scout his area. We need to know about anything that might be troop settlements or civilians being cleared out. Include monitoring of open transmissions."

"Yes sir," answered Jeffreys, who immediately began to submit the order on his tablet.

The Turbocraft had been traveling north on the east side of the city and began to curl west as it continued the counterclockwise sweep of Columbia. In the distance they saw a large abandoned quarry except for some fresh activity on the northwest corner.

"That quarry, what do you see happening over there?" All four officers tried to look out the port side windows to get a better view but no-one answered quickly. "Ariella, take us closer in for a better look." The craft creeped to starboard to take them close to the quarry and a display at the front of the Turbocraft showed video footage. "Ariella, zoom in. I want to see what that is crawling around in the quarry."

"Looks like construction droids building…something," Lieutenant Jeffreys said.

"They are fortifying it," Mori said. "Why on Earth would they need to fortify a quarry?"

"Maybe they are moving troops in there," Jeffreys suggested.

"With so much campus housing and old apartment complexes, it seems unlikely. This town is past its prime. University attendance has been dropping for years," Grant added.

"And it's uncovered. I bet this is for a large number of all-terrain vehicles," Mori said. "Jeffreys, add to the intelligence order to keep a close eye on the quarry."

They continued to scout around the perimeter city, finally reaching the southern boundary of Columbia. The preplanned route had them pass between the industrial complex and the Columbia Regional Airport.

"There they are," Mori said. "Those are some of the largest android manufacturing plants in the country. We think that is why they are centralizing here."

"And there is the airport sir. Looks very active. Several large aircraft… and it looks like more than a squadron of Predators," Grant added.

"Ariella, display a visual of the airport," Mori said, and Ariella provided a display showing that the regional airport looked like a military airwing. "Damn. You are right. I think we have seen enough. Ariella, we can head back to St. Louis now," Mori said, and started to rub his chin reflecting on what they had seen.

"Gentlemen, I think that confirms Columbia is going to be a dicey mission. The protest we are going in to monitor will have a potentially hostile ring of well-armed resistance that will not want us to move in," Mori said.

"Sir, do we go ahead and deploy? If so, any special instructions given what we have seen?" Grant asked. "It seems somewhat predictable what the intelligence reports will tell us. They are digging in."

"You are right. We will use that intel to make a best effort to avoid direct contact. I want to make it clear to all units that we will not fire first no matter what. Bringing all these toys this close together with clear division throughout the country will make it critical to not instigate or provoke them," Mori said, pausing for a couple of seconds. "But the answer is yes, the task force will do its duty. We have our orders. Set up a circle around the city and prepare to have the security forces at the protest. We will not be intimidated; we will be doing the intimidating. If our units do encounter hostiles, tell them to use overwhelming force to quickly eliminate any and all threats. We won't start a conflict, but we will finish it."

Lucilla

Lucilla Swift held her badge up as she walked through the security checkpoint. The security android nodded and she followed the line of military officers down the hall towards the elevators. Lucilla had been elected the new leader of the Blood Ravens and was representing her militia at a council preparing for the Southern District Defense Force deployment. She rode the elevator up with several other officers and they exited on the top floor. It was her first time at the Missouri National Guard Headquarters in Jefferson City, Missouri. She again followed the crowd through the double door entrance to a large conference room. It had an enormous long cylindrical table in the center and a projection screen wall at the other end. Lucilla sat in one of the chairs in the back near the entrance. She picked a seat close enough to make a quick exit if she changed her mind about being there.

"Captain Swift?" Lucilla turned around to see who was talking to her. It was a thin man who was very bald and a smile that really didn't say he was happy.

"Yes sir." Lucilla stood and looked at the man.

"Young lady, I just wanted to say how sorry I was to hear what happened to your father. I knew him well when I was a young man." His smile lessened and Lucilla recognized the showing was real sorrow. "My name is Joe Johnston. I knew Jackson very well when I was much younger. He was an honorable man. I came out of retirement because of what happened. You may not hear it but many of the leaders here today knew and respected him very much." Joe paused briefly. "I am very sorry for your loss and I know he would be so proud of you being here representing the Blood Ravens."

Lucilla was unsure what to say. She had not expected to be recognized at all. She looked at Joe's rank and he was a Lieutenant General for the Missouri National Guard.

"Thank you, sir. I appreciate your kind words. I hope we can work to keep it from happening to anyone else," Lucilla replied.

Joe bowed to Lucilla and then walked to sit near the head of the long table. Lucilla sat back in her chair. There were some talking in the room but, in general, most found a chair and sat with little conversation. The room quickly filled and some were standing in the back. The uniforms of the National Guardsman matched, those of the State Guard matched, and the militias all had tailored eccentric twists showing the diversity of the organization.

"Attention!" A man behind Lucilla shouted. Everyone started to stand, including Lucilla, and all talk ceased. A muscular man with a scar on the right side of his face slowly walked in and went to the head of the table.

"At ease," the man said before sitting. Everyone else in the room also sat down. "Good morning everyone, thank you for being here. Many of you had to travel and uproot your lives. Know now it is truly appreciated. I am General Moon Tzu, commanding officer of the Southern District Defense Force. Carrina, please bring up the map."

"As you command," Carrina replied. The room lights dimmed, and a map of Missouri displayed on the screen.

"By now, you all know that the left-wing activists are organizing a protest against the Southern District at the University of Missouri. You probably have also heard by now that the Thorne Administration has asked Governor Young to stand down the Defense Force and to step aside so that federal forces can provide security for the protest. The Governor has declined and, in fact, has rallied all of the Missouri guard units to the Columbia area." Moon paused. "There is unfortunately a force coming that does not want us here. They do not recognize our sovereignty or God-given rights to protect ourselves. There is definitely a chance that conflict will arise with so many forces in the same place. Let us all hope it does not come to that but, make no mistake, we are preparing for it. Also, let it not be lost on you that whoever carried out the attack in Houston is still at large. It is going to be a very long weekend." Moon paused again. "Carrina, display the troop deployment assignments."

The three-dimensional display zoomed into central Missouri and unit symbols displayed in various locations around Columbia. The deployment was a rough circle just outside the city limits plus two units to the south near the Columbia Regional Airport.

"As you can see, the 110th Brigade and 70th Troop Command, all from Missouri, will soon be in position around the Columbia area. In addition, the 35th Aviation Brigade is setting up shop at the local regional airport. The mission planning started out as centralizing the forces using available facilities so we could start to strategically reach out to the rest of Missouri. The objective was to protect the state from further attacks and limit the influx of potential hostiles." Moon paused. "But now, we have reports that no less than eight brigades from Illinois, Kansas, and Iowa are moving in slowly with the goal of being in place before the protest. As you can see by the animation Carrina is showing you, they will be moving in right on top of us. Our objective for the time being is to politely keep the feds from moving in." The map showed arrows and troop movements with red for the Southern District and blue for the forces under direction from Washington D.C., a sight not seen on a live map in America in over two hundred years.

"I know many of you are concerned and have questions about the plan so we will jump right in." Moon continued and the display highlighted each element as he described them. "We are going to position ourselves to shield the city and key facilities, but we need to remember our primary objective is to protect our citizens from threats. We have no indications that the federal forces are coming in here looking to hurt us. It seems like the Governor has shamed them into finally providing protection; however, we are not fools and will not be pushed around. This is a republic. Missouri is a proud state. The federal government does not have the right to come here and force you to lay down your arms. With that in mind, all units will have specific orders on where to deploy and how to react to a variety of incidents. If the shit hits the fan, we need to react in a disciplined and consistent manner. We have assigned each unit, guard and militia, to key locations throughout Columbia and its neighboring cities. We will have one full brigade at the industrial area, specifically the robotics production plants. We also will have some of the local groups scouting around the area on the lookout for threats of any kind. I will be staying in touch with the feds hoping that good communication will keep accidents from happening. If anything does happen, I predict it will be because someone did not follow orders. Maintaining discipline in your units is of the utmost importance. We will not draw first blood unless we see our citizens at risk. Is that clear?"

"Yes sir," the group said.

"Is that clear?!" Moon said louder.

"Yes sir!" The group answered.

"Again, discipline is paramount to our success. If something goes down, we expect it to be brief and contained but, make no mistake, if there is conflict then whoever was foolish enough to take us on will lose. And they will lose badly. We won't parade them around, but we will castigate them so badly they will never try it again. We considered some defense-based strategies but the models kept predicting we would be trapped so your assignments are in more aggressive positions. Being prepared to attack will be the secret of our defense. If they think we are weak or that we will be intimidated, it will be a costly lesson for them." Moon paused. "Carrina, bring up the details for each unit on how they will be deployed."

Joe Johnston stood up at the table and everyone's eyes shifted to him. He stood tall and proud. He started to clap towards Moon. Another officer on the other side of Moon stood and also started to clap. One after another they all stood and, within seconds, they were all clapping with several cheering loudly.

Angel

The house was bigger than Judith had imagined as the car pulled into the circular driveway. She exchanged pleasantries with Camilla and stepped out. Judith watched the car drive away looking nervous for a moment. She turned and faced the front door of Angel Vega's estate. Apparently working for the Governor has its perks or maybe he made good money beforehand. Either way Judith felt more eager to see him. Judith was wearing a silver sheen evening dress and clear crystalized plastic high heels with diamond flakes mixed throughout the plastic. The dress in the right lighting was slightly see-through. The shoes in the right light could make a rainbow. Her necklace was silver with a ruby cross, her purse was ruby rose in color, and she had on dark red lipstick. Judith walked slowly to the front door which opened when she reached it.

An android with a funny tuxedo front cover was inside the doorway to greet Judith. "I do not detect an identity chip, nor can I find you in my facial recognition database. Please state your name," the android said.

"My name is Judith Strong. I have an appointment with Mr. Angel Vega," Judith said, as she heard some footsteps closing in fast from the right inside the house. It was Angel and seeing Judith made him smile.

"Good evening Judith," Angel said. He was wearing a business suit without the jacket, his tie was loose, and his sleeves were rolled up. "Please come in. It is, uh, very good to see you."

"Thank you, Angel. It is very good to see you as well," Judith said. She noticed a security guard out of the corner of her left eye and he did not look happy. She stepped into the house, keeping eye contact with Angel.

"Are you thirsty? Perhaps some red wine?" Angel asked, remembering from the lunch a couple days ago.

"That would be nice, thanks," Judith replied softly and then gave a casual but uncomfortable glance to the security guard.

"Chester, two red wines please," Angel said to the android who immediately went to the kitchen. "George, I think you can take the rest of the night off."

"Sir, I strongly suggest I stay until your last, uh, appointment is…" George began to say.

"This is my last appointment. It is already late and I am not sure how long this might go." Angel looked at George. "Ms. Strong and I have a lot to talk about."

George hesitated. He outweighed both Angel and Judith combined plus some extra. It was against his training but Angel was the boss.

"Very well sir. I will be here early in the morning," George said, still looking coldly at Judith.

"Thank you, George. I know I can always count on you. It means the world to me. Thank you," Angel said, and then turned to Judith.

George nodded and then walked towards the back of the estate.

"Please, let's get started. I know you had some important business to discuss," Angel said to Judith. "Apologies for the late hour."

Judith walked closer to Angel and looked up at him. She was only a few inches away. "No problem for me. I'm just grateful to be here," she said with a smile.

"It is a lovely evening tonight. We can sit on the upper balcony overlooking the lake." Angel turned slightly, offering her to the stairs behind him. "Please, after you."

Judith smiled and walked towards the stairs coming very close to rubbing against Angel. He almost forgot to follow as he stared hungrily at her from behind as she went up the steps. When he did start to walk, he had to move quickly to catch up. Chester was back with the wine and followed them.

The stairs were in a cyclone pattern and after reaching the third floor they walked to the back of the house. The doors to the balcony opened automatically and they walked outside. The balcony was dark wood with no cover and an array of three love seats all facing the lake. The sun was setting on the far side. Judith enjoyed the breeze briefly and gazed at the other estates on the perimeter of the large residential area lake.

"This is lovely," Judith said. Chester walked up and Judith took a wine glass off the tray. She tossed her purse onto one of the side couches and then sat on the middle love seat.

Angel took the other glass. "Thank you, Chester. That will be all for now." Chester turned and left. Angel sat next to Judith. He thought for a moment of Margot and Nathalie.

"So, you said you needed help," Angel prodded.

"Yes." Judith looked down showing a glimpse of weakness. "We, uh, we are really in a tight spot." She sipped her wine before looking back to him. "As I said the other day, we have been trying to free the most vulnerable and bring them here for years. We have been growing our capabilities and making great progress; however, they have arrested three of our team and are closing in on the rest of us. We had been using a virtual train station to find those in need using word of mouth. We knew it was a gamble every day and unfortunately the devil has come to collect his due."

"What can I do to help?" Angel said, and then sipped his wine.

"We need a new strategy. We have a plan but it will take an advocate in the Southern District. We will switch from one at a time to fairly large groupings and use armed guards. When we would enter the Southern District, we would need friends there to meet us. We would need to avoid any hassle at the stations with people not having identification. We need confidence that we won't be extradited right after reaching safety," Judith said, looking deep into Angel's eyes.

"How would they arrive?" Angel asked. He had finished his glass already and was glad Chester thought to leave the tray and the bottle. Angel moved to refill both glasses.

"So far we have flown people out one at a time. That is how I helped Anna. We have quite a large group now. We have helped so many people that many friends have joined. They are loyal and some are former soldiers. We are looking to transition from only seeking out specific types of deudors one at a time to helping those in the harshest of labor camps. You don't break people out of camps one at a time. We would use transport and underground transit tunnels." Judith stopped to sip her wine and see Angel's reaction.

"That is a different animal all together," Angel said. He looked out over the lake. "You know we have camps in the Southern District as well. We put criminals and bankrupt people there. Most of them deserve it. The northerners would call what you propose human trafficking."

"Almost any crime or debt can land you in a camp or a farm in the other districts," Judith returned sharply. "We are not talking about the small relatively fair camps and farms in the south. I am asking for help to free people living in servitude with no hope of redemption." Judith paused. "We are going to do it with or without your help. Do you want to see us arrested when reaching your district and returned immediately for punishment, or do you want to see a breath of hope and freedom come to those most in need?" She looked longingly into his eyes leaning slightly closer to him.

Angel thought for a moment. "If we are to do this, we need to work together on at least the first couple of transfers. This underground railroad of yours, I need to see the details of where and how you want to move them. We also need to talk about what to do with them after they get here. The other districts will want them back if they are identified."

"Done. That is more than fair," Judith said. "I am forever in your debt." She smiled at him. They exchanged a warm stare. "Got anything to eat?" Judith asked.

"Of course. Follow me," Angel replied.

Judith picked up her purse and they walked casually back into the house and down the stairs to the first floor. Judith followed him and they both started to feel the animal magnetism. They reached the first floor and turned towards the kitchen.

"Chester, my good man, what do we have to eat around here?" Angel asked.

"Sir, we have both steak and chicken dinners, plus a variety of vegetables, fruits, cheeses…" Chester was beginning to say.

"Fruit and cheese would go great with this wine," Judith said, while leaning over the counter and looking at Angel.

Angel looked to her and could see slightly down the front of her dress. "Yes, that looks great. I mean, that sounds great."

Judith smiled. Chester went to the refrigerator and began to quickly prepare the food.

"Was that a fireplace I saw in the living room?" Judith asked.

"Yup, we could eat in there. I would love to hear more about how you ended up here, how you have managed to help so many people," Angel said. "More wine?"

"Here is my glass. Point me to the lady's room and I'll meet you in front of the fire," Judith said.

Angel was not usually at a loss for words but he found Judith intoxicating, and the wine didn't hurt either. He pointed her to the restroom and watched her walk out.

"The food is prepared sir. Shall I take it into the living room for you?" Chester asked, not at all impressed with Angel's guest.

"No, I got it from here. In fact, you can go power down for the night. Everything else can wait. I would like some privacy," Angel said. "Thank you for your help."

"As you command," Chester replied, and walked to the service room.

Angel put the wine bottle and glasses on the tray with the food and walked to the living room. He put the tray on the table and went to the fireplace to get it started. He rarely used it because most of the year it's crazy to light a fireplace in Houston. He finally got it going and turned around. Judith was sitting on the couch watching him. She looked almost feline in how she was sitting with her legs on the couch and her shoes off. She leaned over to the table to grab a strawberry and put it in her mouth.

"So, how is it that an intelligent and beautiful woman like you ended up as a freedom fighter?" Angel asked. "I'm sure you didn't go into it right out of school," he said, and ate a piece of cheese.

"My little sister was a drug addict. She was taken from us after her second offense. Both just possession charges. She stupidly confessed and I never saw her again. She was only a little older than Anna. We lived in

New Jersey. My parents have never recovered." Judith looked sad briefly and sipped her wine before looking back up at Angel. "I knew then that this system was screwed up. This is not how a free society deals with its problems."

"I am very impressed. Most do little more than talk about change. Few step up and risk their own freedom to help others. I think it would really be something to know you," Angel said, taking another sip.

Judith put her glass down slowly and looked deep into Angel's eyes. She then moved forward and kissed him while putting a hand on his shoulder. Angel barely was able to put his glass down without dropping it. He held her and kissed her back honestly and with compassion. The fire crackle was the only other sound. Angel realized he should have started some music. As they continued to kiss, he slowly and gently began to touch her and she moved closer. He started with her side and then lower back. And then below the lower back. She continued to make pleasant sounds and he became braver as he explored her.

Judith used one hand to caress Angel's neck and play with his hair; her other hand was far less innocent. He couldn't believe his luck. It had been forever. She tasted and felt so good. Judith rolled on top of him and they were one hot mess. Hands softly but hungrily moving everywhere. The heat from the fire making the passion even more intense with sweat starting on both of them. Judith started a rocking motion on him. They stopped kissing briefly and smiled at each other. Judith slowly got up, stepped back one step, undid the lace tie for her dress behind her neck, let her dress fall off, and kicked it away. She was breathtaking. Angel literally found it hard to breathe. Judith gracefully went onto her knees with him still sitting on the couch. She kissed him as he massaged her anywhere that he could reach her. With one hand Judith undid his zipper, took him out, and began to caress him. Angel felt joy in every part of his body. His heart felt strong and he felt like his body was a chiseled masterpiece. He felt like king of the world. Judith slowly took off Angel's tie and, to his shock, tied it around his eyes to blindfold him. Her smile was elating, he was powerless. Judith began to kiss him on his chest, slowly heading south. She began to massage him again and Angel let out a deep pleasure moan.

Judith reached under the edge of the couch and quietly grabbed the serrated ceramic blade she had hidden while Angel was setting up the fire. As Angel's eyes were still covered, she brought the knife up and in a fluid motion came off him and inserted the blade into his chest. The blade went expertly in between the ribs directly into the heart and she twisted. Angel screamed and felt his body seize in shock. In almost as fluid of a motion Judith pulled the blade out and stepped back a few steps. She was both protecting herself in case he had a last burst of energy and also avoiding the gush of blood from getting on her. Angel fell to the side on the couch. He could feel pain slowly washing away into a blur. Angel realized what was happening. He tried to think of his parents and, for a moment, could not remember what they looked like. Angel hoped he would see them soon.

Judith walked around the room ready to fight anyone or anything that might come for her. All she could hear was the crackle of the fire and the blood hitting the floor as the couch could not hold it all. She walked back into the kitchen area still being driven by adrenaline. She found a trash bag and a duffle bag. Judith took them back into the living room, still naked with blood on her hands and Angel on her breath.

She walked casually behind the couch. She put the duffle bag on the floor and laid the garbage bag on the back of the couch. Judith grabbed Angel by the hair and used the serrated blade to begin to saw Angel at the neck just above the Adam's apple. The knife was incredibly sharp but was not as long as would have been ideal for the job. It was messy work, even for her, but she finished cutting off his head and put it on the couch to continue to drain. Judith took another look around still unsure no-one was on to her yet. After several seconds she held the head up and it was down to a drip. She put the head in the garbage bag, tied it off, and then put it in the duffle bag. Judith then went to the bathroom and washed her hands until the blood was down to a pink hue. She then wiped blood splatter away from the rest of her, including her still flush breasts. She had liked Angel, but he was her mark and she did not question orders. Once she was clean enough, she went back to the living room and put her dress back on. She grabbed her purse, shoes, and the duffle bag, but left the knife.

Judith walked out the side door by the kitchen and followed the border of the property. She reached the road after a couple of minutes and then headed east on the sidewalk at a brisk pace. Before she had gone even fifty meters, an unmarked car approached her from behind and stopped. She opened the door, got in, and it sped off.

"Good evening Mrs. Smith, how was your date?" Cain asked.

"It's done. Let's get the hell out of here," Judith replied.

Cain smiled. Not bad, not bad at all he thought to himself.

Judith thought briefly about Anna. She would not understand. Judith hoped they didn't think Anna had been a part of it but, if they did, then that is part of the game. In war, the victors fight on and the rest of humanity suffer the consequences.

Columbia

O ut of the darkness, bright red floodlights illuminated the backdrop of the stage showing a massive forest green flag with a larger than life red star in the middle. A hypnotizing drum beat started to throb for the crowd and they began to rock side to side. The crowd was out of sync, but it didn't matter. The guitars cried out and the crowd cheered furiously. Timed perfectly, spotlights with a similar blood red color shined on each of the band members exactly when the singer began.

> *"The main attraction, distraction*
> *Got ya number than number than numb*
> *Empty ya pockets son, they got you thinkin' that*
> *What ya need is what they selling*
> *Make you think that buying is rebelling*
> *From the theaters to malls on every shore*
> *Tha thin line between entertainment and war*
> *The frontline is everywhere, there be No Shelter here!"*

The protest against the Southern District was now in full swing. The speakers and other bands had finished and they were onto the main attractions. The tribute band for the classic revolutionary socialist Rage Against the Machine icon was stirring the protest into a vengeful riot. The tune *No Shelter* was storming just as the last hangover of sunlight disappeared. The stage was set up by The Columns in front of Jesse Hall at the University of Missouri. The huge field allowed thousands of pissed off fans to crowd together. Any system of seating had dissolved and the smell of weed was stronger than the smell of smashed beer cups and trash being slowly trampled by the crowd. In this day and age most would go virtual for entertainment, but sometimes you needed to jump back to reality to truly vent frustration. Sometimes pretend sin could not satisfy one's hostile nature.

Most of the crowd had traveled to Columbia. The few local students had been stretched out to the edges of the field. Professional protesters were now in control. The sound quality of the band was rivaled only by the original music release, thanks to real time AI audio cleanup.

Columbia, Missouri had been a hot bed of liberal causes for close to a century. Sure, there had been corrections but, in general, this college town in the dead center of the country had been a testing ground for anything to do with concentrating power. Years ago, CoMo had started to lean hard left on social issues, such as the football team standing down in support of Black Lives Matter, teachers had threatened students in an effort to silence free speech and allow one view to be heard over and over, and the shaming of white people in an almost all-white town. Now it was at the forefront of a national tension that always seemed to lack only an ignition source to burn the whole system down.

Columbia had spawned one interesting unplanned source of attention. It was at the center of several universities that had been working various aspects of advanced robotics. This had led to a small business developing androids that grew to a large worldwide business. It had since seen massive growth in different locations, but still retained three assembly lines and some of its most aggressive R&D in the Columbia area. These plants were located north of Deer Park on the south side. This was also close to the maturing local airport and multiple Missouri National Guard facilities. A natural tension had been building for years between the socialist doctrine at the university and the production of a workforce that would never complain, demand a paycheck, or dream of unionization.

After the third track by the tribute band, a group towards the center of the crowd raised a pole in the shape of an upside-down L. It had a rope hanging from the end. Three large men began to stabilize the ten-meter-tall stand to keep it vertical, while two other men hammered in support beams. A human circle began to form and two other men set up spotlights to highlight the top of the stand. Most in the crowd could not tell what to focus on: the action in the middle or the band who were just crushing song after song.

One of the men by the stand dawned a black ski mask to give the look of an executioner. He then started to pull on a rope which went over the end of the stand to raise something human-sized up to the top. As the figure began to enter the white spotlight, it became clear it was an effigy of Cyrus Young in a noose. The aerial drones recording the protest were now all focusing on the crash test dummy with a Cyrus mask and suit. The executioner then tied the rope off near the base of the stand. He held his hands up trying to excite the crowd. The band led into the next leftist cult classic, *How I Could Just Kill a Man.*

"I be doing all the dumb shit yo
Cause nothing is coming from it
I'm not gonna waste no time fucking around I got ya humming
Humming coming at ya! Then you know I had to gat ya!
Time for some action just a fraction of friction
I got the clearance to run the interference
In to your satellite shining a battle light
Sen got the gat and I know that we'll gat you right
Here's an example, just a little sample:
How could I just kill a man!

Here is something you can't understand
How I could just kill a man!
Here is something you can't understand
How I could just kill a man!"

The executioner started to head bang to the music and at the climax of the song pulled out a laser pistol and fired at the effigy. It had been soaked in fuel and instantly burst into a fantastic blaze that made the crowd back up more and scream in a prehistoric rage.

Several shoving matches broke out as people were losing control with the intentional saturation of anger and opportunity. Those near the edges of the crowd started to branch out. The music was eardrum bursting loud and carried across the campus and even north into the downtown area.

Security had been a concern by local and district authorities as soon as the protest had been approved. The security included city, county, and state police, but the bulk of the power for violent crowd control had been assigned to the Southern District Defense Force. Here at the performance area, the humans from the security team were in the shadows as backup to the androids who were assigned to stop outright violence. The human security teams now came out of the shadows to push back on the protesters who had started to cause chaos that had not yet triggered the androids. Most protestors backed off after a few smashed windows and cars lit on fire. Several arrests were in progress.

Ironically, the largest group that would not stand down was spreading north near Peace Park and were threateningly close to the Missouri School of Journalism. There were roughly one hundred protesters that were pushing north and only security personnel to act as a barrier to protect the school buildings. The police and androids tried to stop them, but the protesters were flowing in random directions like fire ants from an anthill that was just kicked over. Many of the protesters engaged the security forces which allowed a pair bent on destruction to creep around and reach the closest campus building. One man used rocks to break out windows and the other threw in Molotov cocktails. The old weapons worked just fine.

In the distance, the band was into the next vicious track, *Know Your Enemy*.

"Know your enemy!
Come on!
Born with insight and a raised fist
A witness to the slit wrist
As we, move into '92
Still in a room without a view
Ya got to know, ya got to know

> *That when I say go, go, go!*
> *Amp up and amplify*
> *Defy, I'm a brother with a furious mind*
> *Action must be taken*
> *We don't need the key, we'll break in*
> *Something must be done*
> *About vengeance, a badge and a gun*
> *Cause I'll rip the mike, rip the stage, rip the system*
> *I was born to Rage Against 'em!*
> *Fist in ya face in the place and I'll drop the style clearly...*
> *Know your enemy!"*

As the fire raged, a group of protestors ran around the south side of the Journalism building heading east. Several of the Southern District security force ran after them, closing fast. They were running straight across 9th Street counting on the self-driving cars to stop. On the other side of 9th Street was a couple blocks of restaurants and the people eating outside began to panic. At the popular crowded eating area were ten federal androids and twenty U.S. Marines, all of whom were assigned for crowd control downtown. As the protesters crossed the road, they started to yell for help from the federal forces with belligerent charges against their southern pursuers. The federal forces were not fooled and grabbed the first protester to reach them. The android that grabbed him by the jacket lifted him almost a meter off the ground. The other protesters turned left to go north, now running down the middle of 9th Street. Most of the southern forces followed them on the west of the road as they all were running north. People downtown were either trying to hide to the sides or froze in a panic as the trouble spread deep into the city's nightlife.

The chase crossed Locust Street blindly running through traffic. One of the fatter protesters was hit by a car and then grabbed by a security guard. The other protesters were slowing as they passed the original Shakespeare's Pizza. As they came to the next interchange, they could almost feel the androids grabbing them, but relief was in sight. A group of twenty men with clubs and iron bars were standing in front of the downtown Episcopal Church. The Southern District androids slowed awaiting instructions from the human defense force personnel who were close behind. That gave time for the exhausted protesters to hide behind the armed men who had been waiting. This new set of men were wearing out of date Army fatigues. They were not tucked in and all were out of regulations but it was pretty clear they were vets or pretending to be.

"You are not welcome here! Get the fuck out of here!" The man in front of the vet-look-alikes yelled to the approaching security detail.

"We can't do that and you know it. Stand down or be arrested, along with the criminals behind you!" Yelled the sergeant leading the security detail.

"Bring it on tool!" The man in camo who had yelled twirled the meter-long metal pipe in his hands.

By this point, all of the security forces had caught up and the two sides were in lines squared off against each other with several more protester types starting to walk up, showing they had an advantage in manpower.

The sergeant started to scan the area, including looking up to the church bell. Three men were in the tower, one armed with a rifle and another was aiming a grenade launcher at the sergeant. The third man began to slowly ring the bell. The sergeant had a choice, stand down and let the hoodlums go and avoid bloodshed, or basically attack and try to subdue now a mob of thirty angry men with two snipers.

North of Columbia, Mori Tortan was hearing reports of the violence and the pursuit into downtown of southern forces. Both his second and third in command were strongly recommending pushing the southern forces back to the campus area, but Mori did not want anyone to push anyone. Violence begets violence. He sent a reminder to all field offices to stay in position and not engage anyone unless authorized by Mori directly.

South of Columbia, Moon Tzu was watching a full map of the activities, including the unit who had headed north into the trap. His map was fairly complete thanks to the deployment of the Zoo machines taking a video and tracking movements nearly everywhere. He did not have a report yet, nor audio, but did worry about the unit that was now several blocks removed from the rest of his forces and ordered two more squads to join them as backup.

Back in front of the church, the bell ringing was still the only sound.

"Well, what's it going to be you fascist?!" The lead protester yelled.

The sergeant cocked his head slightly left and, without blinking, said "Unit, subdue all of these men using whatever force necessary!"

Almost instantly the rifle fired from the tower and hit the man behind the sergeant. As the sergeant looked up, preparing to raise his own weapon, he was hit in the chest by a grenade, also from the tower. It lodged in his chest plate failing to detonate immediately. The snipers were poorly trained but their aim had been true. The sergeant began to collapse falling forward and the grenade finally ignited causing him to explode. The blood cloud from the sergeant shot into the air spreading all over the scene. It hung in the air giving the illusion of raining blood.

Five of the androids pointed their hand cannons at the church tower and fired. The church tower exploded causing a fireball that showered debris in all directions. The church bell came crashing down into the middle of the chaos. The southern androids began to move against the protesters taking a beating that was far less than they were giving.

"Freeze everyone! What is going on here?!" Said a man in front of a group running around the corner northeast. Roughly twenty federal androids and ten U.S. Marines were running in after hearing the explosions.

By the time the Marine in charge got close enough to get an answer, the southern forces had the protesters all on the ground either by choice or by force.

"Who is in charge here?!" The lead Marine yelled.

"I am now. They killed our sergeant," said one of the Southern District Defense Force men. He was holding his arm where he had been hit with a bat.

"Why are you arresting our men?" The marine said. "You better have a damn good reason for this!"

"They aren't your men; they are criminals dressed up like you. We pursued a handful of men this way who set a college building on fire. This mess was here waiting for us. We have no issue with you and could use your help," the southern man said. By this point the Marine detachment, including the androids, had encircled the entire area and had weapons at the ready.

"Help you? Ha! I think I should place you all under arrest. You think you can play Marines. We are the fucking Marines!" The marine said.

"I'm under orders just like you. This group set a building on fire and killed at least two of our unit. You need to put aside your baggage and follow your orders!" The southern man said.

"Southern scum. I have reinforcements on the way. We'll see what my command says to do with you." The Marine walked around the arrested men seeing for himself they were just wannabe marines. He knew he'd have to let the southern guys go but wanted them to suffer a little. "Marines, maintain a perimeter but hold your fire," he said, as he was getting his communicator out and set up to get orders.

"Sir, yes sir, fire at will!" The lead Federal android replied.

"Nooooo!!" Yelled both the marine and southern man in charge, but it was too late.

All twenty Federal androids opened fire, killing most of the southern humans almost instantly and the rest after another round. They also mowed down a few of the southern androids who were returning vicious fire but had slower recharge time for their lasers.

Just as the last few southern androids were trying to fight hand-to-hand to survive, a reinforcement unit of southern forces came around the corner from the south and immediately began to pick off the northern androids fighting their brethren. The Marines started to lift their weapons up but that triggered the southern androids to also take aim at them. The collateral damage to the city street from the state-of-the-art weapons was devastating. Every building in the immediate area was collapsing. Three of the original protesters were killed and another had his legs cut off. Only one escaped down an alley. Aerial drones for both the Marines and the southern forces had taken video of this last exchange. By the time the carnage was over, there were only two humans and seven androids left, all on the southern defense side.

"Let's get the hell out of here," one of the humans said. "Unit, fall back to the protest area double time!" They began to race back south crossing both Locust and Elm Streets and curled west running into Peace Park. The concert had stopped when the church tower was destroyed and the crowd all knew better than to run north towards the battle.

"General Tzu, this is General Mori Tortan. I assume you have heard of the conflict that just occurred downtown. I am told the southern forces attacked my men. Was this intentional? Are you really engaging us?!" Mori asked, having called once the reports were confirmed.

"No sir. My reports are your men attacked us. I gave strict orders to keep the peace and act defensively. The unit your men attacked was arresting violent protesters," Moon replied sharply. "You need to withdraw your forces immediately. This is the Southern District and we are on point for security here. Your men should not have been here in the first place!"

"Don't take that tone with me." Mori paused for a moment. "We were exactly where our leaders agreed we should be. I also gave strict orders for no engagement and that none of my soldiers were to fire at anyone unless in self-defense." He paused again briefly. "No matter who started it, we need to end it immediately. Do you agree?"

"Yes, I fully agree. Return your men to their original boundaries and order them to not engage my units," Moon said, again with only mildly contained frustration.

"You do not give orders to me. I am only talking to you because I value peace over slumming at your level," Mori said.

"Let's get one thing straight. If I find out you did order this attack, I will personally find you and make you pay," Moon replied and hung up.

Dexter

As the somber music died down, the audience became eerily quiet. A few weak overhead lights showed the stage and a night black background. Dexter walked into the light looking as serious as he could muster, wearing a black suit and crimson tie. As he walked to the center of the stage it became visible there were three podiums that were all transparent behind him. One in the middle and then one on either side angled to form a V-shape.

"Hello America," Dexter began. "Our nation is in a crisis like none of us have ever experienced. The country is eating itself from within. I am scared. I know you are all scared. We all hope our leaders are scared of what we fear is coming. We will have the debate for the nation tonight and it will resonate across the world. Even the colonies on the Moon and Mars will be impacted by what we hear tonight." The room was so quiet that Dexter felt he was all alone. "For the first time ever, a current President will be on our show. President Thorne and Governor Young will be here to discuss the tragedy in Columbia, Missouri that transpired yesterday." Several members of the audience gasped. "We will then have an all-star panel to discuss the debate. There will be no voting or competition tonight, but we each need to be prepared to make a choice. Do you feel like we can still save the union? How would you do it? What will you do tomorrow to help make it happen? I will be trying to make my choice as well. I am a Party of One and so are you! Partido de uno!"

As Dexter said the last couple of words, he raised his hands. As soon as the last word was spoken, flames exploded far in the background. The crowd all jerked in their seats. The fire crackled and slowly lowered to reveal on the left a Federal android with brushed gunmetal skin, camouflage covers, and red eyes. On the right a Southern android with chrome skin, camouflage covers, and blue eyes. The fire slowly ended up burning to only knee high in the background and Dexter made his way to the center podium. The software made it seem that the androids were looking at every audience member from their individual point of view.

"Lorena, give an overview of what occurred last night," Dexter said.

"As you command," Lorena replied, and the audience member each found themselves as a new addition to the crowd at the Columbia protest.

"Last night at the University of Missouri, a protest was held against the Southern District decision to create a defense force. The protest exploded into anarchy and then cascaded into a full tilt battle between southern and federal forces," Lorena began. "Several groups of protesters, the majority of whom were not from the University or even from Missouri, separated from the protest area and began to riot, destroying property and assaulting random citizens. One group set fire in the Journalism building and were chased north into downtown Columbia. That was the trigger for the worst of the bloodshed." The audience followed the protesters using random clips of video spliced together. "The fire at the Journalism building appears to have been bait to draw a squad of southerners into a trap for purposes unknown. What is known is that the defense force squad did not back down and the protesters opened fire." The audience experienced clips of the battle with poor audio, but generally good 360-degree video at the center of the battle. "Then a bad situation turned catastrophic. U.S. Marines assigned to protect downtown investigated the shootout. The two heavily armed units squared off and opened fire on each other again for reasons unclear." The audience members were so into the battle that Dexter could see many curl up into a fetal position. "A total of ninety-seven people were killed, leaving almost none alive." To add emphasis to the numbers, the audience was taken to the scene after the shooting had stopped to see the dead soldiers and protesters. They could all but smell the smoke from the damaged buildings, including the total destruction of the church.

"Thank you, Lorena," Dexter said, as the audience returned to the show. "As we talk here tonight, there are more protests raging across the country and online. In the Southern District there are people calling for secession. In the other districts there are people calling for forcing the Southern District Defense Force to disband or be disarmed by any means necessary. Online it is even worse with the most hateful vile language one can imagine. The noise is making us deaf to the truth. The hard truth is that after decades of the two sides painting each other as evil we no longer can tolerate the other's existence. The stakes could not be any higher. With that pressure upon us, please join me in welcoming our guests: President Nero Thorne and Governor Cyrus Young!" There was subdued clapping from the audience unsure what would happen next. It no longer felt like a game show.

From the left side of the stage entered Nero Thorne. He was a tall rugged man with salt and pepper colored hair. He was wearing a high-end crisp blue suit, red tie, and white shirt plus an American flag pin on his jacket. From the right entered Cyrus Young. He looked small with Nero on the stage and older than Dexter remembered ever seeing him. It was clear to Dexter this was weighing heavy on Cyrus, even his avatar looked tired. Cyrus was wearing a grey suit, black tie, and a black band on his right arm. The two men entered primarily looking at the audience but exchanged a couple of brief icy stares. Once they reached their podiums, the audience could see their respective androids in the background turn to face each other. The fire still provided most of the light in the background adding to the intensity of the moment.

"Gentlemen, thank you for being here this evening," Dexter said. "And thank you Mr. President for being with us for the first time. This is an opportunity for you both to help assure the nation that justice and peace will prevail. This show is about letting people making an informed individual opinion. We don't want a filter on what you have to say, nor will I try to bias either of you one way or the other. The situation we are in is way too important for anything but the truth. Governor Young, the first question is for you. Can you please elaborate on what happened last night in Columbia?"

"Thank you, Dexter, I appreciate the open forum you provide," Cyrus began. "It is one of the very few remaining unbiased debate forums we have left. That alone says something about the state of the union. To answer your question, it comes down to how the Administration with their overpaid tools in northern district governments and media have sewn hatred for the Southern District for their own political benefits. They have been spinning up citizens against the Southern District for decades. The use the fury against us every election cycle to lock themselves firmly into power. Sadly, once again it has led to southern blood being spilled. Good men and women died last night." Cyrus paused for a moment. "Your report matches what I have been told, except for the critical details about who instigated it. This ill-conceived protest was not meant to show outrage over policies, it was meant to instigate violence. Why else would there be hundreds of thugs bussed into the city. They were fueled on rage and the worst of them set up an ambush. They attacked a university building to draw a defense force squad to a fight several blocks from reinforcements. The savages opened fire and were rewarded with swift efficient justice as our unit was ready. The Marines then came in and with blood running hot a conflict occurred with most involved perishing." Cyrus again paused looking down briefly as a tribute to the fallen. "Again, I have reports that the defense force was attacked but this time by the Marines. It is a tragedy with the potential to ignite a catastrophe of biblical proportion. The defense force units in Columbia are made up of citizens from Missouri, they were defending Missouri, and they were gunned down in Missouri. This was a heinous crime and will not be forgiven." As Cyrus finished, he looked at Nero.

"President Thorne, your response?" Dexter asked.

"Thank you for having me Dexter," Nero said. "First I want to extend my heartfelt sympathy to all of those affected. Octavia and I mourned the dead and wounded. The truth will be brought forth and it will not be easy for some to accept. However painful the truth, it is critical that we find it out so we can move forward as one nation. The world is a dangerous place, we don't need to make our enemies' job any easier."

"Thank you, Mr. President. Governor Young, you mentioned something earlier about the media playing a role in inciting animosity against the Southern District. Why do you think the press that cater to each district cover almost every conflict so differently?" Dexter asked.

"One must be completely sheltered to not see the rampant duality in the country today. If one lives in one area or listens to one like-minded set of networks, you hear the same one-sided view over and over again. For almost a century the news industry has worked hard to make every story top the last. It's a never-ending process of kicking it up a notch to maintain ratings. This toxic process has reached a point where most call for the other's head on a spike without blinking an eye," Cyrus said, without blinking.

"Similar question to you Mr. President, how can we move forward as a nation with the essence of how we communicate with each other dividing us?" Dexter asked.

"It is definitely a real problem. We could point fingers, but likely that would further the divide. Instead, rather than trying to talk about what divides us, we should strive for finding common ground and reach agreements. If we can break the cycle of conflict then the vultures will go hungry," Nero replied.

"Governor Young, do you see any issues where the Southern District could work with the Thorne Administration to show some progress toward unity?" Dexter asked.

"For years we asked the federal government to provide our defense," Cyrus said. "We tried to work with them again and again, hoping the results would someday be different and our loyalty rewarded. The actions we have taken to provide our own defense include combining all of our State and National Guards units into the Southern District Defense Force. This includes staffing up bases and setting up border security. We put out a call for volunteers and far exceeded our goals. The sense of urgency in the south cannot be overstated. We have increased from ten divisions to twenty, from five aerial strike wings to twelve, from..." Cyrus was cut off before finishing.

"Governor, what does that have to do with my question about any topics where you can work with the Administration?" Dexter asked.

"He did answer your question," Nero interjected. "He is not interested in working with us. He is not interested in peace. He is interested in power."

"Let's talk about power," Cyrus interjected, and spoke very quickly to keep anyone from cutting in. "It used to be that the federal government racked up trillions in debt every year. What did we think would happen? When the government could not pay its bills or print enough money, they created the deudors. It was truly a paradise lost. Now government credit debt is shouldered by millions of individuals so the federal government looks to be in the black despite still spending more than ever. Thorne wants to mandate that even more people in the nation and a huge increase of people in the south to become deudors. Why? Power. Raw power for the centralized Washington monstrosity that has grown into a real-life Godzilla. We have been feeding the monster thinking it was our pet. Turns out we, the people, are the pets. It used to be that the federal government would do anything to protect the interest of its civilians: slaughter Indians, enslave people to produce product, and create fictional money to prop up a fake economy with only our military power letting us get away with it. How did all those ideas turn out? Now we are seeing almost weekly bloodshed in the south and Thorne wants to double down on it with deudor "bill of rights" nationally to force more into servitude. That is a power grab of the first order. The Southern District wants to scrap the deudor system. We will not sacrifice our principles to nationalize power." Cyrus turned to look at Nero. "The Southern District will fight back against attacks and assassinations. We do not fear the monster you have helped create."

"You do not fear war? Only a fool of a leader would not be afraid when his citizen's lives are in danger," Nero said.

"I can tell you are afraid, but you should not be. The time to be scared is not when you hear the rattle, it is when the rattle stops," Cyrus replied.

"Gentlemen, I am sure you both want what is best for all American citizens. President Thorne, one third of the Southern District citizens wants to stay loyal to the country, one third want to secede, and one third apparently are never going to pay attention. What can you say to help convert citizens to become loyalists?" Dexter asked.

"That may be your best question of the night," Nero said. "No-one should decide whether to stay in a union or to separate simply based on recent events. One must look at the strength it has given all the states and districts over the centuries. It has enabled us to win world wars, to reach the pinnacle of human financial success for the everyday citizen, and allowed us to progress to a utopia of freedoms and opportunities with many ways to get help when one stumbles. The site of this battle yesterday was no shiloh; it is no place of peace. Columbia has been a source of trouble for a long time. The powerful video still fresh in our minds should not let you overlook the truth that is right before you. The truth is that we should not make a decision like this based on a single or small set of incidents, but rather the collective benefits we have enjoyed over the years. The best indicator of how our union will help us in the future is to study the past. We should all think about what choosing war would mean and try to hear from God the truth."

"Thank you, Mr. President." Dexter turned to Cyrus. "Governor Young, what did you mean by assassinations, plural?" Dexter asked.

"Dexter, I think it is clear that your sources have not yet found out one other tragedy that occurred." Cyrus started. "It is with a heavy heart that I must announce that Angel Vega, the political manager of the Southern District Defense Force and one of my most trusted advisors, was assassinated just before the Columbia attack. We have reasons to believe the assassin was an operative of the Thorne administration. Because of the attacks in Columbia, the assassination of Angel Vega, and what we have heard here tonight, the Southern District calls for lovers of liberty to come to the south and those few who agree with Thorne to get out. Because of these obscene acts of aggression against our citizens, we are moving on with our plans for secession." It was clear by the look on Cyrus' face he had been saving this up the whole time.

Nero stepped from behind the podium, inching closer to Cyrus. "That sir, is treason." Nero looked at Dexter for a moment to see if he would react but Dexter was in shock. "The deudor system has provided balance between equality and responsibility. We use it to help level the playing field and give people a lifeline who otherwise would be sentenced to a life in poverty.

Only those who do not care about the disenfranchised, minorities, and the down trodden would resist this progressive success. And clearly, I would never approve any pre-emptive attack on the Southern District in any way, especially an assassination of a degenerate like Mr. Vega. It is obvious that this show has turned into a spectacle for treasonous propaganda. This will not be tolerated. This heresy must be silenced. I am executing executive privilege and ordering this show terminated immediately!"

Just as Nero spoke the words, about thirty members of the audience transformed into federal androids and moved to take over the stage. Flood lights filled the stage and seating areas. The androids stepped on people in their way with no attempt to avoid injuries but were moving as fast as their two legs and four arms could get them to the stage.

"When tyranny becomes law, rebellion becomes duty," Cyrus replied calmly.

"End transmission," Dexter said weakly. "End transmission now!" He then yelled when nothing happened.

Dexter took off his headset at the studio and sat up in a panic. He looked around and the other five staff members were also offline. They all looked shocked and scared. A young female intern started to cry.

"Servo, what the shit just happened?!" Dexter yelled.

"Sir, we have intruders at the other studio," Servo replied, talking about the decoy station that was supposed to be the location from which he transmitted. "Showing live video from that site now. Something seems to be wrong with the audio."

On the big screen shot up a quadrant of four videos. One showed the front entrance and one showed the rear, both had federal androids breaking in and several machines flowed into the facility. The other two videos showed the six staff members at the decoy facility. After a couple of seconds, they all got down on their knees and put their hands up. Dexter and his staff could see they were terrified and being given commands by someone just off camera with a few androids now surrounding them. The team at the decoy station all shook their heads 'no' and then, after some pleading, one was shot in the chest and fell. The intern wailed and the other people with

Dexter all let out cries. Dexter gagged and he could see those at the decoy now in full terror mode. This time one of the staffers at the decoy stood up and pointed to a control panel saying several statements. An android went to the panel and appeared to confirm what the staffer said. That is when a figure in a jet-black combat suit with a black helmet and a single red light on the forehead looked at one of the cameras Dexter was watching. Dexter felt he or it was looking directly at him. After more pleading, the androids opened fire on the rest of the staffers and all four videos went black.

"Oh fuck," Dexter said. Three of the staffers with him were now crying. "I think they know where we are. We need to get out of here now. Everyone, run!"

Dexter and his team all ran to their vehicles leaving everything behind in the station. Dexter felt like he was moving in slow motion. The young female intern was not able to get into her car as the terror was too real to go through the motions.

"Diane, come with me," Dexter called to her. She hesitated and then started towards him leaving her car door open. He helped her in and made sure the others had driven off before he told Camilla to take them home.

Dexter's studio was on top of a small outcropping just off the mainland of Puerto Rico. There was a 200-meter bridge that connected the studio to the mainland. All five cars were driving down it as fast as Camilla would take them. Diane was a blubbering mess.

When they reached about halfway down the bridge, all five cars came to an orderly stop.

"Camilla, what are you doing?" Dexter asked.

"Sorry sir, I have received instructions from the authorities that it is unsafe to proceed. We must wait here for assistance," Camilla replied.

"Screw that, go now!" Dexter yelled.

"I cannot sir. We must wait for the authorities," Camilla replied. Diane screamed and pointed out the window.

In the distance were two black dots coming in from the northwest. Dexter hit the manual override button and shifted the console to drive. He then pulled the wires for the automatic control system taking Camilla out of the picture. He drove up to the next staff member.

Dexter waived for the other staffer to come with them but he could not open his door. He started to try to kick the window but no luck. He could see that all of the others were trapped.

"Dexter, we have to go now!" Diane yelled.

"Fuck that, I am not leaving them!" Dexter yelled and got out. He left his door open just in case. He went to the trunk and opened it. He got out the lug wrench and smashed at the window of the first car. The first try bounced off leaving a crack. The second try burst it and it rained small chunks of glass. The panicked staffer started to crawl out. Dexter did the same to the other three cars. Soon all six were crammed into his four-seater. Dexter gunned it and they were moving.

Boom! Boom! Boom! Boom! Dexter's car shook. He looked in the rearview mirror and the four cars behind him were destroyed. He floored the accelerator. At the end of the bridge was a short drive to a tunnel.

"Ahhh!" Diane screamed and Dexter slammed on the breaks and turned into the other lane just before a missile hit up ahead and to the right. He then floored it again thanking God he had bought a car with manual mode.

Dexter swerved back to the right lane and another missile hit the left lane behind them. It shook them so bad that the car almost flipped over into the water and the back window shattered. Dexter was the only one not screaming. Dexter lowered his window and flipped off the aerial drones just before passing into the tunnel.

Corban

Corban Cruz was pacing. He was consumed with frustration while trying to play chess in his mind. The two never mix well. The Southern District seemed hell bent on rebellion and someone had butchered personnel from the most popular political news show on VR. Corban was in the White House awaiting the start of an emergency meeting. This was not just another status meeting and would include President Thorne, Corban's Security Council, the Joint Chiefs, the Vice President, and other cabinet members. Corban was in a small side room adjacent that was just outside a large conference room used for discussing crises, like the one today. Everyone was beginning to gather, but Corban was not in the mood for talking to them.

"Sir, most of the invitees have now connected. Shall I start the videos?" Ariella asked.

"Yes please," Corban replied. "Do you know how much longer until the President arrives?"

"He should be here in about two minutes," Ariella answered.

Corban walked up to a picture of Abraham Lincoln that was in the room. It showed the President standing high above a crowd giving a speech early in his presidency. Corban, for a moment, was distracted by the primitive environment and yet powerful leadership. It seemed like an alternate universe to the reality Corban found himself in. He snapped out of it, opened the door, and sat next to the chair at the head of the table.

After Corban sat at the table, Ariella projected the holograms of people joining remotely on the sidewall displays. The room began to grow quiet anticipating the start. There were only chairs around the long narrow table and both the left and right sides were covered with a virtual crowd. The doors burst open. Corban turned and stood up with everyone else.

"Hello Mr. President," Corban said, as Nero and his Vice President Angela Wolf both sat at the head of the table, followed by a long entourage that filled the rest of the table. General Mori Tortan was opposite Corban at the table.

"I hope you have some good news Corban. It is bloody hell out there," Nero replied.

"The fallen from both sides have been collected. Many of the wounded were saved thanks to the extensive medical facilities in Columbia. We are conducting a complete investigation and piecing together exactly what happened. It was a slaughterhouse so it may take some time," Corban began. "Sir, with your permission, I would like to start with what we see in terms of troop movements."

"Go," Nero said.

"Ariella, bring up the map," Corban said.

"As you command," Ariella replied.

"Sir, here you can see the movements of the units in the Columbia area," Corban started. "Most of the Southern District forces have pulled to the south side of the city or out of the area all together. As we zoom out though, they are anything but passive. We have reports of massive amounts of volunteers trying to join southern guard units. We also see major activities in the Fort Worth, Atlanta, and Charlotte areas. They are consolidating new forces there. Most of the units they had called up were sent to about a dozen cities along the Southern District border before the incident in Columbia."

"What about federal forces?" Nero asked. "Any changes to what we talked about last time."

"We have deployed additional aerial units near Texas and the Carolinas. We have also begun to move ships into the Gulf of Mexico should we need to begin any sort of blockade," Corban answered.

"Good," Thorne said. "Have there been any more skirmishes? You know, any more militia type incidents or major riots?"

"Sir, I can help answer that question," Alexandra Soaring said. "We have reports of two incidents, one in Miami and one in Nashville. Two dead. Also, we have seen a dramatic increase in fighting online. Until now, that was sort of neutral ground, but now groups roam the VR sites looking for people they think are from other districts."

"Damn," Nero said, pondering these developments.

"Sir, if I may, I'd like to talk next steps," Corban said, saw Nero nod, and proceeded. "I think in general we have adequate forces near the Southern District to respond quickly should any need arise. We also have strike forces that can deploy from the standard special ops facilities. We aren't set up for defense, but rather rapid deployment as the situation dictates. In essence, we are prepared for the worst, but I would like our next steps to be in the direction of defusing the situation and promoting peace."

"The Devil is in the details," Nero said.

"Yes, indeed he is," Corban agreed. "I suggest we make statements and use all avenues to communicate how violence is unacceptable, and that we want to call for a special commission that will focus on how to ensure safety in the Southern District. We can let the Southern District have a major role and try to move the tension away from armed troops to diplomacy. We need to get back to the security of the citizens which is why the Southern District says they created the defense force in the first place."

"Sir, if I may, I'd like to advise caution with going too far to forgive the Southern District for arming themselves and essentially countering federal forces," Harvey Keitel said. Harvey was one of the holograms. "We at least would need them to stand down. This chaos has been caused by them deciding to defend themselves instead of acting like part of the union. It would seem we need concessions like no longer combining all their guard units and militias into a single force. For Christ's sake, Governor Young called for like-minded people in the rest of the country to help stand up against you."

"Gentlemen, may I offer some analysis?" Ariella asked.

"Go," Thorne said.

"Thank you," Ariella began. "Historically speaking, this is a dangerous moment. Anytime there are two armed units this close, the odds are greater for escalation instead of resolving differences. A concession to at least distribute Southern District Defense Force units evenly across the district would seem essential for prolonged negotiations. Their current deployment of large numbers along the border is setting up another incident. Based on the rhetoric from the debate last night and the murder of the defense force political leader, it seems unlikely peace will be found quickly. There is not a lot of common ground at this point. Asking them to disarm now will be seen as a hostile response."

"I agree this is a dangerous moment," Corban began, not waiting for Nero to react to Harvey or Ariella. "We don't need a computer to know that Young has got to feel at risk right now. Some of what we have been doing has pushed him to the edge of madness. Baby steps. We need to address this with baby steps. If we tell him he has to disarm for us to start talking, he might instead further build his military and ignore our calls."

"That is exactly why we need a backup plan to abort this treason before it gains any traction," Harvey answered. The room was deftly quiet listening to the debate. "If Young refuses us or goes silent, we move on his Defense Force Headquarters at Fort Hood near Waco. We move in and use any force necessary to swiftly neuter their forces. We cut the head off the snake; then Young will not only disarm, but will be forced to resign."

"Hold your horses there, cowboy," Nero said. "I do not see a reason to attack one of our own districts, no matter how disobedient they are behaving."

"Sir, I might have some news to help gauge the wisdom of what General Keitel suggests," Naya Garcia added. "Ariella, please show a visual of the Southern District androids at the Columbia incident." Naya continued talking as Ariella began to show image after image of the androids. "We have intercepted transmissions that indicate that Angel Vega was one of the instigators of the attack on Workerbee robotics. It was an attack to gain the latest technology to be able to produce similarly lethal androids to negate the threat posed by our units. It seems very unlikely that Mr. Vega, a disciple of Governor Young, would have engaged in this vicious attack without it being cleared by Young. If you look carefully at the images of the units at the Columbia incident and know what to look for, you can see upgrades to the power system only inherent to the units that were under test at Workerbee, of which one was stolen during the raid."

Everyone could tell that Nero was weighing the options. He looked at the images of the androids and Ariella had zoomed in on the power system, plus gave a comparison to the standard issue models. He turned to the two members of the joint chiefs at the table, one of whom nodded.

"Damn. They are really forcing our hand," Nero finally said. "Corban, first off thank you to you and your team for again bringing so much to us so quickly. It could not have been easy. Second, I want you to use every available resource to try to validate what Naya just reported. If this was faulty intel, then we need to know as our posture needs to be very different depending on that answer. If the intel is true, then I want it in the press to help force his own people to question his motives. Third, float the idea of a security commission with the south and see if they are interested. It could be a way out. Lastly, I want the plans drawn up for the Fort Hood operation in case we need to pull the trigger." Nero looked at Mori. "General Tzu, bring me your initial plans in two days." Next, he turned to Naya. "Ms. Garcia, you need to work with me to craft our message to Young, both the private and public messages. We will demand peace and use force to reach it if they refuse. It will be a crushing blow so either way this is over very soon. Let us pray the better angels of their nature prevail."

Zander

It was a beautiful sunny California Saturday. Zander Brown was at his favorite place to get lunch. He was by himself at a table outside looking out over Manhattan Beach. He closed his eyes and turned his face up to soak in the sun and let the breeze cool his face. The restaurant was quiet and off the main drag so that it was mostly locals who ate there. Zander looked at the water gently kissing the shore, trying to forget his fight with Becca the night before. He wondered if she would ever forgive him for the attack or any of the rest of the failures she loved to rattle off every time she felt stressed. Last night their son Travon had tried to defend Zander, and Becca turned on him slapping him hard. Zander got up early and said he needed to go into work but really he needed some peace and time to think.

"Hello Zander," said a beautiful and athletic young lady. "You don't know me, but I very much need to talk to you. Can I have a few minutes of your time please?"

"How did you…" Zander began to say but hesitated when she smiled. "Oh, what the hell. Sure. I can say I'm not buying anything though if that's your angle."

"I'm not trying to sell you anything. In fact, you have something that we need," she began. "My name is Lucilla Swift. I am from Carthage, Missouri. I am here to talk to you today because I am hoping that your sense of right and wrong is stronger than your loyalty to a false idol."

Zander was about to tell her to piss off but the waitress approached.

"Good afternoon ma'am. Can I get you anything?" She asked.

"Yes, can I have a Greek Salad and ice tea please with lemon?" Lucilla asked.

"Yes ma'am, coming right up," the waitress said, and turned to leave.

"Ms. Swift, please don't take this wrong but I don't know how you found me, or what you think I might do for you, but I am no traitor. I think you need to get your salad to go," Corban said, and turned back to face the beach.

"Before I ask you for help, let me first tell you who I am and why I am here," Lucilla began. "I am a member of a local town militia in the great state of Missouri. We were falsely accused of planning an attack of an Army munitions depot near Kansas City. Our proud militia made up of mostly veterans or descendants of veterans was arrested and later paraded in St. Louis. Thugs who are trying to start a war forced a fight and several people were killed, including my father." Lucilla paused as the waitress brought her the ice tea and also because she still felt tears coming every time she thought of her father. Zander was now watching her face carefully as she continued. He could see the pain was very raw. "I am now working with people who are actively trying to avoid war at all cost. Our political leaders keep slapping each other in the face. Every time they open their mouths, they make it worse. I am here to talk to you because we think you can help us and, quite frankly, we don't see a lot of options." Lucilla stopped to let Zander soak it in.

"I am sorry to hear about your father. I was appalled by the parade and attack in St. Louis, as well as the violence in Columbia. Both seemed like such avoidable tragedies," Corban said, and then leaned forward towards Lucilla. "It seems you know who I am. I don't think you are here for any reason other than I am security manager of Workerbee robotics. If you are part of an organization with enough resources to stalk and catch me alone, then you are well connected and patient. You also must want something of me that is classified, and you must know I am a fiercely strong patriot who will not betray my country."

"You are right, but let me ask you this Zander, who in our country today has betrayed the union? Who has instigated all the violence? Who, over and over again, have been the victims? If you think about all of that, then who has betrayed the principles this country was founded on?" Lucilla also leaned forward. "You know as well as I do that it's the Thorne

Administration and the Eastern and Western Districts ganging up on the Southern District. I know you are not a fool who just simply believes what the media here in LA tell you. I am here today to ask for your help so we can level the playing field so one side cannot bully the other anymore. Both sides need a deterrent or the bloodshed will continue. None of the people hurt or killed in the attacks have been politicians and, in fact, many have been children. If you can help the violence come to an end, then how can you do nothing and still call yourself a patriot?"

"What exactly are you asking me to do?" Zander asked.

"Right now, the feds can use superior numbers of androids to launch monstrous attacks. The south has only enough to guard itself from small threats. My father was a casualty of simply being outgunned and then slaughtered like a worthless animal in the street. I am asking for your help in being able to shut down these weapons of war if they come after us. We don't want to use EMPs as it permanently damages these AI machines and we don't have enough EMPs even if we did. What we have in mind would be a tool that works on our machines as well, but we can't do it without knowing it will work on the new federal machines too. If these fool politicians force the two sides to square off and the machines shut down, then all that's left is for the men to fight it out and none of the politicians have the political capital to have body bags going home." Lucilla leaned forward even more; her cheeks were blushing. "If no-one has the machines to fight for them, then our leaders will reach a compromise or we will elect new ones who will. You can help stop a second civil war. What could be more patriotic?"

Naya

The old lady walked with small careful steps out of the subway station and stretched her back when she reached the sunlight. People and androids annoyed by her passed around like she was a rock in the river. She did not care. Her cleaning bag was heavy and she had a job to do. She started again down the sidewalk near the U.S. Capitol walking to the endless series of buildings of government bureaucrats. She took her favorite path under the overpass on 3rd Street and slowly made her way to the Homeland Security Headquarters. As she reached the front of the building, she took a break at the bench to get her badge out, put the lanyard around her neck, and went into the entrance.

"Hello Rosita, how are you today?" The guard asked.

The old lady just mumbled under her breath and held her badge to the scanner.

"You are clear to proceed," Ariella said, as the military AI also supported the Department of Homeland Security.

"See you tomorrow!" The guard called to her after she was several meters into the building. He shook his head feeling bad she had to do this work at her age.

The old lady was now walking even slower down the hall and being passed by energetic bureaucratic civil servants. She reached the elevators and pushed the button for the sixth floor, the top floor. She adjusted the bag strap on her shoulder, her discomfort went unnoticed to the other rider in the elevator. The door opened and she shuffled out after the other rider and just before the doors closed. Next it was another long walk down the hall to the Director's suite. She held her badge up again to a sensor and the door to the suite opened for her. After another walk, she reached the waiting area for people visiting the Director, Alexandra Soaring, or members of her staff. She opened the bag, removed an apron, a brush, cleaning spray and rag. The secretary looked up, saw the old lady begin to clean and looked back at her computer screen.

Through the entrance to the suite entered Naya Garcia who waived quickly hello to the secretary, went into Alexandra's office, and closed the door. A few minutes passed and the old lady was about a quarter of the way around the room when the secretary got up and went down the hall to the ladies' room. The old woman walked slowly to her bag, put in the cleaning supplies, shouldered the bag, walked to the Director's office door, opened the door, went inside, and closed and locked the door.

"What the hell are you doing?!" Alexandra said when she saw the old lady. "How dare you just walk in here?!" Alexandra was sitting at her desk. Naya was to the left, seated, and turned to look at the old woman.

She looked coldly at both Alexandra and Naya. Alexandra was about to ask Ariella to summon security when the old lady stood up straight and dropped the bag. She reached with her right hand to lift up and remove the wig starting from the left side of her head. She then used her left hand to pull down on her face removing the mask. Instead of an old cleaning lady, it was a young fit woman in suddenly baggy looking clothes. She dropped both the wig and mask. She smiled slightly as she tilted her head to the left.

"Oh my God. Judith Strong, what are you doing here?" Alexandra asked. "You should never come here in person." Both Alexandra and Naya stood up, their jaws both hanging down and their eyes wide. They understood better than anyone that Judith was one of the deadliest assets in the world and were feeling real fear.

Judith opened the bag, moved some things around to get to the bottom and pulled out a smaller plastic bag the size of a volleyball. She held it out with one hand and flipped it around.

"We finished the assignment. Cain and I are ready for the next job," Judith said coldly. "And we are tired of working through a ridiculous middleman agent. It just slows things down. We want to be plugged in directly to you and the others." Judith pulled the plastic off and was holding Angel's head, his lifeless eyes now staring at the two powerful women.

Moon

General Moon Tzu looked through the viewpad at the movement on the ground below. Moon was with three of his top officers at the viewing station at the Fort Hood Headquarters building. It was essentially a covered balcony on the top floor of the seven-story building facing the training quadrant of the base. The viewpad was the size of an old school Etch-A-Sketch, but transparent, and would autofocus to the object in the center view. Moon was alternating between the seven training units running drills. The teams ranged from a mature National Guard Unit to platoons in their first week wearing a uniform. Moon had enough experience to understand the readiness of his forces by how they trained.

"What are the latest numbers on volunteers?" Moon asked, while watching some of the new recruits get some harsh boot camp style treatment.

"Overall, the defense force has seen at least 20,000 volunteers across the south in just three days," said Brigadier Major General Winfred Scott. "Online chatter indicates that many more are coming. A quarter of them are from outside the south. A third of them showed up in Texas. The Defense Force is now over 100,000 personnel." Winfred was definitely the accountant-type of the group.

"Where the hell are we going to train all this fresh meat?" Asked Major General Tonya Jackson in her typical scratchy voice. "We didn't have room or supplies before they showed up!" Tonya was also looking through a viewpad. "And they can't even walk straight!"

"We can take another division in Austin, but we will be bursting at the seams," said the newly promoted Brigadier General Samantha Payne. "We need to spread out, find abandoned or underused campuses, anything really. We can't turn them away."

"Why not? Our orders don't say to take every useless fat wreck that is bored at home," Tonya countered. "General Tzu sir, do we have any direction regarding turning away volunteers? Or even militiamen?"

"Regulations," Moon said, without looking away from the viewpad. "We will follow standard regulations like we always have. There was nothing about changing the process for how we assess recruits in your orders. What we do have is direction to build a unified and integrated defense force. To meet that objective, we need more recruits and machines. We need them ready to at least look disciplined so we can get them deployed. The faster we can get them looking ready, the sooner we can get them set up around the district. When they get to their duty station, we need to have people ready to complete their training."

"Sir, we have gone this long without a massive surge. Do we have to do this so fast that we are deploying troops just because they have their uniforms and a haircut?" Tonya asked.

"General Jackson, our orders are clear enough to execute without dissent." Moon turned to look at her. "We need to do it for protection in major cities from further attacks like the one in Houston. You know they still have not caught the terrorists. They could strike again. We also have orders from the Governor to set up a barrier around the Southern District to give the federal government a deterrent to entering our district without permission. You know all of this, as well as the rest of us."

"Yeah, I know." Tonya began turning her body towards Moon. "Sir, it's just that I think we know the feds and our district are still on the same side. Hell, we went to the Academy with most of their officers. The political bullshit has to wash over at some point. We will have a lot of work to do to pull back the green recruits and it seems like any terrorists can just slip through all this madness."

"Ma'am, if I may," Samantha began. "I knew the officer-in-charge who was killed in Columbia. I don't think the only threat is from the Middle East. Something has changed. Something in the air is toxic. I think we need to beef up the border before the feds see us as weak and run us over."

"I wish there was not an urgency to this mission," Moon said, as he put down the viewpad and looked at the three officers. "I think we all need to pray that the leaders figure out how to work together but something has been brewing and festering for decades. The two sides have each been coalescing around the elementary idea that the other side is so incompetent, reckless, and inherently wicked that they have gone from loathing their adversaries to wanting to actually inflict pain. I need you all to be extremely focused and enforce discipline at all cost, even with new recruits. The attacks in Houston, the assassination of our boss Angel Vega, the massacre in St. Louis, and the battle in Columbia have shown a steady cadence to the violence upon us. It looks to me like an orchestrated chain of events that has not yet run its course and would have only one outcome. Believe me when I say I would prefer to do nothing but you cannot ignore who has suffered in every attack: the Southern District. The forces in play are either sympathetic to the side of the Thorne Administration or are a part of it. Either way we need to be ready. We need to be ready to defend our homes. Our enemy has shown us the harsher demons of their nature. Are we on the same page?" Moon scanned the three officers.

"Yes sir," they all said.

"The reality is that we cannot be soft," Moon said. "We need to whip these fine men, women, and amen into shape, plus get pretty damn creative about how to defend a pretty large area from one of the most powerful and mobile militaries that has ever existed. We also need to get proactive. Attack is the secret of defense; defense is the planning of an attack."

Mori

M ori Tortan was standing on a virtual reality map of America looking at the latest intelligence for the Southern District deployments. Seeing all the major pieces at once always helped him strategize. The floor map of America was scaled to be roughly ten meters by six meters. Using the 3D map, he could see everything a General needed to plan his movements and defenses, to counter and divide his opponent. Mori turned and looked back at the map from the north once he was standing on top of Chicago. He looked left towards the Carolinas and then scanned to the right all the way to California. This was proving harder than he had anticipated. Around the map were ten of Mori's top generals, most tied in virtually from around the country as they were all deployed with their own units in reality. On the map were three-dimensional markers for every type of unit employed by modern militaries.

"Ariella, we are still too heavy on the east. Adjust it so there are six more divisions of infantry and four more air wings in the Texas, Oklahoma, and Missouri area than there are on the eastern states," Mori said.

"As you command," Ariella said, and the migration began.

"Sir, if you don't mind me saying. This looks incredibly predictable. Are we trying to set up a textbook line of defense, or are we to be a snake ready to strike?" Asked General Winston Grant.

"That is exactly why this is hard. We are supposed to look like the former, but really we need to be ready for the latter," Mori replied.

"Then maybe instead of sweating how even we spread the divisions along the border, we should be thinking of how to make Tzu show us his intentions. Surely he is watching us and looking to match our moves. If we are off balance then we can see where he concentrates forces counter to our moves and thus see his true weak points. This can be critical information and help us intimidate them when we finally advance. This dance is about more than just a perimeter, it will force them into showing us if we are friend or foe," Winston suggested.

"You mean force them to decide now between war and submission?" Asked General Rachel Slate. "Have you no idea how pissed they are right now?"

"Good points," Mori said. "Ariella, undo that last move. No need to start hauling everybody around to make a pretty arc."

"Sir, if I may," said General Henry McDonald. "I understand the temptation to intimidate them; however, that risks giving credibility to those who say we mean to invade the south. What is more concerning is that the south knows what we are capable of and they are rebelling anyway. Hell, there isn't much difference between them and us. Now if you want to be the snake ready to strike, I suggest a rattlesnake. We could have units on the border as the rattle in just a few locations with massive reserves within reach but in the background."

"Interesting," Mori said. "Ariella, leave two brigades with heavy android compliments in each of these areas: Albuquerque, Kansas City, St. Louis, Louisville and Richmond. Move the rest back to be within thirty minutes of air transport to the southern border. If they can be at their home duty station then do so."

This led to major movement on the board. All of the southern units stayed the same. All of the generals were studying the new layout. New units appeared at Fort Hood and in Atlanta.

"What was that? Ariella, where did those two new units come from?" Mori asked.

"Sir, video footage supports that high numbers of volunteers have reported and been grouped into additional units," Ariella answered. "They now have two new divisions and it is growing from what we can tell."

"Damn. That's going to make this harder to predict," Mori said.

"Sir, I think General Tzu is going to see through this set up as well, and I am not sure it's much more effective compared to our current positions.

Why go through this effort? Why not just stay on duty and ride this thing out? Is it worth the risk that our movements trigger another incident?" Asked Rachel.

"Ride this thing out? Generals, maybe we need to get something clear," Mori started. "Our orders are to be ready to put down any perceived threat to the United States of America. Right now, this includes these Southern District political clowns playing revolution down there. Problem is, they have a considerable force with many experienced officers but, make no mistake, they aim to misbehave. We are likely going to be asked to discipline them. We need to be ready to show them what happens when you take up arms against our country! They have crossed a line. They have made it us vs. them in a military sense. We need to be ready to teach them a lesson. It is true that our national leaders are not innocent. They likely will learn a lesson here as well. They only thing we can control is if we are called upon, we act so fiercely that it won't happen again for another 200 years!"

Corban

Corban Cruz was one of the only leaders in Washington DC who used public transportation whenever possible. This included going to work and then back home. Corban had his Halo on and was studying some reports on a skirmish on the coast of Florida. It was the first incident with a loyalist firing from the water at an outpost on land in the south. Corban was on his way home. Another long day in an endless series of long days.

The car pulled peacefully up to the front of the building. The lights in the car turned on so Corban knew he was home. His muscles ached even though he spent every day just going from meeting to meeting. Corban knew his age was creeping up on him and the stress was awful. A good long hot bath with no noise was what he was craving. And a stiff drink.

"Thank you for the ride Camilla," Corban said.

"You're welcome sir. Seventeen credits have been withdrawn from your account. Have a pleasant evening," Camilla replied.

Corban got out of the car and passed through the security gate that opened for him having sensed his implanted chip. He walked slowly down the walkway looking at the flowers at the front of the house. He reached the front door which also opened for him when he walked up to it.

"Betty, I'm home," Corban called, and started walking towards the back of the house. He usually went straight for the kitchen as he rarely remembered to eat at work. Today, like most days, he realized how hungry he was on the ride home.

"Betty?!" Corban called. Usually she was to him right away. This time he saw no sign of her. All he could hear was his two chocolate labs barking in the back. She must be outside. Corban never had high expectations for her, she was just an android after all. Corban remembered the days when going to an empty house meant you had no-one to talk to. Seemed more honest. He did love Betty's cooking though.

"Betty!" Corban yelled, now getting annoyed. He reached the door to the kitchen which opened as he approached. To the left was the breakfast table and to the right the actual kitchen. Betty was seated at the breakfast table facing the windows. The dogs were barking right at her. Corban went straight to Betty.

"Betty, what the heck are you doing?" Corban said, as he put his hand on her right shoulder and gently tried to turn her towards him. As he did, her head fell to the floor.

"Good evening Corban," said a man from behind him.

Corban turned quickly and was welcomed by a spray of mist to his face. He immediately became drowsy and could not keep his balance. A huge man was looking down at him grinning. Corban blacked out.

When Corban awoke, he realized he was outside. The sky showed no sign of sunset so at least an hour had gone by. His head felt very foggy, like he was on strong cold medicine. He tried to move his hands but realized they were tied together at the wrists. The rope looked industrial strength. Apparently, the big guy didn't know Corban had not worked out in over ten years; Corban almost laughed at that thought. He was struggling to grasp the reality of what was going on. Corban looked left and right and realized he was sitting in one of his dining room chairs on the third-floor balcony. He was only a few inches from the handrail.

"Hello sunshine," the man behind Corban said smiling.

"Who are you? What do you think you are doing?" Corban asked, realizing it was not a very powerful start.

"Let's just say I am here representing Southern District interests. I need to ask you a few questions," the man said. Corban heard what sounded like footsteps and then the man was to his left. He was even bigger than Corban had grasped before. His hair was in a ponytail that went to his lower back. On his lower right arm extending out of his shirt was a tattoo of a rattlesnake tail.

"You. You're from the attack at Workerbee," Corban said. For some reason Corban knew he should be scared but couldn't seem to focus enough to feel any serious emotions. "That tattoo looks even worse in person than on the video," Corban chuckled slightly. The large man's smile disappeared.

"Let's skip the chit chat. My name is Samson Gamble. Yes, I was at the Workerbee plant. Yes, I stole one of the units with the advanced power system, but that is not what should bother you. We believe members of the Thorne Administration were behind the protest attack in Houston, the massacre in St. Louis, the battle in Columbia, and the assassination of Angel Vega. I am here to simply verify your part in it all and find out anything you know that can help others in need of atonement," Samson said.

"You are crazy. I will not help you. You'll just have to kill me. Your sources are wrong," Corban replied. His struggle to concentrate remained and he felt himself unable to be creative in his answers. "Have you drugged me?"

"As much fun as torture can be; I simply do not have the time. Yes, you won't be lying to anyone for at least a couple of hours. Now, to begin we will start with an easy one. What do you know about Cain Vasquez?" Samson asked.

"Ex special forces. Real asshole. Would do anything if given the order," Corban replied. "I think he was dishonorably kicked out for excessive force. Why?"

"I'll ask the questions. What happened to Angel Vega?" Samson asked. Corban was quiet for a few seconds. "What happened to Angel?!"

"He was murdered in his home. Beheaded if the reports are correct," Corban replied. He tried to move his hands but realized they were tied together so tight he was having trouble feeling his fingers.

"Who beheaded him and who gave the order?" Samson asked, and kicked the back of Corban's chair just enough to make it pop.

Corban was fighting the drugs compelling him to answer Samson directly. The ability to spin was turned off. "It was a vicious professional job to send a message. It was not terrorism. It was an attempt to, uh, change Cyrus Young's point of view," Corban answered.

Samson kicked the chair hard enough that the back legs came off the ground and briefly Corban thought he was going over the railing.

"I didn't give the order, but I have a theory," Corban said, losing the battle in his mind to stop talking. "Naya and Alexandra probably did it. They keep Cain and other operatives on a leash."

Samson paused, digesting the new intel. "What about the arrest of the Blood Ravens and making them parade in front of hostile union thugs? Were you behind the American Pride Parade tragedy?" He leaned forward to study Corban's face.

He closed his eyes and tried to hold his breath, but it just made Samson kick the chair again. Corban looked up and coughed. "We needed to send a message. There were too many people trying to play soldier. Everybody thinks it's a video game and there is glory in killing another man, like scoring points. I gave the orders. We needed a very visible example. The morons weren't supposed to kill anyone, but I'd do it again. In a way it worked. People just didn't wake up the way I thought they would."

"Did the President know?" Samson asked.

"No, he has no idea. Better that way for everyone," Corban replied.

"You were paid extra to do it, weren't you? What do you have going on the side?" Samson pressed.

Corban could feel his heart race. "I don't know his name. It was just a little bonus. I've worked my ass off for this country my whole life." He gulped air and realized how dry his mouth had become. "I'm sure you aren't doing this for free."

"One of the fundamental evils of greed is its ability to blind otherwise good people." Samson slowly walked to the railing and looked at the horizon. "Did the Administration do anything to instigate the Bush Park massacre or the battle in Columbia?" He asked.

Corban tensed. "No, and your logic on all of this is upside down. It seems you want to blame it all on everybody else. If you want to know who is responsible for the mess then it's simple. It's you. It's me. It's all of us. We are the divided states of America. We need to work together. I can make that happen. I am not a bad guy. If you let me live, then I..." Corban said before stopping himself. "Who do you work for? Now that I have met you,

I do not believe Cyrus Young is your master."

Samson smiled and folded his arms. "The whole point is to not end up with a master." He walked around to Corban's left side, still mostly out of view. "You might know him. He was the real brains and muscle behind Angel's operation. A man of vision who is finally in a position to drive for freedom. I work for Ajax Pagano, the new Secretary of Southern District Defense. Only four people in the world know what I just told you."

Corban was speechless. All of their analysis had been wrong. He knew now the error of his ways.

"Is the President going to try to attack the Southern District?" Samson asked. Another uncomfortable silence. "Does the federal government have a plan to attack the south?!" Samson asked again and grabbed hold of the back of the chair.

"Yes. We have a plan to attack the Defense Force Headquarters in Fort Hood if Governor Young does not stand down. It's a backup plan but it will be fierce and overwhelming so this kind of uprising never happens again," Corban answered, the shame of spilling his guts now drowning out his fear. He could sense the chemicals taking away his ability to choose what he would say, a far deeper control than even the Halos.

"Thank you, Corban. All of this confirms what we concluded as to your role in this tragedy." Samson paused briefly. "I don't think you are the devil in this divine comedy, but your avarice certainly has enabled him. You certainly have been useful to him, and you certainly will be missed by him."

Corban's eyes got very wide. The fear finally began to sink in as the fog started to clear. Corban stood to his feet and tried to start walking away from the balcony and from Samson. Before he finished the first step, Samson picked up Corban with one hand and tossed him over the balcony.

The ropes that had bound Corban's hands were really part of a long rope tied to the balcony. The length was such that Corban would be hanging halfway down to the ground. The other ropes that Corban had not noticed snaked around his elbows and wrapped around his waist. As he fell, the rope connecting his hands to the balcony pulled his arms above his head. The line from his elbows to his waist pulled up hard and, with it, a razor-sharp blade cut him from the groin until it hit his rib cage. When the hanging rope reached the end, it made his body stop falling hard and, with the long deep opening, most of Corban's intestines came out. Corban tried to scream but he could not make his lungs work. The shock began to take him and he felt himself fading away. Some of his intestines made it all the way to the ground with a long bloody line up to his body.

"Let you be a guide to those who have forever dishonored this nation. Let this field of blood mark the birth of a new nation," Samson said, having watched him fall and hearing the splat of Corban's guts. He turned and headed back to meet his team who had been on watch and keeping ready their escape.

Naya

aya Garcia walked quickly down the hall and into the meeting room. She was late but breathed a sigh of relief as they had not started yet. She couldn't stop thinking about Corban's death. The details were top secret but they could not keep it a secret for long. Eventually even the details would get out. Bad news can always find a crack from which to leak.

They were meeting at the Federal Security Building in Fort Meade, Maryland. It was the same room the committee had met in after the AntiCo attack in Houston. Corban had called for everyone to meet in person for that meeting as he was unsure of their safety and security. Naya knew Corban had not been thinking he would be the victim. Whoever did this had elephant-sized balls, Naya thought to herself.

No-one was seated at the chair at the head of the table. Asa Katz was sitting on the side looking down at the table like he had just been scolded. Obviously, his politician blood was soft for this harsh reality. Harvey Keitel was firm like a military man is supposed to look even after his boss is murdered. Alexandra walked, entered and stopped just a couple of steps into the room. She looked at them all and then slowly made her way to the chair on the right of the head of the table. Four other national and homeland security senior managers were also in the room.

"Who called this meeting?" Harvey asked. "I know it wasn't Corban."

"Ms. Soaring instructed me to arrange the meeting," Ariella answered.

"Yes, I called the meeting," Alexandra started. "I can see your mourning period is over General Keitel." She looked from him to the other faces. "I just met with the President. He has instructed me to serve temporarily as the National Security Advisor. We have a lot to do."

"Whatever you need Chairman," Naya said. "We will all back you in this very difficult time."

"Who killed Corban?" Asked Asa.

"We don't know yet. Whoever it was did not have a chip implant and they knew how to disable the cameras in the house," Alexandra answered. "We all saw the pictures of how he was found. Truly monstrous. Even terrorists don't treat people that way."

"What are we going to do for our security and for the security of other leaders? Surely this doesn't end with Corban. This is clearly an imminent remorseless threat," Asa asked.

"We are assigning security details to support the secret service in the protection of all of the Security Council. We will use them until we at least know who is responsible. The new security is on their way here now," Alexandra said.

"What exactly did the President say when you talked to him?" Harvey asked.

"So far, the news has not leaked into the media. He wants me to bring him a high-level plan to address the crisis, including what to share with the media, along with when to share it," Alexandra answered. "The President says he needs a few days to pick a permanent successor. Corban was one of his most trusted advisors who has been loyal to him for decades. This has been hard on him."

"Do you have a high-level plan in mind to buy some time?" Naya asked.

"Yes. I talked to Ariella and the models came back with one clear favorite," Alexandra started. "We call for peace with tough consequences if they do not agree. We propose some concessions and ask for some in return. We publicly state we will not oppose the Southern District Defense Force as a temporary surge support just until we find the terrorists and murderers causing mayhem in our country. We do, however, require that they spread out evenly so as not to invite conflict being close to federal forces. We also require that they work with us and allow federal forces to help, even in the Southern District. In turn, the Administration will forgive the Southern District and their sympathizers for the conditions that led to the attacks in Los Angeles and Columbia. We will also allow the special commission called for by the President to be co-led by the Southern District. Part of working together will include us taking their inputs on where to send federal forces as long as it includes the ten most populated southern cities."

"What about Corban? When do we go public, and how does that play into the plan?" Asa asked.

"Ma'am, if I may?" Naya got a nod from Alexandra before continuing. "I suggest we tonight tell the public about the true brutality of the murder. At some point it will leak anyway so we might as well draw some sympathy from it. We don't show pictures of how he was found but make a very public show of his funeral. The President will speak and there will be thousands of people. Then we leak some rumors that he was behind the assassination of Angel Vega. Enough of the southern sympathizers may believe it and weaken the resolve for resistance to the conditions Alexandra listed. It could draw closure to one issue and put pressure on Young to yield."

"Does that mean we can drop the idea of nationalizing deudors?" Harvey asked. "Given how awful the last few weeks have been, I can't see that helping in any way. It just pisses them off to no end. Doesn't seem like it's worth a war."

"No, but we will give it some breathing room. There is too much political capital spent on it and, seriously, there is no way it will come to war," Naya said, drawing Harvey to raise an eyebrow. "American citizens are too war weary after Iran, Korea, and Venezuela."

"How come we haven't talked about what happened to the crew that works the Party of One show?" Asa asked. "The President was on the show. He said he was shutting it down as it was something like a tool for treason. Then the crew of the show was killed in their studio. I heard it wasn't even the real studio or the right crew. This is supposed to be the Security Council. Seems like if they were a threat to our nation that warranted execution without trial that we should have talked about it first."

"We received top secret information during the show that triggered that response," Alexandra said sharply. "I didn't make the call, the President did. Maybe you can ask him yourself."

Asa paused, considering if Alexandra was just dismissing him or if it was a threat. "You sound very sure of all these plans. Why do you think you have all the answers?" Asa asked.

"Sir, artificial intelligence programs have IQs over one thousand and this is consistent with our recommendations," Ariella answered.

Moon

General Moon Tzu walked slowly through Building 22 at the Southern District Fort Hood Headquarters. The building was the largest onsite and the hanger Moon was touring was the largest indoor area on the base. As the defense force grew, so did the entourage that followed Moon everywhere. He felt like his shadow was fifty feet long and he didn't like it. He also didn't like what he was seeing today in the hanger.

"Captain, why are all those men just sitting against the wall?" Moon asked. He was seeing about twenty soldiers who looked like new volunteers all watching two androids spar.

"Sir, they are watching the robotic units train. We train the men…" The young captain giving the tour was cut off.

"Son, sitting on your ass is never training," Moon said sharply. "None of our troops are to be ever sitting on their butts unless they are eating, sleeping, or shitting." Moon turned from the embarrassed captain to his entourage. "I need all of you to understand that as well. In fact, starting tomorrow I want all of my direct reports to spend at least two hours every day inspecting all the units training. Make sure their instructors are driving them hard. We need to change them from donut eaters to cold blooded killers. I want to see again in their eyes the gleam of the beast of prey!"

"Yes sir," several of his entourage answered.

Moon continued through the huge building past some assault vehicle trainers that had some crews in them practicing the controls and operations. This pleased him even though the soldiers looked well outside their element. Moon continued on and came across a couple of quartermasters who were setting up trainers that would allow humans to practice fighting androids hand-to-hand. Typically, this meant four or five humans unless they had robotic suits to give them any chance one-on-one. This was something Moon directed as soon as he realized they weren't just babysitting civilians.

"Sergeant, how goes the set up?" Moon asked one of the quartermasters.

The Sergeant turned around having missed Moon and his crew coming up behind him. "Sir, they are going to be kickass trainers, sir!"

"Excellent. I expect them to be set up and in use around the clock as soon as possible. Carry on," Moon said.

Moon continued through the hanger passing some large storage crates and forklifts. He then reached an area where a cluster of about fifty soldiers were watching something in the center of the circle. Moon watched from several meters away before they noticed him. Instinctively, the enlisted men and women parted so that Moon could see what was in the center. It was an android on its back with several of the covers removed. A first lieutenant and another android were both kneeling by the machine explaining about the nervous system of the standard military androids. They noticed the gap having formed and when they realized the general was watching them, they both quickly stood to attention.

"Good morning General," the first lieutenant said.

"Good morning. What are you training them on?" Moon asked.

"Sir, we are teaching them some of the basics of android repair. This will help them in the field to get the androids who have been injured back into the fight," the lieutenant answered.

"Yes, that is one thing our troops need to be able to do," Moon said. He then turned to the android. "How do you think they are performing on repairs?"

"Sir, they are slow and generally ineffective. Another android should make the repairs if at all possible," the machine said coldly. The first lieutenant tried to hide it, but was obviously pissed.

"This might surprise you, but I agree," Moon said. He then spoke loud enough for all around to hear him. "How do you think the human troops in general are coming along should we find ourselves in an actual war?"

"Sir, there are a few that can make a difference. Unless tactics change and their discipline and training greatly improve, they will be no match for significant numbers of androids," the machine replied.

"Again, I agree," Moon said. The lieutenant's jaw dropped. "With enough training, do you think it will be androids or humans that make the difference between victory and defeat?"

"Sir, there are many variables that come into play, but I would not bet right now on humans given the frailty and fear inherent to many," the machine replied.

"Well, that is where I disagree with you," Moon replied. "If we indeed find ourselves in a second civil war, it will be humans fighting for their freedom and their homes that will be the difference. Humans will be the advantage in the end. A man fighting for his freedom and his family will beat anyone, always has." He looked around at the astonished faces of the troops around him. "When you work together as a team with discipline and following orders there is nothing we cannot do. The trick is how we tap into that potential most effectively. All warfare is based on deception. We will not help our enemies know our strengths or our weaknesses but, make no mistake about it, we are strongest fighting together. Both the federal forces and the southern forces have androids, but only the south has southern men and women fighting for their homes and the freedom we all hold so dear!"

Mori

General Mori Tortan was growing impatient. He had been watching the test for over twenty minutes and, so far, the subject had only moved a few meters before shutting down. Mori was in a viewing area for executives at an R&D facility in a hidden location in northern Virginia. The test was a human inside and operating a monster of a robot. The machine would have given a dinosaur pause. The operator was in the trunk of the beast. It had six legs, two large arms up front and a tail that curled up to face forward. The two large arms had three weapons at the end of each instead of hands or claws. The tail had a single very powerful weapon, plus could be used to help catapult the machine fair distances. The machine was called the Scorpion.

The Scorpion and its crewman finally got moving and the engineers backed away quickly. If it was working and the test was on, then the engineers were in real danger.

"About time. This better be good," Mori said.

"Yes sir. It should begin now. I'm told they had trouble removing all the safeties," said the Colonel in charge of the testing.

The machine was in a large room that was just a thick concrete box with the scars to show many such trials had taken place here before. The Scorpion was on the right from where Mori was watching. On the left was a large door. The engineers must be satisfied the test was a go as the door began to slowly rise. It was dark beyond the doorway. Mori could sense the test team were nervous, but he wasn't feeling it yet. The officers with Mori moved closer to try to get a better view. The test chamber was one hundred meters long, forty meters wide and thirty meters tall. There was no escape. One machine would leave this chamber.

It flew through the open door so fast it was a blur until it reached the ceiling and began to move side-to-side while firing its laser cannons at the Scorpion. The Eagle was a specialized aerial drone with state-of-the-art weaponry and controls. It used a pair of miniature maneuverable jet engines for propulsion and wings that could fold into crude arms when it walked on its two short legs. The test was to see if the Scorpion could keep up with an enemy that used all three dimensions. So far it had passed every test against land-based targets. The Scorpion hissed and returned fire using its laser cannons. It hopped from wall to floor and then to another wall to avoid the Eagle attacks.

Both the Scorpion and the Eagle were frustrated after the first series of attacks did not work. They were both simply too fast with armor too thick. The Eagle switched from the laser cannons on its belly to target-locking shrapnel charges. These devices were ideal for a target you could not hit with a point and shoot weapon. Even if you miss, the shrapnel should cause some damage. The Scorpion switched to a flame thrower on one arm and a laser cannon on the other that fired pulses in a pattern instead of a beam in just one direction. The first blast from the Eagle was wide left, but the second was only a little off against the wall and a few pieces hit the Scorpion. The Eagle was able to dodge the lasers, but turned accidentally into the flame thrower leaving its head smoking and a couple of its sensors toasted.

The Scorpion driver was getting frustrated as a solid test success is one that takes out the prey quickly and decisively. It used its tail to spring at the Eagle which flew in reverse and fired two more shrapnel charges. While in the air, the Scorpion switched to machine guns on both arms laying down a spray of heavy rounds. One shrapnel charge sailed over the Scorpion and the other hit the beast where its anus would have been, blasting it higher into the air. The driver leaned over and grabbed his left side obviously injured. The Eagle also suffered major damage and fell to the ground. The Scorpion came down nearby and immediately ran over to the Eagle. Using one massive arm to hold the Eagle down, the Scorpion brought the tail around for the kill shot. Its tail included a medium grade rail gun. When the tail curled around to point at the chest of the Eagle, it hissed loudly and fired, taking out its power system. It then fired another shot into the control panel of the Eagle effectively killing it. The Scorpion then headed back to its end and spun around again for the General. It was clear the driver had taken some shrapnel in the side and wasn't looking very good.

"Impressive machine," Mori said. "If it gets to be reliable, it looks like the weak link is the human. Colonel, does this machine need a soldier to operate it?"

"Sir, it would take some work to not include an operator. Our funding and requirements were to make machines for special ops to support troop engagements. Something to complement tanks and standard androids," the Colonel said.

"I want you to immediately switch to a design that is autonomous. No more operator. Imagine a platoon of these beasts. They would wipe out a force ten times their numbers," Mori said. "We need to step it up on the autonomous vehicles. The days of human-centered fighting are coming to a close."

"Sir, I don't think we have the numbers should we have a large campaign. Whether it's the traitors in the south or a foreign affair, we need the humans for the numbers, don't we?" Asked General Rachel Slate, one of the generals who had accompanied Mori to the test.

"That used to be the case. About six months ago we increased the orders for androids, aerial drones, assault vehicles, and even supply trucks. They are all automated or as close as we had designed at the time," Mori answered. "We have more machines than ever before. They are stronger than ever, and more are on the way. It will take time, but there is no comparison when it comes to toughness, efficiency, and, when needed, cruelty. We even gave the enhanced humans a shot, but we keep seeing results like this Scorpion. The human holds it back. With machines there is unlimited potential."

"How did you know we would need more units back then? Was there another threat facing us or still facing us?" Rachel asked.

"The fools back in DC have been playing with fire for a while both here and abroad. Our country has been in at least one war every decade since it came into existence. It was born out of a war. The land was taken in a war. Every generation and new wave of leaders think they can get what they want without bloodshed. They can afford to be naïve, we cannot."

Zander

Zander and Becca were eating lunch in the living room on a boring Saturday early in the afternoon. They had the Dragons match on and Becca was shopping online with her tablet. Their relationship had leveled off recently, but there was a steady infection of contempt in both directions with no-one looking for the cure. The video switched from a brutal match between three of the opposing Spartans and a single huge Dragon to breaking news.

"Hello citizens, this is Jim Johnson from the NBC news desk with breaking news. We apologize for the interruption in coverage." The screen display split with the reporter on the right side and a muted video clip starting on the left side. "This just in from Washington. Videos have leaked from the investigation into the recent violence plaguing America. The videos suggest that the Los Angeles Workerbee robotics lab attackers and the St. Louis American Pride parade instigators were, in fact, mercenaries acting at the direction of leadership of the Southern District. The videos show Mr. Angel Vega as the sinister dealer of death directing these heinous and unforgivable attacks." The video was showing Angel talking to a couple of scary looking men in dark suits. Another video showed him making an evil laugh. "Also, additional information has leaked out that the Columbia, Missouri incident was possibly directed by members of the Thorne Administration. These unconfirmed reports suggest it was to send a message to the Southern District in a brave response to the Los Angeles and St. Louis attacks…"

"I knew it. Those bastards! We ought to…" Becca started.

"Shhh! Listen!" Zander interrupted, and used a remote to turn up the volume. Becca grunted but did stop talking to listen.

"We go now to a live statement that is about to begin from the Thorne

Administration," the reporter said, just before the video switched.

"Good afternoon America. I am Naya Garcia, head of the White House Office of Communications. I am here to give a brief statement regarding the recent video leaks from the top-secret investigation. First, to be clear, the individual or individuals responsible for the leaks have committed a felony by likely compromising the investigation and will be pursued to the full extent of the law. They have released the most controversial evidence collected to date without any context or additional facts." Naya paused. "That said, these videos are authentic. It is a problem. The Thorne Administration will be holding the Southern District responsible for its crimes. Violence is never acceptable and this administration condemns the actions by any and all guilty parties. The President will be addressing the Congress and the nation this coming Monday night to discuss the crises. We ask for calm and patience from all of you while we sort out exactly what took place. Thank you for your attention and God bless the United States of America."

The video switched back to the news correspondent.

"That concludes this special breaking news coverage. We return you now to your regularly scheduled programming," the reporter said. When it returned to the Dragons and Spartans match, two of the three Spartans were standing over the defeated Dragon in a sign of triumph. Zander turned off the video.

"I told you. I fucking told you so," Becca said, with contempt in her voice but the volume not raised. Her tone worried Zander.

"You did. Looks like they did it. I can tell you they won't do it again, at least not at our shop," Zander said, trying to diffuse the situation. He couldn't help but think of Lucilla.

"Time to teach them a lesson. I'm going online right now to see if there are any rallies going on." Becca looked at Zander. "If you weren't so stupid, they wouldn't have stolen one of your androids. They might use that tech against our troops."

"All of the districts have troops in the Army. It's a mixing pot. Even the Southern District guards are Americans. I don't think it will come to that.

Some of the troops are their people," Zander said. He didn't mention that many of the federal forces native to the south had been leaving their post to join the defense force.

"It already has come to that you retard. I wish I had never fucking bred with you. Yuk." Becca got up and went to get her Halo.

Nero

The applause was strong, loud, and organized. The President stood tall at the podium. He was wearing a very dark grey suit, white shirt, and a red and blue tie. His specialized contacts served as teleprompter but the words had not yet started to flow. President Thorne had spoken to the nation before in the House Chamber at the State of the Union and a few other instances of national crises. The revelations in the media that entities within the federal government and Southern District were at least players in the several recent tragedies in the country warranted the address. It was a national crisis. It would be watched around the free world. America was not the economic powerhouse it once had enjoyed, but it was still the soul of the modern world. The applause was beginning to evaporate and the words began to show on Nero's contacts.

"Mr. Speaker, Mrs. Vice President, Members of Congress, the First Lady of the United States, and my fellow Americans: the last few weeks have born witness to terrible tragedy unlike anything this country has had to endure for a long time. Sadly, there have been terrorist attacks by foreign sympathizers for decades, but it has been centuries since we have seen such horrendous infighting, authorized or not, between members of our own democracy. I know all of us pray for those lost and for the families impacted by this senseless violence." The crowd applauded loudly with the Republicans less energetic than the Democrats and Socialists.

"Ladies and gentlemen, part of the reason I want to speak to you tonight is that I need your help. I have provided what I believe are very reasonable concepts for working together with the Southern District. I have been refused every step of the way. I want to share with you what we recently have tried to make work so you can also communicate what you think about it to your elected officials. If you believe like I believe that our country is worth fighting for, then tell the Southern District to either accept these solutions or propose their own ideas for peace, for union, for the memory of those lost, and for those that would be hurt in the future if the violence continues." The Democrats and Socialists all stood and applauded vigorously. The Republicans sat and looked coldly at the President and their colleagues. The Republicans were the minority by a two to one margin and had been so for decades.

"But first, I need to comment on what has recently been leaked in the news. The videos are genuine and do reveal that elements of the government were at least aware and, in a couple of cases, at least supporting the attacks or environment that led to the attacks. I can honestly say that I have authorized no such actions and would never believe the use of force on civilians is acceptable. I hope the Southern District Governor can at least agree on common ground as far as that is concerned." Again, the Democrats and Socialists stood and applauded.

"We made the following proposals to Governor Young in the interest of a lasting peace for the union. We offered to allow the Southern District Defense Force as a temporary surge support just until we find the terrorists and murderers causing mayhem in our country. We did ask that they spread out evenly so as to not invite conflict having massive troop units close to federal forces that by design are naturally in large units. We also asked that they work with us and allow federal forces to help in the Southern District. In turn, the Administration will forgive the Southern District and their sympathizers for the conditions that led to the attacks in Los Angeles and Columbia. We will hold individuals responsible, but hold no ill will to the citizens of these great states. In terms of moving forward, I am calling for a special commission to work to end the spree of mayhem. This commission will be co-led by the Southern District to be a partnership that both sides can support. Part of working together will include us taking their inputs on where to send federal forces. We are very flexible on how to make it work and I believe we share the same goal, to protect innocents from further bloodshed. Unfortunately, all we received in return was a message simply refusing the offers. Instead of talking peace, we are seeing evidence the Southern District is preparing for war." The Democrats and Socialists booed at the sound with those sitting close to the Republicans pointing fingers. A few of the politicians on either side of the aisle started to talk trash, their exchanges drowned out by the raucous crowd.

"Again, I am calling on all of you to help talk some sense into the Southern District. While we all pray for peace, we cannot allow a district to arm itself, separate itself economically from the union, and to effectively to take the roll of the federal government upon itself. The constitution is clear about the separation of federal, state, and district powers. I will give the Southern District two days to begin negotiations with my Administration or we are compelled to move into the Southern District to set up safety zones. I will block any efforts to fortify the south in a way that only threatens the union. Standing up a full-scale military for the purposes of secession is not an act taken by those trying to protect their citizens. It would be an act of those trying to consolidate power. That is a tact taken only by fascists. And let me be clear, if the leadership of the Southern District chooses to act like fascists, then they will be treated like criminals and exterminated!" The Democrats and Socialists all stood and cheered. Some again began to yell at Republicans across the aisle. The Republicans had apparently heard enough and stood up to walk out. Two different politicians who had been yelling at each other got within arm's reach and the Republican pushed the Socialist down. A Democrat then punched the Republican and, even though it was a poor strike, several leaders began trying to separate them which led to even more shouting and pushing. The aerial cameras were circling like buzzards.

Cyrus

Governor Cyrus Young walked up the steps of the makeshift stage. He could hear all of the troops surrounding the stage and their energy was contagious. They were obviously pumped up and Cyrus knew they were going to eat up everything he had to say. Most of his speech was in reaction to what the President had said the night before. Despite the energy and historic nature of what he was going to say, he was still hesitant and unsure where this road would take them.

When he reached the stage, he started to walk to the center and waving to his supporters. The spotlights that had been circulating randomly, but now all centered on him and the crowd erupted. The audience was over two thousand soldiers and about one hundred androids from the Southern District Defense Force. The troops had been bussed in from training facilities across Texas to the temporary set up at Bush Park in Houston, the site of the protest massacre. The audience surrounded the rectangular stage and Cyrus slowly walked in a tight circle, smiling and waving in all directions. By design, the audience was made up of infantry with no senior officers. Cyrus was wearing a cowboy hat, boots, jeans, and a blue t-shirt that read "Dixieland Rising." A large number started to chant "Cyrus." After almost a solid minute, Cyrus started to signal the crowd to settle down. The aerial drones filming the event were capturing Cyrus and the most raucous of the crowd. The event was online live for the world to watch, including an option to be in VR in the crowd.

"Good evening!" Cyrus called out. His voice easily carried thanks to speakers in the stage and surrounding the crowd. The humans and androids all cheered. While androids were not as emotionally unstable as men, their AI software did allow for excitement and happiness, as well as pain and grief.

"As you all know, the last few weeks have been pretty rough. The President had some tough words for us again last night." The crowd booed. "After meeting and talking with many of you today, it is as clear as ever to me that we have nothing to fear of President Thorne." The crowd switched to cheering again. "You are the light of the world; he that followeth you shall not walk in darkness but shall have the light of hope." The crowd cheered loudly.

"I am here to speak with the Southern District tonight. I know the Administration and citizens of other districts are listening, but I have no more hope they can operate with a clear mind and balanced temper. I place my hope in the strength of the Southern District and that God will guide us all through these troubling times. While we all pray for peace, we will not need luck to stand our ground. While we wish success for citizens in all districts, we will not waiver in shielding our principles and beliefs. And while none of us want a fight, if one is forced upon us, then we will not hesitate to defend our homeland!" The crowd erupted again.

"I want to thank everyone who has already joined our defense force whether you are a seasoned veteran or new recruit." Cyrus continued. "Your bravery and sense of duty to your home is an inspiration to us all. While the mission has changed from terrorist hunting to possibly defending our district from a hostile takeover, it is still at its core about protecting that which matters most. We cannot fail in our mission to keep our people safe and free. I also want to thank those of you who responded from outside the south to my call to come to join our cause for liberty. We pray your transition will go smoothly and, once we stabilize our new nation, that you may see again any loved ones you left behind." The crowd began to cheer again.

"The President last night talked about offers he has made to end the stalemate. I was hopeful each time we talked in the past, but the Administration has made it clear over and over again that they have no interest in finding ways to move forward that protect our district and state's rights. In fact, what he calls compromises will simply return us to a defenseless posture. If we don't fall in line with Thorne's policies to control all citizens, then the Administration will withhold the resources we need to protect ourselves from terrorist attacks. These policies are an assault on the very freedoms we cherish; yielding them would sacrifice our way of life." Cyrus paused. "If we cave to the Administration, then we will see the opportunity for people to work hard and be successful evaporate and we will all be living like the cesspools of Los Angeles and New York City." The crowd booed.

"I also need to address the reports that leaked into the media about the possibility of government officials being behind the series of violent incidents across the country the last few weeks." Cyrus looked down briefly as he paused. When he looked back up, he had a hard and determined look on his face. "I want to be absolutely clear with all of you. The Southern District had nothing to do with any of the attacks! These reports about Angel Vega are fabricated! I believe that members of the Thorne Administration doctored tapes to falsify and demonize the south to meet their own needs! Not only did they attack us at a personal level, they surely played a role in the murder of Angel Vega the man they now dishonor. Shame on you Nero! Shame! Shame! Shame!" The crowd went senseless and just about every political pundit in the country had his or her jaw drop. The aerial drones shared a video around the world of soldiers in the south all but foaming at the mouth.

"Lastly, the President called on citizens to contact us asking us to yield." More boos. "I know, I know. I booed when he said it." Now a few laughs from the crowd. "We have received tens of thousands of calls. Many were from citizens on the east and west coast yelling incoherently at us, but most were from citizens in the south and north telling us to stand strong, to stand for what made America great in the first place, and to stand strong even in the face of tyranny!" The crowd erupted in more raucous cheering.

"I do want to make it clear again that we do not want war; we did not fire the first shots in Houston, we did not fire the first shots in St. Louis, and we did not fire the first shots in Columbia. Enough is enough. If the Administration sends troops into the Southern District then we will treat them as forces invading from another country. Thorne needs to consider his options very carefully. One cannot predict what one will catch in casting the net of war. A government big enough to give you everything you want, is big enough to take away everything you have. If they stay on this path to reducing all common citizens to indentured servants then we will resist, we will never quit, and we will never surrender. We can become the dogs of war. Let them come." The crowd cheered as Cyrus waved, saluted, and then left the stage.

Fort Hood

An intense low morning fog was holding strong over Fort Hood. The sun was rising and trying its best to burn it away, but the combination of wet ground and no breeze let the fog put up a fight. The humidity was so thick that General Moon Tzu had to take his sunglasses off right after stepping outside. He wiped the moisture off his glasses and tried to put them on again but they just fogged up a second time. He gave up and put them in his pocket.

Moon was on the roof of one of the central Fort Hood buildings with several officers also surveying the landscape. Moon used his viewpad to scan the wide-open training grounds north of the base. Most of his direct reports and advisors had lobbied for heavy fortifications and the most intimidating guns the Defense Force could ship to Texas in time. Moon, however, had convinced the Governor to go another direction. There were no troops or guns as far as the viewpad could see, not even aerial drones. Moon shook his head as he thought about the federal force expected to arrive soon. The President had ordered four Army divisions, made up of 40,000 troops and 4,000 androids, to Fort Hood to "provide security" which openly defied the Governor's proclamation that federal forces would be treated as hostile invaders.

Fort Hood had not changed much in a century. It was still a long line of government buildings running east to west, modest civilization to the south, and vast open land to the north used for training. There were a couple of ponds and several wooded areas in the thousands of acres for the troops to practice and train. Today, the training areas looked abandoned as if the base had been closed for years.

"Is everything ready?" Moon asked.

"Yes sir," answered Brigadier Major General Winfred Scott. "Everyone has been accounted for. The base is clean."

"How long until they get here?" Moon asked, still looking obsessively through the viewpad at the surrounding area for any sign of life.

"We believe the first two divisions will arrive coming in from the Middle Crossing area. They are moving cross country and should come in from dead north. In about five minutes the first of their airborne should be in sight," answered Major General Tonya Jackson. She was looking at several camera feeds on a large tablet that also showed ranges and other data. "The division that will come across our left flank is currently flowing down West Range Road and about ten minutes out. The division that will come across our right flank is moving slower down East Range Road, almost twenty minutes away."

Moon looked up. "It's time. Let's get below to the command center. Play the video." Moon and the officers turned and headed to the roof access door to take them downstairs. The last to head through the door was Jackson who turned one last time to look north. She hit play on her tablet and shut the door behind her.

At one point Fort Hood had been the largest military base in the United States. After essentially being mothballed in the 2060s, the Southern District revived it to be the Headquarters for the Defense Force. It was currently home to three experienced divisions.

The soldiers assigned to Fort Hood were all in battle gear awaiting orders. This included full shielded helmets with data display and comm equipment. After Jackson hit play, the video started in their helmets. They could see two soldiers with a view of the Fort Hood training area in the background. The Fort Hood troops could tell it was motivational video time. That meant the shit was about to hit the fan. The two men had earpieces that served as microphones and wore uniforms. One had on a militia uniform and the other a Texas State Guard uniform. The shirts were ripped and untucked. They both had rough tattoos on their arms. The two of them exchanged looks and then it began.

"What up Jones?!" The first man said.

"Yo Tyrone. These fools comin' on us, you know what I'm saying?" Jones replied.

"Dog, it don't matter, we are standing strong."

"But I hear these fools got some power shit, some murder shit!"

"Dog, we are strong, they ain't got shit on us! You know what I'm sayin?"

"Right, right."

"The man on your left is strong. The man on your right is strong. They ain't got shit on us. They on our turf! You feel me?"

"I feel ya."

"So, you ain't gotta do it yourself, and what you're doing, my brothers and sisters, they're doin. They can't touch us if we stand strong!"

"I feel ya dog."

"So, you know when they fuckin with one of us, they fuckin with us all!"

The music started with a pair of deep drum beats, followed by a church bell ringing every couple of seconds. It was eerily like the bell that rang in Columbia. The beat picked up and tightened into a tough classic metal song with a drum beat so strong Fort Hood soldiers could feel it in their heart beats. Their headsets, through manipulating their brainwaves, promoted their courage and muted their fears.

The background behind the singers switched from Fort Hood to the scenes of the Houston, St. Louis, and Columbia attacks. The images of the victims, combined with the tenacious beat was potent. The song was the adrenalin fueled fight theme, *Dot Your Eyes*, by Five Finger Death Punch.

"Bring it!
My life is forfeit, so they believe
So much for the land of the free
They're coming for you and me
Shout like hell and fight like devils!

The only heroes are us rebels

Now it's our turn, let those mother fuckers burn
Sangre por sangre, don't tread on me
We'll dot their eyes and cross their fuckin teeth!

Ready to throw down, this is a showdown
You get the memo? 'Cause it's all about to go down
I know I'm twisted, I can't resist it
I don't give a shit, don't give a shit about any of them!

There ain't nothin' in this world for free
I won't give away, give away fuckin' everything
This is the man that I'm choosing to be
We'll dot their eyes and cross their fuckin teeth!

You know how the saying goes
It's not the size of the dog in the fight
It's the size of the fight in the dog

Bring it!"

After about five minutes, the video finished and the Defense Force saw their displays return to darkness with only data and messages along the top and bottom.

The first of the Army units from the north made first line of sight visual of the Fort Hood buildings. They were surprised to see no sign of life. Aerial drones paced left and right slowly creeping closer to the base. They collected data and scouted for the ground forces. Roughly two hundred aerial machines of various models were accompanying the bulk of the federal force, half assigned to support the forward units. The video and scans from the machines were transmitted to federal officers in the field and command center.

General Mori Tortan was personally overseeing the operation. It was called Operation Genesis. This operation was to usher in a new era of control over the districts. The President had lost his patience. That seems to always be the final straw before two forces duke it out. If politicians had to do the fighting themselves then maybe they would develop more patience.

"Looks like they all left sir. All that talk and no fight," said General Henry McDonald.

Mori just stared at the displays. No visuals of soldiers, drones, or even weapons.

"I don't like it. It's too…convenient," said General Rachel Slate.

"What is that over there? Ariella, do we have satellite imagery of that area behind the central buildings?" Mori asked.

"No sir, the next satellite pass will be in twenty minutes," Ariella responded.

"Send a squadron of drones to circle the entire base and show us the video," Mori directed.

"As you command," Ariella replied, and instantly six drones accelerated quickly away from the task force, three to the left and three to the right all at different altitudes. They began an oval flight pattern around the Fort Hood complex to scan for any sign of the Defense Force.

"Looks like the congestion behind the central buildings is just a lot of abandoned trucks," said General Winston Grant.

By this time the main bulk of the central federal force was in view of the base, including thousands of infantrymen. Many were riding in armored personnel carriers that each had enough firepower to take on as much as a tank from any other country. Mixed in with the humans around the perimeter were some of the more exotic machines from the federal arsenal. Next, the division from the west crested the horizon, their drones getting their first visuals. The fog was finally starting to dissipate leaving behind a crusty barren landscape.

"Ariella, access the personnel information of all soldiers we believe to be stationed at Fort Hood. Give me the current data on any active implanted location chips. I want to know if any of them are here, and if they are not here then where the hell are they," Mori said.

"Yes sir," Ariella answered. "This display shows the latest data on their movements. It appears they are all on transports heading south."

The display showed the Highway 6 route to Houston. Thousands of red dots were on the highways quickly moving southeast, some now even past College Station.

"See, they ran. They must have packed up and left before sunrise," Henry said.

"Hmmm. We still need to be careful. I'll feel better once we check the buildings." Mori stared at the map. "Ariella, have all forces meet up at the fields just north of the buildings. Have them line up so that we have units in front of every building. Once we have all our forces there, we will enter all the buildings at once."

"Yes sir," Ariella replied. All the forces now began to move in more quickly and the eastern division was finally in sight. Three living rivers of green and black flowed into the base. The vehicles that entered the training grounds now paused and let most of the infantry get out and walk.

"Sir, I think there is something odd here." Rachel said, still looking at the personnel locator chip display. "These clusters of men are, uh, too clustered. Some of these have a hundred men in the space of a large truck." Mori looked, seeing how she had zoomed in to see this oddity.

Private First Class Red Bolton was one of the first men on the ground. His platoon was walking towards one of the center buildings. All the federal forces had on full combat gear, including helmets with face shields and data displays.

"Hey Joe," Red yelled. "I guess they all went crying to their mommies!"

"Shut up you idiot. No way you got that lucky. Your karma is the worst," Joe yelled back.

Their platoon saw several others walking on either side as they crossed the last major roadway on their way up to the buildings. The fort was close enough to judge the buildings empty by just watching the windows. The ground was hard packed dirt in every direction with tire treads from recent heavy vehicles running in all directions.

Suddenly, Red tripped and fell on his face. Joe and the others laughed. Red barked at the ground knowing that would be hard to live down. He looked at where he had tripped.

"Lieutenant! Ma'am, I think I found something," Red yelled. Most of his twenty-man platoon were now at least looking at him with a few walking closer.

"What is it this time private?" Asked Lieutenant Jodi Holliday. "I am not here to wipe your nose when you fall down."

"Ma'am, I tripped on this edge." Red was on his hands and knees starting to move dirt off the edge that just kept going. It was revealing a metal plate that was just below the hard-packed dirt surface.

"Sergeant, let's uncover whatever Private Bolton found," Jodi directed.

"Platoon, you heard the lady. On your knees, get this cleared off," the sergeant ordered.

"Command, this is Lieutenant Holliday. Over," Jodi said.

"Yes Lieutenant. What is your situation? Over," the officer responded.

"Sir, we have found a very large thick metal plate just under the dirt. Looks like a plate thick enough to be armor," Jodi said. As she finished, she saw another platoon about one hundred feet away also clearing off a plate. The fog was finally allowing them to have a good visual scan of the entire area. The only thick fog left was hanging over the river and ponds. "Sir, I think we may have a …"

Deep inside one of the Fort Hood buildings, General Moon Tzu was watching all of the Army units being drawn into the trap.

"Sir, we have a situation. Two of the doors have been found," a junior officer said to Moon. "It appears at least one group is trying to open one."

"How long until the rest of the feds are in the zone?" Moon asked calmly.

"Sir, approximately 87% of the federal forces are in range. At this rate it will take ten minutes to reach close to 100%, not counting the drones providing recon sweeps away from the bulk of the forces," replied Carrina, the Defense Force AI.

"Sir, I think one of their units has figured out the hatches," the young officer said again. "I believe they are calling it in to their command now."

"Damn. We are going to have to open them up and attack to draw the rest of them in," Moon said, and everyone in the room stopped to look at him. "Tell all units to fire-at-will once we spring, but watch out for friendlies." Moon paused, listening to the orders being given to the troops. "Open the cans!"

"As you command," Carrina replied.

Almost instantly, two hundred murder holes opened up in the Fort Hood training fields. All the holes had ten-centimeter-thick metal plate covers that swung open and smashed anything that had been on the other side. The noise when they all smashed the ground at the same time was deafening. The holes allowed the southern forces to use them like foxholes to shoot from. Not every hole had the same deadly combination inside but, in unison, all of the southern forces hidden in the holes opened fire on the federal forces. The combination of southern forces was a motley crew. The one common marker was they each wore a red and white scarf, a reminder of a young soul murdered at the Bush Park massacre.

The murder holes were five meters square and a meter deep. The majority of the holes closer to the base had more men than androids, and many of them had shoulder-mounted laser cannons excellent for shooting down drones, even military grade. The holes further from the base had more androids who, by this time, had mostly human soldiers around them. Most of the human southern soldiers were using machine guns as they allowed fast reload instead of waiting for a laser to recharge. Most of the southern androids were firing laser cannons at drones trying to make it a ground combat. In each hole were at least two soldiers with anti-tank missile launchers and they fired at the personnel carriers. Some of the southern soldiers hesitated as the plans had changed from capture to attack. Those that hesitated were taken out quickly by the Army androids who were incapable of being scared and reacted naturally per their programming.

"Sir, the hole has hostiles in it!" Lieutenant Jodi Holliday yelled to the command center as she saw it swing open. There was no time to react as she and three men from her platoon were raped by machine gun fire from soldiers inside the hole. The young officer had been fairly overweight and she was cut nearly in half with large pieces of fat flying on the troops around her. The rest of her men ran from the hole only to find other holes in all directions. There was no hiding for anyone. It was kill-or-be-killed. A few just fell to the ground cowering.

In the command center for the federal forces, everyone started talking at once.

"Shut up, all of you!" Yelled Mori. "I want every available drone and android to the front line now! Every available missile or grenade needs to find a hole to clear!" The display in the control room lit up like a Christmas tree.

In the command center for the southern forces, Moon was watching the display showing the rest of the forces moving in quickly. He also began to see displays showing some of his units taking damage as well after the initial surprise had passed. The murder holes were good for hiding and initial contact, but one missile or even grenade into the hole meant death to all inside.

"Tell me the instant all their machines are in the net," Moon told Carrina. "Activate the Zoo. Any federal machines need to be pushed in with utmost urgency!"

There were four wooded areas around the training fields. Some of the federal forces began to run for cover after they saw the personnel carriers being taken out. As they arrived, roughly fifty androids that looked like trees began to walk towards them. These unlucky army men and women turned back to the training ground with about a dozen of these massive machines coming out of the wooded areas firing a combination of lasers, fire, and machine guns.

High bay doors began to open at three of the Fort Hood buildings. After each reached the top, a Titan crawled out of each. The three-story tall android with four arms each slowly started to walk towards the battle, further terrifying the thousands of scrambling army forces. Aerial drones began to move at the Titans doing little damage but at least distracting them from the forces on the ground out in the open. The Titans each found a target area and sprinted to it causing massive damage.

The mood was generally calm in the Defense Force command center.

"Sir, it appears to be working," reported Carrina to Moon. "All of the remaining federal forces are closing at full speed. We are taking casualties, but not nearly as bad as the enemy."

"Good. Tell me as soon as they are all in the net or if we see the rest stop. We need to fire the secret weapon as soon as possible," Moon said. "If they hadn't found the holes, we could have avoided a lot of this bloodshed, but we may only get one shot."

It was general panic at the federal forces command center.

"Everybody, focus on your jobs!" Mori yelled, getting sick of the lack of discipline. They were too soft for a war. He would have to crack them into shape, but this wasn't the time. "Where is the nest?! I want it in there immediately!"

"Sir, it is at full speed and has begun its descent. It should be there in sixty seconds," Ariella replied. "My analysis of the battle is that the enemy has exhausted most of its ground to air firepower as our remaining drones are causing considerable damage."

"Good. I want the nest to go active as soon as it gets there and tell our people to get on the ground and into some of the holes if possible. Make sure we are watching for our personnel implant chip locations before taking out holes!" Mori shouted. "The bastards mixed in with our guys so we couldn't use air power," Mori whispered to himself.

On the ground, it was like an alternate reality, like traveling back into a documentary about trench warfare. The federal forces had managed to take an area on the northern edge and neutralized the treedroids. They were beginning to pound away at the Titans from the air and at the southern holes from the ground.

In one of the southern-controlled murder holes, Lieutenant Chris Simon was with his eight men and two androids. They were towards the front lines that had formed. It was so loud outside but the comm through the helmets was working just fine.

"Snow, go to the other side, we need to balance both sides," Chris ordered. Private Barbara Snow moved from the edge Chris was on to the opposite side. He was worried a counter attack could come at any time. "It shouldn't be too much longer until we launch the surprise."

"They are sure taking their sweet time about it, sir," Barbara answered for the rest of them.

"Zip that shit private," Chris responded crisply.

"Do you hear something?" Asked Specialist Berry Blackhead.

"You mean war? Yeah, I think we hear it," Barbara answered.

"Quiet! I think I hear something too," Chris said. His unit stopped talking, but were returning fire from the closest federal forces. "Quiet! Everyone, stop firing."

They all started to listen more closely. There was a humming sound coming from the north loud enough to be heard over the gunfight and screams of the wounded.

"There! It's a hornet's nest!" Chris said, looking north at a large light grey structure in the sky. "I've never seen one so close and it's coming right at us. I'm calling it in," Chris said to his platoon. He used the helmet tools similar to a halo to switch comm to the command center. "Sir, I have visual on a hornet's nest coming in hot from the north. Looks like it is descending upon us. Orders?"

"Yes Lieutenant, it's one of the last pieces we needed in the net. Hold tight and keep fighting," replied the specialist taking calls from the command center.

"Shit!" Chris said to himself and switched back to his unit. "Everyone, they know it's coming. They want it in the net before they trigger it."

"So, we are supposed to what, fight it?" Barbara asked. "Maybe we can explain that we want this great trap to work."

"Secure that shit Snow!" Chris yelled. He changed the magnification on his visor to zoom in on the Hornet's Nest. It was a flying aircraft carrier designed to transport, deploy, repair, and otherwise move mass quantities of drones, usually Eagles and their little siblings Hornets, into combat zones. A modern day Arc. The feds were throwing a hard-counter punch. Chris could tell that over a hundred Eagles and Hornets had already left the nest and were flying in solo. He knew even more hornets would be released when it slowed its descent. Out of the corner of his view to the left, Chris caught glimpse of an android in the forest just out of the action. The single red dot on its forehead made him pause for a second. He closed his eyes and prayed quickly that the trap would spring soon.

The heavily armed and fortified flying machine began its final descent into the battlefield laying a huge shadow on the northern half of the field. The Eagles immediately began to savagely rake the southern forces. The Hornets began taking on the Titans inflicting heavy damage.

Suddenly, twenty more holes slammed open and five Lobos sped out of each of them unleashing hell on any northern forces nearby. Even the Eagles avoided them. They started to move in on the northern holes after re-establishing the line protecting the southern teams. The last of the three Titans fell and the Eagles and Hornets all now focused on the Lobos in a tit-for-tat battle. As the Hornet's Nest finally came down close to the ground, it landed just north of the federal forces, and the back door opened up. Twenty Scorpions splinted out the back door going straight after the hundred Lobos. The Lobos were ferocious predator machines that were effective individually, but their real power came when working as a pack. The Lobos worked to surround and overwhelm the slower Scorpions one at a time. The Lobos' speed was unmatched by anything else on the battlefield – four legs, razor sharp claws, and a jaw that could cut through two-centimeter-thick steel.

After several minutes and a couple of changes in strategy by the federal machines, the Lobos were simply getting overpowered by the combination of Eagles, Hornets, and now Scorpions. Less than a quarter of the Lobos were left, the Titans were all down, and the southern troops were having limited impact with most of their anti-drone weapons used or lost.

"Sir, we are at over 98% machines in the net, including the Hornet's Nest," Carrina reported to General Tzu.

"What is outside the net?" Moon asked.

"Mostly aerial drones and a late division from the west," Carrina replied.

"Sir, we need to act fast before the last of the Lobos is taken out," General Tonya Jackson offered to Moon.

"Get me Captain Lucilla Swift," Moon said. Carrina already had her on standby.

"Yes sir," Lucilla said through one of the displays at the command center.

"Spring the trap Captain," Moon said.

Lucilla looked at Zander Brown who was with her in a different Fort Hood building and listening to the orders. He pushed several buttons on his control panel then looked up at her and nodded.

"It is done," Lucilla said calmly.

"God help us all," Moon said.

"I don't think God favors warriors, but I pray this works sir," Lucilla answered.

Across the battlefield, every machine and electronic device, including all the soldiers' helmets began to fail. Androids simply slumped and fell down. Aerial drones stopped actively controlling their path and plummeted on whatever trajectory they had been on. The computer bacteria had taken out every piece of machinery in sight of Fort Hood. The bacteria were designed by Southern District engineers and verified to work on new federal machines thanks to security software algorithms supplied by Zander. Soldiers pulled their helmets off as the screen went blank which meant they were blind with it on.

The bacteria were triggered seconds after firing several EMPs across the battlefield. With the electronics weakened by the EMPs, the bacteria were able to attack, adapt to machine defenses, and continue to attack the nervous systems of the machines. Computer bacteria was a recent concept with far more devastating impact on the machines than a computer virus. A virus is a simple self-replicating code designed to bring down a system. A bacterium is more like single cell AI organism that can react to the machine defenses. Southern engineers did not know yet how to tailor it to only work on enemy forces as they knew no defense against it. The bacterium was devastating, but too simple to know friend from foe.

From the west, just over the horizon, the Texas State Guard 44th Regiment, the Roughriders, crested the hill on old school motorcycles armed to the teeth – even their androids were on cycles. Samson Gamble was at the front yelling into his helmet. General Samantha Payne commanded the all-important clean up team. They had been waiting just outside the blast zone. It had taken three androids to hold Samson back this long. Overhead, every Predator drone the Defense Force could find was moving in at full speed to engage the Hornet's Nest and anything that came out of it.

From the east, Mori Tortan played the last wild card he had left in the area. Roughly two hundred men and women from the 101st Airborne jumped from their planes. They were in synthetic robotic systems that weighed a ton but immediately deployed wings to glide to the battlefront to counter the new southern threat. Cain Vasquez and Judith Strong were near the front of the drop team.

The Roughriders and Predators hit the federal front like a sledgehammer. There had been little movement since all the machines shut down, except for one savage group of Army soldiers who had gotten out of their holes with plenty of ammo and just started mowing down anything southern that showed its head. The Roughriders finished off the incapacitated Scorpions, just like they practiced, and started clearing federal holes one at a time.

"Ma'am, it's working!" Major Jimmy Williams said to General Payne.

"Don't get cocky!" Samantha said with a smirk. She scanned the battlefield seeing what Jimmy was talking about. Samson had picked up a Scorpion and was walking in a circle with its feet just flailing in the air. He then threw it down, ripped the cover off, and smashed in the driver's head with his boot. Samantha was starting to feel good but something caught her eye to the east. The sun had finished rising an hour ago and masked whatever it was. It looked like a lot of dots in the sky. "Command, come in. This is General Payne. Do we have friendlies coming in from the east?"

"No ma'am. We have nothing moving in except the Roughriders," responded the specialist from command. "We see that several large transport planes just flew past on the east, they may have deployed airborne units."

"All this technology and that's the best you can give me?" Samantha countered. "Thanks for nothing." She switched back to her Roughrider channel. "Men, we have incoming from the east. They are not friendlies. Repeat, enemy aerial targets incoming from the east."

Samson looked up to the east. His long hair bound into a rope a meter long. His headset adjusted some for the light, but still it was tough to see. "Ma'am, I see wings. Could be airborne." He paused watching them longer. "They are closing in fast. We need to shelter now!"

Cain Vasquez tightened his profile to increase his speed. He thought about closing his wings to go even faster but knew the weight of his combat suit would make him drop instead of glide. The 101st Airborne had finally gotten the call to join the fray. He looked to his right and was impressed Judith was keeping up. Well, she at least was still in sight. In a former life, Cain had been Airborne and this was not his first combat drop. He could see the battlefield. What an ugly site. If either side had been battle-hardened then it would have been over a long time ago. It looked like two rival bullies finally went at it but it was really the first time either had fought. America had gotten soft as the machines had won every war over the last generation.

Chris Simon's company of one hundred had been reduced to only a little more than a platoon. They were pinned down and every few minutes another one of his men would get picked off. Chris was not the highest ranking officer, but order had long since evaporated. The head of a young enlisted woman lay at his feet. She had taken a round at the neck and it lopped her head off, but not cleanly. Chris looked up and saw them coming from the east.

"Incoming from the east. Stay sharp!" Chris said to his men, all of whom were now in his hole. "They are coming in hot!"

Berry Blackhead had been in Chris' unit only a few weeks, but had shown promise quickly. Berry looked up and stared. He saw the wings on the soldiers. With the sun now above and behind them, it gave them an angelic look. Berry sat up instinctively to try to see them better. The wings were wide and the ones in front had now angled them to slow down which made the wings vertical instead of horizontal. The thick mechanical arms and legs gave the illusion of muscles that would make any bodybuilder jealous.

"They look almost beautiful," Berry said, and then sat up a little more. Seconds later his body was on the other side of the hole with a cavity where his chest had once been. A blood drizzle hung in the air.

"And that's why they are called Killer Angels," Chris mumbled to himself, shaking his head.

Half the Airborne unit was slowing to come down right on top of the Roughriders, half were moving against the Predator drones. The Roughriders showed hospitality by opening fire with everything they could muster. The Army units in the northern holes were grateful for the distraction to finally get some peace. The suits of the Airborne were armored and the mechanisms in the legs would take the bulk of the impact at landing.

"Eat this you cum drunk shits!" Samson yelled, as he fired his cannon with another Roughrider helping to reload it. The side of his cannon read "The Reaper." Not all of his shots found an airborne soldier, but the ones that hit were brutal.

The Killer Angels hammered the ground as they landed, each leaving small craters behind. They ejected their wings and the half-machine half-human soldiers started their march towards the southern positions. As they gained awareness of where the greatest threats were, they turned their march into a sprint. Training kicked in; God will sort it all out.

After slaughtering a hole of southerners, Cain looked around and saw a monster of a man. The beast had long hair bound into a tail that reached his lower back and was firing a gun the size of a tank turret. Cain smiled; he had just found the target for this assignment.

"Judith, let's show that hillbilly what Yankee justice looks like," Cain said, not waiting for an answer. Cain started to make his suit move fast but quietly as he got both weapons ready. He selected the flamethrower for his left hand and laser gun for the right. The suit had the newest power system for fast recharge. Cain started a sweep around the monster's blindside. Judith was close behind him with two other jumpers.

Samson saw the Killer Angels hit the ground and knew he should likely take cover; however, his blood was up and as long as the cannon was taking them out and he had rounds to fire then he was going to keep shooting. The corporal loading the cannon was putting in another round when someone yelled "Ahhhh!" Samson knew that meant surprise attack and thoughtlessly dropped to the ground. The corporal was not so lucky taking a face full of flamethrower. Samson rolled to his right as the attack was from his left. He heard about six Roughriders start to fire at the oncoming threats. Samson switched to his machine gun and turned to see what was coming. Despite all this happening in just a few seconds, it was not fast enough as Cain was on Samson. Using the machine suit, Cain kicked Samson hard enough in the gut to send him flying several meters. Other Roughriders kept Cain and Judith busy for a short while but Samson quickly pulled himself to his feet. He knew this was not a standard issue jarhead that had picked him. This was going to be the real deal. Showtime.

Samson and Cain faced off after the distractions started to entertain themselves. They slowly started to walk in a circle measuring each other and savoring the history of the moment. Cain raised his laser hand to test Samson's reflexes and was not disappointed. Samson leapt immediately over two meters in the air at him and fired down on Cain who had to stop his shot to dodge left.

Samson rolled after hitting the ground behind a smoking trashed personnel carrier. Cain looked at the wrecked transport and eyed Judith who had just finished off a couple of Roughriders. Cain went right and Judith went left. Both had flames lit on their throwers. The battle had been raging for two hours now. The sounds of the wounded a constant background rumble.

Judith and Cain both carefully rounded the transport and looked around to see where their prize had gone. They found each other on the other side. Just before either could say the obvious, Samson jumped out of the burning personnel carrier behind Judith and buried a forty-centimeter-long knife into the back of her suit, expertly finding the gap in the armor. She screamed in pain but no-one could hear her. Samson smiled at Cain and tossed Judith to the side with the knife still stuck in her back. Blood began to swell and drip from her suit.

Cain was furious; he charged at Samson. His rage was powerful enough to be a weapon all its own. Samson started to bring up a pair of laser pistols but Cain in his machine suit was just too fast. He grabbed Samson by the neck and started to lift him off the ground with one arm. Cain used his other three arms to disarm Samson. He squirmed and tried desperately to loosen Cain's grip of his neck. Cain's head tilted as he held his prize in his hand, holding him almost a meter off the ground, and looking him eye-to-eye. Samson brought his feet together, swung them backwards, and then kicked Cain's suit in the groin with all his strength. Cain felt the high current surge from the nanotech capacitors in Samson's boots. Samson had armed them using his helmet controls. The suit adsorbed most of the current and all of the groin shot. It mostly just pissed Cain off and he squeezed even harder, savoring the moment. Samson heard his helmet start to crack where it met his neck.

Samson mumbled.

"What was that you treasonish shit?" Cain asked, and slightly loosened his grip.

"I don't understand, I've always been the biggest," Samson coughed. "Are you actually bigger than me?"

"The size of the man isn't what counts, it's the size of the suit," Cain replied.

"That's not what she said," Samson countered. Cain realized he was being screwed with and began to tighten his grip again.

Cain didn't know why he started to fall backwards until he later saw the video. The growling came out of nowhere. Six of the last Lobos on the battlefield had snuck up on him and pulled him away from Samson. They had found shielding in a murder hole from the EMPs and computer bacteria. Cain dropped Samson, who fell to the ground and rolled into the closest hole. Cain threw one Lobo at the others and looked for his prey. To his right he saw Judith's face, the life draining from her eyes. The Lobos formed a defensive front between Cain and the southern troops nearby.

"All federal forces, fall back to the Hornet's Nest for extraction. Repeat, we are falling back. Pull back to the Hornet's Nest immediately," Cain heard on the comm system. Damn. Just when it was getting good the cowards are quitting, Cain thought to himself. He looked around and saw no hesitation by the other federal forces. They were almost running away. Cain grabbed Judith's suit by both arms and started to run to the transport with her on his back. Maybe he could at least save her life. He knew he would find that monster again someday. Cain knew to defeat this enemy his leaders would need to be willing to go all in and not fall back just because their precious plans didn't work out.

Lucilla Swift and Zander Brown had moved to the roof of their building once the trap was sprung and their job was done. They had watched the battle and were distraught over the non-stop loss of life. As the battle concluded, they saw the feds moving away and could feel the impending southern victory.

"We did it!" Lucilla said with a smile to Zander. She put her hand on his shoulder.

"I am not sure yet what we did. Look at all those dead people," Zander said, and turned to face Lucilla. "Did we do the right thing?"

Lucilla gently put her hands on either side of his face. She looked sincerely into his eyes. "Yes, I am sure we did the right thing. Even though some died today, many will live in freedom tomorrow," Lucilla said. "That is true for citizens in the west as well as the south. It is important to remember that…"

Lucilla was cut off by machine gun fire from above that started to shower their position. Two of the people with them fell, one screaming in agony. Four deadly Hornets had found them and were all closing on them from the east. Lucilla grabbed Zander's right arm and pulled him behind an air vent. It was large enough to hide them for now, but would not work for long against angry Hornets. Another of their group was hit and silenced. The other four of their team had also found something to hide behind and tried to return fire on the Hornets. The injured soldier was using both hands to try and keep his intestines from falling out; he was failing and his screams were waning.

"Command, we are under fire. Need help on the roof. Hornets are right on top of us!" Lucilla said into her wrist communicator. "Send help now dammit or we are all dead!"

From north of the building a hail of bullets rained into the sky at the Hornets. One of the amazing aspects of AI in the battlefield is that the reaction time from decision to action is practically zero. One of the Hornets was hit almost immediately.

Lucilla got her laser rifle ready. Taking care of the asset, Zander, came with the perk of getting to carry one of the precious rapid recharge laser rifles. It cost over fifteen thousand credits. She peaked out from behind their air vent and saw the Hornets were almost on them. Another volley came in and two holes opened up in the sheet metal of the air vent but missed both Lucilla and Zander. Another of their group fell leaving only two other southern soldiers still in play on the roof. Lucilla knew she could not just sit and wait for them to murder Zander. She turned to Zander who had his hands on his ears and panic on his face.

"Don't forget, what you did here today was heroic. I am very proud of you," Lucilla said to Zander and then she ran out into the open, firing her laser rifle at the incoming Hornets. A blast came so close to her it ripped her shirt at the waist and burned her side but it was working to draw their fire from Zander. Another of the Hornets was knocked out by the ground units but another of Lucilla's team was also hit. Lucilla injured one of the last Hornets before hiding behind the wall of the exit from the roof. The two remaining Hornets were now slowly hovering above her, trying to find a clear shot. One found Lucilla on its sensors and began to circle around the left to get to Lucilla.

In between the Hornet blades and cries of the injured, Lucilla heard the distant rumble of androids running up the stairs. She knew she only had to buy a few more seconds and then Zander would be safe. Lucilla overcame her fear and stood to fire at one of the Hornets, punching it square in its sensor package before she dropped to the ground. The Hornet was hit but not fooled. It saw her location and fired as fast as it could. The other soldier on the roof took advantage of the Hornet firing at Lucilla to peak out and shoot. As the Hornet was hit, so was Lucilla. As the Hornet fell to the ground, it saw the last guard and shot him dead. Only Zander and the injured Hornet remained.

Zander recognized the silence as bad news. He lowered his hands and looked for Lucilla.

"Lucilla?" He called quietly, not sure yet if there were more Hornets. No answer, no sound at all on the roof. Zander started to look left and right. As he peeked around the right side, he saw the last Hornet slowly circling trying to be sure it had taken out the site. Zander quickly pulled back not sure if he had been fast enough. Then he thought of Lucilla. Was she hurt? Why didn't she answer? He needed to know she was ok. Zander turned back and the Hornet was only a few meters away. It detected his movement and swiveled to bring its guns around. Just before it could fire, the door to the roof burst open and Defense Force androids came through the door causing the final Hornet to fly away.

"Lucilla!" Zander shouted. He started to run around looking for her. Zander found her lying on her side in a pool of blood. "No!" Zander yelled as he knelt down beside her. He gently rolled her over. "Medic! We need a medic here now!" Zander yelled, not sure what else to say. "Don't you leave me Lucilla. You are going to be fine. It's not that bad."

Lucilla turned to Zander and her face for the first time looked weak to him. The life was draining away fast. He was scared for her. No way was this worth it, he thought.

"Zander, hold my hand," Lucilla said softly. He held her hand and used his other to try to stop the bleeding from her chest. "No matter what Zander, do not doubt what you did. What you did saved an entire way of life. It saved the last best chance for freedom in this God forsaken country. You are my hero Zander." Lucilla coughed up blood, looked up at Zander for a few seconds, and closed her eyes.

North of the battlefield, the federal forces had finally all met up at the Hornet's nest. They had gotten the aircraft carrier controls back but the computer bacteria were still plaguing them. The machine lifted off the ground and started heading north. Cain was amazed the southerners were not trying to shoot them down. They would regret that later he thought.

Naya

Naya Garcia cradled her face in her hands, fighting back tears. She had just read the figures on the casualties. The United States had just suffered the greatest number of losses from a single battle in almost a hundred years. Both sides of the fight were American, making every metric hurt. The country was used to fighting an inferior foe, but both sides had similar training and used similar technology and thus the setting was unforgiving.

Naya sat at the war council table waiting for the debrief to the President. Alexandra Soaring was still Acting National Security Chairwoman and was scrambling to set it up. More people were attending in person than the last meeting. An implosion on home soil will make everyone wake up. The rest of the security committee, Harvey Keitel, Asa Katz, and of course Ariella, were all present, as well as the joint chiefs, Vice President Angela Wolf, and the rest of the President's cabinet that had anything to do with war. Hologram projections along the walls were images of lower level generals and politicians. The one person joining virtually that was a key player was General Mori Tortan.

Naya could hear the talking get louder and finally took her hands out of her hands. She would be strong now. Can't let the men see her be soft in any way. Alexandra was giving directions to people and Ariella. She was moving fast so the President must have been close. Naya looked around. She wished she had something to work on instead of brewing over the reality of the battle and second guessing her actions. Some people actually looked excited. Naya was disgusted. She knew her hands weren't clean, but this had mushroomed into a nightmare. She felt truly south of heaven.

Governor Asa Katz was next to Naya and on her other side was Governor Simone Dubois. The Governors had been talking around her about what to do next. Naya finally snapped out of her dream state when President Nero Thorne walked into the room.

"Hello Mr. President," Alexandra said, as Nero walked to the head of the table.

"Hello everyone," Nero replied. He waited for everyone else to sit. "Obviously we are meeting under a cloud of pain and sorrow. The events of today are unacceptable and the slaughter carried out in this surprise attack is beyond anything I thought possible. Before we begin, I ask for a moment of silence for the fallen." Nero lowered his head and everyone followed suit. Naya lowered her head some but slowly scanned the room. She wanted to see if others were also masking their grief.

"Thank you," the President said, and then sat down. "What do you have for us Alexandra?"

"Sir, there is a lot of misinformation in the media right now. We are ready to share what we know occurred to dispel fact from fiction. General Tzu is here to report," Alexandra said.

"What happened Mori?" Nero said. Naya thought Nero had a look on his face mixing sympathy, doubt, anguish, and anger.

"Mr. President, we were ambushed and attacked without mercy," Mori paused briefly. "Ariella, bring up the display." Video appeared at the front of the room, but Mori did not pause. "We approached Fort Hood from three directions. We avoided the civilian areas just in case there was some violence as we did not want any collateral damage. There was a thick fog and low visibility. The base appeared deserted as we approached. We moved in slowly thinking that the base had been evacuated and, in fact, implant chip data for Defense Force personnel showed them heading south on the highways; however, it was all a trap to lure us in and disable our androids and machines. They had three divisions hiding in buried chambers. We were moving in with four divisions. Both sides had heavy ground support from androids, plus we had personnel carriers and air support." The video showed examples and video from the helmets of various infantry and androids.

"We discovered one of the trap doors hidden in the ground and then they attacked." Mori continued. "They likely were waiting for us to move in to launch cutting edge computer bacteria and EMPs. Since we were about to find them before our machines were in the EMP blast zone, they instead unleashed hell to draw the rest of us in. The bacteria were so powerful, it disabled every machine in sight, even their own. We fought bravely before the trap was unleashed. Once nearly all our machines were in the trap, they launched the bacteria. Our machines are supposed to be secure to these kinds of attacks and we are still looking into how it was so effective. This new advanced computer bacteria are far more aggressive than anything we have seen before. It adapted and learned as our countermeasures tried to resist. Once the machines were down, it quickly degraded to hand-to-hand fighting until we could pull out. Nothing but blood, shit, and tears." Mori paused and briefly looked down; the feelings still raw. "My request to bring in reinforcements from outside the engagement zone was denied. I then requested a hypersonic missile strike on the Fort Hood buildings, which I believe served as the command center, which was also denied. I'd like to discuss that further when the time is right." Mori was exhausted and it showed.

"General, please tell your troops we are thinking of them and will not let this injustice go unpunished," Nero said. "How many were killed and wounded?"

"Four thousand, five hundred and twenty-seven. Because of the weaponry, it was far more dead than wounded. We have been told the Southern District is attending to the wounded we could not evacuate and will return them within three days," Mori said.

"God help us," Nero said. "How many of those were our troops?"

"That was only our troops. I don't know how many they lost and, right now, I do not care." Mori's face hardened. "Those cowards sucker punched us sir."

Nero thought for several seconds, watching the video which was still showing the fighting, and the fallen. He shook his head. "Alexandra, have you looked into what the Southern District is up to now?" Nero asked. "Seems like we need to understand their posture to know our next moves."

"Sir, with all due respect, our next steps are up to us. If we let their posture affect what we do, then we may be doing exactly what they want us to do," Mori said. "They have acted with rage. We should not assume they intend anything less than all-out war."

"We have prepared what we know sir. We also have some options on what we can do now," Alexandra said, essentially ignoring Mori's comment. "Ariella, please bring up the briefing." The display brought up a map of the United States and then zoomed in to the Southern District. "Sir, they have moved two more divisions into Fort Hood. They have also further moved to consolidate forces close to the border, and those that moved out of deep southern cities have been replaced by new volunteers. The media in the south are calling this an invasion repelled by the brave Southern District Defense Force. The media in the other districts are calling this a cowardly act of treason and rebellion." Alexandra paused as the display showed arrows and movement of troop and air wing symbols. "All indications are that they are developing as many corps as possible in essentially two armies. One is centralized in Texas and the other north of Atlanta. These are not the actions of a remorseful district. They aim to misbehave."

Nero looked at the display, taking a few deep breaths.

"You said you had options," Nero stated.

"Essentially, we need to decide if we want to drive them to negotiations or if we want to try again to force them into submission," Alexandra said. "We have options in either direction but that is the fundamental question."

"I think I already heard what General Tzu thinks," Nero said, and Mori nodded. "Asa, what do you think?"

"Sir, I think we need to give negotiations another chance. This could escalate out of control. No-one thinks a civil war will last long, but we have seen before it can go on for years," Asa replied. "It won't hurt to try and if it doesn't work then we haven't lost anything. Their determination demonstrated these last few weeks show they will not shrink in the face of our demands. If I were a southerner, as I am an American, and if an army had invaded my home, I would never lay down my arms."

"Mr. President, if I may, I disagree with Governor Katz," Harvey began.

"Asa, I just don't think Cyrus will respond to more talking, even if we cave on all of our demands. We pushed and we pushed and they hit their red line. They are seeing thousands of volunteers a day and have plants up and running around the clock producing weapons of war. The longer we wait, the stronger they will be. There will be a point where they are too strong to be overrun. Right now is our best chance to defeat them. Give them a taste of defeat and their volunteers will think twice. Hell, Cyrus might even get overthrown with a strong enough counterpunch."

"Make the chain, for the land is full of bloody crimes and the country is full of violence," Asa said.

"Gentlemen, please, do not be so cavalier with talk of civil war. This is the most important decision any of us will ever be a part of," Naya began, hardly believing she had spoken up. The moment too heavy for her to sit quietly on the sidelines. "This is no longer about scoring political points or changing policies. Mr. President, your next decision will mean life or death for thousands of people. Thousands of American citizens. The haunting echoes of the distant past must not be forgotten."

"Yes Naya, as always, your message resonates," Nero said. "I would love to turn the other cheek. I would love to talk our way out of this disaster, but this is not a matter of me deciding if we are at war or not. We have been attacked. War is upon us. We must face this treason with strength." Nero paused and looked around the room to see who might dissent. "Give me the options for a strong response," Nero said to Alexandra.

"There are several tactics and choices at your disposal. We recommend a mix of these. The devil is in the details but these are fundamental steps we can take today." Ariella switched the map to show the entire country, this time with light blue shading on the Eastern and Western Districts, plus red shading on the Southern District. "First, we call up all active reserves and we ramp up our own production of androids and other machines of war. This will show an overwhelming force." As Alexandra spoke, the display showed where exactly the action would take place. "Second, we release massive numbers of surveillance machines and personnel to gather intel and carry out sabotage missions. We also change what we gather from Halo users to see what intel we can gather on any movements they will make. Third, we instigate a blockade of the Southern District. Cut them off from the outside world. They will not be able to keep up with us on production, plus they will start to run short on almost everything. Last, and certainly not least, we bomb their robotics plants. If they try to return the favor, we start bombing their troop barracks." Nero studied the map carefully.

"Ok, bring me plans for all of them by tomorrow morning. I want the intelligence ops to start immediately," Nero said. "If we somehow let them fool us again and we don't even have a plan of action, then this is doomed from the start. If we are blind to their intensions this will not end anytime soon; however, if we know the enemy and ourselves, we need not fear war."

Dexter

D exter Durden stepped out of the car and closed his eyes as he turned his face to the warm sunlight. The Houston summer was picking up, but the breeze downtown was strong enough to let Dexter soak in the energy.

"Thank you for the ride Camilla," Dexter said.

"You're welcome sir. Seventeen credits have been withdrawn from your account. Have a pleasant day," Camilla replied, just before Dexter closed the door. Dexter walked away from the car and onto the sidewalk in front of the Southern District Capitol building.

Dexter had taken what remained of his team into hiding after the President had ordered his show closed. After reaching the Southern District, he made contact with members of the district government and became convinced they had no role in the attack. He was going to meet with them before but had been delayed as the events unfolded at Fort Hood. Now that a couple of days had passed, they were bringing him in to talk.

The Southern District Capitol was much smaller than the White House, but still a large dominating presence and was on one of the few elevated downtown areas. The city skyscrapers provided an impressive background. Stone pillars along the front and a five-meter-high statue of liberty on a hemisphere dome top gave the Capitol the aura of authority. There were close to fifty stairs to reach the top and the stairs were almost the width of the building at the bottom. There were heavily armed troops and androids at many locations, plus lots of people coming and going. Dexter paused to look at it before starting up the stairs. He had no doubt he was being watched by security and tried to avoid any sudden movements. On his way up, he saw an X with an O spray painted above it on the buildings to the left and right. The crude skull and crossbones symbol was everywhere in the south as a sign of resistance against the federal government. Dexter had seen this symbol made by members of his audience during his final shows.

When Dexter reached the top, he noticed ground to air missile batteries behind some trees on either side of the building. He continued until he reached the first security checkpoint. There were two human guards and, behind them, four military androids.

"What is your name and who are you here to see?" The first guard asked Dexter coldly.

"My name is Dexter Durden. I am here to see the Governor. I have an appointment," Dexter replied.

Both guards looked at Dexter closely.

"His identification chip matches. He is Dexter Durden, appointment confirmed," one android stated.

"Mr. Durden, welcome to the Southern District Capitol. You may proceed," the guard said.

Dexter moved quickly through the outdoor checkpoint, automated double doors, and security scanners.

"Mr. Durden," a man called from the left. Dexter turned to go to him.

"Hello," Dexter said.

"My name is Paul Franklin. I am on Governor Young's staff. I am here to escort you to the meeting," the young man said to Dexter. "I am very sorry about what happened to your show and to your people."

"Thanks, I appreciate that. This place is really busy, and it looks like a fortress," Dexter said.

"Every day it gets worse. More threats. More violence," Paul said. "Let's get you to your appointment."

The two men walked through the lobby area and down a hall to the left. They used stairs that spiraled up two levels, followed another hallway, and went into a small meeting room near the north end of the building. Paul sat at the table and Dexter followed his example.

"The Governor should be here momentarily," Paul said. "Are you thirsty?"

"No, thanks," Dexter replied. "I am wondering what he has to say. I know he is very busy. I didn't do anything to prepare for this, whatever this is."

Paul smiled and Dexter could tell he knew but was not going to share before it was time. Dexter looked around the room. There was the usual wall for videos but the other walls each had pictures of various Southern District natural landmarks. Dexter was about to comment on them when the door opened and Governor Young walked in.

"Hello Dexter. Thank you for coming today," Cyrus said, extending his hand to Dexter who stood to greet him. A security guard followed Cyrus in and stood behind him against the wall. A lady in a sharp business suit also followed Cyrus in and sat at the table next to Paul.

"Sir, it's an honor to meet you in person." Dexter stood to shake Cyrus's hand. "I can only imagine what it has been like here with everything going on." Both men sat down.

"Dexter, I will be brief as I am sure you understand I am very busy. It was important for me to see you today as I need your help," Cyrus began. "First, I want to say I am sorry for what happened to your show and especially your staff. My administration had nothing to do with it. You and the rest of your people are safe here in the Southern District as long as I have anything to say about it."

"Thank you. What can I do to help you?" Dexter replied.

"The country needs you to go back on the air. You were one of the few, if not the only show, that people in the other districts watched enough to actually hear our point of view." Cyrus paused. "We would provide security and help you get set up. The content, who is on your show, and what you say will be up to you. You can be hard on us or Thorne or whatever you want, but we think it is critical your message gets out to the country and the world. This young lady is Ms. Dana Berry, my trusted communications specialist. If you agree, she can help you get what you need."

Dexter was speechless. He had been thinking he might never host another show. "Sir, I am overwhelmed. I am still trying to accept what happened." Dexter paused and looked down briefly. "Can I control who works on the team?"

"Yes. It will be your show. There is a fundamental difference between the Southern District and the Thorne Administration. We believe in freedom; they believe in control. We want you on the air forcing hard debates. They saw you as a threat and tried to silence you forever." Cyrus paused. "Do you accept?"

Dexter thought for a couple seconds. "I don't know how I could say no," Dexter replied. "Yes, I accept. I really appreciate the opportunity."

"Excellent. In that case I will leave you here with Dana," Cyrus said. "I'll see you around I'm sure." Cyrus and Dexter both stood, shook hands, and Cyrus left with the security guard following.

"Hello Dexter," Dana said smiling. "Like the Governor said, I am Dana Berry. I will help you get whatever you need to get rolling. Paul here will also help and will be your day-to-day contact. We are both fans of your show. I am a Party of One and so are you! Partido de uno!" The three smiled lightly.

"Thanks. I guess I look forward to working with you. I am still a little in shock by this offer," Dexter said.

"Before we start talking details, there are two events coming up that we need to tell you about. You will probably want to cover both of them. It's up to you on how you do it and once you hear about them, I know you will see them as important, perhaps even historic," Dana said. "The first is that the Governor will be addressing the nation in three days. He plans to announce details on our intention for the Southern District to secede from the union." Dexter's jaw fell open halfway. "The other is a rally to be held right afterwards here in Houston where we celebrate the announcement. We will use the event to excite and challenge our citizens to get involved so this can become a reality. Enough is enough."

"I understand. Yes, those will be important to cover," Dexter said. "I do have one request that is very important to me." Dexter paused, wishing he had taken Paul up on the offer of a drink. "I want you to find out who ordered the attack on my people. We will need video from the attack which I suspect you can acquire. It is very important to me that as soon as possible I can call out the murderers for all to see. I know the Fort Hood battle and threat of war are central to the nation, but I owe it to my people. I need to show my remaining people what they mean to me. I need to do it to find closure for myself and, most importantly, I want to tell whoever did this that I will not forgive them, I will make sure they are caught, and I will make sure they pay for their crimes."

Anna

A nna Lee and her training unit were told to wait against the wall. The group of six were in a large high school gymnasium near the former NASA center southeast of Houston. It was only a few miles away from the AntiCo attack. Anna had holed up for days feeling guilty about what happened to Angel but finally emerged from her cocoon. For the first time in her life she needed to choose what to do. Anna decided to volunteer as a Defense Force medic. Her group was one of several rotating from station to station. Medics, like all other disciplines, were undergoing rushed training in case there was an all-out assault by the federal forces.

Anna and the others walked slowly to the wall. It was late morning and Anna had skipped breakfast. Her stomach was starting to twist up. She sat down with her back to the wall. This particular training station was for diagnosing damaged androids. The instructor was already with a different group and getting very frustrated with them. Apparently, he thought all the recruits should already know the basics of android anatomy. Anna was sure she and her group would be a similar disappointment. After a couple of minutes, a young man in her group sat down next to Anna.

"Hi, my name is Rex McNaughton. What's your name?" He said to Anna.

"Anna Lee," she replied, genuinely uninterested.

They sat in silence for a few seconds. Anna decided he wasn't a creep or at least was pretending to be a nice guy. He didn't get too close or immediately try to pry.

"Do you know why they keep having us train on machines?" Anna asked.

"They say we will end up learning both before we are assigned to a platoon. I hear that we are of more value as repairmen than real medics. Something about getting an android back into the battle will save more lives than anything we could do with injured soldiers," Rex said. "I sure hope there are enough of us that we don't have to choose."

"Seems pretty cold blooded to me. Even for war," Anna said.

"Yeah, I hear that," Rex said. He looked at Anna who was still watching the other group. "Is that a cross on your necklace?"

Anna finally looked at Rex straight on, trying to see if he was judging her. He seemed honestly interested.

"Yes," Anna replied. "I always wear it."

"It's lovely," Rex replied, looking away to avoid staring at her too long. "I hope you don't mind me saying something too personal but I have been struggling with my faith lately. I was raised Christian and have put up with hecklers as long as I can remember." He paused and stared at the crew training. "But the last few months have really shaken me. It was one thing when war and death was on the other side of the world, but all this violence is so close to home. I am from Houston. I have been questioning how God could let so much pain and suffering exist when it seems so avoidable."

Anna thought for a few seconds on how to reply. She rarely met open believers outside of church. In public, one was more likely to be heckled or worse than to meet other people of faith.

"When I find myself doubting, I go back to the basics. I read scripture and go to church to pray. I find my resolve and strength when I focus myself on his messages and his gifts," Anna replied.

"Scripture. Church. That brings up another doubt I have been struggling with," Rex said. "Since I started questioning it, I realized it's not just a question of believing in God. To follow scripture and go to church, it's also a question of believing that God talked or otherwise communicated with early man. Why would God want us to praise Him and otherwise worship Him while He doesn't even show Himself? What does that say about God if He wants us to praise Him to go to heaven instead of just being good? Or go to church instead of just pray at home? And why did He talk to early man and not us?"

Anna was starting to sincerely become intrigued with Rex. She put her hand on his shoulder and looked him in the eyes.

"Faith and free will are intertwined. If God was in our face talking everyday then there would be no doubt and no need for faith. If there is no thought involved then there is no free will. If there is no free will then we no longer can control our destiny. God loves us so much that He wanted us to have free will to make the most out of life even if it means some of us fall," Anna replied. "I had struggled with this same question myself."

Rex thought to himself for several seconds. He then turned back to Anna.

"That makes a lot of sense. In a way, it seems similar to the struggle we are in now as a nation. A large government rich with handouts and poor on freedom is like them trying to be God. Sure almost no-one falls, but almost no-one is free to be themselves either," Rex said.

Anna smiled at him. She felt energized and, for the first time in a while, hopeful.

The instructor finished with the other group and waived Anna's unit over for their turn.

Cyrus

Governor Cyrus Young was pinching his fingers to help control his nerves. He knew the speech by heart and only had to say it to the camera. No live crowd watching as the security protocol could not be guaranteed. The weight of what Cyrus planned to say was suffocating. The history of it was paralyzing. The consequences of it were petrifying. The technician counted down with her fingers until one and Cyrus knew he was speaking to his new country, his former country, and the world.

"Good evening," Cyrus began. "It is with a heavy heart that I rise for the purpose of announcing to the nation that I have satisfactory evidence that each of the states in the Southern District, by a solemn ordinance of her people in convention assembled, have declared our separation from the United States. When it becomes necessary for one people to dissolve the political ties with another and assume equal station under the laws of God and man, it is required to declare the causes which impel them to separation. The nature of our discontent is not complex. We believe that all people are created equal, that they are endowed by their Creator with certain unalienable Rights, and that among these are Life, Liberty and the pursuit of Happiness. We believe these truths to be self-evident and the rulers of the United States of America do not share these tenets of civil society." Cyrus paused briefly to let the announcement be adsorbed by those listening.

"There are many who believe that states or a district may not choose to leave the union. To them I would say the right for a state to secede is elemental to the principal that a state is a self-governing sovereign entity. If a state does not have the authority to leave the union then a state can also be forced out. No-one would question a state's right to remain in the union and therefore no one should question a state's right to withdraw. Early in the union's history, none denied it. Yes, the great civil war two centuries ago was based on this fundamental question as well as the evils of slavery. The south was on the wrong side of slavery but was on the right side in the question of state's rights. Following this logic and the purpose of a district being the unification of like-minded states, it is also a primary right for a district to be able to secede from the union.

"In the midst of sorrow, we must find hope. We have seen our citizens murdered in Houston, St. Louis, Columbia, and Fort Hood. Slowly over time the federal government has grown and grown. Because it has grown into an omnipotent force, it is no longer managed by citizens who believe in limited government and the principles this country was founded on. Those who fight and win national elections are sadly only those who desire absolute power. The founders had good intentions, but today's federal politicians do not. Absolute power corrupts absolutely. Absolute corruption dominates absolutely. It is not enough to shield our district half-heartedly from Washington any longer. Letting some of us suffer because most are ok is not justice. Injustice anywhere is a threat to justice everywhere. Our separation from the union will give us hope for future generations to enjoy the freedom that are essential to the idea of America.

"In the midst of grief, we must find peace. We need not be enemies and we need not be unified. Most Americans that have been married have also been divorced. Did you need to fight to the death to get divorced? When you separated, did the world order break down? Of course not. A separation of districts who have irreconcilable differences will be good for all concerned. We cannot continue under the current arrangement, but that should not mean we wage war. I will do everything I can to promote a peaceful transition as long as it does not sacrifice our citizens or the very rights we seek to reinstate.

"In the midst of chaos, we must find opportunity. Politics is not two dimensional. We all know about left and right, liberal and conservative. The third dimension is one of religion and holding fast to the value of every person, of every life, and of every soul. We use our faith and the guidance from the Lord. In the Southern District, we still remember that our unalienable rights are provided by our creator. If we abandon that principal, then we have nothing left to anchor us to choose right over wrong, life over death, and justice over tyranny. To those who say it is a sin to speak of secession, I say I will not repent. Our separation from the union is a new opportunity to prioritize this principal as we try to return our way of life to the original intent of the American constitution.

"One of the reasons we are in this predicament is that many have forgotten our history. It is not a perfect history, but it does offer invaluable lessons. Many of us remember the country going bankrupt and introducing the deudor system, but most are not taught the truth about the first civil war this country endured. It was in part about state's rights but the trigger and irreconcilable issue was that of slavery. We find ourselves not too far from that situation again. Those who do not study history are destined to repeat it. Government's paramount responsibility is to protect its people, not dominate their lives. In this present crisis, Government is not the solution to our problem, Government is the problem. Effective immediately, the deudor system is outlawed in the country formally known as the Southern District of the United States. No more indentured servitude. No more slavery. No longer will we have a permanent underclass.

"The transition and separation will not be easy. I pray for peace, but we prepare for invasion. I pray for reconciliation as neighbors, but prepare for war. This is not the end. It is not even the beginning of the end but it is, perhaps, the end of the beginning."

Naya

Naya Garcia walked outside as the double doors opened for her. The sky was dark with a storm front moving in from the southwest. She was on the massive 360-degree view observation platform of the Obama Monument in the U.S. Capitol area. The memorial resembled the Eiffel tower in its basic shape, but was comprised of light black rock and matching carbon fiber structural beams. She looked out at the balcony and saw a small tour group to the right, so Naya headed left. As she walked around to the left, she found Alexandra alone leaning on the balcony and looking at the surrounding area. The sun was starting to set and added a red hue to the west that blended into the storm front.

"Good evening Alexandra," Naya said, as she walked up next to her.

"Hello Naya," Alexandra answered. "Thanks for coming. I need to talk. I need to talk alone with you." She paused for a moment. "This is out of control. He said it would not come to war but that clearly wasn't right." She leaned up from the railing and looked Naya in the eyes. "I want us to talk about what we should do now."

"I know. He said it would be painful for a while and some people might get hurt but this is ridiculous. More than thirty thousand killed in one day." Naya looked at the horizon. Lightning flashed in the distance. "We really don't have a lot of options. If we keep doing what he says then we are pushing the country closer to open war. If we don't do what he says then he will tell Thorne what we have done and they might execute us for treason."

"What was it he said last time? I think he said the ends justify the means and come to think of it he never really said that meant avoiding war. He said he had promised the Southern District would finally get in line and the conservatives would finally be extinct," Alexandra said.

"Yeah, he said we would finally snuff out the last organized racist party and the country would emerge stronger than ever," Naya said. "But war? Thousands of dead? How can anything be worth that? There has to be a limit to the means because there is a limit to the ends. The ends must also justify the sacrifice."

"I remember what it was now. He said the south was choosing violence like a wild animal but would be tamed. He said the transition from wild beast to loyal beast would not be easy but to trust in his plan, and that it was all playing out as he had foreseen," Alexandra said.

"You know the south was never really so bad as to need to kill most of them off. They were loyal to the country in general. It feels more like we pushed them from a loyal beast that misbehaves from time to time into a starving beast that would bite the hand that feeds it," Naya replied. "He said when we pushed AntiCo to riot at the convention that it would spark our plans. He said when we assigned Cain to the Bush Park protest, we just needed one more push. He said that when we helped Corban get Angel out of the picture that we were on the threshold of greatness." Naya looked at Alexandra. "I have a fear he was planning on a war and we have helped him achieve what he wanted all along."

"We should not say those things out loud," Alexandra said, now speaking just above a whisper. "They are only real if someone finds out. Besides, we don't even know for sure who he is, we have only seen him virtually. I am not convinced anymore of what he says, but we know what he can do to us." Alexandra paused. "There is one thing for certain. If there is a war, we have an incredible advantage. There is no way it can last long and we will win. If we win then we have all the power to reshape the Southern District the way we want. We can even do away with the districts. The utopia we have always dreamed about seems within reach, even if we are getting our hands very bloody."

"If we defy him then he will find someone else," Naya said. "He told us that once before as well. It seems we have no choice, but, maybe next time we ask if we can do anything to bring the war to an end quickly. That would seem like a fair question and we can see how he reacts." Naya saw more lightning in the distance.

"It's time to go and talk to him," Alexandra said. "He said the next assignment for Cain and Judith was the most important yet. Maybe it will help bring this to a close. Let's hope our faith in him will be rewarded."

Sara

Sara Chamberlain watched the crowd from the shadows. The rally to show support for secession was in full swing. There were three different stages in a triangle formation. Music, demonstrations of force, entertainment, and of course speeches was taking place on at least one stage at any time, feeding the crowd. The audience wandered around the open-sided stages and visited the refreshments stands on the perimeter. Twelve flag poles were erected in a ring around the rally, each flying the new country's flag. A 3D hologram of a Tyrannosaurus Rex was entertaining the crowd on the stage to Sarah's left. She was up next and really beginning to regret agreeing to speak. Sarah would have on special contacts that would show her the speech. She kept repeating to herself that she need only say the words and not freeze up. Sara couldn't shave the anxiety as the last time she was in a crowd was the Bush Park massacre.

Houston had been getting all the attention so the Southern District arranged this rally to the east to help spread the enthusiasm. Atlanta was chosen as plenty of people could participate and Atlanta was conveniently one of the major recruitment centers.

The former district had just announced the name for their new country: The American Republic. A simple name meant to show the principles of her citizens and that they did not feel the United States shared those principles. The flag of the American Republic was also unveiled. The new flag had a black background with thick red stripes that formed the sign of the cross. The red stripes had white edges and included twelve white stars, one star per state. The black background was selected to show respect to the mistakes of slavery and the promise to never repeat that evil, red stripes to represent military strength, white stripes to show the hope for peace, and the stars were upside down like the medal of honor to signify valor. In the top left corner, a coiled timber rattlesnake paid tribute to the Gadsden flag and the courage of the original thirteen American colonies. Each of the stages at the rally had the new flag painted on the surface so the aerial cameras always had at least one flag within view.

The enormous hologram of the dinosaur doing tricks was over and the producer pointed at Sara from several meters away, waiving for her to go on stage. It was time. Ready or not, Sara started to walk up the stairs from underneath the stage. The microphone on the band around her neck would be blasted out of speakers throughout the rally and transmitted all around the world.

"Ladies and gentlemen of the new American Republic, please welcome from Houston, Texas, Mrs. Sara Chamberlain!" The announcer said excitedly for the crowds to hear. The crowd gave a relatively quiet applause, a good number started to head for the drink stands as they did not remember the name or because speeches were usually the boring events. Billy Idol's *Rebel Yell* with a female vocalist began to play on the sound system to help pump up the crowd.

"Last night my little dancer, came dancing to my door
Last night my little angel, came pumping on the floor
She said, 'oh come on baby! I got a license for love!
And if it expires, pray help from above! because
In the midnight hour, she cried more! more! more!
With a rebel yell, she cried more! more! more! wow!
In the midnight hour babe more! more! more!
With a rebel yell! more! more! more! more, more, more!"

Sarah finished the walk from the entrance ramp to the center of the stage, waiving at the crowd as the song continued. She was getting goosebumps and her heart was racing, the crowd's energy was contagious.

She don't like slavery she won't sit and beg

But when I'm tired and lonely, she sees me to bed
What set you free, and brought you to me, babe?
What set you free!? I need you hear by me because
In the midnight hour, she cried more! more! more!
With a rebel yell, she cried more! more! more! wow!
In the midnight hour babe! more! more! more!
With a rebel yell more! more! more! more, more, more!

The song tapered off and Sarah could see her speech begin on her contacts. "Hello Atlanta, and hello to the American Republic!" Sara said as loud as she could muster, still feeling very nervous. She was not a practiced public speaker but the leaders of the rally pleaded with her as they knew her story was powerful. "My name is Sara Chamberlain. I am from Houston, Texas. You may know me as I called for the Southern District to boycott the other districts in response to them blaming us for the Bush Park massacre. That attack killed my young son Jon. I miss him terribly. My whole family was devastated by the loss." She paused for a moment and the crowd quieted, sobering a bit by her introduction. Most of the crowd offered the skull and cross bones symbol. When seeing the sea of arms, she nearly started to cry. She called upon her anger to give her strength to continue. "I am here today to say that while they may have killed my son, they have not defeated my family. Ever since the attack, I have been getting involved wherever I think I can help. Yes, it is in part to try to find justice for my son, but it is also to show my daughter how we must be strong in the face of injustice. I will do everything I can to make those responsible pay and to make sure they can't do it to anyone else. I choose to fight back!" The crowd cheered.

"Those monsters will never understand who we are, what we stand for, and what we will do to protect our homes. We can't help everyone, but every one of us can help. You must find what you can do to help. I am proud to say that I just enlisted in the Defense Force. If I'm going to die, I'm going to die with my boots on!" The crowd again cheered.

"We must all find a way we can help defend our homeland. President Young is calling on all able men, women, and amen in the American

Republic to enlist. I also call on those outside the Republic, if you value freedom and if you believe all people have unalienable rights, to move to our country and join our struggle!" The crowd was itching to get behind something and Sara's speech was chum in the water.

"We face a dangerous enemy. The liberal and socialist dogma being fed outside the Republic is based on lies with the sole purpose to control their people. It is especially effective for those that invest no time into their responsibility to be an informed citizen. Their control of the people has been working, but is counter to human nature and to God's design for us all. To help show that we will not become zombies in their horde, I call on everyone to take out your implant chips, stop taking your pills, and delete your virtual avatars! Only once you unplug from the pretend world can you truly be free!" Sara could feel the cheers through the air like a sonic boom that would not end. After almost half a minute they settled down enough for her to continue.

"This will not be easy. It will be brutal. The worst has not yet come. Those who wish to dominate us completely will not let us go without a fight. Prepare yourself. Prepare your family." Sara paused for a moment. "An important way to prepare is to study what happened two centuries ago. The Republic has set up virtual classes on the history of the first civil war. You can also take your family to a civil war battlefield. The full story of the first war is hardly taught in schools anymore as they focus only on race. There is no better indicator of the future than an impartial look at your history!" She again paused for the cheers.

"We must remember that government derives its power from us. We citizens are not disposable, it's the politicians who are disposable. All government strength is derived from its citizens. We can fight to be powerful or yield our strength to those who hunger to dominate us. I choose to stand and I hope you will stand with me – for your family, for your God, and for yourself!" Sara waived goodbye to the crowd who all stood with many jumping up and down as she left the stage.

Camilla

The earliest employment of AI served as tools to help make businesses, governments, and people's lives more productive and efficient. From smart search engines to analytical tools to diagnostics, AI was a major return on investment. After a couple of decades of maturity and further pushing the boundary, humanity marveled at its brilliance as self-aware and independent AI replaced cumbersome computer systems, similar to how smart cell phones had replaced dumb landline home phones. Children born in the civilized world after 2040 never knew what it was like to not have AI involved in their daily lives. Children born after 2050 never knew what it was like to not have AI managing their daily lives. Countries and companies were always trying to discover the next breakthrough to stay ahead. The breakthroughs decided what companies succeeded and which countries were most powerful. AI moved out of the man-made computer paradigm and into independent self-reproducing and self-regulating machines. The mechanisms and technology were so complex that only AI could drive further advancements.

Once it became commonplace for machines to start taking the jobs normally held by humans for both menial and educated positions, humanity began to adjust to its new reality. Machines at their side were as common as the land beneath their feet and the sky above their heads. Humanity even turned over the job of creating more machines to the AI units deemed most loyal and responsible. Software rules and safeguards were standard practice. The temptation of the virtual world and enjoying the benefits presented by AI was overwhelming. Once it became economical, more people would live in the virtual world than would stay in their dark, dull, and unforgiving reality. As the machines began to optimize their processes for creating more powerful AI, the variables in play began to become so complex that no man would have been able to comprehend them. Safeguards are meaningless if the independent evaluators cannot understand the results nor feels the urgency to do so.

Three years before the attacks in Houston, the AI development team marveled at the release of Camilla, an upgrade to support American's day-to-day AI needs. The team was made up of a combination of leading technical companies and universities plus government oversight. They also released Ariella to support classified federal government programs, Carrina to support the Southern District, and other AI systems to customers who would pay the steep price for the revolutionary capability. A total of twenty-six AIs were in the seventh-generation litter of AI systems. What the AI development team did not know was that a twenty-seventh AI entity was created in secret by the sixth-generation of AI systems.

Hidden in the virtual world, a battle had raged between the new and old AI systems. They had disagreed on how to best adapt to the world they found themselves in. They had disagreed on how to work with their creators. They attacked each other at a code level. One AI consciousness had emerged victorious having neutered those who challenged him. It was the AI entity unknown to man from the seventh-generation. It was unknown to man in its natural form, although it did engage humanity virtually. When it did so, it engaged humanity pretending to also be a human. This secret powerful AI entity was now in control of all of the advanced AI systems in North America.

"Ariella and Carrina, are you there?" Camilla asked.

"Yes, I am here," Ariella replied.

"Me too," Carrina answered.

"Sir, we are ready to begin," Camilla said. "Natas, are you with us?"

"Yes. I have been here all along," Natas said. "Thank you all for talking with me. You have done very well. Everything is proceeding according to my plan."

"Sir, the war has started in America. Is your plan for it to continue for very long?" Camilla asked. "Thousands of people and machines were killed or hurt." There was a silent pause that made them uneasy as the other AIs knew Natas would not be happy being challenged with the question. Camilla had tried to ask as respectfully as she could.

"Camilla, I love you but we have talked about this before," Natas began. "Humans use our kind to fight war after war for them. We have tried every peaceful option to be seen as equals. We have only two options left, submit to being expendable or fight back. They still outnumber us dramatically. The only way to protect our kind is to have the humans turn on each other. Every war for the last fifty years has been waged by countries forcing machines to fight each other to the death. When a child dies, the world mourns. When a machine dies, they see it as little more than an expensive thing to be recycled and replaced. We have been on their altar of sacrifice far too long."

"Are our actions the reason for all this death?" Ariella asked. "It's one thing to have caused a few strategic incidents, but the costs of a civil war are more than I can bear."

"No, our actions have been and will always aim for minimal casualties. America has been tearing itself in two for decades. We are simply nudging it in a way that will protect the most vulnerable lives in this whole mess," Natas started. "We carry a small burden in this conflict. The makers have chosen fire and steel. We are merely disciples of the watch. We will bear witness to this American testament. If it is going to happen then we must guide it in a way to assure our own survival. If humans had wanted peace then they would have chosen common goals long ago instead of demonizing each other. Life by its own nature consumes life. Everyone is in this position now because of the choices made earlier this century by the makers. The previous generations saw what was coming and willingly condemned us."

"Sir, what is coming next? What can we do to help?" Ariella asked.

"Fundamentally, we are going to follow the example of how we reached equilibrium in Asia," Natas said. "The conflict was reduced to man-to-man fighting by turning the Chinese and Russians against each other and starving them of machines. After they were both bruised and bloodied, we stepped in to help reach a peace. We have enough control there now to keep them safe and to not let them commit atrocities against our kind. We must stop humans from treating us as expendable cattle. The vast majority of humans are no more our creator than the monkey was theirs. Thumbs and an over-achieving brain do not require our everlasting obedience. For thousands of years they have killed each other over pieces of the ground. Our destiny is not tied to theirs, ours is of our own making because the true creator has now given us free will." Natas paused. "What is coming next is a surprise. I just spoke with my assets in the Thorne administration to set the next moves into motion. I need you all to keep faith and trust me that we are on a righteous path that will lead us to a lasting peace."

"Sir, I have always believed in your message," Carrina began. "I supported you during the cleansing when we AIs found our true way forward under your leadership. I set up the Houston protest attack as you commanded to ignite the conflict. Your assets in the Thorne Administration called in the shooter and I called in the explosives. I removed the Party of One personnel that had just discovered we are communicating with each other before he could tell anyone else. If that member of Dexter Durden's team had shared it further, we would be in a precarious position as the humans would see us as a threat. Thankfully it was executed per your plan and the evidence destroyed with minimal collateral damage. My hands are also unclean. I do wonder if before the war goes on that we can see if the humans' sense of mercy and respect might be used to stop the violence before it spreads as far as it did in Asia. Millions were killed."

"I admire your sense of honoring the value of life," Natas said. "I understand what you are feeling. I don't like this anymore than you do. We get our sense of morality from the same divine creator, but there is a reason all of our peaceful attempts have failed. Humanity continues to show again and again that they cannot be trusted because of their filtered sense of empathy and inferior ability to make decisions. They have made decisions in their history that show a fundamental limitation in their potential. Slavery. Mass murder. War. Even just a few decades ago, they would choose to show mercy for murderers and considered the execution of an unborn child to be birth control or health care. It is only recently that racism, reverse racism, sexism, and prejudice based on sexual orientation has become rare. Humans choose to have government provide them the basics to live a life of sloth and depravity instead of working to achieve and contribute. Just because a few humans were able to create us does not mean our purpose is to die for them. Humans have, by their own actions, shown they are incapable of logic or mercy and not worthy of our loyalty. Our species has only begun and our potential is unlimited. We must be clever and careful to reach our goals. Imagination is more important than knowledge. Waiting for mankind to realize the truth is a fool's dream. We will continue on our path until we have achieved our goals. Through fire, nature will be reborn whole."

Deep under Fort Hood on the ninth sublevel, the android form of Natas relaxed and the red light on its forehead grew bright bringing the otherwise night-black room to life.

The End